ALL NEW

COLORADO'S GOURMET GOLD

cookbook of recipes from Colorado's most popular restaurants

FIRST EDITION
November 1990
©Laika, Inc.
3131 Alameda
Denver, Colorado 80209

We recommend that prospective cooks try the recipe at the respective eatery,
so they will know what the dish is supposed to taste like.

Bon Appetit!

THE ALL NEW COLORADO'S GOURMET GOLD is the sequel to the original COLORADO'S GOURMET GOLD
Cookbook, Volume, I and THE BEST OF COLORADO'S GOURMET GOLD VOLUME II

INTRODUCTION

One new exciting recipe is worth the price of this comprehensive collection of Colorado's outstanding restaurant specialties.

Throughout THE ALL NEW COLORADO'S GOURMET GOLD some of the very best French, Italian, Mexican plus countless ethnic cuisines and contemporary American foods, are revealed in precise recipe form.

"We have come a long way since the fifties when Colorado saw the cuisine of its restaurants evolve." There is a wealth of culinary skill and secrets assembled in THE ALL NEW COLORADO'S GOURMET GOLD. It was made possible only by the abundance of talented Chefs and their assistants in the fine restaurants of Colorado and their willingness to set aside the mystique of some of their highly acclaimed house specialties.

To achieve perfection of the recipes contained in this book, THE ALL NEW COLORADO'S GOURMET GOLD suggests that you visit as many fine establishments as possible, to acquaint yourself with flavors, seasonings and textures, as well as presentations. You might even have the opportunity to meet these culinary stars and obtain a helpful hint or two, to aid your efforts in preparing the recipes in your own home.

THE ALL NEW COLORADO'S GOURMET GOLD is not only a cookbook, it is a passport to extraordinary restaurants all over Colorado — from Denver to Aspen and Vail and beyond.

You would do well to tuck your copy of THE ALL NEW COLORADO'S GOURMET GOLD under your arm and travel from restaurant to restaurant. But, if "dining in" is your preferred lifestyle, follow the recipes and be both "Chef" and "Guest"!

Bon Appetit,

Pierre Wolfe

Pierre Wolfe

CREDITS

Editors:
Linda Ruth Harvey
Jennifer Renolds
Cheryl D. Hammar
Lori Krieger
Elaine St. Louis
Jeanette Landgrauf
Ramona Odierna
Darla Worden
Andrea Siuru

Drawings:
Pat McClure

Art Director — Cover:
Debi Knight, Knight Design Studio

Layout:
Michael Minnix, Art Director, Lambda Graphics

Cover Photo by:
Roger Renolds Photographers — H.B.R. Studios

Typography:
Lambda Graphics (Michael Minnix, Marie Hamill)

Photo Information:
Cover: Cliff Young's Restaurant (Amethyst Room) with Cliff Young

PREFACE

THE ALL NEW COLORADO'S GOURMET GOLD wishes to thank the outstanding restaurants that participated in this book; the many chefs who shared their recipes; and the many guests who dine out frequently to maintain the popularity of these eateries.

Many of the restaurants' descriptions and brief histories have been written by reviewers who know and enjoy them.

A few of the recipes that appear throughout this cookbook are not served nightly at the eatery with which they are identified. Many eateries, such as John's of Boulder, Le Central of Denver, and Abetone's of Aspen, offer daily changing specials; therefore, these special recipes may or may not be offered on a guest's particular visit. Often restaurants allow their creative chefs to offer seasonal menus that may include lighter fare in the summer and heartier presentations in the winter.

Also many of the recipes are the original restaurant's recipes. However, as certain recipes are closely guarded secrets, and also, as some restaurants' recipes were in such large portions, variations on those recipes have been printed and are described as ''variations.''

As this is a Colorado cookbook promoting Colorado restaurants, we strongly urge prospective chefs to use Colorado products whenever possible. In this view, we have altered recipes featuring lamb to use ''Colorado lamb''; recipes calling for ''Idaho potatoes'' to use ''Colorado potatoes''; and ingredients calling for non-dessert vinegars to use ''Colorado's St. Mary's Vinegar'' — all in the spirit of ''Always Buy Colorado,'' the organization promoting the state.

Again **THE ALL NEW COLORADO'S GOURMET GOLD** suggests that prospective chefs enjoy a dish at the eatery which specializes in such before preparing the dish at home. This will provide a fun night of dining out as well as offer a foreknowledge of what the dish is supposed to taste and look like.

Most of the restaurants and their recipes were chosen and/or invited into this book because of an especially outstanding house dish; or excellence by the eatery in its use of quality ingredients and preparation over a consistent period of time; or long Colorado history of the eatery; or a particularly colorful owner, as in the case of 90-year-old Daddy Bruce, who learned to cook from his grandmother.

All eateries in **THE ALL NEW COLORADO'S GOURMET GOLD** have contributed significantly to Colorado's restaurant history and should make enjoyable, delicious and treasured reading.

And finally, **THE ALL NEW COLORADO'S GOURMET GOLD** wishes to thank *Colorado Homes and Lifestyles Magazine* for making this publication possible.

Enjoy!

TABLE OF CONTENTS

I. Appetizers

II. Soups

III. Salads

IV. Omelettes, Quiches and Eggs

V. Breads

VI. Vegetables

VII. Entrées Pasta

VIII. Entrées Seafood

IX. Entrées Fowl

X. Entrées Meat

XI. Desserts

XII. Sauces and Dressings, Etc.

Sectional index located at beginning of each Section

Comprehensive index located at back of cookbook

COLORADO RESTAURANTS BY AREA

ALLENSPARK
Fawn Brook Inn

ASPEN, SNOWMASS, GLENWOOD SPRINGS
Abetone Ristorante
Asia Chinese Restaurant
La Boheme, Snowmass Village
Cache-Cache
La Cantina
Charlemagne
The Chart House
The Copper Kettle
The Golden Horn
Jerome Hotel
The Little Nell
Mayfair Deli and Patisserie
Mezzaluna
Milan's
Motherlode
Pinon's
Poppies Bistro Cafe
Poppycock's
Pour La France! Bistro & Cafe
Primavera Ristorante
The Red Onion
Rennaissance
Smuggler Bar and Restaurant
Sopris Restaurant, Glenwood Springs
Syzygy
Takah-Sushi
Tower-Magic Bar and Restaurant, Snowmass Village
Ute City Banque

BLACK HAWK
Black Forest Inn

BOULDER (and surrounding areas)
Aristocrat Steakhouse
Boulder Salad Company
Flagstaff House
Gold Hill Inn
The Greenbriar
Harvest Restaurant and Bakery
Hotel Boulderado
J.B. Winberie's
John's Restaurant
Orchid Pavilion
Pearl's
Pour La France! Bistro and Cafe
Red Lion Inn
Ristorante Paolino
Rudi's
Walnut Cafe

BRECKENRIDGE
St. Bernard Inn

CASTLE ROCK
China Dragon
The Golden Dobbin

COLORADO SPRINGS (and surrounding areas)
Antonio's Italian Restaurant
Briarhurst Manor, Manitou Springs
Broadmoor Hotel (Charles Court, Penrose Room)
Canterbury Cheese
Chicago Joe's
Craftwood Inn
Golden Dragon
Imperial Wok
La Petite Maison
Olive Branch
Villa at Palmer Lake, Palmer Lake

DENVER (and surrounding areas)
Bibelot
Bistro Adde Brewster
Blue Bonnet
Bob's Pizzeria
Boccalino's
La Bolas
Boyles Bar and Grill
H. Brinker's
Brown Palace
Buckhorn Exchange
Bull & Bush
Cafe Franco
Cafe Giovanni
Le Central
Chao-Praya Thai
Chez Thoa
China Sun Restaurant
China Terrace
Chubby's
Cliff Young's
La Coùpole
Daddy Bruce
Denver Salad Company
Delmonico's
Duggan's
The Egg Shell
Falcone's Restaurant
Fern's Restaurant
Firefly Cafe
Gemini Restaurant
Goodfriend's
Greens Natural Foods
Gussie's
Hal's
Harvest Restaurant and Bakery
House of Hunan
Hunan City
Imperial Chinese Seafood

J.B. Winberies
Lincoln 100
Little Shanghai
Magic Pan Crêperie
Marina Landing
The Market
Mark's Milk Bar
Mary and Lou's Cafe
Maxie's on the Boulevard
Mike Berardi's
Ming's Dynasty
Mexicali Cafe
Monaco Inn
Mostly Seafood
Muddy's Java Cafe
El Noa Noa
Normandy French Restaurant
Off Belleview Grill
The Old Country Inn
Panda Cafe
Park Lane Cafe
Paul's Place
The Peppermill
Philadelphia Filly
Philomena's
A Piece of Quiet
Pomodora
Pour La France! Bistro and Cafe
Red Coral Restaurant
Reiver's
Rick's Cafe
The Riviera
Saucy Noodle
Señor Pepe's
Sfuzzi
Simms Landing
Sorens
Strings
Sushi Den
Tante Louise
Thai Hiep
Transalpin
T-Wa Inn
Twin Dragon
Walnut Cafe
Wellshire Inn
Zenith

DURANGO
Sweeney's
Tamarron Inn, Le Canyon Gourmet Room

ELIZABETH
Botana Junction

EMPIRE
The Peck House

FORT COLLINS
Delfannies Restaurant

GEORGETOWN
The Happy Cooker
The Silver Queen

GOLDEN
El Rancho
Wang's Mandarin House

KEYSTONE
The Ranch at Keystone

LEADVILLE
The Leadville Country Inn

MORRISON
Deacon's Bench
The Fort

PINE JUNCTION
Red Rooster Inn

SILVERTHORNE
Dillon Inn

VAIL - AVON - BEAVER CREEK, EDWARDS, MINTURN
Alfredo's Westin Hotel
Alpenrose
Blu's
Bristol at Arrowhead, Edwards
Chanticler
The Charter's First Season, Beaver Creek
Cyrano's
D-J's Crêpes and Omelets
Fountain Cafe
Golden Eagle Inn, Beaver Creek
Hotel Sonnenalp
Left Bank
Legends, Beaver Creek
Los Amigos
Mataam Fez
Minturn Country Club, Minturn
Mirabelle's, Avon-Beaver Creek
L'Ostello
Patina Grill, Beaver Creek
Pepi's Restaurant
Picasso's
Sweet Basil
Turntable Restaurant, Minturn
The Tyrolean Inn
Uptown Grill
Vail Racquet Club Restaurant
Vendetta's
Wildflower Inn

RESTAURANTS IN ALPHABETICAL ORDER

ABETONE RISTORANTE, Aspen
  *Introduction; Melanzane alla Parmigiana (Vegetables, VI)
  *Fettuccine Abetone (Entrées Pasta, VII)
  *Florida Red Snapper Napoletana (Entrées Seafood, VIII)
  *Scaloppine di Vitella al Marsala (Entrées Meat, X)

ALFREDO'S, Vail
  *Fresh Lochinvar Scottish Salmon with Lavender Butter Sauce (Entrées Seafood, VIII)
  *Lavender Butter Sauce for Lochinvar Scottish Salmon (Sauces and Dressings, Etc., XII)

ALPENROSE, Vail
  *Iced Cucumber Yogurt Soup (Soups, II)

ANTONIO'S ITALIAN RESTAURANT, Colorado Springs
  *Introduction; Tonno con Salsa di Pomodore [Fresh Tuna with Tomato Sauce]
  (Entrées Seafood, VIII)

THE ARISTOCRAT STEAKHOUSE, Boulder
  *Introduction; Nick's Special Omelet (Omelettes, Quiches and Eggs, IV)

ASIA CHINESE RESTAURANT, Aspen
  *Chestnut Chicken (Entrées Fowl, IX)
  *Sweet and Sour Sauce Dip (Sauces and Dressings, Etc., XII)

BIBELOT, Denver
  *Introduction; Tian of Colorado Lamb with Shiitake Mushrooms, Spinach, Tomatoes
  (Entrées Meat, X)
  *Bresaola [Spice Cured Beef Tenderloin] (Entrées Meat, X)
  *Greek Fisherman's Soup (Soups, II)

BISTRO ADDE BREWSTER, Denver
  *Introduction; Salmon Salad (Salads, III)
  *Eggplant Crêpes (Vegetables, VI)

BLACK FOREST INN, Black Hawk
  *Introduction; Roast Venison (Entrées Meat, X)
  *Sauerbraten (Entrées Meat, X)

THE BLUE BONNET CAFE AND LOUNGE, Denver
  *Introduction; Salsa Crude (Sauces and Dressings, Etc., XII)

BLU'S, Vail
  *Introduction; Smoked Salmon Cheesecake (Appetizers, I)

BOB'S PIZZERIA, Denver
  *Bob's Homemade Pasta (Entrées Pasta, VII)
  *Bob's Special Fettuccine (Entrées Pasta, VII)

BOCCALINO'S, Denver
  *Sautéed Scampi and Fettuccine Alfredo (Entrées, Seafood, VIII)

LA BOHEME, Aspen-Snowmass
  *Shrimp Baked with Feta Cheese and Tomato (Entrées Seafood, VIII)

LA BOLAS, Denver
  *Green Chili (Sauces and Dressings, Etc., XII)
  *T.L.C. Butter (Sauces and Dressings, Etc., XII)

BOTANA JUNCTION, Elizabeth
  *Salsa (Sauces and Dressings, Etc., XII)

BOYLE'S BAR & GRILL, Denver area
  *Swiss House Artichoke Hearts (Appetizers, I)

BRIARHURST MANOR INN, Colorado Springs-Manitou Springs
  *Vegetables with Oriental Touch (Vegetables, VI)

BRINKER'S, H., Denver area
  *Introduction; Duck with Orange and Grand Marnier Sauce (Entrées Fowl, IX)
  *Turrine of Fish (Entrées Seafood, VIII)

THE BRISTOL AT ARROWHEAD, Vail-Edwards
  *Introduction; Portuguese Chicken (Entrées Fowl, IX)

THE BROADMOOR HOTEL, Colorado Springs
*Mustard Glazed Salmon Filet on Stirfried Spinach Leaves, Tarragon Butter (Entrées Seafood, VIII)
*Salmon Newburg (Entrées Seafood, VIII)

BROWN PALACE, Denver
*Roast Crown of Lamb Bouquetiére (Entrées Meat, X)
*Steak Tartare (Entrées Meat, X)

BUCKHORN EXCHANGE, Denver
*Spanakopita (Vegetables, VI)

BULL & BUSH, Denver area
*Introduction; Black Bean and Shrimp Salad (Salads, III)
*Apple Mint Salsa served with Lamb Quesadilla (Sauces and Dressings, Etc., XII)
*Banana Split Ice Cream Pie (Desserts, XI)
*Coriander Dressing for Black Bean and Shrimp Salad (Sauces and Dressings, Etc., XII)
*Lamb Quesadilla (Appetizers, I)
*Wafer Crust (Bread, V)

CACHE-CACHE, Aspen
*Vegetable-Cheese Salad with Artichokes (Salads, III)

CAFE FRANCO, Denver
*Crêpe Suzettes (Desserts, XI)

CAFE GIOVANNI, Denver
*Introduction; Sweetbreads aux Marsala (Entrées Meat, X)
*Brown Sauce (Sauces and Dressings, Etc., XII)
*Cream of Zucchini (Soups, II)
*Escargots Maison (Appetizers, I)

CANTERBURY CHEESE, Colorado Springs
*Mayonnaise Variation [Low Cholesterol] (Sauces and Dressings, Etc., XII)
*St. Mary's Cabbage, Artichoke and Caper Slaw (Salads, III)

THE CANTINA, Aspen
*Cantina Rellenos (Vegetables, VI)
*Quesadilla Vegetarian (Appetizers, I)

CASTAWAY'S, Colorado Springs-Manitou Springs
*Smoked Oyster and Shallots Vinaigrette (Entrées Seafood, VIII)

LE CENTRAL, Denver
*Introduction; Pâté Maison (Entrées Meat, X)
*Pâté de Foie (Appetizers, I)
*Poulet Alexander Stuffed Chicken Breasts (Entrées Fowl, IX)
*Rillettes de Portaux Trois Poiver's (Appetizers, I)

CHANTICLER, Vail
*Introduction; Chicken with Orange Sauce (Entrées Fowl, IX)

CHAO-PRAYA THAI RESTAURANT AND LOUNGE, Denver Area
*Kai Yand [Garlic Chicken] (Entrées Fowl, IX)

CHARLEMAGNE, Aspen
*Fish Stock (Soups, II)

THE CHARTER-FIRST SEASON, Vail-Beaver Creek
*Lamb Chops with Barbecue Sauce (Entrées Meat, X)

THE CHART HOUSE, Aspen
*Blue Cheese Dressing (Sauces and Dressings, Etc., XII)
*Chart House Mud Pie (Desserts, XI)

CHEZ THOA, Denver
*Introduction; Vit Quay [Roast Duck] (Entrées Fowl, IX)
*Mang-Tay Nua Cua [Asparagus and Crabmeat Soup] (Soups, II)
*Tom Chien Lan Bot [Hot and Spicy Prawns] (Entrées Seafood, VII)

CHICAGO JOE'S, Colorado Springs
*Summer Pasta Salad (Salads, III)

CHINA DRAGON RESTAURANT, Castle Rock
  *Cashew or Almond Chicken (Entrées Fowl, IX)
CHINA SUN RESTAURANT, Denver
  *Manchurian Beef (Entrées Meat, X)
CHINA TERRACE, Denver
  *Introduction; Ma-Po Style Bean Curd (Entrées Meat, X)
  *Chicken with Garlic Sauce (Entrées Fowl, IX)
  *Egg Roll (Appetizers, I)
  *Hot and Sour Soup (Soups, II)
  *Vegetarian Dim Sum (Appetizers, I)
  *Volcano Shrimp (Entrées Seafood, VIII)
CHUBBY'S, Denver
  *Flour Tortilla (Breads, V)
  *Tortilla Chips (Breads, V)
CLIFF YOUNG'S RESTAURANT, Denver
  *Introduction; Hazelnut Crusted Colorado Rack of Lamb (Entrées Meat, X)
  *Cinnamon Walnut Cookies (Desserts, XI)
  *Dungeness Crab Cakes (Entrées Seafood, VIII)
  *Herbal Buerre Rouge for Hazelnut Crusted Colorado Rack of Lamb
   (Sauces and Dressings, Etc., XII)
  *Rabbit Loin Stuffed with Cornbread and Andoville Sausage (Entrées Meat, X)
  *Wild Rice Potato Cakes (Vegetables, VI)
THE COPPER KETTLE, Aspen
  *Consommé (Soups, II)
LA COUPOLE, Denver
  *Introduction; Chocolate Torte (Desserts, XI)
CRAFTWOOD INN, Colorado Springs
  *Cornish Hen Glazed with Orange and Ginger (Entrées Fowl, IX)
CYRANO'S, Vail
  *Introduction; Cyrano's Egg Mignons topped with Mushrooms (Omelettes, Quiches and Eggs, IV)
DADDY BRUCE, Denver
  *Introduction; Daddy Bruce's Famous Barbecue Sauce (Sauces and Dressings, Etc., XII)
  *Sweet Potato Pie (Desserts, XI)
THE DEACON'S BENCH, Morrison
  *Baked Chicken in Orange-Almond Sauce (Entrées Fowl, IX)
DELFANNIES RESTAURANT, Fort Collins
  *Campaigne Chicken [Friendly Country Chicken] (Entrées Fowl, IX)
  *Chicken Carbonara Fettuccine (Entrées Pasta, VII)
DELMONICO'S, Denver area
  *Pasta Marinara with Shrimp (Entrées Pasta, VII)
D-J'S CRÊPES AND OMELETS, Vail
  *Introduction; D-J's Basic Crêpe Recipe (Breads, V)
  *Cheese Blintzes (Desserts, XI)
  *D-J's Special Avocado, Egg, Cheese, Mushroom, Sprouts Crêpe (Omelettes, Quiches and Eggs, IV)
  *Dessert Crêpe (Desserts, XI)
  *Spinach Italiano (Vegetables, VI)
THE DENVER SALAD COMPANY, Boulder, Denver
  *Chicken Stock Substitute, Vegetarian — Hot and Spicy (Soups, II)
  *Curry Rice Salad with Shrimp (Salads, III)
  *Curry Rice Salad Dressing (Sauces and Dressings, Etc., XII)
  *Pineapple Salsa (Sauces and Dressings, Etc., XII)
  *Santa Fe Tabouli (Salads, III)
  *Thai-Chicken Pasta Salad with Thai-Vinaigrette Dressing (Salads, III)
  *Thai-Vinaigrette Dressing for Thai-Chicken Pasta Salad (Sauces, XII)

DUGGAN'S, Denver area
  *Introduction; Jalapeño Lime Marinated Chicken with Corn Bread Dressing (Entrées Fowl, IX)
  *Country Shrimp and Lemon Corn (Entrées Seafood, VIII)
  *Iron Skillet Peach Cobbler (Desserts, XI)
THE EGG SHELL, Denver
  *Asparagus-Mushroom Omelettes (Omelettes, Quiches and Eggs, IV)
FALCONE'S RESTAURANT AND BAR, Denver
  *Linguine with Tuna-Caper Sauce (Entrées Pasta, VII)
FAWN BROOK INN, Allenspark
  *Baby Canadian Lobster Tails with Curry Sauce (Entrées Seafood, VIII)
FERN'S RESTAURANT, Denver area
  *Cioppino (Entrées Seafood, VIII)
  *Papillotes of Lobster and Shrimp (Entrées Seafood, VIII)
  *Veal with Roasted Red Bell Peppers Buerre Blanc (Entrées Meat, X)
FIREFLY CAFE, Denver
  *Clams and Mussels Luciano (Entrées Seafood, VIII)
  *Fresh Field Greens with Roma Tomatoes and Goat Cheese (Salads, III)
  *Grilled Breast of Chicken with Avocado Cream Sauce with Sundried Tomatoes (Entrées Fowl, IX)
  *Grilled Halibut Filets with Melon and Mango Salsa (Entrées Seafood, VIII)
FLAGSTAFF HOUSE RESTAURANT, Boulder
  *Introduction; Salmon with Lobster and Truffles (Entrées Seafood, VIII)
  *Ahi Tuna in Mustard Crust with Red Pepper Nage (Entrées Seafood, VIII)
  *Flan of Lobster and Scallops with Two Caviars (Entrées Seafood, VIII)
  *Honey Mustard Poppy Seed Dressing (Sauces and Dressings, Etc., XII)
  *Loin of Lamb with Sweet Peppers in Strudel (Entrées Meat, X)
  *Mayonnaise (Sauces and Dressings, Etc., XII)
  *Niçoise Olive Sauce (Sauces and Dressings, Etc., XII)
  *Spinach Salad with Honey Mustard Poppy Seed Dressing and Homemade Mayonnaise
  (Salads, III)
THE FORT, Morrison
  *The Bowl of the Wife of Kit Carson (Entrées Fowl, IX)
FOUNTAIN CAFE, Vail
  *Zucchini Bread (Breads, V)
GEMINI RESTAURANT, Denver
  *Introduction; Swedish Apricot Nut Bread (Breads, V)
THE GOLDEN DOBBIN, Castle Rock
  *Chicken a la King (Entrées Fowl, IX)
  *The Golden Dobbin Meatloaf (Entrées Meat, X)
  *Piquant Green Beans (Vegetables, VI)
GOLDEN DRAGON, Colorado Springs
  *Plum Wine Chicken (Entrées Fowl, IX)
THE GOLDEN EAGLE INN, Vail-Beaver Creek
  *Introduction; Chicken Marengo (Entrées Fowl, IX)
  *Pasta and Broccoli Salad (Salads, III)
GOLD HILL INN, Boulder
  *Roast Leg of Lamb Venison (Entrées Meat, X)
THE GOLDEN HORN, Aspen
  *Pariser Schnitzel (Entrées Meat, X)
GOODFRIEND'S, Denver
  *Ginger Bread (Breads, V)
  *Mediterranean Pasta Salad (Salads, III)
  *New England-Style Clam Chowder (Soups, II)

THE GREENBRIAR, Boulder
 *Broccoli Polonaise (Vegetables, VI)
 *Tournedos Toscana (Entrées Meat, X)
GREENS NATURAL FOODS CAFE, Denver
 *Tabouleh (Salads, III)
GUSSIE'S, Denver area
 *Spicy Lasagne Roll-Ups (Entrées Pasta, VII)
HAL'S, Denver
 *Egg Noodle Dough (Breads, V)
THE HAPPY COOKER, Georgetown
 *Cinnamon Roll (Breads, V)
HARVEST RESTAURANT & BAKERY, Denver, Boulder
 *Scrambled Tofu (Vegetables, VI)
HOTEL BOULDERADO, Boulder
 *Introduction; Cannelloni with Ricotta and Peas (Entrées Pasta, VII)
HOTEL SONNENALP, Vail
 *Pork Cutlets (Entrées Meat, X)
HOUSE OF HUNAN, Denver
 *Szechwan Soup (Soups, II)
HUNAN CITY, Denver area
 *Peppered Chicken (Entrées Fowl, IX)
IMPERIAL CHINESE SEAFOOD RESTAURANT, Denver
 *Roast Pork (Entrées Meat, X)
 *Soy Sauce Marinade (Sauces, XII)
 *Stir-Fried String Beans and Almonds (Vegetables, VI)
 *Szechwan Sauce (Sauces and Dressings, Etc., XII)
IMPERIAL WOK, Colorado Springs
 *Chicken Velvet and Corn Soup (Soups, II)
 *Steamed Egg with Mushrooms (Omelettes, Quiches and Eggs, IV)
JEROME HOTEL, Aspen
 *Chocolate Sauce (Sauces and Dressings, Etc., XII)
 *Chocolate Walnut Crêpe (Desserts, XI)
 *Huevos Jerome and Picante Sauce (Omelettes, Quiches and Eggs, IV)
 *Mexican Cornbread (Breads, V)
 *Picante Sauce (Sauces and Dressings, Etc., XII)
JOHN'S RESTAURANT, Boulder
 *Braised Belgian Endive with Chevre and Niçoise Olives (Salads, III)
 *Chicken with Red Chiles, Mint and Oregon Raspberry Wine (Entrées Fowl, IX)
 *Puree of Leek Soup with Smoked Mussels and Spinach (Soups, II)
 *Ripe Figs with Mascarpone, Toasted Almonds and Port Wine (Desserts, XI)
THE LEADVILLE COUNTRY INN, Leadville
 *Fresh Peach Muffins (Breads, V)
 *Lemon Pecan Tea Bread (Breads, V)
LEFT BANK, Vail
 *Introduction; Côte de Boeuf Bordelaise (Entrées Meat, X)
LEGEND'S, Vail-Beaver Creek
 *Linguine with White Clam Sauce (Entrées Pasta, VII)
LINCOLN 100, Denver
 *Split Pea and Potato Soup (Soups, II)
THE LITTLE NELL, Aspen
 *Introduction; Smoked Trout with Papaya, Avocado and Cucumber (Entrées Seafood, VIII)
 *Chowder of Corn, Wild Rice and Apple Bacon (Soups, II)
 *Grilled Chicken Salad with Apples, Pecans and Lime (Salads, III)
 *Oven Roasted Salmon with Basil Crust and Warm Tomato Chutney (Entrées Seafood, VIII)

LITTLE SHANGHAI, Denver
    *Introduction; Curried Crab (Entrées Seafood, VIII)
    *Kung Pao Chicken (Entrées Fowl, IX)
    *Mongolian Beef (Entrées Meat, X)
    *Steamed Bao (Appetizers, I)
    *Sweet and Sour Pork with Pineapple and Peppers (Entrées Meat, X)
LOS AMIGOS, Vail
    *Chile Relleno Sauce (Sauces and Dressings, Etc., XII)
    *Chile Rellenos with Sauce (Vegetables, VI)
THE MAGIC PAN CRÊPERIE, Denver
    *Crabmeat Salad Crêpe (Salads, III)
    *Strawberry Crêpe Supreme (Desserts, XI)
MARINA LANDING, Denver
    *Introduction; Pine Nut Brown Sugar Cookies (Desserts, XI)
    *Baked Salmon with Tequila Coriander Beurre Blanc (Entrées Seafood, VIII)
    *Chicken Green Chili Stew (Entrées Fowl, IX)
    *Chicken Stock (Soups, II)
    *Lime Vanilla-Bean Ice Cream with Raspberry Sauce (Desserts, XI)
THE MARKET, Denver
    *Marinated Turkey Breast with Coriander-Lime Sauce (Entrées Fowl, IX)
    *Market Curry Chicken Salad (Salads, III)
MARK'S MILK BAR, Denver
    *Mark's Pasta Primavera Salad (Salads, III)
MARY AND LOU'S CAFE, Denver
    *Introduction; Cherry Cheese Danish (Breads, V)
    *Smorgasbord Salad (Salads, III)
MATAAM FEZ AT VAIL, Vail
    *Armenian Shish Kebab (Entrées Meat, X)
    *Moroccan Couscous (Entrées, Meat, X)
MAXIE'S, Denver
    *Chicken Breast Tina Louise (Entrées Fowl, IX)
    *Lamb Chops Parmesan (Entrées Meat, X)
    *Pasta Mangione (Entrées Pasta, VII)
MAYFAIR DELI AND PATISSERIE, Aspen-Snowmass
    *Introduction; Carrot Cake (Desserts, XI)
MEXICALI CAFE, Denver
    *Arroz a la Mexican [Mexican Rice] (Vegetables, VI)
MEZZALUNA, Aspen
    *Pasta Del Giorno [Pasta with Spinach Sauce] (Entrées Pasta, VII)
MIKE BERARDI'S, Denver
    *Avocado Soup with Rock Shrimp (Soups, II)
    *Brodo (Soups, II)
    *Tortellini (Entrées Pasta, VII)
MILAN'S, Aspen
    *Introduction; Hot Shredded Spiced Beef (Entrées Meat, X)
MING'S DYNASTY, Denver
    *Chinese Pancakes (Breads, V)
MINTURN COUNTRY CLUB, Vail-Minturn
    *Introduction; Teriyaki Marinade (Sauces and Dressings, Etc., XII)
MIRABELLE'S, Vail-Avon-Beaver Creek
    *Fettuccine Alfredo (Entrée Pasta, VII)
MONACO INN, Denver
    *Meat Balls with Egg-Lemon Sauce (Entrées Meat, X)

MOSTLY SEAFOOD, Denver
*Chinese Hot and Sour Soup with Shrimp (Soups, II)
*Crab Salad (Salads, III)
*Grilled Jumbo Shrimp with Kentucky Bacon and Fresh Basil (Entrées Seafood, VIII)
*Shrimp Chile Rellenos (Entrées Seafood, VIII)

THE MOTHERLODE, Aspen
*Introduction; Spaghetti with Garlic, Capers and Artichoke Hearts (Entrées Pasta, VII)
*Chicken a la Français (Entrées Fowl, IX)

MUDDY'S JAVA CAFE, Denver
*Introduction; Bolivian Chili (Entrées Meat, X)
*Crème du Broccoli (Soups, II)

EL NOA NOA, Denver
*Guacamole (Appetizers, I)

NORMANDY FRENCH RESTAURANT, Denver
*Cuisses de Grenouilles au Riesling [Frog Legs in Riesling Wine] (Entrées Meat, X)
*Gratin Dauphinois Chez Grand Mere from Bourgogne (Vegetables, VI)
*Grilled Tuna with Herbed Tomato, Garlic, Oil and Lemon Sauce (Entrées Seafood, VIII)

OLIVE BRANCH, Colorado Springs
*Introduction; Scrambled Eggs Benedict (Omelettes, Quiches and Eggs, IV)

OFF BELLEVIEW GRILL, Denver
*Introduction; Red Snapper Louisiane (Entrées Seafood, VIII)
*Caramel Custard (Desserts, XI)
*Summer Salad (Salads, III)

THE OLD COUNTRY INN, Denver area
*Marinated Mushrooms (Appetizers, I)

ORCHID PAVILION, Boulder
*Steamed Meat Dumplings (Appetizers, I)

L'OSTELLO, Vail
*Introduction; Ginger Crème Brûlée (Desserts, XI)
*Bread Stick (Breads, V)
*Chocolate Sorbetto with Raspberry Coulis (Desserts, XI)

PANDA CAFE, Denver
*Introduction; Black Bean Garlic Sauce (Sauces and Dressings, Etc., XII)
*Fried Chili Crabs (Entrées Seafood, VIII)
*Light Ginger Soy Sauce (Sauces and Dressings, Etc., XII)

PAOLINO, Boulder
*Pasta Riviera (Entrées Pasta, VII)

PARK LANE CAFE, Denver
*Introduction; Basic German Pancake (Breads, V)
*Apple Pancake (Breads, V)

PATINA GRILL, Vail-Avon-Beaver Creek
*Crab and Pasta Salad (Salads, III)
*Easy Pasta from Scratch (Entrées Pasta, VII)

PAUL'S PLACE, Denver
*Dijon Mustard Sauce (Sauces, XII)
*Strawberry Base Sauce for Waffle Topping (Desserts, XI)

PEARL'S, Boulder
*Introduction; Potato Skins with Cheese and Bacon (Appetizers, I)

THE PECK HOUSE, Empire
*Introduction; Omelette Florentine (Omelettes, Quiches and Eggs, IV)

PEPI'S RESTAURANT AT GASTHOF GRAMSHAMMER, Vail
*Potato-Stuffed Roast Goose or Turkey (Entrées Fowl, IX)

THE PEPPER MILL, Denver
*Pie Dough (Breads, V)

LA PETITE MAISON, Colorado Springs
  *Introduction; Soup à L'Oignon Gratinee (Soups, II)
PHILADELPHIA FILLY, Denver
  *Chicken Stock, St. Mary's Style (Soups, II)
  *Pot de Crème (Desserts, XI)
PHILOMENA'S, Denver area
  *Vermicelli with Anchovies and Garlic (Entrées Pasta, VII)
PICASSO'S, Vail-Edwards
  *Introduction; Tuna Tartare with Chives (Entrées Seafood, VIII)
  *Almond Gratin with Pineapple (Desserts, XI)
A PIECE OF QUIET, Denver
  *French Mustard (Sauces and Dressings, Etc., XII)
  *Quick Mint Sauce for Lamb (Sauces and Dressings, Etc., XII)
PIÑON'S, Aspen
  *Introduction; Truffled Creamy Mashed Potatoes (Vegetables, VI)
  *Garlic Rice with Pine Nuts (Vegetables, VI)
  *Shrimp Dijonnaise (Entrées Seafood, VIII)
  *Veal with Rosemary Chili Sauce and Walnuts (Entrées Meat, X)
POMODORO, Denver
  *Introduction; Pesce Space Alla Sicilian [Sicilian Style Swordfish] (Entrées Seafood, VIII)
POPPIES BISTRO CAFE, Aspen
  *Poppies Potato Cake (Vegetables, VI)
  *Raspberry Vinegar Demi-Glace Sauce with Fresh Thyme (Sauces and Dressings, Etc., XII)
  *Sauteed Boneless Quail with Poppies Potato Cake, Raspberry Vinegar Demi-Glace Sauce and Fresh Thyme (Entrées Fowl, IX)
POUR LA FRANCE! CAFE & BISTRO, Denver, Aspen-Snowmass
  *Warm Feta Cheese on French Bread (Breads, V)
POPPYCOCK'S, Aspen
  *French Toast Topped with Pecans, Bananas and Grand Marnier (Breads, V)
PRIMAVERA RISTORANTE, Aspen
  *Linguine and Lobster Tails Diable (Entrées Seafood, VIII)
  *Spaghetti and Shrimp (Entrées Pasta, VII)
THE RANCH AT KEYSTONE, Keystone
  *Introduction; Pasta Scampi (Entrées Pasta, VII)
EL RANCHO, Golden
  *Brook Trout, Sauté Meuniere (Entrées Seafood, VIII)
RED CORRAL RESTAURANT, Denver
  *Egg Drop Soup (Soups, II)
RED LION INN, Boulder
  *Caesar Salad (Salads, III)
  *Yorkshire Pudding (Breads, V)
THE RED ONION, Aspen
  *Béarnaise Sauce (Sauces and Dressings, Etc., XII)
  *Swiss Spaghetti (Entrées Pasta, VII)
  *Veal a la Oscar (Entrées Meat, X)
RED ROOSTER INN, Pine Junction
  *Introduction; Melon and Proscuitto (Appetizers, I)
  *Date Nut Roll (Breads, V)
REIVER'S, Denver
  *Dilled Chicken and Potato Salad (Salads, III)
  *Hearty Lentil Soup (Soups, II)
RENAISSANCE, Aspen
  *Salmon a la Provençale with Flageolet Bean Compote (Entrées Seafood, VIII)

RICK'S CAFE, Denver
  *Asian Salad (Salads, III)
  *Asian Salad Dressing (Sauces and Dressings, Etc., XII)
  *Marinated Sirloin Steak (Entrées Meat, X)
THE RIVIERA, Denver area
  *Introduction; Taquitos (Appetizers, I)
RUDI'S, Boulder
  *Introduction; Gâteaux a L'Orange (Desserts, XI)
  *Armenian Cheese Boreck (Appetizers, I)
  *Artichoke Florentine (Vegetables, VI)
  *Aubergines Farci (Vegetables, VI)
  *Avocado Melon Salad (Salads, III)
  *Basmati Rice (Vegetables, VI)
  *Bulghur Pilaf (Vegetables, VI)
  *Carrot Mint Soup (Soups, II)
  *Champignon Elegante (Appetizers, I)
  *Chicken Quenelles with Mushroom Cream (Appetizers, I)
  *Chilled Lime and Honeydew Soup (Soups, II)
  *Date Soufflé (Desserts, XI)
  *Empanada Dough (Breads, V)
  *Hollandaise (Sauces and Dressings, Etc., XII)
  *Honey Walnut Bread (Breads, V)
  *Mornay Sauce (Sauces and Dressings, Etc., XII)
  *Mujedera Lentil Pilaf (Vegetables, VI)
  *Pasta Salad with Basil Pesto (Salads, III)
  *Parmesan Dressing (Sauces and Dressings, Etc., XII)
  *Pecan Pie (Desserts, XI)
  *Salmon Wrapped in Filo with Brie (Entrées Seafood, VIII)
  *Sautéed Cucumbers with Romaine (Vegetables, VI)
  *Strawberry Cream (Desserts, XI)
THE SAUCY NOODLE RISTORANTE, Denver
  *Introduction; Pesto alla Genovese (Entrées Pasta, VII)
  *Marinara Sauce (Sauces and Dressings, Etc., XII)
  *Spaghetti Marinara (Entrées Pasta, VII)
SEÑOR PEPE'S, Denver
  *Pollo Asado a la Parilla (Entrées Fowl, IX)
SFUZZI, Denver
  *Romano Crusted Chicken Salad with Tomato Basil Vinaigrette (Salads, III)
  *Three Cheese Lasagne with Chicken and Porcini Mushrooms (Entrées Pasta, VII)
THE SILVER QUEEN, Georgetown
  *Baked Macaroni and Cheese (Entrées Pasta, VII)
  *Country Mustard (Sauces and Dressings, Etc., XII)
  *Creamy Garlic Dressing (Sauces and Dressings, Etc., XII)
SIMMS LANDING, Denver
  *Introduction; Blackened Tenderloin Caesar Salad (Salads, III)
  *Lemon Proscuitto Shrimp (Entrées Seafood, VIII)
SMUGGLER BAR AND RESTAURANT, Aspen
  *Smoked Mussels in Mustard-Cream Sauce (Entrées Seafood, VIII)
SOPRIS RESTAURANT AND LOUNGE, Aspen-Glenwood Springs
  *Introduction; Beef Stroganoff (Entrées Meat, X)
  *Banana Flambé (Desserts, XI)
  *House Dressing from Sopris Restaurant (Sauces and Dressings, Etc., XII)
SOREN'S RESTAURANT, Denver
  *Dilled Potatoes and Sour Cream (Vegetables, VI)
  *Kapusta (Entrées Meat, X)

ST. BERNARD INN, Breckenridge
    *Introduction; Stuffed Breast of Veal with Marsala Wine Sauce (Entrées Meat, X)
STRINGS, Denver
    *Champagne Vinaigrette served with Charbroiled Eggplant (Sauces and Dressings, Etc., XII)
    *Charbroiled Eggplant with Champagne Vinaigrette (Vegetables, VI)
    *Charbroiled Quail with Shiitake Mushrooms and Wild Rice (Entrées Fowl, IX)
    *Coho Salmon Tortellini with Orange Brandy Cream Sauce (Entrées Pasta, VII)
    *Mountain Meadow Lamb Salad (Salads, III)
    *White Chocolate Boats (Desserts, XI)
SUSHI DEN, Denver
    *Introduction; Sunomono (Appetizers, I)
    *Chilled Noodle Summer Entrée (Entrées Pasta, VII)
    *Sushi Rice (Vegetables, VI)
SWEENEY'S, Durango
    *Introduction; Blue Cheese Dressing (Sauces and Dressings, Etc., XII)
SWEET BASIL, Vail
    *Avocado Pancake Filled with Smoked Duck and Wild Rice (Entrées Fowl, IX)
    *Black Bean Tortilla (Breads, V)
    *Chicken Kiev (Entrées Fowl, IX)
    *Grilled Achiote Chicken with Chipolte Salsa and Shallot Sauce (Entrées Fowl, IX)
    *Grilled Asparagus with Shiitake Mushrooms (Salads, III)
    *Lemon Tarragon Vinaigrette for Grilled Asparagus and Shiitake Mushroom Salad
    (Sauces and Dressings, Etc., XII)
    *Shallot Sauce (Sauces and Dressings, Etc., XII)
    *Tomato Bisque (Soups, II)
SYZYGY, Aspen
    *Introduction; Linguine with Shrimp Sauce (Entrées Seafood, VIII)
TAKAH SUSHI, Aspen
    *Sashimi (Entrées Seafood, VIII)
    *Sukiyaki (Entrées Meat, X)
TAMARRON INN, Durango
    *Introduction; Coquilles Saint Jacques a la Parisienne (Entrées Seafood, VIII)
    *Sesame Chicken Breasts with Lemon Cream (Entrées Fowl, IX)
TANTE LOUISE, Denver
    *Introduction; Salmon Tartare (Entrées Seafood, VIII)
    *Brie Cheesecake on Champagne Crème Anglaise with Fresh Plums (Desserts, XI)
    *Curried Squash Soup (Soups, II)
THAI HIEP, Denver
    *Deep-Fried Prawn with Chiles (Entrées Seafood, VIII)
THE TOWER MAGIC BAR AND RESTAURANT, Aspen-Snowmass
    *Apple-Raspberry Pie (Desserts, XI)
    *John Denver's BBQ Sauce for Grilled Shrimp (Sauces and Dressings, Etc., XII)
    *Tournedos au Poivre Vert (Entrées Meat, X)
TRANSALPIN, Denver
    *Introduction; Trout Poached in Lemon Grass Broth (Entrées Seafood, VIII)
    *Lemon Fish Pie (Entrées Seafood, VIII)
    *Pineapple Ginger Sauce for Trout (Sauces and Dressings, Etc., XII)
TURNTABLE RESTAURANT, Vail-Minturn
    *Ketchup (Sauces and Dressings, Etc., XII)
    *Mini Meat [Ground Turkey] Loaves (Entrées Fowl, IX)
TWIN DRAGON, Denver
    *Fried Rice with Shrimp (Entrées Seafood, VIII)

THE TYROLEAN INN, Vail
    *Applestrudel (Desserts, XI)
    *Escargots Bourguigonne (Appetizers, I)·

T-WA INN, Denver
    *Introduction; Sambal Ulek [Hot Chili Paste] (Sauces and Dressings, Etc., XII)
    *Fish Sauce Variation I and II (Sauces and Dressings, XII)
    *Thai Sausage (Entrées Meat, X)

UPTOWN GRILL, Vail
    *Avocado Red Pepper (Appetizers, I)
    *Smoked Tomato Salsa for Avocado Red Pepper Quesadilla (Sauces and Dressings, Etc., XII)

UTE CITY BANQUE, Aspen
    *Chicken Breast Boursin with Red Wine Sauce (Entrées Fowl, IX)
    *Hearts of Palm and Artichoke Salad (Salads, III)
    *Red Wine Sauce for the chicken Breast Boursin (Sauces and Dressings, Etc. XII)
    *Scallops Parisienne (Entrées Seafood, VIII)

THE VAIL RACQUET CLUB, Vail
    *Introduction; Homemade Spinach Noodles "Al Pesto" (Entrées Pasta, VII)
    *Mussels with Sauce Verte (Appetizers, I)

VENDETTA'S, Vail
    *Zucchini, Mushrooms, and Pimiento Lasagne (Entrées Pasta, VII)

THE VILLA AT PALMER LAKE, Colorado Springs area
    *Introduction; Gnocchi Potato Dumplings (Entrées Pata, VII)
    *Tomato Sauce (Sauces and Dressings, Etc., XII)

WALNUT CAFE, Denver, Boulder
    *Banana Nut Bread (Breads, V)

WANG'S MANDARIN HOUSE, Golden
    *Introduction; Szechwan Hot and Sour Soup (Soups, II)
    *Fried Noodles with Shrimp (Entrées Seafood, VIII)

WELLSHIRE INN, Denver
    *Cream of Artichoke Soup (Soups, II)
    *Demi-Glacé Sauce (Sauces and Dressings, Etc., XII)
    *Leo's Spinach Salad (Salads, III)
    *Mustard Dressing (Sauces and Dressings, Etc., XII)
    *Tournedos Diane (Entrées Meat, X)

WIENERSTUBE RESTAURANT, Aspen
    *Broiled Barberry Duck Salad "Framboise" (Salads, III)
    *Chicken Vegetable Soup (Soups, II)
    *Raspberry/Walnut Dressing for Broiled Barberry Duck Salad "Framboise"
     (Sauces and Dressings, Etc., XII)
    *Salzburger Nockerl (Desserts, XI)
    *Wiener Schnitzel (Entrées Meat, X)

THE WILDFLOWER INN, Vail
    *Introduction; Lamb Shanks for Six (Entrées Meat, X)
    *Mosaic Nut Torte (Desserts, XI)
    *Oysters with Crackling for Six (Entrées Seafood, VIII)
    *Scallops Niçoise (Entrées Seafood, VIII)
    *Torta Regina (Desserts, XI)

J.B. WINBERIE, Denver, Boulder
    *Pita Chips with Artichoke (Appetizers, I)

ZENITH, Denver
    *Introduction; Roast Garlic Tamales (Appetizers, I)
    *Black Bean Sauce (Sauces and Dressings, Etc., XII)
    *Blue Corn Pancakes with Caramelized Apples and Bananas (Desserts, XI)
    *Chocolate Bread Pudding (Desserts, XI)
    *Goat Cheese Tart (Desserts, XI)

APPETIZERS I

APPETIZERS, I

Armenian Cheese Boreck (Rudi's) — p. 1
Avocado Red Pepper (Uptown Grill) — p. 1
Champignon Elegante (Rudi's) — p. 2
Chicken Quenelles with Mushroom Cream (Rudi's) — p. 3
Egg Roll (China Terrace) — p. 4
Escargots Bourguignonne (The Tyrolean Inn) — p. 4
Escargots Maison (Cafe Giovanni) — p. 5
Guacamole (El Noa Noa) — p. 5
Kiwi Scallops Cointreau (Delfannies Restaurant) — p. 6
Lamb Quesadilla (Bull & Bush) — p. 6
Marinated Mushrooms (The Old Country Inn) — p. 7
Melon and Prosciutto (Red Rooster Inn — Introduction) — p. 7
Mussels with Sauce Verte (The Vail Racquet Club) — p. 8
Pâté de Foie (Le Central) — p. 9
Pita Chips with Artichoke (J.B. Winberie) — p. 9
Potato Skins with Cheese and Bacon (Pearl's — Introduction) — p. 10
Quesadilla Vegetarian (Cantina) — p. 10
Rillettes de Porc aux Trois Poivrés (Le Central) — p. 11
Roast Garlic Tamales (Zenith — Introduction) — p. 12
Smoked Salmon Cheesecale (Blu's — Introduction) — p. 13
Steamed Bao (Little Shanghai) — p. 14
Steamed Meat Dumplings (Orchid Pavilion) — p. 14
Sunomono (Sushi Den — Introduction) — p. 15
Swiss House Artichoke Hearts (Boyle's Bar & Grill) — p. 15
Taquitos (The Riviera — Introduction) — p. 16
Vegetarian Dim Sum (China Terrace) — p. 17

RUDI'S

4720 Table Mesa Drive
Boulder, Colorado 80303
(303) 494-5858

Chef Faith Stone

Armenian Cheese Boreck

1   pound ricotta cheese
½   pound feta cheese
4   ounces sharp cheese, Kesseri or Swiss
1   egg
a few sprigs of fresh dill
a pinch of cinnamon
salt and pepper to taste
1   box filo dough
1   pound butter, melted
pastry brush

Combine all ingredients except for the filo and butter.

Lay the filo out flat and cover with plastic wrap to prevent from drying. Take 1 sheet of filo and lay separately, brush lightly with butter to cover but not too heavily. Add a second layer and brush with butter and then a third. With a knife cut the buttered sheets of filo in 4 vertical strips. Place a large tablespoon of cheese filling in the corner of each strip and fold over to form a triangle with the filling inside. Continue folding over into triangles (as you would fold a flag) up the length of the strip. Repeat this procedure with the remaining filo and filling. Brush the tops of the Borecks lightly with butter and bake at 350° until the triangles are browned and puffed.

UPTOWN GRILL

472 East Lionshead Circle
Vail, Colorado 81659
(303) 476-2727

Avocado Red Pepper Quesadilla
with Smoked Tomato Salsa (see Sauce section)

8   6½-inch hand-formed flour tortillas
1   sweet red pepper
2   ripe avocados
1   pound pepper jack cheese
½   bunch fresh cilantro
1   tablespoon ground cumin
1   teaspoon garlic powder
1   teaspoon salt
1   teaspoon black pepper

Roast and peel red pepper, deseed and dice. Peel avocado, slice thin. Grate cheese. Chop cilantro and add to cheese, add cumin, garlic powder, salt and pepper. Mix well.

To build quesadilla: In the tortilla, put the cheese, avocado, red pepper and cheese. Top with another tortilla. Saute in skillet with hot oil. Brown and flip. Cut the quesadilla into sixths and top with smoked tomato salsa. Garnish with cilantro sprig. Enjoy! Serves 4.

RUDI'S

4720 Table Mesa Drive
Boulder, Colorado 80303
(303) 494-5858

Chef Faith Stone

Champignon Elegante
(Original recipe)

3   pounds mushrooms
6   tablespoons butter
¼   cup onion—minced
2   cloves garlic—minced
1   stalk celery, thinly sliced
1   ounce slivered almonds, toasted
½   pound Brie cheese, cut into small chunks

Seasonings

¼   teaspoon dill
1 or 2 dashes Tabasco
pinch of chervil
salt and pepper to taste

Frangipane

½   cup unbleached flour
3   egg yolks
1¼   tablespoons butter—melted
pinch nutmeg
pinch pepper
½   cup scalded milk, hot

To make frangipane, combine flour, egg yolks, nutmeg and pepper in food processor; process until yolks and flour are thoroughly combined and mixture resembles wet sand, about 10 seconds. With motor running, add melted butter; process until butter is absorbed. With motor running, add milk in a steady stream; process until mixture is thick and completely smooth and pale yellow. Place frangipane in a skillet over medium heat; stir constantly until lumps begin to form. Continue stirring until mixture forms thick mass and leaves sides of pan, forming thin film on bottom. Reduce heat to low: continue stirring until mixture turns waxy yellow, about 3 minutes. Transfer mixture to flat plate; press into thick pancake. Refrigerate, covered, until completely chilled, about 2 hours or overnight.

Wipe mushrooms with a damp towel and remove stems and reserve for another use. Saute caps in a few tablespoons of butter until barely cooked.

Saute onions, celery and garlic in remaining butter until tender.

In a bowl combine chilled frangipane, sauteed onion mixture, almonds, Brie and seasonings. Mix thoroughly.

Fill mushroom caps with Brie mixture, chill to set, 20 minutes, and bake at 375° for 20-30 minutes, or until browned and hot. Serve hot.

RUDI'S

4720 Table Mesa Drive
Boulder, Colorado 80303
(303) 494-5858

Chef Faith Stone

Chicken Quenelles with Mushroom Cream

1½ pounds raw chicken breasts, skinned and boned
3   eggs
1½ cups heavy cream
¾   teaspoon tarragon
¾   teaspoon salt
dash freshly grated nutmeg
½   teaspoon ground white pepper
2   dashes Tabasco
3   cups chicken stock

garnish—2 tablespoons green onions, sliced
         1 tablespoon freshly grated Romano

Chop the raw chicken meat. Put it in the container of a blender or food processor with the eggs and cream and process to a smooth paste. Mix in the tarragon, salt, nutmeg and Tabasco.

Chill the mixture while making mushroom sauce. Recipe follows.

Keep sauce warm while heating stock for poaching quenelles. Bring the stock to a simmer and drop in quenelles mixture 1 tablespoon at a time. Poach for 10-15 minutes or until cooled through. Cut one in half to check. Cook the quenelles in several batches to keep them from overcrowding the pan.

Drain the cooked quenelles and keep warm on a platter. Spoon the hot mushroom cream over the platter and garnish with sliced green onions and a sprinkle of Romano.

Mushroom Cream

3   tablespoons butter
½   pound Colorado mushrooms wiped to remove dirt
2   cloves garlic
2   cups heavy cream
½   teaspoon salt
pinch pepper and grated cheese
¼   cup sherry
pinch of nutmeg

In a heavy saucepan bring the cream to a simmer and cook until reduced by half. Meanwhile melt the butter in a skillet and sauté the garlic and mushrooms until tender, but not mushy. Then stir the mushrooms into the reduced cream and season with salt, pepper, cheese nutmeg and sherry. Serves 6.

CHINA TERRACE

1512 Larimer Street
Denver, Colorado 80202
(303) 592-1032

Egg Roll

5   pounds cabbage
5   pounds celery
1   pound roast pork
1   pound baby shrimp
1½ ounces salt
2½ ounces sugar
¼   teaspoon white pepper
4   teaspoons sesame oil
25 egg roll wrappers
3   eggs, beaten
4   cups soybean oil

Cut cabbage into very thin slices and chop celery finely. Put cabbage and celery in boiling water for 15 seconds. Drain, then rinse thoroughly with cold water. Squeeze out excess water until very dry. Chop the roast pork finely. Mix together pork, cabbage, celery, shrimp, salt, sugar, white pepper and sesame oil. Spoon ½ cup of the mixture across one corner of each egg roll wrapper. Brush eggs evenly over all edges of wrappers. Roll wrappers around filling, folding in the corners. Heat soybean oil in wok until very hot. Fry about 5 to 7 egg rolls at a time until they turn golden, about 4 to 6 minutes. Drain on absorbent paper. Makes 25 egg rolls.

THE TYROLEAN INN

450 East Meadow Drive
Vail, Colorado
(303) 476-2204

Escargots Bourguignonne

2   dozen escargots
1   clove garlic, chopped
1   shallot, chopped
4   ounces red wine
½   pound butter, melted
dash salt and pepper
1   teaspoon worcestershire sauce
juice from one lemon
2   ounces parsley, chopped
2   cloves garlic, chopped

Rinse escargots well. In a small skillet, saute garlic (one clove) and shallot for 1 minute. Add wine and escargots and cook for 2 minutes. In a bowl, combine the remaining ingredients with the two cloves garlic to make garlic butter. Place escargots in stone snail dish and cover with the garlic butter. Bake in 375° oven until golden brown (about 8 minutes).

CAFE GIOVANNI

1515 Market Street
Denver, Colorado 80202
(303) 825-6555

Escargots Maison

24 French snails
2   tablespoons butter
2   cloves garlic, minced
1   shallot, minced
2   tablespoons cognac
2   egg yolks
2   cups heavy cream
1   tablespoon minced fresh parsley
salt to taste
white pepper to taste

Place snails, butter, garlic and shallot in a sauté pan and sauté over medium heat for 2 minutes. Add cognac to the pan and allow to flame. Add the cream and lower the heat. Allow the cream to come to a boil. In a separate bowl, lightly beat egg yolks. Add ¼ cup of the hot cream to the egg yolks and mix well. Return this mixture to the pan and allow the snails to simmer until the sauce is thick. Add the parsley and salt and pepper to taste. Use imagination when serving the escargots: try a puff pastry shell or wrap them in parchment paper. Cafe Giovanni cuts a doubled piece of parchment paper into a half-heart shape, as one would to make a valentine. Beginning at the point and extending half or two-thirds of the way up, double-fold the two edges together to form a pocket between the layers. Put the escargots in the pocket and close the remaining edges. Fasten with paper clips. Butter the paper and bake at 450° until golden brown, about 5 minutes. Remove paper clips before serving. Serves 6.

EL NOA

722 South Santa Fe Drive
Denver, Colorado 80204
(303) 623-9968

EL NOA NOA

1920 Federal Boulevard
Denver, Colorado
(303) 455-6071

For festive, authentic Mexican food, Noa Noa is the place. Here is a variation of their delicious guacamole.

Guacamole

1   tablespoon chopped jalapeno or serrano peppers
2   medium avocados, peeled and seeded
1   small onion, finely diced
2   cloves garlic, minced
1   tablespoon lemon juice
dash of Tabasco

Place above in blender and blend till smooth. Transfer to a bowl and chill till serving time. Makes 1¼ cups. Serve as dip with tortilla chips (see Bread section).

DELFANNIES RESTAURANT

215 East Foothills Parkway
Fort Collins, Colorado 80525
(303) 223-3354

Kiwi Scallops Cointreau

5-6 ounces Bay or Sea scallops
1½ ounces Cointreau
2   ounces lemon juice
pinch salt
pinch black pepper
1   kiwi, sliced

Combine all ingredients in a saute pan. Cook over medium heat until scallops are no longer opaque. Garnish with thin slices of kiwi. Serves 1.

BULL & BUSH

Cherry Creek Drive at Dexter
Denver, Colorado
(303) 759-0333

Lamb Quesadilla
with Apple Mint Salsa (see Sauce section)

1   pound ground lamb
½   cup diced onion
½   cup peeled fresh apple, diced
¼   teaspoon sage
1   teaspoon salt

1   teaspoon black pepper
8   flour tortillas
2   cups grated Jack cheese
8   ounces cream cheese

In large frying pan saute lamb, onion, apple, sage, salt and black pepper until lamb is cooked. Pour off fat. Cover one flour tortilla with ¼ cup grated Jack cheese and ¼ cup lamb mix. Dot with 3 to 4 tablespoons of cream cheese. Top with another flour tortilla and grill until cheese melts. Cut into four pieces. Serve with Apple Mint Salsa. Serves 6.

THE OLD COUNTRY

134 Union Boulevard
Lakewood, Colorado
(303) 986-5531

Marinated Mushrooms

½   cup St. Mary's Gourmet Vinegar
1   teaspoon tarragon
3   cups olive oil
1   teaspoon dry mustard
2   tablespoons garlic salt
2   tablespoons garlic powder
2   tablespoons oregano
juice from one fresh lemon
1   dash Tabasco
1/8 cup sugar
2   pounds button mushrooms
3   red bell peppers, sliced

Mix all of the above ingredients, except for the mushrooms and bell pepper slices, in a blender. Wash mushrooms and shake off excess water. Put liquid mixture into a gallon crock, not stainless steel. Add mushrooms and bell peppers. Mix well. Let stand 6 to 8 hours before serving. Serves 8 to 10.

RED ROOSTER INN

16 Mountain Evans Boulevard (off Hwy 285)
Pine Junction, Colorado 80470
(303) 838-4537

For more than 27 years, mountain residents as well as travelers through Colorado's Front Range have fallen in love with the Red Rooster Inn—even when it was a trolley car serving only chicken.

In 1963, the Rhodes converted a streetcar (named Desire at the time) into a restaurant located in Pine Junction along U.S. 285, 35 miles southwest of Denver. Today the restaurant is larger, incorporating the old trolley, and offers award-winning selections from the gourmet menu.

Dinner, lunches, breakfasts and special events all receive special attention from a dedicated staff. The Red Rooster Inn—a Rocky Mountain Treasure.

Melon and Prosciutto

1½ inch slices of cantaloupe or honeydew melon
strips of prosciutto

Wrap the prosciutto around the melon, fasten with a toothpick, and serve as an appetizer. Serves 2 to 6.

Pasta and Dressing

½   pound packaged pasta shells, cooked and well rinsed
½   cup Italian-style salad dressing
¼   cup olive oil
¼   cup prepared mustard

THE VAIL RACQUET CLUB

East Vail
Vail, Colorado
(303) 476-4700

The Vail Racquet Club has long been one of Vail's finest restaurants. Here is a variation of one of their continental seafood appetizers.

Mussels with Sauce Verte

1½ dozen mussels

Sauce Verte

1   cup mayonnaise (see Sauce section)
½   cup chopped spinach
1/3 cup chopped parsley
1/3 cup chopped watercress
1   tablespoon snipped fresh chives
1   tablespoon snipped fresh dill
2   teaspoons dried tarragon leaves
1   tablespoon lemon juice
dash salt
½   cup water
½   clove garlic, crushed

Pasta and Dressing

½   pound packaged pasta shells, cooked and well rinsed
½   cup Italian-style salad dressing
¼   cup St. Mary's Gourmet Vinegar
¼   cup olive oil
¼   cup prepared mustard

Check mussels, discarding any that are not tightly closed. Scrub well under cold running water to remove sand and seaweed. With a sharp knife, trim off the "beard" around edges. Let soak 1 to 2 hours in cold water.

Meanwhile, make sauce verte: Combine all ingredients in blender or food processor, and process until smooth. Turn into a small bowl; refrigerate, covered. Makes 1¼ cups.

Lift mussels from water, and place in a colander. Rinse with cold water; let drain.

Place mussels in large skillet; add ½ cup water and garlic.

Cook, covered, over high heat 5 to 8 minutes. Shake skillet frequently, so mussels will cook uniformly.

With slotted utensil, remove mussels to dish; refrigerate, covered, 1 hour.

Meanwhile prepare dressing and mix with pasta. Have pasta as an accompaniment.

To serve: Spoon 1 teaspoon sauce verte on top of each mussel in shell. Reserve remaining sauce. Turn shells onto serving platter. Mound filled mussels in the middle. Pass reserved sauce.

Serves 6 appetizers.

LE CENTRAL

112 East Eighth Avenue
Denver, Colorado 80203
(303) 863-8094

Pâté de Foie

1½ pounds chicken liver
½ cup Port wine
½ cup milk
2 small white onions, finely minced
¼ pound butter
1 teaspoon leaf thyme
1 teaspoon fresh dill
1 bay leaf, crumbled

½ cup brandy or sherry
1¼ pounds sweet butter, softened
¼ cup cream
1 teaspoon ground coriander
salt and white pepper to taste
small handful fresh chopped parsley
2 hard-boiled eggs
½ cup finely minced walnuts

Wash, clean and trim livers; add Port wine and milk. Let stand overnight. Mince onions and saute them in ¼ pound butter with thyme, dill and bay leaf. Cook slowly until tender and turn up heat to deglaze with brandy or sherry. Add marinated livers and cook until medium-rare to medium. Remove from heat and cool completely. Pour off any accumulation of liquid and turn mixture into mixing bowl or food processor. Blend with softened sweet butter and cream. Add remainder of spices and eggs. Mix until smooth. Add walnuts and mix one minute longer. Transfer to desired container and cool. May be served out of container or shaped into desired form. Serves 6 to 8.

J. B. WINBERIE'S

1247 Pearl Street Mall
Boulder, Colorado 80302
(303) 444-4884

Pita Chips with Artichoke Dip

To prepare Pita Chips

Using 6″ or 7″ loaves of Pita bread, cut each loaf into 6-8 wedges, separating the two halves of each wedge. Bake in 350° oven until golden brown. Salt lightly.

To prepare Artichoke Dip

8 ounces cream cheese, room temperature
4 teaspoons dijon mustard
3 tablespoons mayonnaise
1 1/8 teaspoon herb salt
4 hearts artichokes, drained, cut in ½-inch pieces

Beat cream cheese on medium speed, 1-2 minutes, until smooth.

Add mustard, mayonnaise and herb salt; continue to beat on medium speed until thoroughly combined.

Remove from mixer; fold in artichokes by hand until thoroughly combined. Refrigerate until ready to assemble.

To assemble:

On a platter or large dinner plate, place a mound of pita chips spread to the edge.

Place a scoop of Artichoke Dip in the center.

Sprinkle with diced greed onions and diced tomato.

Sprinkle shredded Monterey Jack cheese evenly over entire platter.

Place under broiler until cheese melts.

Enjoy!

PEARL'S

1125 Pearl Street
Boulder Mall
Boulder, Colorado
(303) 443-4548

Pearl's is a delightful three-story, art nouveau-art deco, eatery and elegant saloon. Unique house specialty drinks, as well as casual munchies and contemporary meals such as Chicken in Champagne Sauce, fried onion rings and more, regularly grace guests' tables. Adorning Pearl's walls are lovely commissioned oil paintings. A large oil painting of a reclining nude beauty, Pearl, with exquisite flaming red hair, had to be reclothed with a drape because of protests from offended Boulderites opposed to Pearl ''au naturel.'' This fun Boulder eatery with its paintings, art nouveau decor, specialty drinks, and good food is a great place to make a habit.

Potato Skins with Cheese and Bacon

This unusual appetizer is an exciting finger food that works great for parties and special occasions.

2	jumbo white potatoes	3	ounces cooked bacon, crumbled
8	ounces grated cheddar cheese	8	ounces sour cream with chives

Bake two jumbo San Luis Valley potatoes (Idaho white) at 400° for approximately 1 hour and 15 minutes or until soft. Home ovens vary quite a bit so feel the potatoes periodically. Let cool ½ hour and slice in half lengthwise. Scoop out meat of potato leaving approximately ¼ inch of meat attached to skin. Cut each half into thirds lengthwise. Arrange the 12 pieces skin side down on a cookie sheet and sprinkle with grated cheddar cheese. Feel free to substitute favorite cheese. We use cheddar because we like the flavor with the potato skin and bacon. Sprinkle 3 ounces of cooked bacon on top of cheese. Put back in oven for approximately 10 minutes until cheese is bubbling and brown. Serve with a side dish of sour cream and chives. Eat these baked potato skins with your fingers. Serves 2 to 4 people.

CANTINA

411 East Main Street
Aspen, Colorado 81611
(303) 925-3663

Quesadilla Vegetarian

2	12-inch flour tortillas	green chiles, finely chopped
3	ounces grated cheddar cheese	green onions, chopped
3	ounces mozzarella cheese	guacamole (see Appetizer section)
	chopped mushrooms	salsa crude (see Sauce section)
	spinach, chopped	

On grill or oven, put one tortilla on bottom. Top with grated cheese, chopped mushrooms, spinach, green chiles and onions. Place one tortilla on top and heat through. Serve with guacamole and salsa crude in center.

LE CENTRAL
112 East Eighth Avenue
Denver, Colorado 80203
(303) 863-8094

Rillettes de Porc aux Trois Poivres
(Mild, spreadable Pork Pâte)

3   pounds pork shoulder, 2/3 lean, 1/3 fat
1   tablespoon salt
½   teaspoon black whole peppercorns
½   teaspoon green whole peppercorns
½   teaspoon pink whole peppercorns
¼   teaspoon coriander
¼   teaspoon crushed garlic
2   cloves
6   bay leaves
1   bottle white, dry wine

Cut pork into 2- to 3-inch chunks. Put all ingredients in heavy saucepan with enough white wine to reach 1 inch above the meat. Bring to boil, cover, and simmer slowly 5 ½ to 6 hours. Cool. Blend together in a food processor or blender. Serve cold with dijon mustard, croutons, and a white Loire wine. Serves 12.

ZENITH

901 Larimer
Denver, Colorado
(303) 629-1989

Zenith is the ticket. Located in the tower above the renovated Tivoli Brewery, Zenith offers an unobstructed view of the Denver skyline as well as the Rocky Mountains.

Voted by *Westword* editors and readers as "1990 Best Restaurant Overall," "Best New Restaurant on its way up in 1989," and also "Denver's Best New Restaurant of 1988." Zenith offers fine dining with a varied menu of grilled items, fresh fish, poultry and pastas at an affordable price.

Under the guidance of Chef-owner Kevin Taylor and owner Janet Wright, Zenith will create a special menu to ensure that guests' meals are nothing less than spectacular. Whether it is for business, a special occasion, or just for fun, Zenith is the ticket.

Roast Garlic Tamales
with Black Bean Cumin Sauce
(see Sauce section)

soaked corn husks
½   clove roasted garlic
½   cup shortening
½   cup masa harina (corn flour)
½   cup blue cornmeal
2   cups fresh corn kernels
½   cup chicken stock or bouillon
½   teaspoon cumin
¼   teaspoon cayenne pepper
salt and pepper to taste

Roast garlic clove in oven until slightly brown and squeezes out easily from skin. Blend in food processor with shortening until fluffy. Remove to mixing bowl. Blend half of corn until smooth and milky and fold into shortening mix. Add rest of corn and dry ingredients and mix thoroughly. Add stock or bouillon and season.

Mixture should be somewhat pasty but won't stick to hands when worked with (if too dry, add more liquid; if too sticky, add cornmeal).

Roll into soaked corn husks and tie both ends. Steam in the steamer basket until inserted knife comes out clean (about 10 minutes). Or microwave for 2 minutes. Cut open and push up bottom like a baked potato to make eating easier. Serve with black bean sauce (see Sauce section).

BLU'S

193 East Gore Creek Drive
Vail, Colorado
(303) 476-3113

Reasonably priced creative cuisine, an extensive wine list, friendly, efficient service and a casual, pleasant atmosphere are all ingredients of Blu's. From eggs, sandwiches and full entrees to salads, soups and appetizers, the brunch/lunch selections will appeal to any size appetite. At dinner, Chef Blu expands the menu to include fresh fish, pasta, steak, veal and chicken entrees. As an added enticement, the food and wine are priced affordably. Blu's is ideal for a snack or full meal, any time of the day.

Smoked Salmon Cheesecake

This appetizer is not sweet as the name may imply, but it is an unusual marriage of salmon and cheese. It is best served slightly chilled with one's favorite bottle of white wine.

Crust

2   cups dry bread crumbs
½   cup butter, melted
1   tablespoon fresh parsley, chopped
½   teaspoon salt

Filling

2½ cups sour cream
1   pound cream cheese
3   large eggs
1   teaspoon salt
½   teaspoon white pepper
1½ tablespoons lemon juice
8   ounces smoked salmon, boned, skinned and finely diced

Sauce

8   ounces sour cream
1   tablespoon dill weed

Mix ingredients for crust and press into the side and bottom of a 10″ springform pan. With an electric mixer, cream softened cheese, adding one egg at a time. Add remaining ingredients except salmon and pour half of mixture into pan. Add salmon to the remaining mixture and pour into pan. Bake at 325° for 45-55 minutes. Remove from oven and cool for 15 minutes. Refrigerate at least four hours (preferably overnight) before cutting. Mix sauce and spoon over cut wedges. May be garnished with capers and chopped red onion. Serves 12.

LITTLE SHANGHAI

460 South Broadway
Denver, Colorado
(303) 722-1292

Steamed Bao

Dough

1 to 1½ pounds flour
1 cup cold water

1 cup hot water

Ingredients

½ cup chopped green onion
¼ pound chopped pork
¼ ounce ginger, chopped
¼ to ½ pound chopped cabbage

3 tablespoons soy sauce
1 tablespoon salt
1 teaspoon black pepper

Mix water and flour into a regular dough. Mix all the rest of ingredients thoroughly and let stand about 20 minutes. With the dough, make 3-inch diameter, thin pancakes. Put a spoonful of filling ingredients on each pancake. Steam for 15 to 20 minutes and serve. Serves 2.

ORCHID PAVILION

1050 Walnut Street
Boulder, Colorado
(303) 449-4353

Steamed Meat Dumplings

1 pound ground pork sausage
1 pound fresh ground pork
2 teaspoons salt
15 water chestnuts, finely chopped
1-2 tablespoons minced fresh ginger
½ cup cornstarch
½ cup chicken broth
1 tablespoon light soy sauce
1 tablespoon salted turnips, finely minced
4 tablespoons sugar
1 teaspoon teriyaki sauce
1 teaspoon sherry
1 teaspoon sesame oil
½ cup Chinese parsley, finely chopped
1 stalk green onions, finely chopped
1 package wonton skins or 1 recipe of egg noodle dough

Preparation: Mix all ingredients except wonton skins. Sauté mixture in skillet until pork is cooked.

Wrapping: Trim off 4 corners of wonton skins to form circles. Drop 1 teaspoon mixture onto middle of the skin, gather up skin sides, letting the dough pleat naturally. Press together. Steam 10 to 15 minutes and serve. Makes 10 dozen dumplings.

SUSHI DEN

1469 South Pearl Street
Denver, Colorado
(303) 777-0826

Toshihiro Kizaki's Sushi Den has a reputation for having sushi rivaling the best in the nation. Sushi aficionados from New York, San Francisco, and Japan nightly thrill to the cuisine of the Sushi Den. Toshi personally checks all ingredients and carefully prepares sushi supervising his staff. The menu is varied offering salmon teriyaki, shrimp tempura and much more.

Sunomono
(Vinegared Cucumber)

1	green cucumber
3	tablespoons rice wine vinegar or St. Mary's Gourmet Vinegar
1	tablespoon water
2	teaspoons sugar
½	teaspoon salt
½	teaspoon finely grated fresh ginger
2	tablespoons light soy sauce
2	tablespoons cooked crab or octopus, diced (optional)

Peel cucumber, cut in half lengthwise and remove seeds. Slice crosswise into thin slices. Combine all other ingredients and marinate cucumber in the mixture for at least an hour. Serve small helpings as an appetizer.

BOYLE'S BAR & GRILL

4042 East Virginia Avenue
Denver, Colorado 80222
(303) 322-3025

Swiss House Artichoke Hearts

1	teaspoon fresh garlic, minced
3-4	ounces butter
4	whole artichoke hearts, quartered
3	ounces Swiss cheese
	chopped parsley

Saute garlic in butter for 1-2 minutes. Add artichoke hearts, saute for additional 2-3 minutes or until hot. Place in au gratin dish, cover with Swiss cheese and melt under broiler. Top with chopped parsley.

THE RIVIERA

4301 East Kentucky
Glendale, Colorado
(303) 758-9719

No Colorado restaurant history would be complete without mention of the Riviera, which has long been a favorite watering hole for Coloradans. This inexpensive, unpretentious little spot regularly holds shoulder-to-shoulder packed crowds of beer drinkers, margarita enthusiasts, and Mexican food aficionados.

Although the proportions are not exact, here is the recipe for Taquitos, one of the many popular items at the Riviera.

Taquitos

3   corn tortillas (see Bread section)
1   cup shredded beef, cooked season to taste
¾   cup guacamole (see Appetizer section)

Sprinkle 1/3 cup of beef into each corn tortilla. Add onions and seasoning. Roll stuffed tortillas. Quickly deep-fry stuffed tortillas in hot oil. Top with guacamole. Serves one.

CHINA TERRACE

1512 Larimer Street
Denver, Colorado 80202
(303) 592-1032

Vegetarian Dim Sum

6   dried Chinese mushrooms
3   tablespoons peanut oil
¼   cup finely chopped spring onions
1   clove garlic, crushed
1   teaspoon finely grated, fresh ginger
2   cups finely sliced cabbage
½   cup finely chopped bamboo shoots and/or water
    chestnuts
2   tablespoons light soy sauce
2   teaspoons sesame oil
2   tablespoons cornflour
2   eggs, beaten
8   ounce wonton wrappers (see Bread section Egg Noodles)

Stuffing mixture: Soak mushrooms in hot water for 30 minutes. Then remove and discard stems, chop caps very finely. Heat peanut oil in a wok or large frying pan and fry spring onions, garlic and ginger on low heat for a minute or two. Add cabbage and continue to fry, stirring, until cabbage is soft. Add bamboo shoots, water chestnuts and mushrooms and cook for a minute or two longer. Remove from heat, put into a large bowl and add seasonings, cornflour and enough beaten egg to bind the mixture together.

Take a wonton wrapper in the palm of your hand. Put a tablespoonful of mixture in the center and gather up the pastry to enclose filling. With the back of a teaspoon, press points of the dough down to cover. Squeeze dumpling firmly to make dough adhere to filling. Put in an oiled steamer and steam for 10 minutes.

These may be served at once, or refrigerated for a day or two and deep fried, or reheated by further steaming before cooking. Makes 36.

SOUPS II

P. McClure

SOUPS, II

Avocado Soup with Rock Shrimp (Mike Berardi's) — p. 1
Brodo (Mike Berardi's) — p. 1
Carrot Mint Soup (Rudi's) — p. 2
Chicken Stock (Marina Landing) — p. 2
Chicken Stock, St. Mary's Style (Philadelphia Filly) — p. 3
Chicken Stock Substitute, Vegetarian — Hot and Spicy (The Denver Salad Company) — p. 3
Chicken Vegetable Soup (Wienerstube Restaurant) — p. 4
Chicken Velvet and Corn Soup (Imperial Wok) — p. 5
Chilled Lime and Honeydew Soup (Rudi's) — p. 5
Chinese Hot and Sour Soup with Shrimp (Mostly Seafood) — p. 6
Chowder of Corn, Wild Rice and Apple Bacon (The Little Nell) — p. 6
Consommé (The Copper Kettle) — p. 7
Cream of Artichoke Soup (Wellshire Inn) — p. 7
Cream of Zucchini (Cafe Giovanni) — p. 8
Crème du Broccoli (Muddy's Java Cafe) — p. 8
Curried Squash Soup (Tante Louise) — p. 9
Egg Drop Soup (Red Coral Restaurant) — p. 9
Fish Stock (Charlemagne) — p. 10
Greek Fisherman's Soup (Bibelot Restaurant) — p. 10
Hearty Lentil Soup (Reiver's Restaurant) — p. 11
Hot and Sour Soup (China Terrace) — p. 11
Iced Cucumber Yogurt Soup (Alpenrose) — p. 12
Mang-Tay Nua Cua (Asparagus and Crabmeat Soup) (Chez Thoa) — p. 12
New England-Style Clam Chowder (Goodfriends) — p. 13
Purée of Leek Soup with Smoked Mussels and Spinach (John's Restaurant) — p. 14
Soup à L'Oignon Gratinee (La Petite Maison — Introduction) — p. 15
Split Pea and Potato Soup (Lincoln 100) — p. 15
Szechwan Hot and Sour Soup (Wang's Mandarin House — Introduction) — p. 16
Szechwan Soup (House of Hunan) — p. 17
Tomato Bisque (Sweet Basil) — p. 17

MIKE BERARDI'S

2115 East Seventeenth Avenue
Denver, Colorado
(303) 399-8800

Avocado Soup with Rock Shrimp

6 to 8 large shrimp, boiled, rinsed, shelled, deveined and cut
into chunks and set aside in refrigerator.

Broth

2   cups chicken broth (see this section)
2   medium avocados, deseeded, peeled and cut up
½   cup chopped onions
½   cup lime juice
3   cloves minced garlic

In a blender, combine chicken broth, avocados, onions, lime juice and garlic until smooth.
Refrigerate soup until ready to serve. Just before serving, add chunks of shrimp and stir. Float
thin slice of fresh lemon or lime and parsley sprigs atop each bowl of soup. Serves 4.

Brodo*
(Basic Broth)

1½ pounds beef shoulder
1   pound veal
½   capon
2   carrots
2   stalks celery
1   medium-size onion
4   quarts water
2   teaspoons salt
salt and pepper to taste

Arrange the beef shoulder, capon, carrot, celery, and onion in a deep soup kettle. Cover with
the water, add the salt, and bring to boil. Simmer, covered, for 3 hours. Season with salt and
pepper to taste. Remove the beef and capon, reserving for another use. Strain the stock and
discard the vegetables. After the stock has cooled, skim off the fat, use as much or as little of this
stock as you need at one time. Serves 8. (See Tortellini in Pasta section.)

*variation

RUDI'S

4720 Table Mesa Drive
Boulder, Colorado 80303
(303) 494-5858

Chef Faith Stone

Carrot Mint Soup

6-8 carrots (1½ pounds) peeled and cut into chunks
1   onion quartered and thinly cut into chunks
3   cloves garlic minced
8   cups vegetable or chicken stock
½   cup cream
2   teaspoons salt
½   teaspoon pepper
¼   cup fresh minced mint leaves or 2 teaspoons dried mint
2   tablespoons brown sugar

Combine the carrots, onions, garlic and stock in a soup pot. Bring to a simmer and cook for 40 minutes or until carrots are tender. Purée the carrot chunks in a blender until smooth and return to the pot. Stir in cream, salt, pepper, mint and brown sugar. Mix well. Taste and adjust seasonings.

MARINA LANDING

8101 East Belleview
Denver, Colorado
(303) 770-4741

Chicken Stock
(for Chicken Green Chili Stew)

large saucepan
1   large boiling fowl giblets
1   carrot
1   small onion
2   cloves garlic, peeled
10   peppercorns
2   teaspoons salt
1   cup leafy celery

Cut the fowl into pieces. Clean and slice the vegetables. Cover all the ingredients with cold water and bring them to a boil, lower the flame and simmer for about 3½ hours.
Let the ingredients cool off in the broth and then strain the broth. Set aside until cooled. Skim the fat from the top and store until ready to use.

PHILADELPHIA FILLY

278 South Downing Street
Denver, Colorado
(303) 733-2208

Chicken Stock, St. Mary's Style

2 to 4 skinless chicken breasts
½   cup St. Mary's Gourmet Vinegar
½   cup light soy sauce
6 - 8 cups water

Place above ingredients in pot, making certain chicken is covered in liquid and bake 1 hour at 350°.

Remove chicken and enjoy or save and shred for cold salad dish.

Refrigerate broth for chicken stock (add 2 more cups of water when prepared to use in recipes).

Or freeze chicken stock in ice tray and use each ice cube of frozen stock for bouillon and add 1 cup water to each chicken stock cube.

THE DENVER SALAD COMPANY

2700 South Colorado Boulevard
Denver, Colorado
(303) 691-2050

THE BOULDER SALAD COMPANY

2595 Canyon Boulevard
Boulder, Colorado
(303) 447-8272

THE DENVER SALAD COMPANY

14201 East Public Market Drive
Aurora, Colorado
(303) 750-1339

Chicken Stock Substitute,
Vegetarian — Hot and Spicy

1   cup St. Mary's Cajun Vinegar
5   cups water
1   large carrot, chopped
2   quartered onions, peeled
2   cloves garlic
1   stalk celery, chopped
1   bay leaf
1   leek (green part discarded, thoroughly washed and chopped)

Place in large pot and bring to boil. Reduce heat and simmer 2 hours. Cool the stock and strain.

WIENERSTUBE RESTAURANT

633 East Hyman Avenue
at Spring Street
Aspen, Colorado 81611
(303) 925-3357

Chicken Vegetable Soup

One of Jill St. John and Robert Wagner's favorite soups!

1   large fresh whole chicken, 1 to ½ pounds
3   bay leaves
crushed peppercorns
1   tablespoon dry Italian seasoning or the fresh equivalent in herbs finely
     chopped (parsley, thyme, basil, oregano,
     marjoram, 1 whole sprig of rosemary)
1   clove of garlic, crushed
1   cup diced scallions, including the green part
2   cups of diced celery, ¼ to ½-inch chunks
2   cups of diced carrots, ¼ to ½-inch chunks
salt to taste

Take a large 4 quart stock pot, fill half with cold water and wash the whole fresh chicken, place it in the water and under moderately high heat, bring to a slow rolling boil. Add crushed peppercorns and bay leaves and simmer for at least one hour until chicken is done. Remove chicken from broth and let cool. De-bone and skin the chicken, dice the meat into ½-inch cubes and set aside in refrigerator.

Continue to simmer the strained broth down to about a quart and a half of liquid. Then add diced scallions, celery, carrots, fresh herbs and other spices and simmer until vegetables are done, but still firm. Add the diced chicken meat, adjust the soup to your liking with salt. This soup may be made ahead and then served piping hot with some fresh, crisp French or Austrian farmers' rye bread. Thanks to Mr. Arthur Langenkampf for letting us peek into his kitchen! Serves 4 to 8.

IMPERIAL WOK

5674 North Academy Boulevard
Colorado Springs, Colorado
(719) 548-0300

Chicken Velvet and Corn Soup*

1   whole small chicken breast, skinned, split, and boned
2⅔ cups chicken stock
1½ teaspoons cornstarch
¹/₈ teaspoon pepper
1   egg white
1   8-ounce can cream-style corn
2   tablespoons cold water
1   tablespoon cornstarch
½   teaspoon sesame oil (optional)
1   thin slice boiled ham, finely chopped

Place chicken breast pieces between two sheets of plastic wrap. Working out from center, pound chicken pieces to ¼-inch thickness. Remove plastic wrap. With sharp cleaver or knife, finely chop chicken.

In mixer bowl, combine chicken, ¼ cup chicken broth, the 1½ teaspoons cornstarch, salt, and pepper. Beat with electric mixer till well blended. With clean beaters, beat the egg white till fluffy but not stiff; fold into chicken mixture.

In large saucepan or Dutch oven, bring remaining 2½ cups chicken broth to boiling. Stir in cream-style corn. Slowly blend cold water into the 1 tablespoon cornstarch. Stir into broth along with sesame oil, if desired, and the chicken mixture. Cook and stir for 2 minutes. To serve, garnish with finely chopped boiled ham. Makes 3 to 4 servings.

*variation

RUDI'S

4720 Table Mesa Drive
Boulder, Colorado 80303
(303) 494-5858

Chef Faith Stone

Chilled Lime and Honeydew Soup

1   honeydew melon — peeled, seeded and chopped
juice of 6 fresh limes, or ⅓ cup
1   cup apple juice
½   cup sour cream
1   teaspoon fresh grated ginger

Purée the melon with lime and apple juice. Transfer the mixture to a serving bowl and stir in sour cream and ginger. Serve well chilled. Garnish individual servings with a thin slice of lime and sprig of fresh mint.

MOSTLY SEAFOOD

303 Sixteenth Street
Denver, Colorado
(303) 892-5999

Chinese Hot and Sour Soup with Shrimp

1   pound large shrimp, peeled and deveined, tail on
6   dried Chinese mushrooms
1   pound bean curd (tofu) cut into ½ inch squares
¾   cup canned bamboo shoots cut into slender strips
      an inch long
1 ½   quarts chicken stock
2   tablespoons soy sauce
3   tablespoons rice wine vinegar
2   eggs, beaten
3   tablespoons cornstarch mixed with 3 tablespoons
      cold water
1   tablespoon sesame oil
3   scallions, coarsely chopped

In a bowl cover mushrooms with warm water. Let them soak for half an hour. When they are soft, drain and cut into thin strips. In a deep pot combine stock, soy, mushrooms, and bamboo shoots. Bring to a boil, then reduce to a simmer. Add the shrimp, bean curd, vinegar and pepper. Simmer 3 minutes, add ½ of the cornstarch. Use more if thicker soup is desired. While stirring pour the beaten egg into the broth. Divide equally into soup bowls and put a little sesame oil in each bowl. Garnish with green onions. For a variation try scallops. Serves 6.

THE LITTLE NELL

675 East Durant Avenue
Aspen, Colorado
(303) 920-4600

Chowder of Corn,
Wild Rice and Apple Bacon

4   ears of corn (cut off cob)
½   cup wild rice
½   cup onion, diced
¼   cup applewood smoked bacon (or regular), diced
1   quart chicken broth (see Soup section)
1   quart heavy cream
1   talespoon fresh sage, chopped
salt
white pepper
¼   cup cornstarch, dissolved in water

In a 4-quart saucepan, saute bacon and onions until bacon is crisp and onions soft. Pour off half of the grease. Add remaining ingredients and simmer ½ hour. Add enough cornstarch to thicken. Season and serve.

THE COPPER KETTLE

535 East Dean Avenue
Aspen, Colorado 81611
(303) 925-3151

Consommé

6   cups chicken consommé
1   bay leaf
1   cup clam bouillon
¼   cup dry white wine
1   carrot, peeled and shredded
1   celery stalk (with leaves) sliced thin
1   bell pepper (red or green), seeded and slivered
2   scallions (tops included), sliced thin on the diagonal

Combine chicken consommé, bay leaf and clam bouillon in a saucepan; cover and bring to a boil. Lower heat and simmer 15 minutes; remove bay leaf. Add wine. Divide vegetables between bowls; pour steaming hot broth over them and serve. Serves 6.

WELLSHIRE INN

3333 South Colorado Boulevard
Denver, Colorado
(303) 759-3333

Cream of Artichoke Soup

1   can artichoke hearts, packed in brine
1   cup half & half
3   cups chicken broth, strained
salt and pepper
cornstarch in cold water

Drain artichoke hearts and place in blender. Add 1 cup chicken broth and blend to purée. While blending, heat half & half and add the remainder of the chicken broth. Combine puréed hearts and seasoning and simmer for 15 minutes. Add cornstarch mixture to thicken. Serves 6.

CAFE GIOVANNI

1515 Market Street
Denver, Colorado 80202
(303) 825-6555

Cream of Zucchini

1   pound zucchini, sliced
1   cup chicken stock
4   tablespoons chopped onion
2   tablespoons butter
2   cups half & half
½   teaspoon sugar, granulated
salt to taste
white pepper to taste
roux

In a saucepan combine the zucchini, chicken stock, sugar and ½ teaspoon salt. Bring to a boil and simmer for 15 minutes. In a separate pan saute the onion in butter until just tender. Puree both the onion and zucchini (with liquid) in a blender or food processor. Add the half & half and slowly bring the soup to a near boil. Add only enough roux to thicken as desired. Serve either hot or chilled.

MUDDY'S JAVA CAFE

2200 Champa Street
Denver, Colorado 80202
(303) 298-1631

Crème du Broccoli

1   bunch (about 1¾ pounds) broccoli, chopped
1   cup mushrooms, chopped
½   cups beef stock
4   cups chicken stock
4   ounces butter
dash of worcestershire sauce
pinch of nutmeg

Bring the stock, butter and seasonings to a boil. Add the vegetables and cook lightly until the broccoli is fork tender, about 20 minutes. Remove from heat and add the following:

1   teaspoon capers
2   ounces (1 small jar) pimientos

Let cool and blend. Return blended ingredients to pot and reheat. Stir in the following:

2   cups sour cream
1   cup half & half

Heat to boiling point. DO NOT BOIL. Garnish with a dollop of sour cream or chopped parsley.

In the summer, serve the soup chilled and with pumpernickel bread. Creme du Broccoli makes a great light supper. Yields 8 servings.

TANTE LOUISE

4900 East Colfax Avenue
Denver, Colorado 80220
(303) 355-4488

Curried Squash Soup

6   whole acorn squash
3   large onions, sliced
3   tablespoons curry powder
olive oil
2   cups dry white wine
2   quarts homemade chicken stock
salt and pepper
2   tablespoons chopped fresh cilantro

Roast acorn squash until soft. Cut in half, remove seeds and discard. Scoop out nearly all of the squash, leaving a little to give the squash cup some stability. Refrigerate squash cups. Meanwhile, in a large, thick saucepan, heat the olive oil and saute the onions until they begin to caramelize. Add the curry powder and saute about 2 minutes with the onions. You may need to add more olive oil. Deglaze the pan with the white wine and add the squash. Cover with the chicken stock and bring it to a boil. Simmer about 30 minutes, purée the soup and season with salt and pepper. Reheat the squash cups in a steamer or in the oven, being careful not to break them. Bring the soup back to the boil, fill the squash cups with the soup and garnish with chopped fresh cilantro.

RED CORAL RESTAURANT

1591 South Colorado Boulevard
Denver, Colorado
(303) 758-7610

Egg Drop Soup

1   quart chicken broth
1   tablespoon cornstarch
1   well-beaten egg
2   tablespoons sliced green onion

In saucepan slowly stir the cornstarch into the chicken broth. Cook, stirring constantly, till slightly thickened. Slowly pour in the well-beaten egg; stir once, gently. Remove from heat. garnish with green onion. Makes 4 servings

CHARLEMAGNE

400 West Main
Aspen, Colorado
(303) 925-5200

Fish Stock*

6   pounds of fresh fish, including bones, head, and flesh
2   medium-size onions
2   leeks
3   quarts water
1   cup white wine
1   small bay leaf
2   teaspoons fennel seed
1   cloves
1   teaspoon salt

Place all ingredients in a deep kettle and bring to a boil. Lower the heat and simmer for 45 minutes. Strain the stock, cool, and store tightly covered in the refrigerator. Makes 12 cups.

*variation

BIBELOT

Restaurant

1424 Larimer
Larimer Square
Denver, Colorado 80202
(303) 595-8400

Greek Fisherman's Soup

5   cups clam juice
1   cup water
2½ cups white wine
½   cup orange juice concentrate
2   cups diced tomatoes
2   tablespoons dried orange peel
1   teaspoon crushed saffron
pinch crushed red pepper
1   teaspoon white pepper
2   carrots, diced
2   potatoes, diced
1   leek, cut in half and sliced julienne crosswise
½   ounce Pernod
1   ounce extra-virgin olive oil
2   cups assorted poached seafood and cooked shellfish (shrimp, scallops, etc.)

In a large pot, add clam juice, water, white wine, orange juice concentrate, diced tomatoes, orange peel, saffron, red peppers and white pepper. Bring to boil. You may thicken slightly with arrowroot and water.

Add carrots, leek, Pernod and olive oil when original liquid boils. Poach 20 minutes.
Just before serving, add cooked seafood mixture (shrimp, scallops, etc.).
Enjoy!

REIVER'S RESTAURANT

1085 South Gaylord
Denver, Colorado 80210
(303) 733-8856

Hearty Lentil Soup

2½ cups lentils (soak for 1 hour)
½ medium onion, diced
1 carrot
3 celery stalks (with leaves) coarsely chopped
3-4 potatoes, unpeeled, washed, ½-inch pieces
1 tablespoon butter
3 tablespoons dry sack sherry
1 teaspoon garlic powder
1 bay leaf

2 teaspoons black pepper
2 teaspoons thyme
2 teaspoons parsley
1 cup ketchup
1 cube beef bouillon
½ cup St. Mary's Gourmet Vinegar
beef or pork bones — scraps if desired

Sauté onion, celery, carrot, and potatoes in butter. Add spices and bouillon. Add lentils, water to cover (beef and pork scraps also). Add ketchup and vinegar. Let simmer for 1 to 2 hours, adding water if necessary for desired thickness. May be served with cruet of vinegar and thick slice of bread and butter. Makes 10 to 12 cups.

CHINA TERRACE

1512 Larimer Street
Denver, Colorado 80202
(303) 592-1032

Hot and Sour Soup

20 wan yee (tree) mushrooms
1 quart water for broth
4 ounces bean curd, cut in thin slices
3 ounces pork, shredded
3 ounces bamboo shoots, shredded
2 teaspoons vinegar
½ teaspoon salt
1½ teaspoons sugar
2 teaspoons soy sauce
¼ teaspoon white pepper
2 teaspoons cornstarch dissolved in 6 tablespoons water
1 egg, beaten

Soak wan yee mushrooms in a small amount of water for ½ hour. Pour quart of water into soup pot. Add bean curd, pork, bamboo shoots and wan yee. Cook until water boils. Add vinegar, salt, sugar, soy sauce and white pepper. Stir in cornstarch mixture and egg. Add sesame oil. Serves 4.

ALPENROSE

100 East Meadow Drive
Vail, Colorado 81657
(303) 476-3194

Iced Cucumber Yogurt Soup

3   cloves garlic, minced
1   teaspoon salt
2   tablespoons olive oil
2   cups plain yogurt
1   cucumber, peeled and chopped
juice from ½ lemon
2   cups water
¼   cup chopped parsley
½   cup chopped walnuts
salt and pepper

Combine garlic, salt and olive oil. Stir this mixture into the yogurt. Combine cucumber, lemon juice and rind with the water. Stir well and add to the yogurt mixture. Add parsley, walnuts, salt and pepper. Serve in cups; put an ice cube in each. Serves 4.

CHEZ THOA

159 Fillmore
Denver, Colorado 80206
(303) 355-6464 or 355-2323

Mang-Tay Nua Cua
(Asparagus and Crabmeat Soup)

3   quarts water
3   pounds pork bone
1   tablespoon fish sauce (Nuoc Maui)
2   tablespoons cornstarch, dissolved in ½ cup water
½   can (16 ounces) white asparagus, cut in small chunks or 16 ounces, approximately
     2 cups, of fresh asparagus which has been steamed for 7 to 10 minutes or boiled
     for 3 to 5 minutes and cut into small chunks
2   cups cooked crabmeat
2   green onions, chopped
black pepper
few drops soy sauce

Bring water to a boil and add the pork bones. Remove the scum and continue to cook the bones for 1 hour. Pour the stock through a fine strainer. Discard the bones. Season stock with fish sauce in a saucepan. Bring the stock to a boil, stir in the cornstarch and water mixture, stirring constantly for 5 minutes.

Add crabmeat and white asparagus, keep stirring until the soup comes to a boil again. Sprinkle the green onion and black pepper over soup before serving, seasoning with a few drops of soy sauce. Serve hot. Serves 6.

GOODFRIENDS

3100 East Colfax Avenue
Denver, Colorado 80206
(303) 399-1751

New England-Style Clam Chowder

½   diced yellow onion
2   stalks of celery, diced
3   pounds peeled and diced potatoes
2   pounds chopped clams (frozen or canned, not drained)
4   ounces sherry
4   ounces clam base
¼   teaspoon white pepper
¼   teaspoon granulated garlic
¼   teaspoon thyme
1   pound butter
¾   quart flour
1   quart milk
1   pint half & half
1   cup cream
3   quarts and 1 pint water
oyster crackers for garnish

Combine 4 ounces butter and ¾ quart flour in a saucepan over low heat to make roux; set aside.

Sauté onion, celery and spices in remaining butter in a large saucepan or kettle (at least 10 quarts).

Add potatoes and 1 pint water, cook for 5 minutes, but do not brown potatoes.

Add chopped clams, sherry, clam base and 3 quarts water. Bring to a boil and cook until potatoes are tender.

Heat combined milk products to 120-140°F while potatoes are cooking.

Stir in roux to potato and clam mixture slowly thickening. Slowly add heated milk products, stirring constantly. Remove from heat and serve.

JOHN'S RESTAURANT

2328 Pearl
Boulder, Colorado 80304
(303) 444-5232

Purée of Leek Soup
with Smoked Mussels and Spinach

4	medium-sized leeks
3	ounces of butter
2	shallots
1	large potato, peeled, diced and boiled
2	ounces of dry sherry
12	fresh blue mussels
1½	quarts of water
4	ounces of chardonnay
1	bay leaf
8	smoked mussels, washed and bearded
1	cup spinach, fine chopped
sprinkle of fresh grated nutmeg and fresh ground white pepper	
4	ounces half & half

In saucepan bring water, white wine, and bay leaf to a boil. Drop in mussels, cover pan and simmer five minutes until mussels open.

Wash leeks and slice thin. Chop shallots. Sauté in heavy saucepan shallots and leeks very slowly in butter (being careful not to brown the shallots or leeks). Add dry sherry and diced boiled potato. Add broth from the mussels. Blend ingredients in blender till very smooth. Return blended soup to pot and add chopped fresh and smoked mussels, plus finely chopped spinach. Simmer five minutes on low heat. Skim and season to taste with salt, fresh ground white pepper and nutmeg. Finish with half & half.

LA PETITE MAISON

1015 W. Colorado Avenue
Colorado Springs, Colorado
(719) 632-4887

Holly and Jeff Mervis oversee every exquisite detail of the contemporary cuisine served in this country French setting. Here is a popular, classic French onion soup recipe.

Soupe à L'Oignon Gratinee

4   onions, thinly sliced
6   tablespoons butter or olive oil
6   cups beef broth, hot
½   cup sherry
6   slices French bread, toasted or stale
½   cup grated Gruyere cheese
grated Parmesan cheese

Sauté onion in butter or oil until brown. Add broth and sherry.
Place a slice of toast in each of 6 bowls.
Pour soup over; sprinkle with cheese. Bake at 350° for 5 minutes. Serves 6.

LINCOLN 100

100 East Ninth Avenue
Denver, Colorado
(303) 894-0600

Split Pea and Potato Soup*

1   tablespoon unsalted margarine
1   medium-size yellow onion, chopped
2   cups chicken broth
2   cups water
½   cup dried split green peas, rinsed and sorted
2   medium-size potatoes, peeled and quartered
¼   teaspoon black pepper

In a large heavy saucepan, melt the margarine over moderate heat. Add the onion and cook, uncovered, until soft — about 5 minutes. Stir in the chicken broth and water and bring to a boil — about 4 minutes. Add the peas and potatoes; adjust the heat so that the mixture bubbles gently, cover, and cook for 30 minutes or until the peas and potatoes are tender. Remove from the heat and cook for 10 minutes.

In an electric blender or food processor, purée the soup in 5 batches, whirling each batch about 15 seconds. Return to the pan, set over low heat, and bring to serving temperature, stirring often. Add the pepper. Serves 4.

*variation

WANG'S MANDARIN HOUSE

25958 Genesee Trail Road
Genesee Towne Center
Golden, Colorado 80401
I-70 Exit 254
(303) 526-9111

Not only does Wang's have marvelous Chinese food overlooking a romantic mountain view, but it also has dancing and live piano music nightly at modest prices.

Szechwan Hot and Sour Soup*

6   cups chicken stock
2   ounces cellophane noodles, soaked
1   cup finely chopped cooked pork or chicken, or mixture
     of both
4   dried Chinese mushrooms, soaked and chopped
1   small can bamboo shoots, chopped
1   teaspoon finely grated fresh ginger
1   tablespoon cornflour
4   tablespoons cold water
1   egg, slightly beaten
2   tablespoons light soy sauce
½   teaspoon salt or to taste
2   tablespoons vinegar
ground black pepper to taste
pinch of chili powder, optional
2   teaspoons sesame oil
2   spring onions, finely chopped
3   tablespoons green onions, chopped

Bring stock to a boil in a large pan and add noodles cut in short lengths, pork or chicken, mushrooms, bamboo shoots, green onions, and ginger, Stir the cornflour and the cold water together to blend thoroughly and add to simmering soup, stirring constantly until it boils and clears. Dribble the beaten egg into soup, stirring rapidly with chopsticks or fork so that it sets in fine shreds.

Remove soup from heat, add remaining ingredients and mix well. Serves 6.

*variation

HOUSE OF HUNAN

440 South Colorado Boulevard
Denver, Colorado
(303) 329-9955

Szechwan Soup

2   cups soaked cellophane noodles
15   dried Chinese mushrooms
1   tablespoon oil
½   cup finely chopped cooked pork
1   tablespoon dark soy sauce
2   teaspoons sugar
¼   cup hot water
½   cup chopped cooked prawns
½   cup fresh bean curd, chopped
6   cups chicken or pork stock
1   tablespoon light soy sauce
1   tablespoon Chinese sweet vinegar or other mild vinegar

1   tablespoon Chinese wine or dry sherry
1   teaspoon chili oil
2   eggs, beaten
1½   tablespoons cornflour
6   tablespoons cold water
salt and pepper to taste

Cut soaked noodles into short lengths. Soak mushrooms in hot water for 30 minutes. Cut off and discard stems, then slice mushroom caps finely.

Heat oil in a saucepan and fry mushrooms and pork, stirring constantly, until they start to turn slightly brown. Add dark soy sauce, sugar and ¼ cup water and simmer, covered, until mushrooms have absorbed almost all the liquid. Add prawns and bean curd and stir fry for 1 minute. Add stock and noodles, bring to a boil, then reduce heat and simmer for 3 minutes. Add light soy, vinegar, wine and chili oil. Dribble beaten eggs into simmering soup, stirring constantly so that egg separates into fine shreds. Mix cornflour smoothly with cold water, then add to soup away from heat. Return to heat and stir constantly until soup is thickened. Season to taste with pepper and salt. Serve immediately. Serves 6 to 8.

SWEET BASIL

193 East Gore Creek Drive
Vail, Colorado 81657
(303) 476-0125

Tomato Bisque

4   ounces butter
1   onion, chopped
1   clove garlic, minced
1   green pepper, chopped
2   stalks celery, chopped
6   tablespoons flour

4   cups tomatoes, peeled and diced
3   cups chicken stock
2   teaspoons thyme
2   teaspoons rosemary
salt and pepper
½   cup heavy cream

Melt butter in an iron pot and saute onion, garlic, green pepper and celery until soft. Mix in flour and cook over low heat 5 minutes. Add tomatoes, chicken stock and seasonings. Cook over medium heat, stirring occasionally until soup thickens (about 30 minutes). Puree soup in a blender. Add cream and serve.

SALADS III

SALADS, III

Asian Salad (Rick's Cafe) — p. 1
Avocado Melon Salad (Rudi's) — p. 1
Black Bean and Shrimp Salad with Coriander Dressing (Bull & Bush — Introduction) — p. 2
Blackened Tenderloin Caesar Salad (Simms Landing — Introduction) — p. 3
Braised Belgian Endive with Chevre and Niçoise Olives (John's Restaurant) — p. 4
Broiled Barberry Duck Salad "Framboise" (Wienerstube Restaurant — Introduction) — p. 5
Caesar Salad (Red Lion Inn) — p. 6
Crabmeat Salad Crêpe (The Magic Pan Crêperie) — p. 6
Crab Salad (Mostly Seafood) — p. 7
Crab and Pasta Salad (Patina Grill) — p. 7
Curry Rice Salad with Shrimp with Curry Rice Salad Dressing (The Denver Salad Company) — p. 8
Dilled Chicken and Potato Salad (Reiver's Restaurant) — p. 8
Fresh Field Greens served with Roma Tomatoes and Goat Cheese (Firefly Cafe — Introduction) — p. 9
Grilled Asparagus with Shiitake Mushroom Salad with Lemon Tarragon Vinaigrette (Sweet Basil) — p. 10
Grilled Chicken Salad with Apples, Pecans and Lime (The Little Nell) — p. 10
Hearts of Palm and Artichoke Salad (Ute City Banque) — p. 11
Leo's Spinach Salad (Wellshire Inn) — p. 11
Market Curry Chicken Salad (The Market) — p. 12
Mark's Pasta Primavera Salad with Oil Free Dressing (Mark's Milk Bar) — p. 13
Mediterranean Pasta Salad (Goodfriends) — p. 14
Mountain Meadow Lamb Salad with Raspberry Vinaigrette (Strings) — p. 15
Pasta and Broccoli Salad (The Golden Eagle Inn) — p. 16
Pasta Salad with Basil Pesto (Rudi's) — p. 17
Red Onion Potato Salad (The Denver Salad Company) — p. 17
Romano Crusted Chicken Salad with Tomato Basil Vinaigrette (Sfuzzi) — p. 18
Salmon Salad (Bistro Adde Brewster — Introduction) — p. 19
Santa Fe Tabouli (The Denver Salad Company) — p. 20
Smorgasbord Salad (Mary and Lou's Cafe) — p. 21
Spinach Salad with Honey Mustard Poppy Seed Dressing and Homemade Mayonnaise (Flagstaff House Restaurant)—p. 21
St. Mary's Cabbage, Artichoke and Caper Slaw (Canterbury Cheese) — p. 22
Summer Pasta Salad (Chicago Joe's) — p. 22
Summer Salad (Off Belleview Grill) — p. 23
Tabouleh (Greens Natural Foods Cafe) — p. 23
Thai-Chicken Pasta Salad with Thai-Vinaigrette Dressing (The Denver Salad Company) — p. 24
Vail Mountain Summer Salad Served with a Fresh Wild Blueberry-Dijon Vinaigrette (Alfredo's — Introduction) — p. 25
Vegetable-Cheese Salad with Artichokes (Cache-Cache) — p. 26

RICK'S CAFE

80 South Madison
Denver, Colorado 80209
(303) 399-4448

Asian Salad
(Rick's Cafe House Specialty)

1	pound spaghetti	1	green bell pepper, cut into thin strips
1	bunch fresh basil	1	red bell pepper, cut into thin strips
1	bunch scallions	1	small can water chestnuts
½	bunch fresh cilantro	1	small jicama, cut into thin strips
1	stalk bok choy, cut into thin strips	1½	pounds cooked turkey (optional)

Cook, drain and chill the spaghetti. Chop the basil, cilantro and scallions. Cut the bok choy into thin strips diagonally across the stalk. Cut the peppers into thin strips. Cut the jicama into thin strips after peeling. Drain the liquid off the water chestnuts. If adding turkey, cut into thin strips. Prepare the Asian Salad Dressing (see Sauces and Dressings section). Then combine everything in a large bowl with the entire batch of Asian Salad Dressing and serve. For hotter seasoning, sprinkle with crushed red pepper. Serves 4 as an entree, 6 to 10 as a side dish.

RUDI'S

4720 Table Mesa Drive
Boulder, Colorado 80303
(303) 494-5858

Chef Faith Stone

Avocado Melon Salad

3   avocados
1   large honeydew or cantaloupe
3   scallions
12   ounces fresh spinach
2   ripe tomatoes
olive oil
1   clove garlic, minced
3   lemons
a few sprigs of fresh mint
a few sprigs of fresh basil

Prepare 6 plates with a bed of washed spinach.
Cut melon and avocado in chunks, mince scallions, mint and basil. Toss the melon, avocado and herbs in a bowl with enough olive oil to lightly coat. Place several spoons of the mixture on each plate of spinach and squeeze lemon over the plates. Serve immediately. Serves 6.

BULL & BUSH

Cherry Creek Drive at Dexter
Denver, Colorado
(303) 759-0333

The Bull & Bush is known as the "Granddaddy of Watering Holes" in Denver and will be celebrating its 18th anniversary this year. Playboy Magazine voted the Bull & Bush as one of the top 100 taverns in the country.

This restaurant-pub is meant to be casual and fun. It was modeled after a centuries-old London pub of the same name built in 1645.

Sports fans already know that this pub is the best sports bar in town. For the last three years it has been awarded "Favorite Sports Bar or Restaurant" by the *Denver Post* Dining Survey. With three satellite dishes and ten televisions the Bull & Bush loyal patrons can come to socialize, and watch all the important games simultaneously.

What makes this pub so different is their outstanding food. The chef creates great Southwestern specialties including BBQ ribs, New Mexican dishes, and great sandwiches and salads. Guests must try the famous steak sandwich or steak cooked on a rock!

The Bull & Bush serves lunch, dinner and weekend brunch. Don't forget to try the great variety of English beers on tap and enjoy the weekend live entertainment.

Black Bean and Shrimp Salad
with Coriander Dressing (see Sauce section)

1 ²/₃ cups dried black beans, washed, picked over, soaked
1   onion, chopped coarse
2   garlic cloves, chopped
1   3-inch cinnamon stick, halved
1½   teaspoons chopped fresh thyme leaves or ½ teaspoon
     crumbled dried thyme
¼   teaspoon cayenne pepper
1   bay leaf
½   teaspoon salt
½   pound snow peas, strings removed, sliced into julienne
     strips
1   small cantaloupe, seeded, peeled and cut into small
     chunks
6   scallions, trimmed and sliced thin
3   tomatoes, peeled, seeded, coarsely chopped and drained
1   small red bell pepper, seeded and chopped
20   large shrimp, cleaned and steamed with 1 slice lemon,
     salt, and black pepper about 3 minutes or until just
     cooked. Chill
1   head red leaf or bib lettuce, leaves separated, washed and
     spun or patted dry

Put the beans in a heavy 4-quart saucepan with the onion, garlic, cinnamon, thyme, cayenne pepper, bay leaf and salt. Add enough water to cover the beans by 2 inches, bring it to a boil, and boil for 10 minutes. Reduce the heat and skim off the foam that rises to the surface. Cover and simmer just until the beans are tender — 1 to 1½ hours. Drain the beans and rinse under cold water. Remove the cinnamon and bay leaf, and drain the beans again.

Prepare the Coriander Dressing (see Sauce section).

Blanch the snow peas in boiling water for 15 seconds and refresh them under cold, running water for a few moments; drain and place on paper towels to dry.

In a large bowl, combine the cantaloupe, scallions, tomatoes, red bell pepper, shrimp, snow peas and black beans. Pour 1 cup of the Coriander Dressing over the salad and toss lightly. To serve, mound the salad on lettuce leaves arranged on individual plates or on a platter, and pass the remaining dressing separately. Serves 6.

SIMMS LANDING

West Sixth Avenue at Simms
Lakewood, Colorado
(303) 237-0465

Simms Landing is one of Denver's most popular and award — winning restaurants, where one can dine overlooking the city lights. It is one of the crowd-pleasing restaurants that renews food critics' faith in the meaning of their jobs. After Simms celebrated its 12th anniversary in 1988, it was again awarded a "4" Star Rating.

The food is fresh, original, delicious, and the chef's talent is bringing together interesting ingredients in new ways to create exciting dishes.

The informal elegance of Simms is duplicated in its menu selections; Slow Cooked Prime Rib, Grilled Raspberry Chicken Salad, Pasta with Lobster in Brandy Champagne Sauce, Blackened Trout finished in a shrimp and pecan butter sauce, Fresh Salmon baked with Fresh Herbs and Vegetables cooked in parchment paper and served with dijon mustard and dill Hollandaise sauce.

The sauces at Simms are marvelous and the decision of ordering can be difficult, but whatever the dish the consistency of the kitchen will be one's assurance of getting a great meal.

A decadent close after a meal at Simms would by "sharing" one of their exceptional desserts — may we suggest the Chocolate Pate covered with a raspberry sauce, or perhaps the famous Pineapple Pie topped with macadamia nut ice cream.

It is no wonder Simms Landing has been awarded "Favorite Overall Restaurant," "Favorite for Seafood, Weekend Brunch, Lunch," "Favorite for Romantic Meal," and "Favorite Restaurant to take Out-of-Town Guests" — you are invited to be Simms Landing guests.

Blackened Tenderloin Caesar Salad

Caesar Salad Dressing

2   eggs
1   teaspoon garlic powder
1   tablespoon black pepper
½   tube anchovy paste
¼   cup lemon juice
½   teaspoon salt
1/8   cup red wine
4   cups olive oil
¼   cup Parmesan cheese

Combine all ingredients except oil and cheese in the blender and blend for 30 seconds. Scrape down. Add oil and cheese and blend for 10-15 seconds

Combine 6 ounces of Caesar dressing with 1 bunch of Romaine lettuce, torn into small pieces. Mix with ½ cup croutons and freshly grated Parmesan.

Divide salad onto 4 serving plates, top each with 3 ounces of sliced grilled beef tenderloin and ¼ cup of Parmesan cheese. Serves 4.

JOHN'S RESTAURANT

2328 Pearl
Boulder, Colorado 80304
(303) 444-5232

Braised Belgian Endive
with Chevre and Niçoise Olives

4   Belgian endive
24   nicoise olives, pitted and coarsely chopped
2   anchovy filets, mashed
1   garlic clove, mashed or fine chopped
1   tablespoon chopped parsley
2   tablespoons bread crumbs
2   tablespoons olive oil
2   tablespoons of capers
½   teaspoon of ground oregano
4   ounces mild chevre (goat cheese)
½   lemon
salt to taste

Wash and slice endives in half lengthwise. Coat skillet with one tablespoon olive oil and a sprinkle of salt. Quickly brown the endives on the flat side.

Turn endive over and add to skillet remaining olive oil, olives, capers, garlic, anchovies and parsley. Sauté one minute on medium heat.

Remove endive and place on oven-proof platter. Spread the flat sides of endive with the chevre.

Add bread crumbs to the skillet with olives and capers, stir and spoon over the endive. Bake five minutes in the oven at 375°.

Remove from the oven and sprinkle lightly with lemon juice. Serve immediately.

WIENERSTUBE RESTAURANT

633 East Hyman Avenue
at Spring Street
Aspen, Colorado 81611
(303) 925-3357

The story of the Wienerstube Restaurant begins in a small Austrian village called Villach, Carinthia, where the hosts and chefs, Gerhard Mayritsch and Helmut Schloffer, spent their childhood. After leaving Villach, both men served chef apprenticeships and decided to move to Aspen, Colorado, to open a restaurant in 1965. The result of this Austrian experience is the "Stube," as Aspen residents call it.

The word "Stube" in German means "to be at home." Wienerstube means "a Viennese living room." Gerhard and Helmut have created what every Austrian farmhouse has — a gathering place, a pleasant place for family and friends. The Wienerstube is warm and cozy — gemutlich.

Another Austrian custom is represented here. As guests enter the restaurant they notice a large table in one corner that is called the "Stammtisch." That word means "to belong to" in German; in Aspen, it is called "the locals' table." In Europe, Stammtisch refers to a certain clientele, repeat customers, who want to sit at a special table and do not want to wait to be seated. Aspenites who know the custom eat many breakfasts, lunches and dinners here and the discussions at the "Stammtisch" are often lively and always interesting.

Beyond the comfort and pleasant atmosphere, Gerhard and Helmut have made excellent food and consistency their hallmark. They use strictly fresh ingredients, spices and flavorings. The food is simple and delicious. After all, the Wienerstube has served over 2,800,000 customers over the years, and that many customers can't be wrong!

Guests are welcomed at the Wienerstube, where their attentive hosts, Gerhard and Helmut, are waiting to serve them.

Broiled Barberry Duck Salad "Framboise"*

fresh lettuce medley (enough for appetizer or main course)
2   whole fresh Barberry duck breasts 10 to 12 oz. each
salt and pepper to taste
2   tablespoons of oil

Wash and spin fresh lettuce medley (corn lettuce, bib lettuce, red-leaf lettuce, egghorn lettuce, radicchio, curly endive, arugula, tatsai, mitsuna and red or regular mustard greens, nasturtium leaves and flowers, johnny-jump-up viola/pansy, and other available tender greens. To assure crispness place cleaned dry lettuce in a bowl covered with plastic wrap into the refrigerator for at least two hours before serving.

Cut the pair of deboned duck breasts in half, in the direction of the removed breast bone, make criss-cross shallow cuts in the duck skin, brush with oil and place it skin side down on a broiler or in a preheated skillet with a small amount of oil. Over high heat brown skin and turn once, and place in preheated oven at 375° and roast about ten minutes for medium done. Hold in a warm place until ready to serve for about 5 additional minutes.

Assemble in a stainless mixing bowl the salad greens and toss with just enough dressing (see Sauce section) to coat the leaves lightly. Place on a chilled large plate in center, garnish with nasturtium flowers, fresh raspberries and coarsely chopped walnuts. Place roasted duck breasts on a slicing board and slice on an angle thinly in strips. Place around the lettuce in the form of a spiral. Serve at once. Additional dressing may be served on the side.

Serve with freshly baked French bread. A sparkling glass of "Blanc de Blanc" goes well with this salad entree. Serves 4 to 8.

*See "Framboise" in Sauce section.

RED LION INN

Highway 119
Boulder, Colorado
(303) 442-9368

Caesar Salad

3   small heads romaine lettuce, washed, dried and chilled
1   cup crisp croutons
1   cup freshly grated Parmesan cheese
½   teaspoon salt
3   cloves garlic
8   anchovy filets
1   teaspoon dry mustard
1   cup olive oil
⅓   cup St. Mary's Gourmet Vinegar
3   eggs, coddled
1   teaspoon Worcestershire sauce
juice of 1½ medium-size lemons
freshly ground pepper

   Tear romaine into pieces and place in a large salad bowl. Top with croutons and cheese. Combine salt and garlic in a small bowl and mash. Add anchovies and mustard and mix together until a paste is formed. Add the oil a little at a time, stirring constantly. Add vinegar, eggs, Worcestershire sauce and lemon juice. Mix well. Pour dressing around inside edge of salad bowl. Toss well with greens. Grind pepper over all. Serves 6.

THE MAGIC PAN CRÊPERIE

1465 Larimer
Denver, Colorado
(303) 534-0123

Crabmeat Salad Crêpe

14   ounces cooked crabmeat
½   cup mayonnaise
½   cup celery
2   teaspoons horseradish
2   tablespoons chopped green onions
¼   teaspoon salt
¼   teaspoon pepper
chopped parsley

   Combine the above ingredients except parsley. Cover and chill. Spoon onto crêpes (see Basic Crêpe) and roll. Garnish with small dab of mayonnaise and sprinkle with chopped parsley. Makes 12 crêpes.

MOSTLY SEAFOOD

303 Sixteenth Street
Denver, Colorado
(303) 892-5999

Crab Salad

1   pound crab meat
¾   cup diced celery
¼   cup diced onion
1   tablespoon lemon juice
¼   teaspoon black pepper
1   tablespoon minced parsley
3-4 tablespoons mayonnaise

In a bowl mix the celery, onion, lemon juice, pepper, parsley and mayonnaise. Add the crab meat and mix gently and thoroughly. Serves 4.

For crab and seafood salad follow same recipe but substitute one pound of crab and white fish blend for the crab meat.

PATINA GRILL

Hyatt Regency
Vail-Beaver Creek, Colorado
(303) 949-1234

Crab and Pasta Salad

6   ounces vermicelli or other thin pasta
2   tablespoons Oriental sesame or peanut oil
1   medium-size sweet red or green pepper, cored, seeded,
       and cut into matchstick strips
2   cloves garlic, minced
3   green onions, sliced thin
6   ounces fresh, thawed, frozen, or canned crabmeat, picked
       over for bits of shell and cartilage
1   small head romaine or other lettuce (about ½ pound),
       torn into bite-size pieces
2   tablespoons reduced-sodium soy sauce
2   tablespoons St. Mary's Gourmet Vinegar
1   tablespoon medium-dry sherry or white wine
$1/8$ teaspoon cayenne pepper

Cook the vermicelli according to package directions, omitting the salt. Drain and transfer to a serving bowl.

Meanwhile, heat 1 tablespoon of the sesame oil in heavy 10-inch skillet over moderately high heat for 1 minute; add the red pepper and garlic and stir-fry just until limp — about 3 minutes. Add the green onions and stir-fry 30 seconds longer.

Combine the vermicelli, red pepper-green onion mixture, crabmeat, and lettuce in a large bowl. In a small bowl, whisk together the remaining sesame oil and the soy sauce, vinegar, sherry and cayenne pepper. Pour over the past mixture, tossing gently to mix. Serves 4.

THE DENVER SALAD COMPANY

2700 South Colorado Boulevard
Denver, Colorado
(303) 691-2050

THE DENVER SALAD COMPANY

14201 East Public Market Drive
Aurora, Colorado
(303) 750-1339

THE BOULDER SALAD COMPANY

2595 Canyon Boulevard
Boulder, Colorado
(303) 447-8272

Curry Rice Salad with Shrimp
with Curry Rice Salad Dressing

6	cups uncooked white rice
12	cups water
1	pound bay shrimp, cooked and peeled
2	cups chopped celery
2	cups snow peas
¼	cup finely chopped red onions
½	cup black olives, sliced

Cook rice in water. Note: cook rice first to allow adequate time to cool. Once cool, prepare Curry Rice Salad Dressing (see Sauces and Dressing section) then mix dressing with rice, then add shrimp, celery, snow peas, red onions, and black olives.

REIVER'S RESTAURANT

1085 South Gaylord Street
Denver, Colorado
(303) 733-8856

Dilled Chicken and Potato Salad

2	whole chicken breasts, boned and cooked
1½	pounds small new potatoes, cooked in chicken broth
2	green peppers, chopped
1	bunch scallions, trimmed and sliced
1	cup thinly sliced celery
¼	cup chopped dill
¼	cup drained capers
1	cup olive oil
⅓	cup St. Mary's Gourmet Vinegar
1	teaspoon sugar
2 to 3	tablespoons of dijon mustard

salt and pepper

Cut chicken into large bite-size pieces. Mix with potatoes, peppers, scallions, celery, dill, and capers. Beat oil with vinegar, sugar and mustard until smooth and thick. Pour over salad and toss. Chill and serve with sliced plum tomatoes and Greek olives.

FIREFLY CAFE

5410 East Colfax Avenue
Denver, Colorado 80220
(303) 388-8429

The Firefly Cafe has been in existence since December 1981 at its present location. Formerly a bar and Mexican food restaurant, it has undergone an about face and become an oasis on East Colfax Avenue. With a new dining room and a very popular and well-planted garden and patio, the Firefly Cafe continues to provide good, fresh food at a reasonable price in the beginning of its ninth year.

Breakfast, lunch and dinner are served seven days a week with a well-received breakfast menu served until 3:00 p.m. on weekends. Fresh baked goods, wonderful desserts from the pastry case, and fresh ground coffee make it a good choice all day. The menu provides a good selection of homemade soups, fresh garden salads, sandwiches, fresh seafood, pastas and pizzas and many other items. The specials of the day usually number between eight and twelve different creations.

The dress is nicely casual. There is a piano in the dining room and oftentimes someone may sit down and play for tips, dinner and a bottle of wine for an hour's worth of tickling the ivories. This has been the policy for many years. As has been said, it is better to have no money, the Firefly Cafe and its piano, than to have money and no Firefly Cafe.

Fresh Field Greens served with
Roma Tomatoes and Goat Cheese

This salad which has already proven to be popular is a new addition to the menu. One may use any variety of greens. The Firefly Cafe likes the mixture of baby red leaf lettuce, radicchio (endive), arugula and chou frise' (curled Savoy cabbage).

4-5 ounces goat cheese
¼   cup toasted pine nuts
olive oil for sauteing, the fruitier the better, about 2 ounces
2-3 ripe Roma tomatoes
2-3 ounces of hazelnut liqueur (preferably Frangelico)
mixed greens to make 4 good-sized salads

In a saute pan heat the oil to just below the smoking point and add the goat cheese which has been cut into rounds or small chunks. Add the pine nuts and allow them to brown slightly.

As the cheese begins to melt stir with wooden spoon or spatula and add the liqueur. The mixture should begin to resemble a dressing. Allow it to reach a boil and reduce the heat. After this mixture cools slightly, toss with the greens. Serve on plate garnished with the tomatoes.

The salad as described above is on the sweet side and the greens are just wilted slightly. If one prefers a little tang with it, serve with a small amount of Balsamic or St. Mary's Gourmet Vinegar. Serves 4.

SWEET BASIL

193 East Gore Creek Drive
Vail, Colorado 81657
(303) 476-0125

Grilled Asparagus
and Shiitake Mushroom Salad
with Lemon Tarragon Vinaigrette
(see Sauce section)

6   ounces shiitake mushrooms, no stems
24 asparagus spears, about 5 inches long
mixed greens for 4
8   Belgian endive leaves

Prepare the Lemon Tarragon Vinaigrette (see Sauce section).

Brush the asparagus and shiitake with olive oil, season with salt and pepper and grill over charcoal or gas, turning once or twice for 2-3 minutes.

Cut the mushrooms into bite size pieces and toss, hot, with the greens and a little dressing, and divide among four plates garnished with endive leaves.

Place 6 hot asparagus spears on top of each salad, sprinkle some more tarragon around the edge of the salad and serve at once. Serves 4.

THE LITTLE NELL

675 East Durant
Aspen, Colorado 81611
(303) 920-4600

Grilled Chicken Salad
with Apples, Pecans and Lime

1½ pound chicken breast, boneless
1   red onion, julienned
¼   cup of pecans, chopped (roasted at 200° for 20 minutes)
juice of 2 limes
½   cup mayonnaise
4   tablespoons cilantro, chopped

Grill chicken over hot charcoals on both sides until cooked. Chill. Julienne chicken and toss with remaining ingredients. Season with salt and white pepper.

UTE CITY BANQUE

501 East Hyman
Aspen, Colorado 81611
(303) 925-4373 or 925-3621

Chef David Zumwinkle

Hearts of Palm and Artichoke Salad*

½ cup hearts of palm in vinegar, drained and diced
½ cup artichoke hearts in vinegar, drained and diced
2 avocados, peeled, deseeded and cut into halves

Mix artichoke hearts and hearts of palm. Fill center of avocados and keep on top of avocados the hearts of palm and artichoke heart mixture. Prepare vinaigrette.

Tomato-Basil Vinaigrette

⅓ cup St. Mary's Gourmet Vinegar
⅓ cup prepared mustard
⅓ cup olive oil
1 cup fresh tomatoes, finely diced
2 tablespoons chopped basil

Mix above ingredients and spoon over each filled avocado.

*variation

WELLSHIRE INN

3333 South Colorado Boulevard
Denver, Colorado
(303) 759-3333

Leo's Spinach Salad

8-10 large spinach leaves
½ cup sliced mushrooms
5 slices of bacon, crisply fried and drained

Take fresh spinach, trim stems and wash thoroughly. Drain and chill. Slice fresh mushrooms, crumble cooked bacon. Use mustard dressing (see Sauce section). Top spinach leaves with fresh mushrooms and bacon. Serves 1.

THE MARKET

1445 Larimer
Denver, Colorado 80020
(303) 534-5140

Guests flock to The Market for great pastries, coffees and deli items. Gary, the owner and chef, creates daily specials which vary with availability of fresh ingredients, but which never lack creativity.

Here is one of their most popular dishes.

Market Curry Chicken Salad

2   pounds boneless chicken, cooked and cut into chunks
3   ounces raisins
3   ounces walnuts
1   cup blanched broccoli, chopped
1   teaspoon chopped garlic
4   ounces scallions, chopped
1   ounce curry powder
1   teaspoon ginger
½   cup mayonnaise
1   ounce sour cream
2   ounces fresh orange juice
½   cup chutney

Combine chicken, raisins, walnuts, broccoli, garlic and scallions in a bowl. In another bowl combine curry powder, ginger, mayonnaise, sour cream, orange juice, and chutney. Pour sauce over chicken salad and serve on bed of lettuce or on sandwiches.

MARK'S MILK BAR

1529 South Pearl
Denver, Colorado
(303) 777-7927

Over the years Mark Haber has come a long way. He began with a small ice cream and sandwich shop and today has expanded and has an intimate European eatery, still offering ice cream and sandwiches, but also so much more: cappuccinos, oil-free pasta salads, and healthful entrees that are great in a wonderful atmosphere — one of those special places that becomes a secret "find."

Mark's Pasta Primavera Salad
with Oil Free Dressing

3   cups cooked pasta, well rinsed
½   cup red onion, finely diced
½   cup tomatoes, chopped
½   cup cauliflower
½   cup broccoli florets, chopped
1½ cups St. Mary's Oil-Free Dressing

Toss above ingredients and enjoy!

Variation:
Instead of vegetables, substitute diced, canned hearts of palm, artichoke hearts, capers, pimiento and chopped fresh onions.

GOODFRIENDS

3100 East Colfax Avenue
Denver, Colorado 80206
(303) 399-1751

Mediterranean Pasta Salad

1   bunch green onions, diced
½   red onion (sliced very thin)
1   pound sliced cucumbers
1 ½ cups pepperoncinis, drained
1 ½ cups diced tomatoes
1   pound pasta shells (i.e., shell macs, gnocci shells)
1 ½ cups quartered artichoke hearts, drained

Marinade:

⅓   cup oregano
⅓   cup lemon juice
⅔   cup Italian vinaigrette dressing

Cook pasta shells al dente, rinse with cold water and drain well.
Combine oregano, lemon juice and Italian vinaigrette dressing.
Combine all other ingredients with pasta shells.
Toss mixture with marinade liquid, mix well.
Chill for two hours, serve over bed of mixed greens, garnished with feta cheese and red
bell peppers if desired. Serves 8.

STRINGS

1700 Humboldt
Denver, Colorado 80218
(303) 831-7310

Mountain Meadow Lamb Salad
with Raspberry Vinaigrette

1   head bib lettuce
1   radicchio
½   pound mache or lamb's lettuce
1   Belgian endive
16   pieces yellow pear tomatoes
½   pint raspberries
4   sprigs of fresh thyme
16-24 pieces edible flowers
4   4-ounce loins of lamb (remove fat or silver skin)
1   ounce olive oil
salt and pepper
fresh thyme
1   teaspoon mustard

Raspberry Vinaigrette (1 cup)

8   raspberries
¼   cup raspberry vinegar
1   teaspoon honey
½   teaspoon brown sugar
¼   cup olive oil
½   cup cottonseed oil
pinch of salt and pepper
juice from ¼ of a lemon
blend all together

To prepare lamb:
Sprinkle loin of lamb with fresh thyme, mustard and salt and pepper. Sear in hot skillet and place in roasting pan. Place in a 400° oven until rare (approximately 5 minutes). Store and keep warm. (Allow to rest, do not slice meat as juices will be lost).
To prepare salad plate:
Wash all lettuce and place on towel to dry.
Arrange leaves of endive, radicchio and bib around side of plate.
Toss lettuce with ¾ of raspberry vinaigrette and place in center of plate.
Arrange thin slices of lamb on lettuce.
Garnish with halved yellow pear tomatoes, raspberries and fresh edible flowers.
Sprinkle with raspberry vinaigrette. Serves 4.

THE GOLDEN EAGLE INN

Village Hall
Vail-Beaver Creek, Colorado
(303) 949-1940

Pasta and Broccoli Salad

1   tablespoon Oriental sesame or peanut oil
1½   teaspoons St. Mary's Gourmet Vinegar
1   teaspoon dried marjoram, crumbled
1   clove garlic, minced
¼   teaspoon black pepper
1   cup broccoli florets
8   ounces elbow macaroni, fusilli, rotelle, or medium-size
     pasta shells
1   small sweet red pepper, cored, seeded, and cut into strips
     2 inches long and ½ inch wide
1   small yellow onion, sliced thin
2   ounces Swiss cheese, cut into strips 2 inches long and ½
     inch wide
1   tablespoon chopped walnuts

To make the dressing, combine the sesame oil, vinegar, marjoram, garlic, and black pepper in a large heatproof bowl and whisk to mix; set aside.

Cook the broccoli for 3 minutes in a large kettle of boiling unsalted water; scoop out with a small strainer, shake to remove excess water, and add to the dressing.

In the same kettle of boiling water, cook the macaroni according to package directions, omitting the salt. Drain well and add to the broccoli, along with the red pepper, onion, cheese, and walnuts. Toss well, cover, and refrigerate until needed. Serves 4.

Variations:

Pasta and Green Bean Salad — Substitute 1 cup trimmed green beans, cooked for 4 minutes, for the broccoli. Substitute toasted slivered almonds for the chopped walnuts.

Pasta and Snow Pea Salad — Substitute 1 cup trimmed snow peas, cooked for 2 minutes, for the broccoli. Substitute sunflower seeds for the chopped walnuts.

RUDI'S

4720 Table Mesa Drive
Boulder, Colorado 80303
(303) 494-5858

Chef Faith Stone

Pasta Salad with Basil Pesto

6   ounces unusually shaped pasta (spirals, shells, wheels, etc.)
2   large tomatoes — wedged
½   bunch green onions — minced
3   tablespoons St. Mary's Gourmet Vinegar
3   tablespoons olive oil
½   head of romain or bib lettuce — torn into bite-size pieces

Pesto

2   ounces fresh basil, washed, stems removed
2   ounces walnuts
¼   cup fresh grated Parmesan cheese
2   large cloves garlic

½   teaspoon salt
¼   teaspoon pepper
½   cup olive oil
½   cup water

Grind pesto ingredients together in a blender to make a thick paste. Pesto will keep one week in the refrigerator, several weeks in the freezer.

Combine cooked pasta, tomatoes, green onions, lettuce, olive oil and vinegar. Toss with sufficient pesto to taste.

THE DENVER SALAD COMPANY

2700 South Colorado Boulevard
Denver, Colorado
(303) 691-2050

THE DENVER SALAD COMPANY

14201 East Public Market Drive
Aurora, Colorado
(303) 750-1339

THE BOULDER SALAD COMPANY

2595 Canyon Boulevard
Boulder, Colorado
(303) 447-8272

Red Onion Potato Salad
(Oil and Cholesterol Free)

6   medium potatoes, peeled, cooked and sliced
1   cup sliced celery
1   cup thinly sliced red onion
1   cup chopped parsley

¼   cup St. Mary's Oil Free Dressing
3   tablespoons St. Mary's Gourmet Vinegar
1   cup red bell peppers, chopped

In large bowl, combine hot potatoes with remaining ingredients. Refrigerate to chill. Serves 6.

TIP: Marinate hot potatoes in dressing while they chill to bring out full flavor — you will need less dressing!

SFUZZI

3000 East First Avenue
Cherry Creek Mall
Denver, Colorado
(303) 321-4700

Romano Crusted Chicken Salad
with Tomato Basil Vinaigrette

12	ounces chicken breast, boneless, skinned (4 3-ounce pieces)
8	ounces asparagus, blanched and chilled
2	large tomatoes, beefsteak, sliced ½-inch thick
4	ounces arugula
4	ounces frisee
4	ounces radicchio
1½	cups bread crumbs
3	ounces romano cheese, grated
1	tablespoon oregano, fresh, chopped
2	tablespoons basil, fresh, chopped
3	whole eggs, beaten
½	cup flour
½	cup olive oil
salt and pepper to taste	

Place trimmed chicken breast between sheets of plastic wrap and flatten with meat pounder until ¼-inch thick. Mix together bread crumbs, romano cheese, oregano, basil, salt and pepper. Dredge each piece of chicken in flour, then egg, then bread crumbs. Heat olive oil in large saute pan. When olive oil is near smoking point, place chicken breast in pan and immediately reduce heat to medium. Cook chicken approximately 2 minutes on each side, being careful not to burn. Remove chicken from pan, drain on paper towels and keep warm until ready to assemble salad. Serves 4.

BISTRO ADDE BREWSTER

250 Steele
Cherry Creek North
Denver, Colorado 80206
(303) 388-1900

''Bistro Adde Brewster has leaped onto the serious nosher's must try list'' thus raves the *Denver Post* of one of Denver's hottest new restaurants. Adde Bjorkland, a Swede, has a marvelous restaurant history of experience as does his partner Brewster Hauson. This winning combination packs crowds during every meal for some of the best fare in Colorado in one of the warmest settings. No wonder it is not just a ''must try'' but is fast becoming a habit for food aficionados.

Salmon Salad

prepare Bistro Vinaigrette (see below)
mixed greens
diced mango
diced avocado
pecan pieces
feta cheese
tomato wedges
grilled or sauteed salmon

Put your favorite proportions. Toss and enjoy.

Bistro Vinaigrette

4   eggs
2   tablespoons dijon mustard
1   tablespoon salt
1   tablespoon pepper
1   tablespoon oregano
1   tablespoon ground thyme
1   tablespoon lemon juice
1   tablespoon lime juice
½   cup red wine vinegar
½   cup balsamic vinegar
4   cups olive oil

Mix just 10 ingredients in the bowl and slowly whip in the olive oil.

THE DENVER SALAD COMPANY

2700 South Colorado Boulevard
Denver, Colorado
(303) 691-2050

THE DENVER SALAD COMPANY

14201 East Public Market Drive
Aurora, Colorado
(303) 750-1339

THE BOULDER SALAD COMPANY

2595 Canyon Boulevard
Boulder, Colorado
(303) 447-8272

Santa Fe Tabouli

1	cup bulgur wheat
2	cups vegetable stock or water
1	bunch cilantro, chopped coarse
¼	cup jicama, diced
¼	cup carrots, diced
1	cup canned kidney beans, drained
¼	cup red bell peppers, chopped fine
¼	cup red onions, diced

Dressing:

1	cup olive oil
1	cup lime juice
2	teaspoons cayenne pepper
1	teaspoon onion powder
1	teaspoon garlic powder
2	teaspoons cumin
2	teaspoons chili powder
½	cup water

Pour bulgur wheat into large mixing bowl. Mix up dressing in stove pan and bring to a boil. Pour dressing on bulgur, mix, let stand until bulgur is cooked (about 30 minutes). Cover pan.

After bulgur is cool, mix in cilantro, jicama, carrots, kidney beans, red bell peppers and red onions. Mix in 3 cups of pineapple salsa (see Sauce section) and mix well.

MARY & LOU'S CAFE

82 Broadway
Denver, Colorado 80203
(303) 733-7389

Smorgasbord Salad

2   cups diced tomatoes (1 inch dice)
2   cups diced peeled cucumbers
1   cup diced green peppers
½   cup diced red or white onions
Oil and Vinegar Dressing (see recipe below)

Oil and Vinegar Dressing

1   cup of olive or peanut oil
1   cup St. Mary's Gourmet Vinegar

Use wire whip to blend vinegar and oil. If you do not use St. Mary's, use apple cider. Mix with vegetables and marinate for at least one hour. Serve on a bed of lettuce.

FLAGSTAFF HOUSE RESTAURANT

1138 Flagstaff Road
Boulder, Colorado 80302
(303) 442-4640

Spinach Salad
with Honey Mustard Poppy Seed Dressing
and Homemade Mayonnaise

1   patch fresh spinach leaves
garnishes:
   cooked bacon
   sliced hard boiled eggs
   sliced Mandarin oranges
   sprouts

Rinse and tear cold spinach leaves. Garnish with cooked bacon, slices of hard boiled eggs, Mandarin oranges and sprouts. Prepare Honey Mustard Poppy Seed Dressing (see Sauces and Dressing section) and pour over salad. Toss and enjoy!

CANTERBURY CHEESE

26 North Tejon
Colorado Springs, Colorado
(719) 635-3337

This great little deli has a sit-down area of 20 tables for continental breakfasts or deli-lunches, or great for take-out including dinner items.

St. Mary's
Cabbage, Artichoke and Caper Slaw

3   cups shredded cabbage
1   cup diced artichoke hearts, canned in vinegar and drained
½   cup green onions
¼   cup chopped pimientos
¼   cup capers

Dressing

⅓   cup prepared mustard
⅓   cup olive oil
⅓   cup St. Mary's Gourmet Vinegar

Toss salad ingredients in large bowl. Prepare dressing and pour over salad. Enjoy. Serves 4.

CHICAGO JOE'S

775 West Bijou
Colorado Springs, Colorado
(719) 633-5637

Summer Pasta Salad*

4   ounces tiny pasta shells, elbow macaroni, or ditalini
4   teaspoons olive oil
¼   cup minced fresh basil or parsley
$1/_8$ teaspoon black pepper
1   small red onion, chopped fine
1   medium-size cucumber, peeled, seeded, and chopped
1   large ripe tomato, cored, seeded, and cut into ½ inch cubes

In a large saucepan, cook the pasta according to package directions, omitting the salt. Drain, rinse under cold running water to stop the cooking, and drain again. Transfer the pasta to a large bowl; add the olive oil, basil, and pepper, and toss well to mix.

Add the onion, cucumber, and tomato, and toss well again. Serve at room temperature. Serves 4.

*variation

OFF BELLEVIEW GRILL

East of I-25 on Belleview
Denver, Colorado
(303) 694-3337

Summer Salad

1	clove garlic	4	heads bib lettuce, well-washed
1	egg yolk	¼	cup bacon, cooked and crumbled
½	teaspoon ground white pepper	1	cup croutons
1	cup olive oil	12	cherry tomatoes
¼	cup green onions, chopped		
¼	teaspoon fresh mint, chopped		
¼	teaspoon oregano		
½	cup freshly grated Parmesan or Romano cheese		

Sprinkle salt in a large wooden salad bowl. Rub bowl with garlic. Discard garlic.

In the bowl, vigorously whip the egg yolk, lemon juice, and white pepper (salt, if necessary). Slowly add olive oil.

Mix in green onions, mint, oregano and ¼ of the cheese.

Add lettuce and toss. Portion onto chilled plates. Sprinkle with bacon, croutons and remaining cheese. Garnish with tomatoes. Serves 4.

Preparation: 20 minutes.

"A refreshing change from Caesar!"

GREENS NATURAL FOODS CAFE

320 East Colfax
Denver, Colorado
(303) 831-1315

Here is a refreshing salad of Middle Eastern origin.

Tabouleh

1   cup bulgur
2   cups boiling water
4   teaspoons lemon juice
2   teaspoons olive oil
2   medium-size ripe tomatoes, cored, seeded, and chopped, or 1 cup canned low-sodium tomatoes, drained and chopped
¼   cup minced fresh mint or 1 tablespoon mint flakes
3   tablespoons minced parsley
½   small red onion, sliced thin
2   green onions, including tops, chopped fine
¼   teaspoon each ground coriander and cumin
$^1/_8$ teaspoon hot red pepper sauce

Place the bulgur in a large heatproof bowl and pour the boiling water over it. Cover and let stand for 30 minutes. Drain off any liquid that remains.

In another large bowl, mix the lemon juice, olive oil, tomatoes, mint, parsley, red onion, green onions, coriander, cumin and red pepper sauce. Add the bulgur and toss well to mix. Serves 6.

THE DENVER SALAD COMPANY
2700 South Colorado Boulevard
Denver, Colorado
(303) 691-2050

THE DENVER SALAD COMPANY
14201 East Public Market Drive
Aurora, Colorado
(303) 750-1339

THE BOULDER SALAD COMPANY
2595 Canyon Boulevard
Boulder, Colorado
(303) 447-8272

Thai-Chicken Pasta Salad
with Thai-Vinaigrette Dressing (see Sauce section)

4	cups garden spiral pasta, cooked, well-rinsed and chilled
1½	cups cooked chicken breast meat, sliced thin
1	teaspoon fresh ginger root, peeled and diced
½	cup green onions, finely chopped
½	cup medium red onion, diced
2	tablespoons cilantro, coarsely chopped
1	tablespoon cannola seeds, optional
1	cup Thai-Vinaigrette Dressing (see Sauce section)
½	teaspoon red pepper flakes to taste

Once pasta has cooled, add all ingredients, add Thai-Vinaigrette (see Sauce section) and toss to mix. Serves 12 to 24.

ALFREDO'S

The Westin Resort
1300 Westhaven Drive
Vail, Colorado 81657
(303) 476-7111

The best Sunday brunch in the Vail area is regularly served at Alfredo's at the Westin Hotel — a smorgasbord of pasta salads, hearts of palm, platters of shrimp, wheel of Brie, fish entrées, chicken entrées, vegetable dishes of stuffed tomatoes, potatoes au gratin, baron of beef, fresh fruit, egg dishes, a mind-boggling table of incredible desserts and much more. Champagne, orange juice, coffee, a lovely view of the mountains and a posh setting is included for the fixed brunch price. It is no wonder Denverites are known to spend a leisurely Sunday mini-vacation driving to Vail, brunching at Alfredo's and returning to Denver, enjoying the majestic vistas of the Rocky Mountains.

Vail Mountain Summer Salad Served with a fresh Wild Blueberry-Dijon Vinaigrette

The Salad

1	head radicchio	1	scallion (slivered lengthwise)
1	head butter lettuce (washed and cleaned)	4	ounces finely slivered carrot and cucumber slices
1	large Roma tomato (washed and cleaned)	8	fresh Nasturtiums
1	cantaloupe (cut into 8 attractive spears)		
4	small bunches sprouts		
1	pack (approximately 4 ounces) Snow puff mushrooms		

Tear off the whole leaf from each head of butter lettuce and radicchio and combine (green under purple) in the form of a "Cup," and place one cup on each 9″ salad plate. Place the slivered vegetables, the mushrooms and scallion slivers inside attractively.

Now place the sprouts on the side, the tomato and cucumber spears underneath the lettuce (seemingly "blossoming" from the center of the plate). Garnish with two nasturtiums per salad and chill.

The Vinaigrette

2	egg whites	¼	cup finely chopped scallions
16	ounces olive oil	4	ounces apple juice
4	ounces Grey Poupon dijon mustard		

Reduction Ingredients:

8	ounces Burgundy wine
3	ounces St. Mary's Gourmet Vinegar
2	ounces chopped shallots
½	ounce chopped garlic
1	teaspoon freshly cracked black peppercorn
1	teaspoon finely chopped rosemary needles
1	cup fresh blueberries

Place all the reduction ingredients in a saucepan and reduce on low heat to approximately 3 ounces liquid. Let cool.

Make an emulsion with the reduction and add all remaining ingredients, thinning with apple juice if needed.

This salad is quite large and can be made as a summer lunch entree, or kept smaller and used for a dinner salad. This salad and the vinaigrette are in the style of "HealthMark"...in other words - no salt, no cholesterol, no sugar, no meat — an item popular with the *nutrition-minded*. The salad is also as beautiful as a summer meadow...and the dressing is bright purple...very different and very attractive. Serves 4.

CACHE-CACHE

205 South Mill Street
Aspen, Colorado 81611
(303) 925-3835

Vegetable-Cheese Salad with Artichokes*

1   cup broccoli florets
2   teaspoons olive or walnut oil
1½   teaspoons balsamic or St. Mary's Gourmet Vinegar
¾   teaspoon dried tarragon, crumbled
lean artichoke hearts in vinegar, drained
1/8 teaspoon black pepper
6   cherry tomatoes, halved
½   cup sliced Jerusalem artichokes or water chestnuts
2   ounces part-skim mozzarella cheese, cut into ½-inch cubes

   In a large bowl, combine the oilve oil, vinegar, tarragon, and pepper. Add the broccoli, artichoke hearts, cherry tomatoes, Jerusalem artichokes, and cheese. Toss well, cover, and refrigerate at least 6 hours before packing for a picnic or brown bag lunch. Serves 4.

*variation

OMELETTES EGGS IV

P. McClure

OMELETTES, QUICHES & EGGS, IV

Asparagus-Mushroom Omelets (The Egg Shell) — p. 1
Cyrano's Egg Mignons topped with Mushrooms (Cyrano's — Introduction) — p. 2
D-J's Special Avocado, Egg, Cheese, Mushroom, Sprouts Crêpe (D-J's Crêpes and Omelets) — p. 2
Huevos Jerome and Picante Sauce (Jerome Hotel) — p. 3
Nick's Special Omelet (The Aristocrat Steakhouse — Introduction) — p. 3
Omelette Florentine (The Peck House — Introduction) — p. 4
Scrambled Eggs Benedict (Olive Branch — Introduction) — p. 5
Steamed Egg with Mushrooms (Imperial Wok) — p. 6

THE EGG SHELL

1520 Blake
Denver, Colorado 80202
(303) 623-7555

Asparagus-Mushroom Omelets

1	large egg
5	large egg whites
1	tablespoon minced fresh chives
2	tablespoons cold water
¼	teaspoon black pepper
2	tablespoons unsalted margarine
¼	cup finely chopped cooked asparagus or broccoli
¼	cup finely chopped mushrooms
¼	cup finely chopped ripe tomato
¼	cup minced parsley

In a medium-size bowl, combine the egg, egg whites, chives, water, and pepper; whisk just enough to mix lightly.

Melt ½ tablespoon of the margarine in a heavy 7-inch skillet over moderately high heat. Add ¼ each of the asparagus and mushrooms and cook, stirring for 1 minute.

Add ¼ of the egg mixture (about ½ cup) and shake the skillet over the heat, stirring, for 30 seconds; then let the omelet cook, undisturbed, for 30 seconds more or until the edges and bottom are set.

With a spatula, either fold the omelet in half or roll it to the edge of the pan and invert it onto a heated plate. Make 3 more omelets in the samy way. Top each omelet with the chopped tomato and sprinkle with the parsley, dividing the total amount evenly. Serves 4.

Variation:

Herb-Mushroom Omelet.
Omit the asparagus and add 1 tablespoon minced fresh dill, oregano, basil, sage, tarragon, or chervil (or 1 teaspoon dried herb, crumbled) to the egg mixture just before cooking.

Tip:

To judge the freshness of eggs, look at their shells. Old eggs are smooth and shiny; fresh ones are rough and chalky by comparison.

CYRANO'S

298 Hanson Ranch
Vail, Colorado
(303) 476-5551

Cyrano's, over the years, has become the classic breakfast place in Vail, even if guests enjoy breakfast at 3 o'clock in the afternoon. Of course, Cyrano's offers casual brunches, dinner and a great social bar. Here is a variation of an egg entree.

Cyrano's Egg Mignons topped with Mushrooms

1   muffin tin with 12 cups
olive or butter or paper muffin liners
12   strips of soft fried bacon, not crisp
12   raw eggs
2   cloves garlic, minced
1   cup fresh mushrooms, chopped
cracked white pepper

Place a teaspoon of butter or olive oil or paper liner into each muffin tin. Line the sides of each muffin cup with a strip of soft fried bacon. Crack a raw egg into each muffin cup. Sprinkle the top of each muffin cup with a pinch of minced garlic, a teaspoon or more of fresh, chopped mushrooms and white pepper. Bake 15 minutes at 350° or until eggs are opaque. Serve 2 eggs with champagne mimosas. Serves 6.

D-J'S CRÊPES AND OMELETS

Concert Hall Plaza Building
Vail, Colorado 81657
(303) 476-2336

D-J's Special Avocado, Egg, Cheese, Mushroom, Sprouts Crêpe

¼   avocado, sliced
1   scrambled raw egg
2   ounces grated white Wisconsin cheddar cheese (or cheese preference)
2   ounces sauteed sliced mushrooms
Add 1 handful of fresh sprouts

Heat a 12-inch Teflon or silverstone omelet pan over a moderately high flame for a least 1½ minutes or until water drops bead and bubble away. (Tip: A well-heated pan is the secret to good, consistent crêpes.) To the pan, add at least 5 ounces of crêpe batter (see Basic Crêpe). Swirl around the pan to cover and pour off excess. Add egg on top of crêpe. Immediately lower heat to low. Add cheese and mushrooms. Cook until corners of the crêpe begin to curl or until egg is cooked. Loosen the crêpe with a spatula. Cover and cook for a few minutes. Remove cover; add avocados and sprouts. Fold crêpe in half and cook until done. NOTE: Avocados and sprouts do not want to be cooked for long. Top with sour cream or a cream sauce of your choice. Serves 1 generous portion.

JEROME HOTEL
330 East Main
Aspen, Colorado 81611
(303) 920-1000

Huevos Jerome and Picante Sauce

3   eggs
3   tablespoons picante sauce (see Sauce section)
2   ounces grated cheese

Crack 3 eggs into small greased omelet pan over medium heat. After a white film has set, top with picante sauce and cheddar cheese.

Cover with a tight lid. Cook until cheese has melted. Serve on a flour tortilla (see Bread section), garnish with sour cream. May substitute scrambled eggs for basted eggs. Heat tortilla, eggs, sauce and cheese under broiler — do not cook. Serves 1.

THE ARISTOCRAT STEAKHOUSE
2053 Broadway
Boulder, Colorado
(303) 444-8688

Christie and Paul Boryames supervise a great breakfast-lunch, steak-and-eggs eatery in Boulder. The low prices, generous portions and good taste have created such a following that daily the place is packed. Nick's Special Omelet is reputed to be the biggest omelet in Colorado and, certainly, one of the most popular.

Nick's Special Omelet

3   tablespoons butter
6   large eggs
½   cup chopped onions
½   cup chopped tomatoes
½   cup chopped green pepper
½   cup grated Swiss cheese
½   cup chopped cooked ham
1   tablespoon sour cream — as topping

Heat 2 tablespoons butter in omelet frying pan over low, even heat. Beat eggs until frothy, and salt and pepper to taste. Set aside. In another skillet with 1 tablespoon butter, grill onions, peppers, tomatoes, and ham. Pour frothy eggs into buttered, heated omelet pan and cook over low heat. When omelet begins to bubble around edges, pour grilled ingredients throughout center. Sprinkle the Swiss cheese over the grilled ingredients. Fold omelet in half and serve topped with a tablespoon of sour cream.

NOTE: Be careful not to scorch omelet as this completely changes the egg flavor. An ''easy'' omelet is better than a ''too-done'' scorched omelet.) Serves 1 gigantic appetite.

THE PECK HOUSE

83 Sunny Avenue
Empire, Colorado
(303) 569-9870

The Peck House of Empire, like the Stanley Hotel of Colorado, is a historic stop-over for guests and has an early-mining-days beginning and various mysterious stories connected with the individuals who traveled through its doors. The Peck House has an exquisite gourmet dining room and superb Sunday brunches. Here is a variation of one of their popular brunch items: the Omelette Florentine.

Omelette Florentine

1   cup chicken broth
2   large eggs
1   tablespoon sour cream
1   tablespoon butter
salt and pepper to taste

Omelette Florentine Filling

3   torn spinach leaves per omelette
2   tablespoons butter
1   tablespoon Parmesan cheese

Saute filling ingredients over very low heat while preparing omelette.

Omelette: Break eggs into bowl and add broth. Put butter in omelette pan and heat butter. Whip eggs and mash in sour cream (30 strokes) with table fork. Pour egg mixture into hot skillet. As the edges of the omelette cook, pull them into center of the omelette. Spatula-turn the omelette when there is no more runny eggs mixture. Cook for approximately 30 seconds on flip side. Place on serving plate. Add Florentine filling to white sauce. Place filling and sauce into omelette and fold in half and top with more white sauce. Sprinkle with Parmesan cheese and serve. Serves 1.

White Cream Sauce

$^1/_8$ pound butter
4   tablespoons flour
2   cups cold milk
$^1/_2$ teaspoon salt
$^1/_8$ teaspoon pepper

Melt butter in skillet. Stir in flour. Cook-stir for 3 minutes without browning. Add cold milk, salt and pepper. Stir until mixture thickens slightly. Remove from heat.(Use with Ham a la King Crepe — see Crepe section).

OLIVE BRANCH

2140 Vickers Drive
Colorado Springs, Colorado
(719) 593-9522

The Olive Branch is a friendly neighborhood restaurant serving wholesome breakfast favorites such as whole grain pancakes and yogurt, omelettes, lox and bagels. *The Best of the Springs* voted the Olive Branch, "Best Eggs Benedict and breakfast meeting place."

Scrambled Eggs Benedict*

4   thin slices reduced-sodium ham (about ¼ pound)
1   cup low-sodium chicken broth
3   tablespoons unsalted margarine
2   tablespoons flour
1   tablespoon lemon juice
$1/_8$ teaspoon plus pinch black pepper
1   large egg
4   large egg whites
2   tablespoons skim milk
2   English muffins, split
2   tablespoons minced parsley

Preheat the oven to 350°. Wrap the ham slices in aluminum foil, place in the oven, and heat for 10 minutes. In a small saucepan, heat the chicken broth until it just starts to simmer.

Meanwhile melt 2 tablespoons of the margarine in another small heavy saucepan over moderate heat. Add the flour and cook, stirring constantly, for 2 minutes. Whisk in the hot chicken broth and the lemon juice; bring to a simmer and cook, stirring, for 2 minutes or until the sauce has thickened. Stir in $1/_8$ teaspoon of the pepper.

In a small bowl, beat together the egg, egg whites, skim milk, and the pinch of black pepper. Melt the remaining tablespoon of margarine in a heavy 10-inch skillet over low heat, add the egg mixture, and cook, stirring often, for 4 to 5 minutes or until the eggs are set.

While the eggs are cooking, toast the muffins, then place a slice of ham on top of each one. Place ¼ of the scrambled eggs on top of each slice of ham, spoon the sauce over all, and sprinkle with the parsley. Serves 4.

Note: This has only a quarter of the cholesterol of standard Eggs Benedict. You can reduce the sodium by 200 mg if you substitute chicken or turkey for the ham.

*variation

IMPERIAL WOK

5674 North Academy Boulevard
Colorado Springs, Colorado
(719) 548-0300

Steamed Egg with Mushrooms

4	dried Chinese mushrooms
½	cup soaked cellophane noodles
4	ounces crab or prawn meat
4	ounces cooked pork
5	eggs
2	spring onions, finely chopped
2	teaspoons finely chopped fresh coriander leaves
½	teaspoon salt
$^1/_8$	teaspoon black pepper

Soak mushrooms in hot water for 30 minutes. Discard stems, squeeze excess water from caps and slice finely. Soak a small amount of cellophane noodles in hot water for about 10 minutes, then measure half cup. Flake crab meat and discard any bony bits, or chop the shelled and deveined prawns into small pieces. Chop pork finely.

Beat eggs until yolks and whites are well mixed but not frothy. Stir in the chopped spring onions, coriander, salt and pepper and the prepared mushrooms, noodles, seafood and pork. Put into a heat-proof dish and steam until firm, exact time depending on the depth of the mixture in the dish. Serve with rice. Serves 3 to 4.

BREADS V

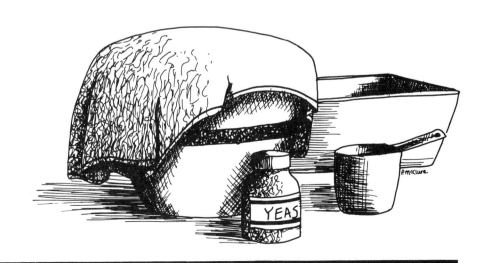

BREADS, V

Apple Pancake (Park Lane Cafe) — p. 1
Banana Nut Bread (Walnut Cafe) — p. 1
Basic German Pancake (Park Lane Cafe — Introduction) — p. 2
Black Bean Tortilla (Sweet Basil) — p. 2
Bread Sticks (L'Ostello) — p. 3
Cherry Cheese Danish (Mary and Lou's Cafe — Introduction) — p. 4
Chinese Pancakes (Ming's Dynasty) — p. 5
Cinnamon Rolls (The Happy Cooker) — p. 5
Date Nut Roll (Red Rooster Inn) — p. 6
D-J's Basic Crêpe Recipe (D-J's Crêpes and Omelets — Introduction) — p. 7
Egg Noodle Dough (Hal's) — p. 7
Empanada Dough (Rudi's) — p. 8
Flour Tortillas (Chubby's) — p. 8
French Toast Topped with Pecans, Bananas and Grand Marnier (Poppycock's) — p. 9
Fresh Peach Muffins (The Leadville Country Inn) — p. 9
Ginger Bread (Goodfriends) — p. 10
Honey Walnut Bread (Rudi's) — p. 10
Lemon Pecan Tea Bread (The Leadville Country Inn) — p. 11
Mexican Cornbread (The Jerome Hotel) — p. 11
Pie Dough (The Pepper Mill) — p. 12
Swedish Apricot Nut Bread (Gemini Restaurant — Introduction) — p. 12
Torotilla Chips (Chubby's) — p. 13
Wafer Crust (Bull & Bush) — p. 13
Warm Feta Cheese on French Bread (Pour La France! Cafe & Bistro) — p. 13
Yorkshire Pudding (Red Lion Inn) — p. 14
Zucchini Bread (Fountain Cafe and Restaurant) — p. 14

PARK LANE CAFE

305 South Downing
Denver, Colorado 80209
(303) 777-7840

Apple Pancake

German pancake batter (see Basic German Pancake)
2   tablespoons butter
1   sliced raw apple
sugar
cinnamon

In a large frying pan melt butter and coat bottom and sides. Pour in 3 tablespoons batter, or enough for very thin coating. Tilt pan to spread batter evenly and cook 1 minute. Cover with apple slices. Pour 3 tablespoons batter over apple. Turn cake when browned and brown other side. Turn pancake out on a hot platter and fold over or roll loosely. Dash with sugar and cinnamon. Cut in half to serve 2.

WALNUT CAFE

338 East Colfax Avenue
Denver, Colorado
(303) 832-5108

WALNUT CAFE

3073 Walnut Street
Boulder, Colorado
(303) 447-2315

This popular breakfast spot is well known for this banana-nut bread which accompanies all egg dishes.

Banana Nut Bread*

½   cup butter
¾   cup sugar
2   eggs, separated
3   medium bananas
3   tablespoons buttermilk (or sour milk with 1 teaspoon St. Mary's Gourmet Vinegar)
2   cups sifted flour
¼   teaspoon salt
½   cup chopped walnuts
1   teaspoon baking soda

Cream butter with sugar, beat egg yolks, and add. Mash bananas and add to mixture. Add baking soda to buttermilk, salt with flour and add to mixture, also nuts. Beat egg whites stiff, fold into mixture. Bake in greased 10 x 5 x 3 loaf pan in 350° oven for 1 hour. Recipe doubles beautifully, and is a most delicious, moist nut bread.

* Variation

PARK LANE CAFE

305 South Downing
Denver, Colorado 80209
(303) 777-7840

Park Lane Cafe is one of the most cheerful breakfast spots in Denver. Great coffee and prices. Here is a variation on one of their most popular offerings.

Basic German Pancake

1	tablespoon sugar	6	large eggs
1½	cups sifted flour	2	cups milk
¼	teaspoon salt		

Beat eggs in large bowl. Beat in flour, salt and sugar. Gradually add milk and beat several minutes. Pour batter into a pitcher or glass measure and let stand for 30 minutes. Any batter not used can be stored covered in refrigerator.

1	tablespoon butter		powdered cinnamon
1	jar (14¾ ounces) lingonberries, heated		juice of ½ lemon
	confectioners' sugar	¼	cup Jamaica rum or kirsch (optional)

In large crepe pan melt butter over medium heat. When butter begins to turn golden, pour in about ½ cup batter. Quickly swirl pan to coat bottom with a large, thin pancake. Cook until brown, turn with large pancake turner, and brown on other side. Slip onto hot platter. Sprinkle thickly with confectioners' sugar, cinnamon and lemon juice. Spread with hot lingonberries and roll like jelly roll. Sprinkle with more sugar and cinnamon. If desired, sprinkle with kirsch or rum and ignite. Cut pancake in half for 2 servings.

SWEET BASIL

193 East Gore Creek Drive
Vail, Colorado 81657
(303) 476-0125

Black Bean Tortilla

2	tablespoons vegetable shortening
2	cups sifted flour
1	tablespoon baking powder
½	teaspoon sugar
½	teaspoon salt
1½	cup poaching liquid from black beans reduced by half

Mix the dry ingredients in a bowl. Cut the shortening into the flour with a fork until the flour becomes coarse. Add the liquid until a dough forms. Knead for 5 minutes, then let rest for 20 minutes. Roll with a rolling pin as thin as possible and cut into 5″ circles. Cook in a hot, dry skillet 30 seconds on both sides.

L'OSTELLO

705 West Lionshead Circle
Vail, Colorado 81657
(303) 476-2050

Pastry Chef Raymond A. Arter

Bread Sticks

1	ounce fresh yeast		¼	teaspoon chopped garlic
7	cups all-purpose flour		2	cups lukewarm water
½	cup Parmesan cheese		1	tablespoon salt
¼	teaspoon cayenne pepper			

Dissolve yeast in water. Add the rest of the ingredients together in separate bowl. When the yeast is sufficiently dissolved, add the rest of the ingredients into it and knead. When the dough comes to a ball, put into a lightly oiled bowl and cover. Let rise for 45 minutes. Punch the dough down and roll into thin stick form and place on a pan. Let rise for 20 minutes. Bake in oven at 350° until light brown.

MARY AND LOU'S CAFE

82 Broadway
Denver, Colorado
(303) 733-7389

Mary and Lou's Cafe is a real Broadway landmark. Everybody that's anybody eats at Mary and Lou's Cafe — Pat Schroeder, the late radio personality Alan Berg (this was his favorite restaurant); street people, neighborhood people, laborers, yuppies, policemen, politicians, judges, et al.

Mary and Lou's has grits on the menu 24 hours a day. It also has waitresses who look like characters out of a Charles Dickens novel.

Mary and Lou Poboheski both came from restaurant backgrounds. Mary trained chain restaurant waitresses. Lou worked his way up from dishwasher to district manager in the same chain. They secretly married, bought a small two thousand dollar restaurant and hence have loved and nurtured Mary and Lou's.

Money and profit are not the name of the game with this eatery. Feeding people with good food at a more-than-fair price is the secret of Mary and Lou's Cafe long-term success (over 20 years).

If guests wish real potatoes, not powdered, the place to go is Mary and Lou's.

Mary is an extremely handsome lady who graciously attends guests who daily attend this funky, yet real restaurant. (Many restaurants start with marble and great decor and poor food and high, high prices) — yet Mary and Lou's has great value, real food and funky decor.

Cherry Cheese Danish

Basic French Puff Dough Pastry

1   pound (4 sticks) butter or margarine, well chilled
4¼ cups sifted all-purpose flour
1   cup ice water
2   tablespoons lemon juice

Cut ½ pound (2 sticks) of the butter/margarine into flour with a fork or pastry blender in a large bowl until mixture is crumbly and pale yellow. (Keep remaining 2 sticks of butter well chilled for later use.)

Stir ice water and lemon juice all at once into crumbly mixture. Continue stirring with a fork until mixture is completely moistened and pastry is very stiff. Wrap in waxed paper, foil or plastic wrap; chill for 30 minutes.

Unwrap the pastry and roll out to an 18 x 12-inch rectangle, on well-floured pastry cloth or board. Pastry should be ¼ inch thick. Roll straight, lifting the rolling pin each time as you reach the edge, so pastry will be evenly thick.

Slice reserved ½ pound of very cold butter into thin, even pats over two-thirds of pastry to form a 12-inch square.

Fold uncovered one-third of pastry over middle one-third; fold opposite end over top. Then fold pastry in thirds crosswise to make a block. Now you have 9 layers of pastry with pats of butter between each. Roll out again to an even 18 x 12-inch rectangle; repeat folding as above; chill 30 minutes.

Repeat rolling, folding and chilling 3 more times. Pastry is stiff and cold, so first pound firmly with rolling pin to flatten, watching carefully to keep thickness even. After rolling and folding the last time, wrap and chill pastry overnight or several days, then shape. (Time of preparation is cut to a minimum when you buy convenient, frozen puff pastry.)

Cream Cheese Filling

8   ounces creamed cheese, softened
½   cup sugar
2   tablespoons lemon juice
dash of salt

Cream sugar and cheese well. Blend in lemon juice and salt.

Powdered Sugar Icing

Combine 1 cup of sifted powdered sugar, ¼ teaspoon vanilla and enough milk for drizzling.

Canned cherry pie filling for topping (may use peach, apple or blueberry filling in place of cherry).

Use 1 pound of puff dough and roll out to a 20-inch square. Cut into 4-inch squares. Spread 1 tablespoon filling diagonally across each square. Fold opposite corners toward middle across filling. Flute inside corners to seal.

Place on ungreased cookie sheet pan.

Brush with eggwash and bake at 425° for 10 minutes.

Reduce heat to 350° and cook for 15 minutes longer.

Place 1 tablespoon of cherry pie filling in each corner.

Cool to room temperature. Drizzle with icing.

MING'S DYNASTY

4251 East Mississippi
Denver, Colorado
(303) 757-4923

Chinese Pancakes

2   cups flour
¾   cup boiling water
1   tablespoon sesame oil

Place unsifted flour in bowl. Bring water to boil and pour into flour, stirring with chopsticks or the handle of a wooden spoon for a few minutes. As soon as it is cool enough to handle, knead for 10 minutes until the mixture is smooth dough. Place dough on board and cover with a bowl for 30 minutes.

Roll dough into cylindrical shape and cut into 10 slices of equal size. Take 1 slice and divide into 2 equal pieces. Roll each piece into a ball, then, on a floured base, roll it into a circular, thin crêpe — approximately 3 inches in diameter. Brush each circle lightly with sesame oil and cover each pancake with plastic as it is made. Heat an ungreased frying pan over low heat and place individual crepes in one at a time. Cover over low heat until pancake develops small bubbles. Turn frequently so that it cooks on both sides. Pancakes should be soft and pliable, not brittle.

To serve, fold each pancake in quarters. Cover pancakes tightly until ready to serve or they will dry out. Makes 20 pancakes to serve 4 or 5 people.

THE HAPPY COOKER

412 Sixth Street
Georgetown, Colorado
(303) 569-3166

Cinnamon Rolls

4   cups flour
1   teaspoon salt
¼   cup sugar
1   cup butter

1   cake yeast
¾   cups very warm water
3   egg yolks, beaten
1   cup milk, scalded and cooled

Place flour, salt and sugar in large bowl. Cut in butter with mixer, until is looks like meal. Dissolve yeast in warm water. Add to flour mixture along with eggs and cooled milk. Beat well. Chill overnight in refrigerator. (This dough is sticky.) Divide dough in half. Roll each half into 10 x 12-inch rectangles. Spread with melted butter. Sprinkle on rolled dough:

¼   cup sugar   ¾   teaspoon cinnamon

Roll up lengthwise into 1-inch slices. Place in greased muffin tins, cover and let set 1 hour. Bake 20 to 25 minutes at 375°.

Glaze

1½ cups powdered sugar
2   tablespoons butter

2   tablespoons milk
1½ teaspoons vanilla

Spread on rolls when they are cooled.

RED ROOSTER INN

16 Mountain Evans Boulevard (off Hwy 285)
Pine Junction, Colorado 80470
(303) 838-4537

Date Nut Roll

Combine in saucepan:

1	cup snipped dates	¹/₈	teaspoon salt
¼	cup sugar	1	cup water

Bring to a boil. Cook and stir until thick. Cool to room temperature.

In mixer bowl:

4   eggs

Beat on high speed for 5 minutes. Gradually add:

½   cup sugar

In another bowl blend:

1	cup flour	½	teaspoon salt
1	teaspoon baking powder	½	teaspoon allspice

Fold the flour mixture into the egg mixture. Add cooled dates.
Spread into 15 x 10 x 1-inch greased and floured pan. Top with nuts. Bake at 375° for 12 to 15 minutes.
Turn out on a towel sprinkled with powdered sugar. Roll up — start with small end. Cool. Unroll. Spread with cream cheese.

Filling:

Beat together

6	ounces cream cheese	½	teaspoon vanilla
4	tablespoons butter	1	cup powdered sugar

Reroll. Dust with powdered sugar. Decorate with nuts, etc.

D-J'S CRÊPES AND OMELETS

Concert Hall Plaza Building
Vail, Colorado 81657
(303) 476-2336

Doug McCadam, whose favorite restaurants in the east were certain compact-efficient diners, missed them when he came to the west in 1970. In Vail, Colorado, a blatant need for a light, inexpensive dinner other than burgers and pizza was apparent. Doug, an experienced cabinet maker, and his good friend and partner Jay Arcand, a successful Boston restaurateur, combined their ingenuity and created D-J's Crêpes and Omelets. Voila! A cheerful, friendly Vail eatery (diner-style) was born. Amidst this delightful ambience, guests receive freshly squeezed orange juice and a variety of exquisite delicacies of quality ingredients and view the spectacle of the meal preparation — at very low prices. Today, this popular place packs Vail regulars and visitors morning, noon and night (until 3 a.m.) for good eating and good times.

D-J's Basic Crêpe Recipe

2	eggs	1	cup all-purpose flour
2	tablespoons salad oil	½	teaspoon salt
1⅓	cups milk		

Mix or blend all ingredients except flour. Slowly mix or blend in flour to avoid lumping. Batter keeps well for 4-6 days in refrigerator. Makes 10-12 crêpes.

HAL'S

5115 Federal Boulevard
Denver, Colorado
(303) 455-8239

Egg Noodle Dough*

3   extra-large eggs
2⅔ tablespoons water
3   cups unsifted all-purpose flour

To make dough by hands: Beat eggs with water, then add flour. Beat in the first 2 cups in your mixer and the last cup by hand, as the dough is very dry. Mix until the ingredients adhere. Knead on board (no need to flour the board) for at least 10-15 minutes, until dough is smooth. Divide dough into 2 balls, keeping one covered while you work with the other. Makes 1½ pounds of egg noodles or 80 to 100 sheets wonton wrappers (3- to 3½-inch) square or 25 sheets egg roll wrappers (5- to 5½-inch square.)

*Variation

RUDI'S

4720 Table Mesa Drive
Boulder, Colorado 80303
(303) 494-5858

Chef Faith Stone

Empanada Dough

2½ cups whole wheat flour   ½ cup yogurt
1½ cups unbleached white flour   ½ teaspoon salt
¾ cup water   ½ cup oil
a wok of hot oil for frying empanadas (optional)

Mix the ingredients by hand or with a mixer to get a smooth dough. Knead the dough for 5 minutes by hand or 2 minutes in the mixer. Let the dough rest for a bit. Pull off a small ball of dough (about 1¼ ounces for appetizer size, 2½ ounces for entree size) and roll in a circle. Fill the center with vegetable filling. Moisten the edges with water and press together. With a fork press the edges to tightly seal. Bake turnovers at 350° for 20 minutes or until browned and hot through.

CHUBBY'S

1231 West 38th Avenue
Denver, Colorado
(303) 455-9311

Flour Tortillas

4   cups flour
2   teaspoons salt
6   tablespoons shortening
1 to 1½ cups lukewarm water

Sift flour and salt. Work in the shortening and water. Form a ball. Knead dough on floured surface. Make dough into balls the size of golf balls. Let these stand 15 minutes. Roll these dough balls out until they are flat and the size of a plate. Bake on hot, ungreased griddle or skillet for 2 minutes on one side, turn and cook about 1 minute on the other side.

POPPYCOCK'S

609 East Cooper
Aspen, Colorado
(303) 925-1245

Poppycock's is a breakfast treat and a haunt of Aspen locals. Here is a variation of one of their great breakfast favorites.

French Toast Topped with Pecans, Bananas and Grand Marnier

4   eggs, raw but well blended
4   slices rye or whole wheat bread
2   tablespoons olive oil

Heat skillet to medium. Add oil. Dip bread into egg batter and lightly fry bread on each side. Heat topping in a separate skillet and place atop each slice of French toast. Serves 2 to 4.

Topping

1   fresh banana, sliced   ¼   cup Grand Marnier
½   cup shelled pecans, chopped   ½   cup orange juice

Heat and spoon over French toast.

THE LEADVILLE COUNTRY INN

127 East Eighth Street
Leadville, Colorado 80461
(719) 486-2354

Fresh Peach Muffins

¼   cup butter   1   large egg, beaten
¾   cup milk   ½   cup fresh peaches, chopped

2   cups flour   ½   teaspoon salt
⅔   cup sugar   ½   teaspoon cinnamon
1   tablespoon baking powder   ¼   teaspoon nutmeg

Mix dry ingredients. Mix wet ingredients. Mix wet and dry ingredients until lumpy. Bake at 425° for 20 minutes.

GOODFRIENDS

3100 East Colfax Avenue
Denver, Colorado 80206
(303) 399-1751

Ginger Bread

1 ¼ cups Grandma's molasses (or any unsulfured molasses)
¾ cup vegetable oil
¾ tablespoon ground ginger
3 ³/₈ cups all-purpose flour
½ teaspoon salt
1 ¼ cups hot water
½ tablespoon baking soda
¹/₈ cup milk
1 egg

Mix ¼ cup hot water and baking soda. Combine all other ingredients, mix well, then add water and baking soda mixture. Pour into a 9 x 9 x 2-inch baking pan that has been sprayed with vegetable spray (i.e., Pam, Vegeline, etc.) and lightly floured.
Bake at 300° for 40-45 minutes. Brush top with melted butter as soon as removed from oven.
Serve topped with whipped cream and sliced bananas. Serves 8.

RUDI'S

4720 Table Mesa Drive
Boulder, Colorado 80303
(303) 494-5858

Chef Faith Stone

Honey Walnut Bread

2 ½ cups whole wheat flour
1 tablespoon baking powder
1 teaspoon salt
1 cup milk
1 cup honey

2 eggs beaten
¼ cup softened butter
½ cup chopped walnuts
1 loaf pan

Sift together flour, baking powder and salt.
Beat together milk, honey, eggs and butter.
Stir dry ingredients into wet ingredients until well blended. Fold in the nuts.
Place dough in a greased loaf pan and bake at 350° for 50 minutes to an hour or until a toothpick inserted in the center comes out clean. Cool before slicing.

THE LEADVILLE COUNTRY INN

127 East Eighth Street
Leadville, Colorado 80461
(719) 486-2354

Lemon Pecan Tea Bread

1	stick butter	2	cups flour
1¼	cup sugar	1	teaspoon baking powder
3	eggs	½	teaspoon salt
1	teaspoon vanilla	⅛	teaspoon mace
1	tablespoon lemon zest	¾	cup buttermilk
1	tablespoon lemon juice	½	cup nuts

Use mixer and beat butter, sugar. Add eggs one at a time. Add flavorings. Mix flour, baking powder and spices together. Add flour mixture, alternating with buttermilk. Add nuts.
Bake at 350° for 55 minutes.

JEROME HOTEL

330 East Main
Aspen, Colorado
(303) 920-1000

Mexican Cornbread

1½	cups corn meal	1	can (16½ ounces) creamstyle corn
¾	teaspoon salt	1	cup sharp cheddar cheese, grated
½	teaspoon baking soda	1	large onion, chopped
1	cup skim milk	1	clove garlic, minced
2	egg whites	1	can (4 ounces) green chiles
1	egg	2	tablespoons softened butter or olive oil

Preheat the oven to 350°. Combine corn meal, salt and baking soda. Stir in remaining ingredients and spoon into 9 by 13-inch baking dish that has been greased and sprinkled with cornmeal. Bake 45 minutes. Let cool 5 minutes before serving. Serves 12 to 20.

THE PEPPER MILL

5959 South Willow
Englewood, Colorado
(303) 741-1626

Pie Dough*

1	cup flour	1	egg
½	teaspoon salt	2	teaspoons cold water
½	cup butter		

Sift flour and salt together and cut in the butter. Beat egg and water together and stir into flour mixture. Pat together into a ball and chill.

Divide chilled dough in half and roll very thin. Fit bottom crust into 9-inch pie pan. Pour in the filling (your favorite) and top with crust. Flute the edges and brush with yolk and milk. Bake at 400° until brown. Serves 4 to 6.

*Variation

GEMINI RESTAURANT

4300 Wadsworth
Wheat Ridge, Colorado
(303) 421-4990

Gemini, a family-owned eatery, strives to bring quality, nutritional dishes to guests. The eatery provides a choice of smoking or non-smoking areas, meats or vegetarian dishes, alcoholic or fresh fruit drinks. No refined sugar or over-processed foods are used. The menu features fresh fruits and vegetables and exquisite creations at comfortable prices, served artfully and tastefully in an atmosphere of pure air and pleasant surroundings.

Swedish Apricot Nut Bread*

1	cup dried apricots	½	to 1 cup brandy, as needed
1	cup raw sugar	2	tablespoons softened sweet butter
1	egg, lightly beaten		grated rind of 1 lemon
½	cup strained orange juice	2	cups whole wheat flour
½	teaspoon baking soda	½	teaspoon salt
¾	cup chopped walnuts		

Soak apricots in brandy to cover for 2-3 hours. Drain, cut each apricot half into 6 small pieces and reserve ¼ cup brandy in which they soaked. Cream sugar and butter until light and fluffy. Add egg and lemon rind and beat until mixture is smooth and well-blended. Add reserved ¼ cup brandy and orange juice. Sift flour with baking powder, soda and salt. Re-sift into batter gradually, stirring well between additions. Fold in nuts and cut-up apricots. Butter an 8-inch loaf pan, line with brown paper and pour in batter. Let stand 20 minutes. Bake in preheated 350° oven, 1 hour, or until top is golden brown and a tester comes out clean. Turn out of pan while hot, peel off paper and cool on a rack. Let mellow for 24 hours before cutting.

*Variation

CHUBBY'S

1231 West 38th Avenue
Denver, Colorado
(303) 455-9311

Tortilla Chips — Oven Crisp

4   flour tortillas (see recipe in this
     section)

Cut flour tortillas into wedges with kitchen shears or a knife. Place the wedges on an ungreased cookie sheet and toast in a 350° oven for 10 to 12 minutes until dry and crisp.

BULL & BUSH

Cherry Creek Drive at Dexter
Denver, Colorado
(303) 759-0333

Wafer Crust

5   tablespoons softened butter
6   ounces vanilla wafers
¼   cup sugar

Coat one 9-inch springform pan with one tablespoon butter. Put the wafers and sugar in food processor and process to crumbs. Melt the remaining butter and process into the crumbs. Press crumb mixture evenly over the bottom of the springform pan.

POUR LA FRANCE! CAFE & BISTRO

730 South University Boulevard   1001 Pearl Street   413 E. Main
Denver, Colorado 80209   Boulder, Colorado 80302   Aspen, Colorado
(303) 744-1888   (303) 449-3929   (303) 920-1151

Warm Feta Cheese on French Bread
with Sun-Dried Tomatoes & Greek Olives

6   slices of Pour La France! French bread (no more than ½-inch thick)
6   tablespoons feta cheese
6   sun-dried tomato slices
1   Greek olive
3   teaspoons basil pesto
red grapes (optional)
lettuce leaf

Spread ½ teaspoon basil pesto on each bread slice. Top with 1 tablespoon feta cheese, 1 sun-dried tomato slice and 1 Greek Olive sliver. Broil for 1 minute or until soft. Garnish with lettuce leaf and red grapes.

RED LION INN

Boulder Canyon
Boulder, Colorado
(303) 442-9368

Yorkshire Pudding

2   cups all-purpose flour, sifted
1   teaspoon salt
1   cup milk
1   cup light cream
4   eggs
8   tablespoons butter or pan drippings from roast beef

Combine the sifted flour and salt, and sift again. With an egg beater, gradually blend in the milk and cream, beating after each addition until the mixture is smooth. Add the eggs, one at a time, beating at least 1 minute for each. Set the liquid batter in the refrigerator, covered with a cloth or aluminum foil, for at least 2 hours. Preheat the oven to 450°, and bake for 10 to 15 minutes. When the pudding turns crispy brown and light in texture, cut into squares and serve immediately. Serves 8.

FOUNTAIN CAFE AND RESTAURANT

223 Gore Creek Drive
Vail, Colorado
(303) 476-5885

Zucchini Bread

3   eggs, beaten
2   cups sugar
2   teaspoons vanilla
1   teaspoon baking soda
½   teaspoon cinnamon
1   cup cooking oil

2   cups grated zucchini
2   teaspoons baking powder
3   cups sifted flour
½   cup chopped nuts
     pinch of salt

Preheat oven to 325°. Grease and flour 2 loaf pans. Beat eggs, then add oil, sugar and vanilla. Cream together, add zucchini. Measure flour, baking soda and baking powder and add to creamed mixture. Add nuts and bake for 1 hour. Makes 2 small loaves.

VEGETABLES
VI

P. McClure

VEGETABLES, VI

Arroz a la Mexican (Mexican Rice) (Mexicali Cafe) — p. 1
Artichoke Florentine (Rudi's) — p. 2
Aubergines Farci (Rudi's) — p. 3
Basmati Rice (Rudi's) — p. 3
Broccoli Polonaise (The Greenbriar) — p. 4
Bulghur Pilaf (Rudi's) — p. 4
Cantina Rellenos (Cantina) — p. 5
Charbroiled Eggplant with Champagne Vinaigrette (Strings) — p. 5
Chili Rellenos with Sauce (Los Amigos) — p. 6
Dilled Potatoes and Sour Cream (Soren's Restaurant) — p. 6
Eggplant Crêpes (Bistro Adde Brewster) — p. 7
Garlic Rice with Pine Nuts (Piñon's) — p. 7
Gratin Dauphinois Chez Grand Mere from Bourgogne (Normandy Restaurant) — p. 8
Melanzane Alla Parmigiana (Abetone Restaurant — Introduction) — p. 9
Mujedera Lentil Pilaf (Rudi's) — p. 10
Piquant Green Beans (The Golden Dobbin) — p. 11
Poppies Potato Cake (Poppies Bistro Cafe) — p. 11
Sautéed Cucumbers with Romaine (Rudi's) — p. 12
Scrambled Tofu (Harvest Restaurant & Bakery) — p. 12
Spanakopita (Buckhorn Exchange) — p. 13
Spinach Italiano (D-J's Crêpes and Omelets) — p. 13
Stir-Fried String Beans and Almonds (Imperial Chinese Seafood) — p. 14
Sushi Rice (Sushi Den) — p. 15
Truffled Creamy Mashed Potatoes (Piñon's) — p. 16
Vegetable Empanadas (Rudi's) — p. 17
Vegetables with Oriental Touch (Briarhurst Manor Inn) — p. 18
Wild Rice Potato Cakes (Cliff Young's Restaurant) — p. 18

MEXICALI CAFE

1453 Larimer
Denver, Colorado
(303) 892-1444

Arroz a la Mexican*
(Mexican Rice)

1½ cups (abour 10½ ounces) unconverted long-grain rice
1   cup (½ pound) finely chopped unskinned tomatoes
2   tablespoons finely chopped white onion
2   garlic cloves, peeled and roughly chopped
⅓   cup olive oil
3½ cups chicken broth, approximately
⅓   cup carrot rounds, optional
½   cup fresh peas or diced zucchini, optional
sea salt to taste

Put the rice into a bowl and cover with very hot water,. Stir and leave to soak for about 10 minutes. Drain, rinse in cold water, and drain again.

Put the tomatoes, onion and garlic into a blender jar and blend until smooth. Set aside.

Heat the oil in a heavy pan. Give the rice a final shake and stir into the oil. Fry over fairly high heat until it begins to turn a light golden color. Strain off any excess oil, stir in the tomato puree, and fry, scraping the bottom of the dish to prevent sticking, until the puree has been absorbed — about 8 minutes. Stir in the broth and vegetables and cook over fairly high heat, uncovered, until all the broth has been absorbed and air holes appear in the surface. Cover the surface of the rice with a towel and lid and continue cooking over very low heat for about 5 minutes. Remove from the heat and set aside in a warm place for the rice to absorb the rest of the moisture in the steam and swell — about 15 minutes. Dig gently to the bottom and test a grain of rice. If it is still damp, cook for a few minutes longer. If the top grains are not quite soft, sprinkle with a little hot broth, cover, and cook for a few minutes longer.

Before serving, turn the rice over carefully from the bottom so that the flavored juices will be distributed evenly. Serves 6.

*variation

RUDI'S

4720 Table Mesa Drive
Boulder, Colorado 80303
(303) 494-5858

Chef Faith Stone

Artichoke Florentine

6   artichokes
6-8 cups water or vegetable stock
2   cups white wine
4   tablespoons olive oil
3   cloves garlic — minced

Trim the artichokes, removing the stalks and tough outer leaves. Trim the barbs off the remaining leaves and smooth artichoke bottoms with a knife. Cover the bottom of a pot, which will hold the artichokes in a single layer, with a thin layer of olive oil and garlic. Place the artichokes, bottoms down, in the pan and brown the bottoms. Then invert the artichokes (heart up) and fill the pot with stock or water up to the base of the leaves. Then fill the pot to cover the bottoms with wine and more water as needed. Weight the artichokes down with a plate to keep them from flipping over. Cover the pot, bring to a boil and simmer for 45 minutes or until a leaf will pull away easily and is tender to eat. Drain and make filling.

Florentine

1   pound spinach, 2 cups cooked
2   cups Mornay sauce (see Sauce section)
4   ounces grated cheddar cheese
1   tablespoon grated Romano
¼   teaspoon pepper
a dash Tabasco

Wash the spinach and remove tough stems. Cook in the water that clings to the leaves until just wilted, about 5 minutes. Refresh the spinach under cold water, squeeze off excess moisture and chop. Stir the chopped spinach, cheddar, Romano, Tabasco and pepper into the hot Mornay sauce.

Remove the fuzzy thistles from the artichokes and fill the cavities with Florentine. Serve with dipping butter for the artichoke if desired.

RUDI'S

4720 Table Mesa Drive
Boulder, Colorado 80303
(303) 494-5858

Chef Faith Stone

Aubergines Farci
(A Rudi's Original)

2   ripe eggplants, peeled and cut lengthwise into ½ inch slices
3   pounds fresh asparagus, snap off tough ends and peel stalks unless very tender
½   pound Gruyere cheese grated
olive oil
seasoned flour (1 cup flour, 1 teaspoon basil, Romano cheese,
     rosemary and a pinch of salt and pepper

   Steam or boil asparagus for 3-5 minutes until only slightly tender and set aside.
   Dredge eggplant slices in seasoned flour and fry until browned on both sides in oilve
oil. Drain on paper towels.
   Roll asparagus spears in the slices of browned eggplant and place in a baking dish. Top
with grated Gruyere cheese and bake at 350° for 15-20 minutes or until hot and bubbly.
Top with Hollandaise sauce (see Sauce section) and serve.

RUDI'S

4270 Table Mesa Drive
Boulder, Colorado 80303
(303) 494-5858

Chef Faith Stone

Basmati Rice

1½ cups basmati
3   cups water
2   tablespoons cashews
½   stick cinnamon
2   tablespoons butter
½   teaspoon salt
pinch of salt
½   cup green peas (optional)

   Rinse basmati twice. Bring water to a boil in a heavy gauge pot with tight fitting lid.
Add cashews, cinnamon, butter, salt and pepper. Add rice and bring to a boil. Cover and
turn heat to low. Cook for 20 minutes. Stir in peas and serve.

THE GREENBRIAR

North Foothills Highway
Boulder, Colorado
(303) 440-7979

Broccoli Polonaise

3   tablespoons butter
1   hard-boiled egg, chopped
2   teaspoons garlic paste or 1 clove garlic, chopped
sprig fresh parsley, chopped
salt to taste
1   tablespoon white bread crumbs
3 to 4 flowerettes of broccoli, steamed 10 minutes

   Melt butter. Saute garlic; add chopped egg and bread crumbs to thicken slightly. Add chopped parsley. Pour over steamed broccoli. Serves 1.

RUDI'S

4270 Table Mesa Drive
Boulder, Colorado 80303
(303) 494-5858

Chef Faith Stone

Bulghur Pilaf

3   ounces vermicelli, break into small (2 inch) pieces
3   cups bulghur
¼   cup olive oil
2   tablespoons butter
1   onion, thinly sliced
6   cups vegetable stock or water

   Heat olive oil in a skillet or sauce pan and fry raw vermicelli until browned. Add 6 cups stock or water, bring to a boil and cook 5-7 minutes until vermicelli is tender. Add bulghur, and cook for 5 minutes over low heat. Turn off heat, cover and let stand for 10 minutes.
   In a separate pan saute onion in 2 tablespoons butter until tender. Stir onion into the pilaf and serve.

CANTINA

411 East Main Street
Aspen, Colorado 81611
(303) 925-3663

Cantina Rellenos*

8   Anaheim chiles
1   cup shredded cheddar cheese
1   cup shredded beef, cooked
⅓   cup raisins
⅓   cup pecans
salsa verde (see Sauce section)

   Fill large Anaheim chiles with shredded beef, raisins, and pecans. Sprinkle with salsa
verde and cheese. Bake in oven 15 minutes at 300° or grill.

*variation

STRINGS

1700 Humboldt
Denver, Colorado 80218
(303) 831-7310

Charbroiled Eggplant
with Champagne Vinaigrette (see Sauce section)

1   eggplant
olive oil
salt and pepper to taste
½   garlic clove, minced
4   tomatoes, sliced
8   ounces Buffalo mozzarella, diced
lemon juice
freshly cracked pepper
6   basil leaves, julienned
pinch of parsley

   Slice eggplant into 8 slices. Brush with olive oil and season lightly with salt and pepper.
Add garlic for just a hint. Charbroil and place on plate.
   Slice tomatoes and dice cheese. Take 2 ounces Champagne Vinaigrette and a squeeze of
lemon juice with fresh cracked pepper, basil leaves and pinch of parsley.
   Toss together and serve with the eggplant. Serves 4.

LOS AMIGOS

318 East Hanson Ranch Road
Vail, Colorado
(303) 476-5847

Chili Rellenos
with Sauce (see Sauce section)

4   whole stem chiles
4   slices Monterey Jack cheese (2½ inches wide)
egg batter (see below)
peanut oil
1   cup cheddar cheese
chili rellenos sauce (see Sauce section)

Remove skins from chiles by placing them over a flame until skins sizzle. Slit chiles at the top to open and stuff jack cheese through slit. Heat about 1 inch of oil in fry pan to 350°. Dip chiles in egg batter, then fry in hot oil for 3 minutes on each side or until brown. Remove. Place chiles in baking dish, cover with cheddar cheese and bake at 500° until cheese melts (about 10 minutes). Remove from oven and cover with hot chili relleno sauce and serve. Serves 4.

Chili Rellenos Egg Batter

2   eggs, separated
pinch of salt
pinch of baking soda

In a bowl, beat egg whites until very stiff. Fold in beaten egg yolks very carefully. Add salt and baking soda. Continue folding until batter reaches a smooth consistency.

SOREN'S RESTAURANT

315 Detroit
Denver, Colorado 80209
(303) 322-8155

Dilled Potatoes and Sour Cream

4   potatoes, diced
1   pound sour cream or non-fat yogurt
2   tablespoons dill
1   teaspoon salt
1   teaspoon pepper

Boil diced potatoes until tender. Drain potatoes. Combine sour cream, dill, salt and pepper. Add to cooked potatoes. Chill. Serves 6-8.

BISTRO ADDE BREWSTER

250 Steele
Cherry Creek North
Denver, Colorado 80206
(303) 388-1900

Eggplant Crêpes

1   large eggplant (approximately 2 pounds) sliced lengthwise ¼ ″ thick
1   tablespoon salt
2   cups olive oil
¼   cup bread crumbs (dry)
½   cup chopped parsley
1 ¾ cups grated mozzarella
½   cup grated Parmesan
1   egg, beaten
fresh pepper
1 to 2 cups Marinara Sauce (see Sauce section)

   Layer eggplant slices in colander and sprinkle with salt and let drain for at least 2 hours. Dry with paper towels. Brown eggplant slices in olive oil and drain again on towels. Preheat oven to 375 ° — combine crumbs, garlic, parsley, mozzarella and Parmesan. Stir in eggs and season with salt and pepper. Place about 1 tablespoon of cheese filling in each crêpe and roll and place in baking dish, seam side down. Top with marinara and some grated Parmesan and bake until hot and bubbly. Serves 6-8.

PIÑON'S

105 South Mill
Aspen, Colorado
(303) 920-2021

Garlic Rice with Pine Nuts*

1   small green pepper, cut in strips
1   small red pepper, cut in strips
¼   cup pine nuts or slivered almonds
1   clove garlic, minced
1   tablespoon butter or margarine, melted
2   cups cooked rice (cooked in chicken broth)*
2   tablespoons snipped fresh parsley

   Cook peppers, pine nuts, and garlic in butter in large skillet over medium-high heat until peppers are tender crisp and nuts are lightly browned. Add rice and parsley; stir until thoroughly heated. Serves 4.

Basic Rice Preparation*

   Combine 1 cup uncooked regular-milled long grain rice with 1 ¾ to 2 cups liquid.
   Add an optional teaspoon of salt or optional tablespoon of butter or margarine in a 2-to 3-quart saucepan. With a cup of regular-milled medium or short grain rice, use 1 to 1 ½ cups of liquid and the optional salt and butter or margarine.
   Heat to boiling, stirring once or twice. Lower heat, simmer, cover with tight-fitting lid.
   If rice isn't tender in 15 minutes, or liquid not absorbed, replace lid and cook 2 to 4 minutes longer. Fluff with fork.

*variation

NORMANDY FRENCH RESTAURANT

1515 Madison Street
Denver, Colorado 80206
(303) 321-3311

Gratin Dauphinois Chez Grand Mere
From Bourgogne

3   pounds white potatoes, peeled and very thinly sliced
3   cups milk
1   clove garlic, peeled and halved
freshly ground black pepper to season
½   cup creme fraiche or heavy cream
1   cup Gruyere cheese, grated
1½ teaspoons salt
2   large eggs, lightly beaten

Preheat oven to 375°.

Rub the inside of oval porcelain dish with the garlic. Arrange potatoes in an even layer in the dish.

Mix the milk, eggs, salt and pepper and pour over potatoes.

Bake, occasionally cutting the crust that forms on top and gently folding it into the potatoes until the gratin is golden, approximately 55 minutes.

Remove the dish from the oven, sprinkle with the grated cheese, then dab the gratin with creme fraiche or heavy cream.

Return the dish to the oven and bake until the top is very crisp and golden, about 15 minutes. Serves 6 to 8.

ABETONE RESTAURANT

620 East Hyman Avenue
Aspen, Colorado
(303) 925-9022

Abetone Ristorante, serving authentic classical Northern Italian cuisine, opened its doors to Aspenites and visitors during the ski season of 1978.

Aptly named, Abetone is a ski resort of note, located on the eastern side of the great Italian mountain range, the Apennines, between Florence and Bologna.

The similarity of cities doesn't end with a reputation for first-rate skiing, as Italy's premier ski area lies in the richest gastronomic region of the country. The authentic cuisine of that region has been discovered over the last few years in Aspen at Abetone Ristorante, which serves imported pasta, fresh seafood (including live lobsters flown in from the New England coast), prime veal and beef along with a variety of seasonal specialties — all served with fresh vegetables and salad.

Melanzane Alla Parmigiana
(Eggplant Parmigiana)

½   cup milk
2   eggs
salt and pepper
1   medium eggplant, peeled and cut into ½-inch slices
1   cup all-purpose flour
1   cup fine, unflavored bread crumbs
1   cup olive oil
2   cups fresh tomato sauce
8   slices mozzarella cheese
½   cup grated, imported Parmesan cheese

Mix milk, eggs, salt and pepper in a bowl. Dip eggplant slices in flour, then in egg mixture. Lightly coat with bread crumbs. Fry eggplant in hot olive oil in a heavy skillet until golden on both sides. Pat with paper towel to dry excess oil. Pour tomato sauce to cover the bottom of a baking dish. Alternate eggplant slices with mozzarella in layers. Cover with remaining sauce. Sprinkle with Parmesan. Bake at 350° for 15 minutes. Serves 4.

RUDI'S

4720 Table Mesa Drive
Boulder, Colorado 80303
(303) 494-5858

Chef Faith Stone

Mujedera Lentil Pilaf

1 cup lentils	¼ cup olive oil
3½ cups vegetable stock or water	pinch cayenne
1 cup fine cut bulghur	salt and pepper to taste
2 onions minced	

Soak lentils in water (not the stock) for 5 minutes. Discard any imperfect beans that float and drain off soaking water.

In a heavy bottomed pot bring the lentils and stock or water to a boil. Reduce heat and simmer 1 hour or until lentils are tender. Stir in bulghur and add a little more water if needed. Cook for an additional 5 minutes until bulghur is tender. Cover and remove from heat.

Cook minced onions in olive oil until tender and stir into the lentil and bulghur pilaf. Season with cayenne. Salt and pepper to taste.

Can be served hot as is or cold with fresh lemon, a drizzle of olive oil and pita bread.

THE GOLDEN DOBBIN

519 Wilcox
Castle Rock, Colorado 80104
(303) 688-3786

Piquant Green Beans

1   package French cut green beans
4   strips bacon
2   tablespoons diced pimientos
¼   teaspoon sugar
¼   teaspoon dry mustard
1   tablespoon worcestershire sauce
Tabasco sauce (2 drops)

Cook beans according to directions on package. Cook chopped bacon until crisp and add to drained beans. To bacon fat add rest of ingredients and bring fat to boil, stirring constantly. Pour over beans and mix well. Serve hot. Serves 3-4.

POPPIES BISTRO CAFE

834 West Hallan
Aspen, Colorado 81611
(303) 925-2333

Poppies Potato Cake

5   potatoes
whole thyme sprigs
½   cup clarified butter
2   teaspoons olive oil

Peel potatoes. Cut on a mandoline, as a potato chip. In a black steel pan, pour clarified butter and olive oil. Shingle potatoes around the edge and spiral inward. Make 4 layers. Sauté over high heat. When the potatoes start to brown, cut the flame in half. Flip over. Cook for 3 minutes. Put in 350° oven for 10 minutes. Remove from pan onto cutting board. Cut into wedges like a pie. Serve warm with Sautéed Boneless Quail (see Fowl section).

RUDI'S

4720 Table Mesa Drive
Boulder, Colorado 80303
(303) 494-5858

Chef Faith Stone

Sautéed Cucumbers with Romaine

2   cucumbers peeled, cut in half and seeded
1   head Romaine lettuce
juice of 1 lemon
1   teaspoon dill
2   tablespoons sunflower seeds
2   tablespoons sesame oil
salt and pepper to taste

Chop cucumbers into ¼-inch slices. In a wok or wide skillet heat sesame oil and lightly brown sunflower seeds. Add cucumbers and stir-fry 2 minutes, until cucumbers start to clear and are barely tender. Add Romaine and stir-fry until Romaine wilts. Remove from heat and toss with lemon juice, dill, salt and pepper to taste.

HARVEST RESTAURANT & BAKERY

1738 Pearl
Boulder, Colorado
(303) 449-6223

HARVEST RESTAURANT & BAKERY

7730 E. Belleview Avenue
Greenwood Village, Colorado
(303) 779-4111

HARVEST RESTAURANT & BAKERY

430 S. Colorado Boulevard
Denver, Colorado
(303) 399-6652

Scrambled Tofu *

½   cup tofu cut into strips
½   cup green onions, chopped
½   cup fresh tomatoes, chopped
½   cup mushrooms

¼   cup lite soy
2   tablespoons sesame oil
¼   teaspoon fresh ginger
1   teaspoon sesame seeds

Soak tofu in soy and transfer to hot skillet with sesame oil and ginger. Sear on all sides of tofu. Add remaining ingredients to skillet and heat thoroughly. Serve at once with rice. Serves 1.

* Variation

BUCKHORN EXCHANGE

1000 Osage
Denver, Colorado 80204
(303) 534-9505

Spanakopita

2	pounds frozen chopped spinach		1	teaspoon Maggi seasoning
1	small onion, diced		¼	teaspoon nutmeg
4	green onions, chopped		1	teaspoon sasoned salt
½	pound feta cheese		¼	teaspoon white pepper
3	medium eggs		¼	teaspoon granulated garlic
⅓	cup milk		6	ounces streusel dough leaves
¼	cup dill weed			

Cook and drain spinach. Saute onions. In mixing bowl combine onions, spinach, crumbled feta cheese, and seasonings. Beat together eggs and milk, add to filling. Layer ½ of streusel leaves in bottom of a buttered 2-inch baking pan. Butter each layer. Add filling, top with remaining streusel leaves, buttering between each layer. Bake at 375° for 1 hour. Cut into 3 x 6 inch pieces. Serves 6.

D-J'S CRÊPES AND OMELETS

Concert Hall Plaza Building
Vail, Colorado 81657
(303) 476-2336

Spinach Italiano

3   cups chopped fresh spinach
1   tablespoon olive oil
½   cup finely chopped onions
1   cup ricotta cheese (cottage cheese may be substituted)
2   tablespoons grated Parmesan cheese
⅓   cup light cream
salt and pepper
cream of celery soup
nutmeg
basic crêpes (see Basic Crêpes recipe — makes 10 to 12)
D-J's Italian Sauce (see Sauce section)

In a saucepan, combine all filling ingredients (except celery soup and nutmeg). Cook and stir until well blended. Add cream of celery soup to attain a smooth, but not soupy, texture. Add a dash or more of nutmeg, seasoning to taste. Cook on low to medium heat until hot and onions are cooked. Ladle about 8 ounces of mixture into each crêpe and fold. Top with Italian Sauce and Parmesan cheese. Serves 10 to 12 large crêpes.

IMPERIAL CHINESE SEAFOOD

1 Broadway
Denver, Colorado
(303) 698-2800

Stir-Fried String Beans and Almonds
(with Soy Sauce)

1   pound string beans (or 1 package, 10 ounces, frozen)
2   tablespoons peanut or vegetable oil
3   slices ginger, chopped
1   cup blanched, peeled almonds
1   tablespoon soy sauce
½   teaspoon sugar
¼   cup chicken stock
salt and pepper

If beans are fresh, parboil and dry before frying. If frozen, thaw and dry. In skillet, heat oil. Add ginger and almonds and stir-fry for 1 minute. Add string beans and stir-fry for 1 minute. Add soy sauce, sugar and chicken stock. Boil until liquid reduces and thickens to coat a spoon. Season and serve. Serves 4.

SUSHI DEN
1469 South Pearl
Denver, Colorado
(303) 777-0826

Sushi Rice

Rice

3 ⅓ cups short-grain rice
4   cups water

Vinegar mixture

5   tablespoons plus 1 teaspoon rice vinegar
5   tablespoons sugar
4   teaspoons salt

Wash the rice until the wash water runs clear and drain in a colander for 1 hour. Place the drained rice in a rice cooker or in a pot with a close-fitting lid and add water. Cover and bring the water to a boil over a medium heat.

Cover tightly and boil over high heat for 2 minutes. Reduce heat to medium and boil for another 5 minutes. Over low heat, cook for 15 minutes or until all the water has been absorbed. Remove from heat. Take off the lid, spread a clean kitchen towel over the top of the pot, replace the lid and let stand for 10 to 15 minutes.

While the rice is cooking, combine the vinegar ingredients in an enamel bowl and heat slowly till the sugar has dissolved, stirring constantly. Remove from heat. To cool quickly, place the enamel bowl in a bowl of ice cubes.

Empty the rice into a hangiri (or other non-metallic) tub and spread it evenly over the bottom with a shamoji or a large wooden spoon. Run the spatula through the rice in right and left slicing motions to separate the grains. As you do this, slowly add the vinegar mixture. You may not need all of it. Avoid adding too much; the rice must not be mushy.

Continue the slicing motions with the spatula as you add the vinegar. All the while you do this, have a helper fan the rice with a fan (uchiwa) or a piece of cardboard.

The fanning and mixing take about 10 minutes, that is, until the rice reaches room temperature. Do not refrigerate the rice, but keep it in the tub, covered with a clean cloth, until you are ready to use it. Sushi rice lasts only one day and does not lend itself to leftovers.

PIÑON'S

105 South Mill
Aspen, Colorado
(303) 920-2021

Chef Robert Mobilian has earned Piñon's the reputation for being one of the finest restaurants in Colorado. Pheasant Quesadillas; sautéed soft shell crab; ahi with macadamia nut breading; and truffled mashed potatoes are only a few of the wonderful dishes, prepared to perfection, that nightly grace guests' tables at this fabulous restaurant.

Chef Robert Mobilian keeps his recipes top secret. But here's a hint or variation of that top secret.

Truffled Creamy Mashed Potatoes

3   cloves garlic, crushed
4   medium-size all-purpose potatoes (about 1 pound), peeled and sliced thin
1   bay leaf
1   tablespoon unsalted butter
¾   cup cream (or ½ cup buttermilk and 3 tablespoons non-fat yogurt)
1   tablespoon truffles
1   tablespoon chopped mushrooms

In a medium-size heavy saucepan, bring 3 cups unsalted water to a boil. Add the garlic, potatoes, and bay leaf, and cook, partially covered, over moderate heat for 12 minutes or until the potatoes are fork-tender. Drain, reserving 3 tablespoons of cooking water, and discard the bay leaf.

Transfer the potatoes to a large mixing bowl. Add the butter and cream (or low cholesterol substitute of buttermilk and yogurt) and beat with an electric mixer.

In a skillet poach truffles and mushrooms in reserved water.

Add to mashed potatoes.

Thoroughly fold in and enjoy.

RUDI'S

4720 Table Mesa Drive
Boulder, Colorado 80303
(303) 494-5858

Chef Faith Stone

Vegetable Empanadas

½ bunch broccoli, 1½ cups buds
1   small cauliflower, 1½ cups buds
1   small onion, 1 cup, chopped
1   small green pepper
1½ cups squash, winter or summer, chopped
1   cup sliced mushrooms
4   ounces spinach, washed, stems removed
4   ounces Brie cheese, cut small
1   clove garlic — minced
salt and pepper to taste
4   tablespoons butter

Sauté the onion and green pepper in butter until tender. Add the broccoli, cauliflower and squash with ½ cup water, cover and steam for 15 minutes or until veggies are tender. Add the mushrooms, garlic and spinach and cook for 5 minutes more. Remove from heat and drain off any vegetable liquids. Transfer to a bowl and stir in the Brie and salt and pepper to taste. Refrigerate until ready to use. Prepare the Empanada Dough (see Bread section). Fill turnovers with the above vegetable mixture and bake 20 minutes at 350° or until browned and hot through.

BRIARHURST MANOR INN

404 Manitou Avenue
Colorado Springs-Manitou Springs, Colorado
(719) 685-1864

A visit to Colorado must include a meal at this historic restaurant where Chef Sigi Krauss brings his award-winning international culinary background to Briarhurst Manor Inn.

Vegetables with Oriental Touch

1   large carrot, peeled and cut into julienne strips
3   ounces leek, cut into julienne strips
3   ounces zucchini, cut into julienne strips
1   small onion, diced
1   ounce sesame seed oil
2   ounces butter
pinch nutmeg
pinch salt
dash white pepper
garnish with chopped green onions

In a sauté pan, place oil and butter; heat. Add julienne vegetables and seasoning and sauté 2 to 3 minuts. Transfer to serving platter and garnish with green onions. Serves 4.

CLIFF YOUNG'S
RESTAURANT

700 East Seventeenth Avenue
Denver, Colorado 80210
(303) 831-8900

Chef Dave Query

Wild Rice Potato Cakes

2   potatoes
2   egg yolks
2   egg whites (beaten soft peaks)
½   cup cooked wild rice
salt, pepper, chives

Cook two potatoes and mash. Separate eggs, fold in beaten egg whites with the potatoes. Whisk egg yolks, salt, pepper and chives into an egg wash. Separate potato mixture into small cakes. Dip with egg wash. Then dip into cooked wild rice and bake 10 minutes at 350°.

PASTA VII

P. McClure

ENTRÉES PASTA, VII

Baked Macaroni and Cheese (The Silver Queen) — p. 1

Bob's Homemade Pasta (Bob's Pizzeria) — p. 1

Bob's Special Fettuccine (Bob's Pizzeria) — p. 2

Cannelloni with Ricotta and Peas (Hotel Boulderado — Introduction) — p. 2

Chicken Carbonara Fettuccine (Delfannies Restaurant) — p. 3

Chilled Noodle Summer Entrée (Sushi Den) — p. 3

Coho Salmon Tortellini with Orange Brandy Cream Sauce (Strings) — p. 4

(Easy) Pasta from Scratch (Patina Grill) — pp. 5-6

Fettuccine Abetone (Abetone Restaurant) — p. 7

Fettuccine Alfredo (Mirabelle's at Beaver Creek — Introduction) — p. 8

Gnocchi Potato Dumplings (The Villa at Palmer Lake — Introduction) — p. 8

Homemade Spinach Noodles ''Al Pesto'' (Vail Racquet Club Restaurant — Introduction) — p. 9

Linguine with Tuna-Caper Sauce (Falcone's Restaurant & Bar) — p. 10

Linguine with White Clam Sauce (Legends) — p. 11

Pasta Del Giorno (Pasta with Spinach Sauce) (Mezzaluna) — p. 12

Pasta Mangione (Maxie's) — p. 13

Pasta Marinara with Shrimp (Delmonico's — Introduction) — p. 14

Pasta Riviera (Ristorante Paolino) — p. 14

Pasta Scampi (The Ranch at Keystone — Introduction) — p. 15

Pesto alla Genovese (The Saucy Noodle Ristorante — Introduction)) — p. 16

Spaghetti Marinara (The Saucy Noodle Ristorante) — p. 16

Spaghetti with Garlic, Capers and Artichoke Hearts (The Motherlode — Introduction) — p. 17

Spaghetti and Shrimp (Primavera Ristorante at Aspen Mountain) — p. 17

Spicy Lasagne Roll-Ups (Gussie's) — p. 18

Swiss Spaghetti (The Red Onion) — p. 19

Three Cheese Lasagne with Chicken and Porcini Mushrooms (Sfuzzi) — pp. 20-21

Tortellini (Mike Berardi's) — p. 22

Vermicelli with Anchovies and Garlic (Philomena's) — p. 23

Zucchini, Mushroom and Pimiento Lasagne (Vendetta's — Introduction) — p. 24

THE SILVER QUEEN

500 Sixth Street
Georgetown, Colorado
(303) 569-2961 — local
(303) 670-1307 — metro

Baked Macaroni And Cheese

6	ounces elbow or other small macaroni
1	tablespoon unsalted margarine or butter
1	teaspoon dried marjoram, crumbled
½	teaspoon dried thyme, crumbled
pinch ground nutmeg	
pinch paprika	
3	tablespoons flour
2	cups skim milk
1	tablespoon country mustard (see Sauce section)

½	cup grated Parmesan cheese
1	cup low-fat cottage cheese

Preheat the oven to 350°. Cook the macaroni according to package directions, omitting the salt; rinse with cold water and drain well.

Meanwhile, melt the margarine in a small heavy saucepan over moderate heat; add the marjoram, thyme, nutmeg, and paprika, and cook, stirring, for 1 minute. Remove from the heat and set aside.

In a small bowl, whisk the flour with ¼ cup of the milk. Add another ¼ cup milk and whisk until blended. Pour the mixture into the saucepan with the margarine and herbs, set over moderate heat, and add the rest of the milk in a steady stream, whisking constantly. Bring to a simmer and cook, stirring constantly, for 2 minutes or until slightly thickened. Remove from the heat and stir in the mustard and all but 2 tablespoons of the Parmesan cheese.

Stir the sauce into the macaroni and mix well. Add the cottage cheese and mix well again. Spoon into an ungreased 8 x 8 x 2 baking pan and sprinkle with the remaining 2 tablespoons of Parmesan cheese. Bake, uncovered, for 30 minutes or until bubbly and golden. Serve with a green salad. Serves 4.

Variation: stir in minced green onions or pimientos.

BOB'S PIZZERIA

1824 South Sheridan
Denver, Colorado
(303) 936-0911

Bob's Homemade Pasta

1	pound flour
enough water to make a hard dough	
salt to taste	

3	eggs
2	tablespoons olive oil

Mix dough together and blend well by hand. Make a hard dough. Roll dough out with rolling pin on floured paper. Roll the dough then into one big roll, like a gigantic cigar. At this point the dough may be placed in the freezer in a bag or in the refrigerator for 7 days — although it will turn dark. When ready to use pasta dough, slice the rolled dough into thin strips with the meat slicer (this works better then spaghetti or pasta machines). Uncurl the slices and drip the spaghetti into rapidly boiling, salted water. Remove spaghetti, drain off water and serve on hot platter and top with favorite sauce. Serves 4 portions of spaghetti.

BOB'S PIZZERIA

1824 South Sheridan
Denver, Colorado
(303) 936-0911

Bob's Special Fettuccine

1	pound fettuccine noodles		1	dash chopped garlic
½	cup soft sweet butter		⅓	cup Parmesan cheese
⅔	cup heavy cream			Romano cheese
1	teaspoon salt			

Precook fettuccine noodles and drain. To make sauce, combine all ingredients (except Parmesan cheese) in a large skillet and heat on medium heat until mixture starts to bubble. Add Parmesan cheese. Stir rapidly for 1 minute. Add noodles to sauce. Divide onto 5 plates and sprinkle with Romano cheese. Serves 5.

HOTEL BOULDERADO

13th and Spruce
Boulder, Colorado
(303) 442-4344

This is an historic downtown hotel with three places to sit: the Bar at Winston's — an old fashioned pub; The Mezzanine Lounge upstairs; and the Catacombs downstairs. Here is a vegetarian pasta variation on their daily changing specials.

Cannelloni with Ricotta And Peas

12 cannelloni shells or 8 manicotti shells
¼ cup fresh or frozen green peas
1 cup part-skim ricotta cheese
2 tablespoons golden raisins
1 large egg
3 medium-size ripe tomatoes, peeled, cored and chopped
    or 1 can (1 pound) low-sodium tomatoes, drained and chopped
3 tablespoons minced fresh mint or parsley
½ teaspoon black pepper
2 tablespoons tomato paste

Preheat the oven to 350°. Cook the cannelloni shells in boiling unsalted water for 6 minutes or until partially softened. Drain and set aside.

Bring an inch of water to a boil in a small saucepan, add the peas, and cook for 2 minutes. Drain. In a medium-size bowl, combine the peas, cheese, raisins, egg, egg white, ⅓ cup of the tomatoes, 1½ tablespoons of the mint, and ¼ teaspoon of the pepper, and mix well. Fill the cannelloni shells with the mixture.

Combine the remaining tomatoes, mint, and pepper with the tomato paste in a small bowl; mix well. Pour ¾ cup of the mixture into the bottom of an ungreased 8″ x 8″ x 2″ baking pan and place the filled pasta shells on top. Pour the remaining mixture over all. Cover with aluminum foil and bake for 20 minutes. Uncover and bake 10 minutes longer. Serves 4.

DELFANNIES RESTAURANT

215 East Foothills Parkway
Fort Collins, Colorado 80525
(303) 223-3354

Chicken Carbonara Fettuccine

1   six-ounce boneless, skinless chicken breast cut into strips and floured
2   green onions, diced
4   strips crisp bacon, diced
pinch salt
pinch black pepper
pinch dried parsley
2   ounces clarified butter
1   tablespoon dijon mustard
1½ ounced white wine
½   cup heavy cream
2   ounces Parmesan cheese
6   ounces cooked fettuccine

   In a saute pan, cook chicken strips in butter, salt, pepper and parsley until well done. Add bacon, green onions, mustard, and deglaze with white wine. Add cream. Reduce until sauce will coat the back of a spoon. Add grated Parmesan cheese and fettuccine and toss. Serve with garlic bread and grated Parmesan cheese. Serves 1.

SUSHI DEN

1469 South Pearl Street
Denver, Colorado
(303) 777-0826

Chilled Noodle Summer Entrée

1½ cups fine noodles (3 ounces)
½ cup thinly sliced green onion
½ cup chicken stock

2   tablespoons soy sauce
1   tablespoon dry sherry
½   teaspoon grated ginger root

   Cook noodles according to package directions; rinse thoroughly with cold water and drain well. Cover with ice water; let stand until noodles are chilled. Drain well. Combine noodles and green onion; set aside.
   Combine chicken stock, soy sauce, dry sherry, and ginger root.
   Serve noodles with chicken stock mixture. Serves 3 or 4.

STRINGS

1700 Humboldt
Denver, Colorado
(303) 831-7310

Coho Salmon Tortellini with Orange Brandy Cream Sauce

Pasta

8	ounces flour	salt	
8	ounces Semolina	pepper	
2	eggs	nutmeg	
2	ounces white wine		

Mix

4	ounces cooked spinach	¼	ounce Parmesan cheese
4	ounces sliced mushrooms	1	ounce grated ricotta
½	pound Coho salmon (diced)		zest of ½ orange

Sauce

	juice of 2 oranges	1	pint half & half
1	ounce brandy	1	ounce grated Parmesan
1	pint cream		

Garnish

2	oranges (segmented)	1	pound Coho salmon

Pasta:

Combine all ingredients. Roll into a ball. Cover with a damp cloth and allow to rest for 1 hour. Roll out pasta into thin sheets. Place ¼ teaspoon of filling mix for each tortellini. Cut with round cutter. Fold over and seal sides. Egg wash one side. Allow to rest for 15 minutes. Poach in gentle boiling water for 2-3 minutes.

Sauce:

Combine cream and half & half and reduce by one third. In a separate pan reduce orange juice by half. Add tortellini and the brandy and flame it. Add to cream sauce. Sprinkle with Parmesan and arrange on a serving plate. Decorate with orange segments and sauteed pieces of Coho salmon.

PATINA GRILL

Hyatt Regency
Vail-Beaver Creek, Colorado
(303) 949-1234

(Easy) Pasta From Scratch*

Egg Pasta

3 cups unsifted all-purpose flour	1 tablespoon salad or olive oil
½ teaspoon salt	2-3 tablespoons lukewarm water
4 eggs	

Sift flour with salt into medium bowl. Make a well in center. Add eggs and oil. Pour water in gradually, and mix with fork until well combined. Dough will be stiff. Form into a ball.

Turn out on lightly floured wooden board. Knead dough until it is smooth and elastic — about 15 minutes. Cover with bowl; let rest at least 30 minutes (this makes it easier to roll out). Makes 1½ pounds.

To shape: Divide dough into four parts. Keep covered with bowl until ready to roll out; or refrigerate in plastic bags.

On lightly floured pastry cloth or board, roll each part into a rectangle about 16 by 14 inches and about 1/16 inch thick. Work quickly, because dough dries out. From long side, roll up loosely as for jelly roll.

With thin, sharp knife, cut roll crosswise, 1/8 inch wide for fettuccine. For lasagne, cut the rolled dough into strips 2 inches wide, 6 inches long. For wide noodles (tagliatelle), cut into strips ¾ inch wide. For narrow noodles, cut ¼ inch wide. Unroll noodles, and wind loosely around fingers. For fresh pasta, cook immediately. Or freeze in plastic bags for a week.

To dry pasta, arrange on ungreased cookie sheets; let dry overnight. Store pasta in a covered glass jar in a cool place.

To cook pasta: In large kettle, bring 3 quarts of water, 1 tablespoon each of salt and salad oil to rapid boil. Add pasta; bring back to boiling; cook, uncovered and stirring occasionally with long fork to prevent sticking, just until tender — 3 to 5 minutes for fresh pasta, 7 to 10 minutes for dried. (Do not thaw frozen pasta.) Do not overcook. Drain well. Rinse.

Note: For food processor, place all ingredients in processor container. Process about 1 minute, or just until mixture leaves sides of container. Continue with step 2, turning out on lightly floured wooden board.

Spinach or Broccoli Pasta

1 package (10 ounces) frozen chopped spinach or broccoli
3 cups unsifted all-purpose flour
½ teaspoon salt
2 eggs
1 tablespoon salad or olive oil

Cook spinach according to package directions; drain well. Puree in food processor or blender. Follow directions for making Egg pasta, adding pureed spinach along with eggs and oil and omitting water. (If dough seems sticky, add more flour to board during kneading.)
Makes 1½ pounds.

Tomato Pasta

3 cups unsifted all-purpose flour	1 can (8 ounces) tomato sauce
½ teaspoon salt	1 tablespoon salad or olive oil
2 eggs	2 teaspoons dried basil leaves

Follow directions for Egg Pasta, adding tomato sauce and basil with eggs and oil, omitting water. (If dough is sticky, add more flour to board during kneading.)
Makes 1½ pounds.

Whole Wheat Pasta

2	cups whole wheat flour	4	eggs
1	cup unsifted all-purpose flour	1	tablespoon salad or olive oil
½	teaspoon salt	3-4	tablespoons lukewarm water

Follow directions for Egg Pasta.

Parmesan-Cheese Pasta

3	cups unsifted all-purpose flour	3	eggs
¼	cup grated Parmesan cheese	1	tablespoon salad or olive oil
½	teaspoon salt	5-6	tablespoons lukewarm water

Follow directions for Egg Pasta. Add Parmesan with flour and salt.
Make 1½ pounds.

Carrot Pasta

2	cups sliced carrots	2	eggs
3	cups unsifted all-purpose flour	1	tablespoon salad or olive oil
½	teaspoon salt		

In small saucepan, cook carrots, covered, in 2 inches boiling water until tender. Drain; puree in food processor or blender. Cool completely; use 1 cup.
Follow directions for making Egg Pasta, adding 1 cup carrot puree along with eggs and oil and omitting water. (If dough seems sticky, add more flour to board during kneading.)
Makes 1½ pounds.

Asparagus Pasta

1   package (10 ounces) frozen asparagus
3   cups unsifted all-purpose flour
½   teaspoon salt
3   eggs
1   tablespoon salad or olive oil

Cook asparagus according to package directions; drain well. Puree in food processor or blender. Follow directions for making Egg Pasta, adding pureed asparagus along with the eggs and oil, omitting water. (If dough seems sticky, add more flour to board during kneading.)
Makes 1⅔ pounds.

Orange Pasta

3	cups unsifted all-purpose flour	1	tablespoon salad or olive oil
½	teaspoon salt	2	tablespoons grated orange peel
3	eggs	3-4	tablespoons orange juice

Follow directions for making Egg Pasta, substituting orange juice for water. (If dough seems sticky, add more flour to board during kneading.)
Makes 1¼ pounds.

* Variation

ABETONE RESTAURANT

620 East Hyman
Aspen, Colorado
(303) 925-9022

Fettuccine Abetone

6	quarts water		salt and pepper to taste
salt		1	cup heavy cream
2	tablespoons olive oil	½	cup grated, imported Parmesan cheese
1	box imported fettuccine (egg noodles)	¼	cup chopped parsley
1	pound cooked, fresh lobster meat		

Bring water to a boil in a large pot. Add salt and oil; add fettuccine and cook for 12 minutes. Meanwhile, melt butter in a large skillet. Add lobster meat and salt and pepper. Sauté over medium heat for 5 minutes. Add cream and Parmesan; mix. Simmer 5 minutes. Add drained fettuccine; mix again. Simmer 2 minutes longer. Put in serving bowl. Sprinkle with parsley. Serve immediately. Serves 4.

MIRABELLE'S AT BEAVER CREEK

55 Village Road
Vail-Beaver Creek, Colorado
(303) 949-7728

This romantic Victorian house offers some of Colorado's finest classic continental dining. Here is a variation of classic Fettuccine Alfredo.

Fettuccine Alfredo

1	pound noodles
6	tablespoons butter
1	teaspoon olive oil
4	tablespoons heavy cream
3	cloves minced garlic
6	tablespoons freshly grated Parmesan cheese

Boil water with the oil to prevent sticking. When water boils, add pasta and cook until pasta is done. Place colander in sink with running cold water. Pour hot pasta into colander and rinse thoroughly.

In a skillet, melt butter and olive oil and minced garlic. Stir in the cream. Add drained, cooked noodles and mix well. Just before serving, stir in Parmesan cheese. Serves 4.

THE VILLA AT PALMER LAKE

75 Highway 105
Colorado Springs-Palmer Lake, Colorado
(719) 481-2222

The drive from Colorado Springs to Palmer Lake makes a romantic night out. The Villa specializes in tastefully prepared northern Italian cuisine which has earned a good reputation for great food.

Gnocchi Potato Dumplings*

4	pounds potatoes, peeled	5	cups flour

enough water to make crumbly dough, if necessary

Boil and dice potatoes. Gradually add 5 cups of flour. Knead until a smooth, manageable dough is obtained. If necessary, add a little more flour.

Roll dough into long rope-like strips, about ¾ inch thick; cut into ¾ inch pieces; dip in flour.

Boil in 8 quarts of rapidly boiling water for about 10 minutes. Drain. Place on large platter or individual plates.

Serve with tomato sauce (see Sauce section) and sprinkle with grated Parmesan cheese. Serves 6 to 8.

*Variation

VAIL RACQUET CLUB RESTAURANT

Racquet Club Drive
East Vail, Colorado 81657
(303) 476-7000

The luxurious Racquet Club Restaurant in East Vail has a reputation for superb continental cuisine and it is no wonder. The international cuisine that graces the tables nightly creates a memorable gastronomic experience for Vail residents and Colorado visitors.

Homemade Spinach Noodles "Al Pesto"

Noodles

1	pound flour		2	ounces salt
3	eggs		2	ounces oil
6	ounces fresh spinach puree			a little water

Combine all ingredients except water in mixer bowl with dough attachment or mix by hand. Add water while mixing until dough reaches a well blended, smooth but not sticky, consistency. Using a rolling pin or pasta machine, roll out the dough very thin with use of flour, cutting noodles to desired width. Place in boiling water with a bit of salt and oil. Boil approximately 2 minutes until done. Strain well, top with pesto and serve immediately.

Pesto

¼ cup olive oil
¼ cup butter
6 ounces fresh grated imported Parmesan cheese
2 tablespoons fresh chopped parsley
2 tablespoons fresh chopped basil
3 ounces finely chopped walnuts

Combine all ingredients in pan over heat, melting butter and heating lightly. Serve over noodles. Serves 4 to 6.

FALCONE'S RESTAURANT & BAR

1096 South Gaylord
Denver, Colorado 80209
(303) 777-0707

Linguine With Tuna-Caper Sauce*

1	tablespoon olive oil
1	clove garlic, minced
1	can (1 pound) low-sodium crushed tomatoes, with their juice
1	teaspoon dried oregano, crumbled
¼	teaspoon red pepper flakes
1	can (6½ ounces) water-packed light tuna, drained and flaked
2	tablespoons capers, chopped
2	tablespoons minced parsley
6	ounces linguine or spaghetti

In a heavy 10-inch skillet, heat the olive oil over moderate heat for 30 seconds; add the garlic and cook for 30 seconds. Stir in the tomatoes, oregano, and red pepper flakes. Bring to a boil, then lower the heat until the mixture barely bubbles; simmer, uncovered, for 7 to 8 minutes or until slightly thickened.

Stir in the tuna, capers, and parsley, and simmer 5 minutes longer.

Meanwhile, cook the linguine according to package directions, omitting the salt; drain well and transfer to a heated bowl. Pour the tuna sauce over the pasta and toss well. Serves 4.

Variation:

Linguine with Shrimp-Caper Sauce — Substitute ¾ cup chopped cooked shrimp for the tuna. Vary the flavor, if desired, by substituting minced fresh basil (or 1 teaspoon dried basil) for the parsley, and 1 teaspoon marjoram for the oregano.

* Variation

LEGENDS
Poste Montane Lodge
Vail-Beaver Creek, Colorado
(303) 949-5540

Linguine With White Clam Sauce*

8   ounces linguine or spaghetti
1½ tablespoons olive oil
½   small yellow onion, finely chopped
6   cloves garlic, minced
2   tablespoons flour
¼   cup dry white wine
¼   cup clam juice or low-sodium chicken broth
1   cup low-sodium chicken broth
1   can (6½ ounces) minced clams, drained, rinsed well, and drained again
¼   cup grated Parmesan cheese
2   tablespoons minced parsley

Cook the linguine according to package directions, omitting the salt. Rinse with cold water, drain, and set aside.

Meanwhile, heat the olive oil in a heavy 10-inch skillet over moderate heat for 1 minute; add the onion and garlic and cook, uncovered, until the onion is soft — about 5 minutes. Blend in the flour and cook, stirring constantly, for 1 minute. Add the wine and cook for 2 minutes, stirring constantly. Add the clam juice and chicken broth and cook, stirring, 4 minutes longer. Stir in the clams and cheese.

Add the reserved linguine and cook 1 minute longer, tossing well until heated through. Mix in the parsley and serve with a tossed green salad and crusty bread. Serves 4.

Variation:
Linguine with Red Clam Sauce — Omit the flour. In step 2 add 1 cup drained and chopped canned low-sodium tomatoes along with the clam juice and chicken broth. Cook and stir for 6 minutes or until slightly thickened, then proceed with the recipe as directed.

* Variation

MEZZALUNA
600 East Cooper Avenue
Aspen, Colorado 81611
(303) 925-5882

Pasta Del Giorno (Pasta with Spinach Sauce)*

8   ounces linguine
1   tablespoon olive oil
1   small yellow onion, chopped fine
2   cloves garlic, minced
1   pound fresh spinach, trimmed and chopped, or
    1 package (10 ounces) frozen chopped spinach, thawed and well drained
½   cup skim milk
½   cup low-sodium chicken broth
¼   cup grated Parmesan cheese
¼   teaspoon black pepper

In a large kettle, cook the linguine according to package directions, omitting the salt.

While the linguine is cooking, heat the olive oil in a small heavy saucepan over moderate heat for 1 minute; add the onion and garlic and cook, uncovered, until the onion is soft — about 5 minutes. Add the spinach, milk, chicken broth, cheese, and pepper. Bring the mixture to a boil; reduce the heat and simmer, uncovered, for 3 minutes or until the sauce thickens slightly.

Pour the sauce into an electric blender or food processor and whirl until the mixture is pureed. Pour the sauce back into the saucepan and reheat over moderate heat until the mixture starts to simmer — about 1 minute.

Drain the linguine and return it to the kettle. Add the spinach mixture and toss well with two forks to mix. Transfer to a heated platter and serve. Serves 4.

* Variation

MAXIE'S

Cherry Creek Inn
600 South Colorado
Denver, Colorado 80222
(303) 759-3341 ext. 755

Pasta Mangione

1	package spinach noodles	1	tablespoon oil
½	pound bacon	¹/₈	cup jalapeños, finely diced
½	onion, finely chopped	¼	teaspoon basil
¼	cup shallots, finely chopped	½	teaspoon marjoram
½	cup diced green chiles	½	teaspoon chervil
1½	cups artichoke hearts, quartered	1	bunch green onions, diced
½	cup black olives, finely diced	1	cup shrimp, cooked and peeled
2	tomatoes-peeled, seeded and diced		

Vinaigrette

¼	cup white wine	¼	cup olive oil
2	tablespoons St. Mary's Gourmet Vinegar	¼	cup Pernod
2	tablespoons lemon juice		salt to taste

Cook spinach noodles al dente (7-10 minutes) in a large pot of boiling water to which a few drops of oil have been added. Drain, rinse well with cold water and set aside to chill.

Fry bacon, drain off grease, saute onions, shallots, green chiles with basil, marjoram, and chervil. Dice bacon and add all to noodles.

Add artichoke hearts, olives, tomatoes, green onions and shrimp. Prepare vinaigrette by mixing vinaigrette ingredients with whisk. Pour vinaigrette over salad and toss.

DELMONICO'S

Aurora's Finest!
3140-B S. Peoria
at 225 and Peoria in the Regatta Plaza
Aurora, Colorado
(303) 755-9437

Family owned and operated, Delmonico's offers an extraordinary variety of Italian and American specialties.
Enjoy fine dining in an informal setting at affordable prices. Treat yourself to century-old Italian favorites: succulant prime rib, char-broiled filets and exceptional scampi, lunch and dinner Monday through Saturday.
The following recipe, "Pasta Marinara with Shrimp" is a favorite. Always prepared with freshest of ingredients, it is reminiscent of Regatta dining off the shores of the Italian boot.

Pasta Marinara with Shrimp

Prepare the following ingredients for 6.

6   cups slices fresh mushrooms
6   cups diced fresh tomatoes
6   sliced fresh cooked or canned artichoke per person
6   peeled large shrimp per person

Heat ½ cup olive oil. Add 1 minced garlic clove. Add ½ cup dry white wine. Add ½ teaspoon onion salt. Add 1 teaspoon fresh chopped basil. Add 1 teaspoon fresh chopped oregano. Add salt and pepper to taste.
Saute above ingredients in seasoned olive oil-wine mixture al dente.
Pour over fresh salted cooked pasta and top with grated parmesan.

RISTORANTE PAOLINO

3100 Arapahoe Avenue
Boulder, Colorado
(303) 444-0999

Pasta Riviera*

4   ounces small pasta shells
1½ quarts boiling water
¼   cup dry white wine
1   garlic clove, finely minced
1   green bell pepper, seeded and cut into strips
1   red bell pepper, seeded and cut into strips
1   small zucchini, sliced
1   7-ounce can water-packed tuna, drained and broken into chunks or 1 cup cooked and peeled shrimp or other seafood

2   tablespoons chopped fresh parsley leaves
1   tablespoon drained capers
½   teaspoon dried thyme
½   cup cherry tomatoes, halved

Gradually add the small pasta shells to rapidly boiling water so that the water continues to boil. Cook, uncovered, stirring occasionally, until tender. Drain in a colander. Meanwhile, pour the wine into a large frying pan. Add the garlic, green and red peppers, and zucchini. Cook and stir until the vegetables are just tender. Stir in tuna, parsley, capers, and thyme. Cook until just heated through. Add the cooked pasta shells to the pan and mix thoroughly. Just before serving, add the halved cherry tomatoes. Serves 2.

* Variation

THE RANCH AT KEYSTONE

Keystone, Colorado
(303) 468-4161

Meander over the hills and the golf course at Keystone Ranch to this huge log house, situated on a former working ranch. Dinner feels like eating in someone's private home. You will go through a six-course meal of Chef Chris Wing's choice of appetizers, beef, veal, game, shellfish, fish or lamb and all the rest of it. Wing specializes in what he calls "new Rocky Mountain cuisine" and accommodates his menu to mountain dining in ways unique, splendid and creative. Dessert after dinner sweetens a visit to an anteroom and the fireplace around which the huge log home was first built.

Pasta Scampi*

1	tablespoon olive oil	¼	teaspoon dried oregano
1	garlic clove, minced	1	tablespoon chopped fresh parsley leaves
½	pound shrimp, peeled and cleaned	4	ounces spaghetti
¼	cup dry white wine	1½	quarts boiling water
1	tablespoon fresh lemon juice		

Heat the oil in a nonstick frying pan. Add the garlic and shrimp and saute stirring frequently, until the shrimp turn pink. Add the wine, lemon juice, oregano, and parsley and cook for several minutes longer. Meanwhile, gradually add the spaghetti to rapidly boiling water so that the water continues to boil. Cook, uncovered, stirring occasionally, until tender. Drain in a colander. Serve the spaghetti topped with the shrimp and any remaining liquid. Serves 2.

* Variation

THE SAUCY NOODLE RISTORANTE

727 South University Boulevard
Denver, Colorado 80209
(303) 733-6977 or 778-9735

The Saucy Noodle was established in 1960 and drew pasta lovers to Jim Badis' colorful Italian eatery. Homemade pastas, great garlic bread and Marinara Sauce, pizzas, and hickory pit barbecued ribs soon developed a following of regular Saucy Noodle fans who frequented this antique-laden, unpretentious eatery for years. Word spread and today this award-winning, highly acclaimed eatery attracts so many guests and packs such crowds that many are lucky to enjoy take-out service from this delightful neighborhood spot.

Pesto alla Genovese

½ to ⅔ cup fresh basil leaves
6   cloves garlic
¼   cup pine nuts
½   cup grated Pecorino (often called Romano) or Parmesan
         cheese, or a mixture of the two
⅓ to ½ cup olive oil
a little boiling water
1   pound thin spaghetti noodles, boiled and drained*

Chop basil leaves, garlic, pine nuts and walnuts, then put into a mortar with grated cheese and pound to a paste. Then add olive oil, drop by drop at first and then in a thin trickle, stirring (as with mayonnaise) until it becomes a thick sauce. Thin with a spoonful or so of boiling water. Serve over pasta or thin spaghetti. It is essential to use fresh basil in this recipe. Serves 4.

*Boil pasta with drop of oil to prevent noodles from sticking. Rinse thoroughly in cold water.

Spaghetti Marinara

1 pound spaghetti	1 clove garlic
1 large can plum tomatoes	2 ounces grated Romano
4 tablespoons olive oil	¼ teaspoon oregano
2 sliced onions	¼ teaspoon sugar
salt and pepper to taste	2 filets of anchovy

Saute onion and garlic in hot oil about 5 minutes or until soft; remove garlic; add tomatoes; cook rapidly for 5 minutes. Then lower flame and simmer for one hour. Add anchovies cut into small pieces. Use very little salt and pepper; add sugar and cook slowly for 10 minutes. Add oregano; stir. Keep hot over low flame until ready to serve.

Cook spaghetti as usual. Drain; arrange on hot platter and pour sauce over spaghetti. Sprinkle with grated cheese. Serves 4 to 6.

THE MOTHERLODE

314 East Hyman
Aspen, Colorado
(303) 925-7700

The Motherlode resides in an historic building erected in 1886 and specializes in wonderful "free-style" Italian cuisine.

Spaghetti with Garlic, Capers and Artichoke Hearts*

1	pound spaghetti
4	tablespoons garlic, minced
1	can of artichoke hearts in vinegar, opened, drained and chopped
1	bottle capers, drained
1	small can pimientos, drained and chopped
½	cup olive oil
¼	cup St. Mary's Gourmet Vinegar
4	tablespoons chopped parsley

Boil water with teaspoon of oil to prevent sticking. When water boils, add pasta. Cook until tender. Place colander in sink and run cold water. Pour pasta into colander and rinse thoroughly. Place vinegar and olive oil in skillet with garlic and other ingredients except pasta. Add cooked pasta. Mix thoroughly. Heat and serve. Serves 2 to 4.

* Variation

PRIMAVERA RISTORANTE AT ASPEN MOUNTAIN

600 South Spring Street
Aspen, Colorado
(303) 925-6602

Spaghetti and Shrimp

1	pound uncooked, peeled shrimp	½	cup white wine
4	plump, ripe tomatoes	2	tablespoons tomato sauce
¼	cup olive oil	1	teaspoon oregano
1	onion, minced	2	tablespoons chopped parsley
2	cloves garlic, minced	½	tablespoon crushed red pepper
1	crushed bay leaf	½	teaspoon salt
1	teaspoon black pepper	1	tablespoon lemon juice
1	pound spaghetti		

Blanch and peel tomatoes. Saute the onion and garlic in the olive oil. Add the tomatoes (chopped), seasonings and wine. Let the sauce simmer for 5 minutes until well-blended. Add the shrimp and cook for another 5 minutes. Do not overcook the shrimp. Cook the spaghetti in oiled, rapidly boiling water. Arrange the sauce over the spaghetti and serve hot with Parmesan cheese.

GUSSIE'S

2345 West 112th Avenue
Westminster, Colorado 80234
(303) 469-5281

Spicy Lasagne Roll-Ups

1	tablespoon olive oil
1	large yellow onion, chopped fine
1	teaspoon dried basil, crumbled
½	teaspoon dried marjoram, crumbled
1	bay leaf, crumbled
2	cloves garlic, minced
¾	teaspoon black pepper
½	skinned and boned chicken breast (about 4 ounces), chopped fine
1	can (1 pound) low-sodium tomatoes, chopped with their juice
2	tablespoons low-sodium tomato paste
8	ruffle-edge lasagne noodles (about 4 ounces)
½	cup grated Parmesan cheese
1	cup part-skim ricotta cheese
½	pound fresh spinach, trimmed and chopped, or ½ 10-ounce package frozen chopped spinach, thawed and drained
¼	teaspoon ground mace or nutmeg
¼	teaspoon cream of tartar

Heat the olive oil in a heavy 10-inch skillet over moderate heat for 1 minute. Add the onion, basil, marjoram, bay leaf, half the garlic, and ¼ teaspoon of the pepper; cook, uncovered, until the onion is soft — about 5 minutes. Remove 2 tablespoons of the mixture from the skillet and set aside.

Add the chopped chicken to the skillet and cook, stirring, for 3 minutes. Reduce the heat to low, add the tomatoes, and tomato paste, and cook, uncovered, for 20 minutes, stirring occasionally. Set aside.

Meanwhile, cook the lasagne noodles according to package directions, omitting the salt. Rinse with cold water and drain.

Preheat the over to 375°. To prepare the filling, combine 5 tablespoons of the Parmesan cheese in a medium-size bowl with the ricotta cheese, spinach, mace, cream of tartar, the remaining garlic and pepper, and the reserved onion mixture. Mix well.

Spoon half the tomato sauce into an ungreased 9 x 9 x 2 baking pan. Spread 3 tablespoons of the cheese filling on each noodle, roll up as for a jelly roll, and place seam side down in the pan. Repeat until all the noodles are used. Top with the remaining sauce.

Cover with aluminum foil and bake for 25 minutes. Uncover, sprinkle the remaining Parmesan cheese on top, and bake, uncovered, 5 minutes longer. Serves 4.

THE RED ONION

420 East Cooper Street Mall
Aspen, Colorado
(303) 925-9043

Swiss Spaghetti

2	tablespoons butter		salt and pepper
½	onion, diced	2	tablespoons cornstarch
2	garlic cloves, diced	½	cup red wine
	dash rosemary	4	slices Swiss cheese
	dash thyme	8	cups cooked spaghetti
32	ounces of canned tomatoes in puree		

Melt the butter in a large skillet. Add the onion, garlic, rosemary and thyme. Saute for 2 minutes. Next add the tomato puree and cook for ten minutes. Add salt and pepper to taste. Mix the cornstarch with the red wine and add to the puree. Cook for several minutes and correct the seasonings. Pour the sauce over the spaghetti in a buttered casserole dish and cover with the Swiss cheese. Put under the broiler until the cheese is golden brown. Serves 6.

SFUZZI

3000 East First Avenue
Cherry Creek Mall
Denver, Colorado
(303) 321-4700
Executive Corporate Chef Steven Singer

Three Cheese Lasagne with Chicken and Porcini Mushrooms

In Sfuzzi restaurants we make the lasagne individually in special rings which hold all the ingredients in layered form. The dimension of these rings is 4″ diameter by 1¾″ high. If you can acquire rings similar to this, it makes for a unique presentation; if not, use a glass baking dish 13 x 9 x 2 or a similar dimension.

Mushroom/Spinach Filling

1½ ounces Porcini mushrooms, dried
4   ounces mixed fresh mushrooms (table, shiitake or oyster)
1   3-pound chicken, roasted
12   ounces spinach, freshly washed and de-stemmed
1   tablespoon garlic, chopped
¹/₈ cup oregano, freshly chopped
1   tablespoon salt
2   teaspoons pepper, black, coarse ground
3   ounces extra virgin olive oil

Preheat oven to 400°. Salt and pepper the cavity of chicken and stuff with 1 lemon cut in half, 1 medium red onion halved and a sprig of fresh rosemary. Truss the bird and rub with olive oil, salt and pepper. Place bird on roasting rack in oven and roast 30 to 35 minutes. Remove and allow to rest 30 minutes. Remove all meat in chunks from bones and discard along with skin and excess fat. Reserve the meat.

Soak the porcini mushrooms overnight in cool water. When softened, rinse carefully as dried porcini many times hold bits of sand and earth. Cut mushrooms into slices. Slice the fresh mushrooms and chop garlic.

Heat 3 ounces olive oil in large saute pan. Add fresh mushrooms and garlic. Cook 2-3 minutes. Add porcini and cook a few minutes more. Add washed spinach, reduce heat and cook slowly until almost all liquid evaporates. Add oregano, salt and pepper. Remove from heat and mix in chicken. Reserve for assembly.

Cheese Mixture for Filling

1   pound mozzarella, fresh, diced small   4   ounces romano (Pecorino), grated
1   pound ricotta cheese, fresh   ½   cup fresh basil, chopped

Mix all ingredients together well and reserve for assembly.

For the pasta sheets: Purchase or make fresh sheets (5 each) 12″ x 6″ x ¹/₁₆″. Heat 6 quarts of water (salted heavily and should taste like ''ocean water'') and bring to a boil. If using fresh sheets, cook 1½ minutes. Cook 1 sheet at a time and remove from water carefully so as not to tear. Coat each sheet after cooking with olive oil so they do not stick together. Reserve for assembly. If making this recipe ''in the round'' at this time, cut circles to get the rings. You will need 4 pasta circles for each portion.

For the assembly: If you are using a baking dish, lightly olive oil the bottom surface. If using rings, oil a sheet pan and the sides of the rings. Place rings on oiled sheet pan. Assembly as follows: place one layer of pasta down first. On top of the pasta spread ½ the cheese mixture evenly. Follow by a layer of pasta, then the total spinach mushroom mixture. Follow again by a layer of pasta, then the remaining cheese mixture followed by another pasta layer (the top). Sprinkle the top layer with an additional 4 ounces of shredded mozzarella. The lasagne is ready to bake.

Place lasagne in preheated 375° oven and bake uncovered for 30 minutes. The lasagne is done when the top is thoroughly browned and the center is very hot.

To make the sauce:

1   small carrot, sliced thin
2   ounces red onion, diced fine
2   ounces leeks, sliced thin
2   pounds roma tomatoes, peeled, seeded and diced
1   teaspoon garlic, chopped fine
3   ounces extra virgin olive oil
4   ounces dry white white
6   ounces chicken stock
pinch red chili flakes
1   bay leaf
8   ounces butter, unsalted
½   bunch Italian parsley, chopped
salt
pepper, black coarse ground

Heat olive oil in a large saucepan. Add carrots, onion and leeks. Cook 5 minutes until soft. Add tomatoes and garlic. Cook 5 more minutes. Add chicken stock, wine, bay leaf and chili flakes. Cook on high heat for 6-8 minutes or until thick. Remove from heat and place in food processor and blend until very smooth. Transfer back to saucepan and whisk in butter over medium heat. Season with salt and pepper. Add parsley.

To serve: Divide sauce evenly on serving plates. Place warm lasagne on top of sauce. Garnish with chives, cut in 1″ lengths. Serves 6.

MIKE BERARDI'S

2115 East Seventeenth Avenue
Denver, Colorado
(303) 399-8800

Tortellini*

1	pound flour	4	eggs

Directions for tortellini dough: Place flour in a large bowl, mix in the eggs, and work together with your hands to make a stiff dough. Turn the dough out on a floured pastry board and knead until smooth. Roll the dough as thin as possible and cut into squares. Place a tablespoon of stuffing in the center of each square. Starting at one end of the tortellini, bring a corner up to form the tortellini into a triangle. Then, with both corners of the base or widest end of the triangle secured, wrap the tortellini around a finger and tuck one corner into the other. The apex or point of the triangle should remain upright, and the tortellini should fit your finger like a ring. A little practice will produce a perfect tortellini, an inspiration to behold.

Tortellini Stuffing:

2	tablespoons butter	1	ounce very lean prosciutto ham
¼	pound pork loin, boned	2	egg yolks
2	ounces chicken breast, boned	¼	pound imported Parmesan cheese, grated
¼	pound mortadella (Italian cold cut)		pinch of salt and nutmeg

Directions for Tortellini Stuffing: Heat the butter in a large skillet. Add the pork loin and chicken breast and saute for 10 minutes. Place the mortadella and prosciutto in the skillet and saute all the meat for 5 minutes more. Cool slightly, and grind all the meat together 2 or 3 times in the meat grinder. Stir the egg yolks, imported Parmesan, salt and nutmeg into the ground meat mixture. Put all ingredients together in the grinder and grind once more. Arrange a tablespoon of meat stuffing on each tortellini square of dough. Shape the tortellini as directed. Serves 8.

9	cups Brodo (see Soup section)		stuffed tortellini

Directions for Soup: Bring 9 cups of Brodo to a boil in a large kettle. Drop stuffed tortellini into the broth, reduce to very low heat and simmer for 5 minutes, or until the tortellini are cooked through. Spoon some tortellini into each soup plate, pour the broth over them, and serve immediately. Serves 8.

* Variation

PHILOMENA'S

10471 South Parker Road
Parker, Colorado
(303) 841-4456

Vermicelli with Anchovies and Garlic*

1   pound vermicelli
10 to 15 anchovy filets (2 cans) or other canned fish
6   cloves garlic, chopped
½   cup olive oil
2   teaspoons black pepper
1   teaspoon chopped parsley

¼   cup Parmesan cheese
¼   cup fresh breadcrumbs
¼   cup olive oil

Saute the garlic in ½ cup olive oil until soft. Add the anchovies, but try not to mash them. Stir gently with a fork. Add the pepper and parsley. Cook the vermicelli until al dente, in boiling salted water. Drain and add to the skillet, tossing the pasta until it is well covered. Serve with Parmesan cheese mixed with toasted breadcrumbs and olive oil.

* Variation

VENDETTA'S

291 Bridge Street
Vail, Colorado 81657
(303) 476-5070

Vendetta's has developed a reputation as Vail's premier Italian restaurant. Part-owner and manager John Wayne Brennen wishes to welcome visitors from around the world to Vail. The staff at Vendetta's has been a major reason for the restaurant's great success: their warmth and amiability create its casual atmosphere. Chef Ray Jay Benoit and his staff take great pride in serving creative Northern Italian cuisine. They offer the best-quality food at the most reasonable prices, guests' satisfaction is their goal.

Zucchini, Mushroom and Pimiento Lasagne

2	bulbs (entire heads) garlic
4	ounces lasagne noodles
1	tablespoon olive oil
1	medium-size yellow onion, chopped
1	medium-size zucchini (about ½ pound), halved lengthwise and sliced thin
½	pound mushrooms, sliced thin
1	cup fresh or frozen green peas
2	teaspoons lemon juice
½	teaspoon black pepper
1	jar (4 ounces) pimientos, drained and sliced lengthwise into ½ inch strips
1½	cups skim milk
2½	tablespoons flour
½	teaspoon dried oregano, crumbled
¼	cup grated Parmesan cheese

Preheat the oven to 375°. Wrap each unpeeled garlic bulb in aluminum foil, set in the oven, and roast for 20 minutes. Cook in the foil until easy to handle, then pull off the garlic cloves one by one and pinch, squeezing the flesh into a small bowl; mash the garlic and set aside.

Cook the lasagne noodles according to package directions, omitting the salt. Rinse with cold water and drain.

Meanwhile, heat the olive oil in heavy 10-inch skillet over moderate heat for 1 minute; add the onion and zucchini and cook, uncovered, until soft — about 5 minutes. Add the mushrooms and cook, uncovered, 3 minutes longer; add the peas and cook 3 more minutes. Stir in the lemon juice, pepper, and pimiento and remove from the heat.

In a small saucepan, whisk the milk into the flour; set over moderately low heat and cook, stirring for 4 minutes or until thickened. Mix in the oregano, cheese, and reserved garlic. Measure out ½ cup of the sauce and reserve. Combine the rest with the zucchini mixture.

To assemble the lasagne, line the bottom of an ungreased 8 x 8 x 2 baking pan with the cooked lasagne noodles, cutting them to fit and reserving the scraps. Spread half the zucchini mixture over the noodles, add a second layer of noodles, spread with the remaining zucchini mixture, then top with the noddle scraps.

Finally, smooth the reserve sauce evenly. Cover with aluminum foil and bake 20 minutes at 375°. Then remove foil and bake 10 minutes longer. Serves 4.

SEAFOOD VIII

P. McClure

ENTRÉES SEAFOOD, VIII

Ahi Tuna in Mustard Crust with Red Pepper Nage (Flagstaff House Restaurant) — p. 1
Baby Canadian Lobster Tails with Curry Sauce (Fawn Brook Inn) — p. 2
Baked Salmon with Tequila Coriander Beurre Blanc (Marina Landing) — p. 3
Brook Trout, Saute Meuniere (El Rancho) — p. 4
Clams and Mussels Luciano (Firefly Cafe) — p. 5
Cioppino (Fern's Restaurant) — p. 5
Coquilles Saint Jacques A La Parisienne (Tamarron Inn — Introduction) — p. 6
Country Shrimp and Lemon Corn (Duggan's) — p. 7
Curried Crab (Little Shanghai — Introduction) — p. 8
Deep-Fried Prawns with Chiles (Thai Hiep) — p. 9
Dungeness Crab Cakes (Cliff Young's) — p. 9
Flan of Lobster and Scallops with Two Caviars (Flagstaff House Restaurant) — p. 10
Florida Red Snapper Napoletana (Abetone Ristorante) — p. 10
Fresh Lochinvar Scottish Salmon with Lavender Butter Sauce (Alfredo's) — p. 11
Fried Chili Crabs (Panda Cafe) — p. 11
Fried Noodles with Shrimp (Wang's Mandarin House) — p. 12
Fried Rice with Shrimp (Twin Dragon) — p. 12
Grilled Halibut Filets with Melon and Mango Salsa (Firefly Cafe) — p. 13
Grilled Jumbo Shrimp with Kentucky Bacon and Fresh Basil (Mostly Seafood) — p. 13
Grilled Tuna with Herbed Tomato, Garlic, Oil, and Lemon Sauce (Normandy French Restaurant) — p. 14
Lemon Fish Pie (Transalpin) — p. 15
Lemon Prosciutto Shrimp (Simms Landing) — p. 15
Linguine and Lobster Tails Diable (Primavera Ristorante at Aspen Mountain) — p. 16
Linguine with Shrimp Sauce (Syzygy — Introduction) — p. 16
Mustard Glazed Salmon Filet on Stirfried Spinach Leaves, Tarragon Butter (The Broadmoor Hotel) — p. 17
Oven Roasted Salmon with Potato Basil Crust and Warm Tomato Chutney (The Little Nell) — p. 18
Oysters with Crackling for Six (The Wildflower Inn) — p. 19
Papillotes of Lobster and Shrimp (Fern's Restaurant) — p. 19
Pesce Space Alla Siciliana (Sicilian Style Swordfish) (Pomodoro — Introduction) — p. 20
Red Snapper Louisiane (Off Belleview Grill — Introduction) — p. 21
Salmon A La Provençale with Flageolet Bean Compote (Renaissance) — p. 22
Salmon Newburg (The Broadmoor Hotel) — p. 23
Salmon Tartare (Tante Louise — Introduction) — p. 24
Salmon with Lobster and Truffles (Flagstaff House Restaurant — Introduction) — p. 25
Salmon Wrapped in Filo with Brie (Rudi's) — p. 26
Sashimi (Takah Sushi) — p. 26
Sauteed Scampi and Fettuccine Alfredo (Boccalino's) — p. 27
Scallops Niçoise (The Wildflower Inn) — p. 27
Scallops Parisienne (Ute City Banque) — p. 28
Shrimp Baked with Feta Cheese and Tomato (La Bohéme) — p. 29
Shrimp Chile Rellenos (Mostly Seafood) — p. 30
Shrimp Dijonnaise (Piñon's) — p. 30
Smoked Mussels in Mustard-Cream Sauce (Smuggler Bar and Restaurant) — p. 31
Smoked Oysters and Shallots Vinaigrette (Castaway's) — p. 32
Smoked Trout with Papaya, Avocado and Cucumber (The Little Nell — Introduction) — p. 32
Tom Chien Lan Bot (Hot and Spicy Prawns) (Chez Thoa) — p. 33
Tonno Con Salsa Di Pomodoro (Fresh Tuna with Tomato Sauce) (Antonio's Italian Restaurant — Introduction) — p. 33
Trout Poached in Lemon Grass Broth (Transalpin — Introduction) — p. 34
Tuna Tartare with Chives (Picasso's — Introduction) — p. 35
Turrine of Fish (H. Brinker's) — p. 36
Volcano Shrimp (China Terrace) — p. 37

FLAGSTAFF HOUSE RESTAURANT

1138 Flagstaff Road
Boulder, Colorado 80302
(303) 442-4640

Ahi Tuna in Mustard Crust with Red Pepper Nage

Mustard Crust Tuna

2 8-ounce slices of sushi quality tuna	dijon mustard

bread crumbs seasoned with the following:

cumin	fresh thyme
mustard seed	cayenne pepper
garlic	salt and pepper

Brush tuna with mustard and spread seasoned bread crumbs over the mustard. Cook the tuna to desired temperature, which is preferably rare.

Red Pepper Nage

1	quart fish fume	fresh thyme
3	red peppers	star anise
1	cup dry vermouth	black pepper
½	pound butter	bay leaf
salt and pepper		strainer

Sweat red peppers in pan on low heat. Add dry vermouth and reduce. Cover with fume and herbs. Simmer for 15-20 minutes. Blend with butter; then strain. Season to taste.

Fumé

5	pounds fish bones (washed and gilled)		bay leaf
2	carrots		thyme
1	celery		black pepper
2	leeks	1	cup white wine
2	onions		

Sweat fish bones for approximately 4-6 minutes. Then, add vegetables and sweat. Cover with water and wine. Simmer for 40 minutes. Strain. Serves 2.

FAWN BROOK INN
Allenspark, Colorado
(303) 747-2556

This marvelous restaurant has superb Swiss, German and French cuisine. Here's a variation on one of their fabulous creations.

Baby Canadian Lobster Tails with Curry Sauce

2	quarts water		2	bay leaves
1	cup dry white wine		2	cloves
1	ounce brandy		1	ounce butter
1	small carrot, peeled and halved			salt and pepper
1	stick celery		1	pinch oregano
1	small onion, peeled and halved		1	teaspoon sugar
1	clove garlic		½	teaspoon Knorr fish aromat
3	sprigs parsley			

Put all the court-bouillon ingredients in a large heavy pot. Bring to a boil and boil for 15 minutes. Remove from heat and keep warm.

16-20	baby lobster tails or langoustine		1	tablespoon dry white wine
1	ounce unsalted butter		1½	teaspoons good curry powder
4	teaspoons onion, finely chopped		1½	cups whipping
¼	teaspoon garlic, finely chopped			salt

In a sauce pan melt the butter and saute the onion until transparent. Add the garlic and sauté for another minute until cooked but not brown. Off the heat add the curry powder and mix well. Then add the wine, stirring thoroughly, and the cream. Return to stove and add the salt. Let the mixture boil for two minutes and keep hot. Bring the court-bouillon to a boil and drop in the lobster tails. Let them simmer for 2-3 minutes, depending on the size.

Bring the curry sauce to a boil and little by little thicken with the beurre manie. The sauce should have the consistency of a light cream. Serve the lobster on a hot plate with the sauce on the side and garnish with parsley. Serves 4.

Beurre Manie:
1   tablespoon butter blended in a paste with 1 tablespoon flour.

MARINA LANDING

8101 East Belleview
Denver, Colorado 80237
(303) 770-4741

Baked Salmon with Tequila Coriander Beurre Blanc

For the Beurre Blanc:

¼ cup dry white wine
¼ cup tequila
2 tablespoons St. Mary's Gourmet Vinegar
1 tablespoon minced shallot
1 stick (½ cup) cold unsalted butter cut into 8 pieces
lemon juice to taste
1 tablespoon jalapeño seasoned salt

In a small heavy saucepan combine the wine, the tequila, vinegar, and boil until it is reduced to about 3 tablespoons. Reduce the heat to moderately low and whisk in the butter, 1 piece at a time, lifting the pan from the heat occasionally to cool the mixture, adding each new piece of butter before the previous one has melted completely. Season the beurre blanc with the lemon juice and jalapeño seasoned salt and keep it warm set over a pan of hot water.

For the Salmon:

1 3-4 pound salmon filet (about 1¼ inches thick)
salt and freshly ground white pepper
lemon slices or lime slices
fresh cilantro
1 avocado, peeled and seed removed

Preheat oven to 350°. Line baking pan with foil. Place salmon on foil, skin side down. Sprinkle generously with salt and pepper. Bake until fish is just opaque in center.

Transfer salmon to platter. Spoon sauce over salmon. Garnish with avocado cut into quarters and fanned, lemon slices or lime slices, and fresh cilantro. Serves 6.

EL RANCHO

El Rancho Rural Branch, Exit 252, off I-70
Golden, Colorado 80401
(303) 526-0661

El Rancho's aim has been to offer good food, good service, and good value to increasing numbers of regular guests. It specializes in steaks, lobster, prime rib, shrimp, and trout. Here is a variation of the trout recipe.

Brook Trout, Sauté Meuniere

1   trout per portion
flour
clarified butter (directions below)
fresh lemon
chopped parsley
2   tablespoons butter

Clean the trout, cut off fins and tail, but leave the head on. Dip lightly in flour and fry in clarified butter until browned. Place on platter, squeeze fresh lemon over the fish, and sprinkle with finely chopped parsley. Add two tablespoons of butter to the pan in which the trout is cooked. When the butter takes on a brown color, pour it over the fish and serve immediately.

Clarified Butter:

Heat butter very slowly for about 30 minutes until solid particles settle out. Strain through very fine sieve or cloth.

FIREFLY CAFE

5410 East Colfax Avenue
Denver, Colorado 80220
(303) 388-8429

Clams And Mussels Luciano

This is a simple dish that highlights the simple pleasures of these abundant mollusks.

20 fresh mussels, bearded and scrubbed
20 fresh clams, scrubbed well (littlenecks or manila)
½ cup olive oil
½ tablespoon minced garlic
¼ cup chopped parsley
1/8 cup minced fresh basil
½ cup dry white wine
½ teaspoon crushed red pepper
salt - just a pinch

Heat a medium sized sauté pan over high heat and add the oil. When the oil is hot add the garlic and saute briefly, not allowing to brown. Add the cleaned clams and saute for about 2 minutes, add wine, parsley and basil. Then add mussels and cover the pan until both the mussels and clams have opened wide. Finish with the red pepper and salt. Serve on a platter with good French or Italian bread.

This recipe is also excellent as a main course served over pasta. The Firefly Cafe prefers angel hair or linguine.

FERN'S RESTAURANT

DENVER HILTON SOUTH
Ferns's Restaurant
7801 East Orchard Road
Englewood, Colorado 80111
(303) 779-6161

Sous Chef Jeanette Landgraf

Cioppino

4 shrimp
8 to 12 scallops
6 clams
½ cup onions, diced
3 stalks celery, diced
12 Roma tomatoes, blanched and seeded

1 clove garlic, crushed
1 cup fish stock
basil, dried
oregano, dried
salt and pepper
dash cayenne pepper

Sauté onions and celery until translucent. Add chopped garlic and cook a little bit more. Do not brown. Deglaze pan with red wine. Add seafood. Cover pot until clams open. Add fish stock, Roma tomatoes and herbs and spices to taste.

Serves 2.

TAMARRON INN

Le Canyon Gourmet Room
40292 U.S. Highway 550
Durango, Colorado
(303) 247-8801, ext. 1122

Le Canyon's gourmet dining room at the Tamarron Inn has received "rave" reviews and praise for their exquisite continental cuisine from visitors to the Western Slope and residents of the area. Here is a variation on one of their nightly-changing gourmet specialties.

Coquilles Saint Jacques A La Parisienne

½	pound of fresh mushrooms, chopped	1½	cups dry white wine
1	onion, finely chopped	2	pounds scallops, chopped
2	tablespoons butter	2	tablespoons water
1	tablespoon chopped parsley	1	teaspoon lemon juice

Simmer scallops in wine for 3 minutes. Drain, but save the broth. Put mushrooms, onion, butter, water, parsley and lemon juice in a covered pan. Simmer 10 minutes. Strain. Add liquor to broth. Make veloute sauce with the broth mixture. Add vegetables and scallops. Fill scallop shells or ramekins with mixture. Sprinkle with bread crumbs; dot with butter. Brown at 400° or under the broiler. Serves 6.

Sauce Veloute
Basic White Sauce with Stock

3   tablespoons butter
¼   cup flour
1   tablespoon onion
2   cups chicken, veal or fish stock, depending on dish
salt and pepper

Wilt onion in butter; blend in flour; cook three minutes; add stock and season to taste. Stir constantly until sauce reduces to 2 cups.

DUGGAN'S
South Federal at Belleview
Denver, Colorado
(303) 795-1081

Country Shrimp and Lemon Corn

2½ pounds medium shrimp, peeled with tails intact
1   small bay leaf
½   teaspoon crushed peppercorns
1   lemon, halved
4   cups sweet yellow corn
½   cup thinly sliced scallions
1   lemon, thinly sliced
3   tablespoons jalapeño seasoned salt

Vinaigrette

½   cup fresh lemon juice
1¼ cup olive oil
¾   teaspoon salt

1   teaspoon sugar
1   teaspoon black cracked pepper

Mix everything together but oil. Add oil, mix well.

Jalapeño Seasoned Salt

¾   cup garlic salt
½   cup celery salt

⅔   cup jalapeño powder
2   tablespoons salt

Mix all ingredients together well.

To prepare: In a large saucepan, place the shrimp in 1 quart of water.
Add the bay leaf, peppercorns, the halved and squeezed lemon, and jalapeño seasoned salt. Bring to a boil over moderately high heat. Add the corn and remove from the heat. Drain and turn into large bowl.
Remove and discard the halved lemon and bay leaf. Fold in the scallions and lemon slices.
Pour vinaigrette over the corn and shrimp, tossing to coat. To serve, mound the shrimp and corn on red lettuce leaves arranged on individual plates. Serves 4.

LITTLE SHANGHAI

460 South Broadway
Denver, Colorado
(303) 722-1292

Several years ago the Little Shanghai opened its doors on Broadway. The immense popularity of the eatery was immediate. Because of the demand for sensational Szechuan cuisine, the family-owned restaurant has steadily grown into one of the consistently best Chinese food restaurants in Colorado.

Curried Crab

about ½ gallon soy bean oil
2 to 3 pounds any kind of crab with shell (Alaskan King Crab is recommended)
¼   ounce ginger, chopped
1   teaspoon salt
1   teaspoon curry powder
¼   cup chopped green onions
1 to 2 ounces carrots, sliced
¼   teaspoon sugar
2   teaspoons cornstarch mixed with a small amount of water (optional)

Heat salad oil in a frying pan over medium heat. Fry crab in oil for 3 to 4 minutes. In another frying pan, heat 3 to 4 ounces oil. Add ginger, salt and curry powder. Cook for 30 seconds, then add all the rest of the ingredients. Cook, covered, for 7 to 8 minutes. Add cornstarch and water mixture if there is an excess of sauce in the frying pan and if thicker sauce is preferred. Serve immediately. Serves 2.

THAI HIEP

333 South Federal Boulevard
Denver, Colorado 80202
(303) 922-5774

Deep-Fried Prawns with Chiles

1	pound raw prawns	1	tablespoon sugar
3	fresh red chiles	1	tablespoon light soy sauce
2	cloves garlic	1	tablespoon Chinese wine or dry sherry
2	teaspoons finely grated fresh ginger		oil for deep frying

Shell and devein the prawns, rinse and dry well on paper towels. Slit the chiles and remove seeds, then chop them finely. Crush garlic with a little of the measured sugar and mix with the chiles and ginger.

Heat about half cup oil in a wok until very hot and deep fry the prawns a few at a time for 2 or 3 minutes, or just until the color changes. Remove from pan and drain on paper towels. Pour off most of the oil from pan, leaving only about a tablespoon. Add the chiles, garlic and ginger and fry on low heat, stirring. Add the remaining sugar, soy sauce and wine, then add prawns and stir only until reheated. Serve immediately with rice or noodles. Serves 4.

CLIFF YOUNG'S
RESTAURANT

700 East Seventeenth Avenue
Denver, Colorado 80203
(303) 831-8900

Chef David Query

Dungeness Crab Cakes

½	pound Dungeness crab meat	1	ounce chopped basil
4	ounces bay scallops	1	ounce shiitake mushroom, sliced
2	ounces peeled, deveined shrimp	1	egg
2	ounces chopped onion		pinch cayenne
2	ounces roasted green pepper, chopped		salt and pepper to taste
2	ounces roasted red pepper, chopped	1	ounce white wine

Pureé scallops and shrimp. Sauté onions and mushrooms in a small amount of butter. Add wine and reduce until wine has evaporated. Cool onion mixture and fold into shrimp and scallop pureé with roasted peppers, basil, egg and seasoning. Mix well and fold in dungeness crab carefully so crab meat does not break apart. Make 6 patties, using all crab mixture and sauté in hot olive oil until golden brown on both sides. Serve with a butter sauce, aioli or infused oil and lime wedges. Serves 6.

FLAGSTAFF HOUSE RESTAURANT

1138 Flagstaff Road
Boulder, Colorado 80302
(303) 442-4640

Flan of Lobster and Scallops with Two Caviars

Custard

1	cup whipping cream	½	teaspoon garlic
1	cup milk	1	sprig tarragon, chopped
5	eggs		pinch cayenne pepper
pinch nutmeg			salt and pepper to taste
			pinch saffron

4   deep sea scallops
1   lobster, cooked and diced
4   flan molds, teflon coated and buttered
½   teaspoon per custard of American sturgeon caviar
½   teaspoon per custard of salmon caviar

Add all custard ingredients together and whip. Let stand for five minutes, then strain.
Slice scallops into three pieces each and place in the molds. Add the same amount of lobster. Pour in the custard and bake at 350° for 15-20 minutes, in a water bath.
Unmold and serve, garnished with the caviars. Serves 4.

ABETONE RISTORANTE

620 East Hyman Avenue
Aspen, Colorado 81611
(303) 925-9022

Florida Red Snapper Napoletana

2   pounds filet of genuine American red snapper from Florida cut in 4 8-ounce slices, skin off
½   cup black olives, pitted
2   tablespoons of capers, rinsed
4   ripe tomatoes, peeled
½   cup chopped onions
¼   cup extra virgin Italian olive oil
¼   cup all-purpose flour
¼   cup white wine
1   tablespoon chopped parsley
salt and pepper

Dredge the filets of red snapper in flour, then saute in skillet with ½ of the oil over medium heat until golden on both sides and set aside in a baking dish. Add the rest of the oil to the skillet with the onion and cook until transparent. Add capers, olives and chopped tomatoes, wine, salt and pepper and cook over medium heat until liquid is reduced. Pour over fish and bake for 10 minutes in preheated 350° oven. Sprinkle parsley over and serve. Serves 4.

ALFREDO'S

The Westin Resort Vail
1300 Westhaven Drive
Vail, Colorado 81657
(303) 476-7111, ext. 7014

Fresh Lochinvar Scottish Salmon
with Lavender Butter Sauce (see Sauce section)

10 7-8 ounce filets Lochinvar Scottish salmon
10 flat pieces puff pastry (¼ ″ thick, 8″ x 8″)
salt and white pepper
2   eggs
6   ounces clarified butter

Place ½ of the clarified butter in a skillet or saute pan, and bring to very hot temperature. Lightly season the filets with salt and white pepper and quickly sear for 10 seconds on each side, then cool.

Place the 10 pastry sheets out on a working table and place one salmon in the center of each sheet (the top side should face down). Whisk the two eggs briskly and with a pastry brush lightly brush the pastry — then overlapping it around each salmon into a nice, neat package. (The egg mixture will work like glue.)

Place the salmon, top side up, on an oiled sheet pan and lightly brush the top of each one. Bake in a 350°-370° oven for 12-14 minutes until pastry is golden brown.

Remove and serve on a bed of Lavender Butter Sauce. Garnish with fresh lavender or chervil if desired.

PANDA CAFE

1098 South Federal Boulevard
Denver, Colorado 80219
(303) 936-2500

Fried Chili Crabs*

2   medium-size raw crabs
½   cup peanut oil
2   teaspoons finely grated fresh ginger
3   cloves garlic, finely chopped
3   fresh red chiles, seeded and chopped

¼   cup tomato sauce
¼   cup chili sauce
1   tablespoon sugar
1   tablespoon light soy sauce

Wash crabs well, scrubbing away any mossy patches on the shell. Remove hard top shell, stomach bag and fibrous tissue and with cleaver chop each crab into 4 pieces, or 6 pieces if they are large.

Heat a wok, add oil and when oil is very hot, fry the crab pieces until they change color, turning them so they cook on all sides. Remove to a plate. Turn heat to low and fry the ginger, garlic and red chiles, stirring constantly, until they are cooked but not brown. Add the sauces, sugar, and soy sauce, bring to a boil, then return crabs to the wok and allow to simmer in the sauce for 3 minutes. Add a little water if sauce reduces too much. Serve with white rice. Serves 4.

* Variation

WANG'S MANDARIN HOUSE

25958 Genesee Trail Road
Golden, Colorado
(303) 526-9111

Fried Noodles with Shrimp

1 teaspoon salt	2 teaspoons sherry or rice wine
4 tablespoons water	½ cup shredded bamboo shoots
dash of sugar	6 ounces egg noodles or fried egg noodles
4 teaspoons soy sauce	½ pound shrimp, shelled and washed
½ cup mushrooms, sliced	

Boil the noodles until they are soft. Be careful not to overcook. Heat 3 tablespoons oil and fry noodles as one big pancake until both sides turn light brown. Prepare and saute shrimp until they turn reddish in color and remove from heat. Saute mushrooms and bamboo shoots and add remaining ingredients with a little cornstarch to thicken the gravy and pour over fried noodles.

TWIN DRAGON

3021 South Broadway
Denver, Colorado
(303) 781-8068

Fried Rice with Shrimp

1 teaspoon salt	6 tablespoons peanut or salad oil
1 teaspoon sugar	3 medium-size onions, coarsely chopped
3 eggs, beaten	1 pound of shrimps, shelled and diced
3 tablespoons soy sauce	3 dried mushrooms, soaked and sliced;
3 cups cold, cooked rice	or 3 ounces fresh mushrooms, sliced;
½ teaspoon pepper to season	or 1 small can of mushrooms

Wash shrimp thoroughly. Heat skillet with oil, bring up the heat and pour shrimp to brown or turn color. Remove shrimp. Under low heat, pour beaten eggs into pan. When firm and cooked, remove and fold like jelly roll. Cut eggs into thin shreds when cool. Return pan to heat, add salt, pepper, onions and mushrooms, then add shrimp, mix thoroughly and stir frequently. Add rice, soy sauce, and sugar. Cook over medium heat for 5 minutes and stir constantly. Return shredded eggs to rice mixture. Serve hot.

FIREFLY CAFE

5410 East Colfax Avenue
Denver, Colorado 80220
(303) 388-8429

Grilled Halibut Filets with Melon and Mango Salsa

6   boneless Alaskan halibut filets 6 ounces each

Mango Salsa

1	small cantaloupe		pinch of red pepper flakes
1	medium mango	2	ounces olive oil
1	small red onion, diced	1	teaspoon minced garlic
1	bunch coarsely chopped cilantro	2	ounces tequila

Heat the olive oil in a saute pan and saute the garlic and onion. Deglaze with the tequila and allow the tequila to nearly evaporate. Allow to cool. Peel and seed the cantaloupe and mango, dice the flesh and toss with the onion and garlic. Finish with the cilantro and allow the salsa to cool to room temperature. The salsa can be prepared ahead and will stay in the refrigerator up to 4-5 days covered.

When ready to serve, season the halibut filets with salt and white pepper and sauté in a lightly oiled skillet about 6 minutes per side. Serve with ¼ cup of the salsa and garnish with vegetables and starch of choice. Serves 6.

MOSTLY SEAFOOD

303 Sixteenth Street
Denver, Colorado
(303) 892-5999

Grilled Jumbo Shrimp with Kentucky Bacon And Fresh Basil

16   jumbo shrimp, peeled and deveined, tail on
16   strips of bacon
32   fresh basil leaves
olive oil

Slit the back of each shrimp lengthwise to the tail. Penetrate the incision halfway into the shrimp. Stuff 2 basil leaves into the slit of each shrimp. Wrap a strip of bacon around each shrimp and secure with a toothpick. Dip each shrimp in olive oil, drain and place on hot grill. Grill about 4 or 5 minutes to each side. Remove toothpicks and serve.

NORMANDY FRENCH RESTAURANT

1515 Madison Street
Denver, Colorado 80206
(303) 321-3311

Thon Grille Sauce Vierge (Grilled Tuna with Herbed Tomato, Garlic, Oil, and Lemon Sauce) from Pays Basque

Tuna:

1   pound fresh tuna steak, sliced three inches thick
1   tablespoon extra virgin olive oil

Sauce:

3   tomatoes, peeled, cored, seeded and chopped
salt to season
3   garlic cloves, minced
½   cup extra virgil olive oil
3   tablespoons freshly squeezed lemon juice
large handful of fresh herbs (chervil, tarragon, parsley and chives)

Combine the tomatoes, lemon juice, garlic and olive oil in a bowl; stir to blend. Season with salt to taste; allow flavors to blend for 1 to 2 hours. Add the herbs and stir to blend just prior to cooking the tuna.

Preheat the broiler. Prepare a grill for grilling, or heat a dry cast iron skillet over high heat.

Brush the tuna with the olive oil. Cook the tuna for 1 minute on each side. The tuna will be very rosy and rare on the inside and charred on the outside.

Remove tuna to a large, preheated platter and top with half of the sauce. Cut the tuna into thick strips and serve with additional sauce. Serves 4.

Note: This is delicious cold the next day, served as is, or mixed with warm pasta.

TRANSALPIN

Seventh Avenue at Logan Street
Denver, Colorado 80203
(303) 830-8282

Lemon Fish Pie

1   pound fresh thick fish
1   medium onion, sliced
2   carrots, thinly sliced
½   cup water
1   tablespoon butter or olive oil
1   tablespoon flour
1   cup skim milk
juice of 1 lemon
1½ pounds potatoes, cooked and mashed with skim milk
lemon twists and parsley for garnish

Cut fish into bite-size pieces. Place in a saucepan with onion, carrots, and water. Bring mixture to a boil, reduce heat and simmer for 15 minutes until the fish flakes with a fork and carrots are soft. Meanwhile, prepare the mashed potatoes. Drain the fish and vegetables and measure the fish stock, adding milk to yield 1½ cups. Melt butter, add flour and cook gently until mixture bubbles. Quickly stir in the liquid, cook over low heat until the mixture thickens, stirring continuously. Add lemon juice, parsley, fish, and vegetables. In a lightly greased quart casserole, spread the potatoes over the bottom and up the sides to make a potato crust. Pour the fish filling into the center. Top with crushed crackers or bread crumbs. Bake in a preheated 350° oven for 20 minutes or until the top is golden brown. Garnish with lemon twists and parsley. Serves 4.

SIMMS LANDING

West Sixth Avenue at Simms
Lakewood, Colorado
(303) 237-0465

Lemon Prosciutto Shrimp

16   large shrimp, peeled
16   slices of prosciutto
8   tablespoons Scampi Prep (chopped shallots and garlic)
6   teaspoons lemon zest
4   ounces of vodka
4   teaspoons lemon juice
8   ounces cream
4   ounces of grated Parmesan cheese
16   ounces of cooked fettuccine

Broil shrimp wrapped in prosciutto. Heat butter in sauté pan and add shallots, lemon zest. Saute until glossy.
Deglaze with vodka.
Add cream and reduce.
Add fettuccine. Toss and add Parmesan cheese.
Sprinkle top of pasta with Parmesan cheese and parsley. Top with prosciutto wrapped shrimp.

PRIMAVERA RISTORANTE AT ASPEN MOUNTAIN

600 South Spring Street
Aspen, Colorado
(303) 925-6602

Linguine and Lobster Tails Diable

8	lobster tails	4	tomatoes
1	onion, minced	¼	cup Parmesan cheese
1	teaspoon black pepper	½	cup white wine
½	cup olive oil	½	teaspoon salt
3	cloves garlic	4	basil leaves
1	pound linguine	1	teaspoon chopped parsley
1	teaspoon red pepper	1	tablespoon lemon juice

Drop the lobster tails into boiling salted water. Cool and split down the middle and remove the meat. Blanch and peel two tomatoes. Brown the garlic, parsley and onion in the olive oil. Add the tomatoes, basil, seasonings and white wine. Cook for 5 minutes. Add the chopped lobster meat and simmer for another 5 minutes. Cook the linguine in rapidly boiling water and drain and rinse through a colander under cold water. Return to the pot and add a bit of the sauce. Toss the linguine until well-covered. Serve the linguine on separate warm plates. Spoon the sauce and lobster over the top of the pasta and serve with Parmesan cheese.

SYZYGY

520 East Hyman Avenue (second floor)
Aspen, Colorado 81611
(303) 925-3700

Guests enter an intimate room with a wall of glassed waterfalls and experience the creative cuisine of Chef Jean Dwyer. Appetizers of carpaccio of beef (paper thin beef topped with capers and peppercorns and served with olive bread, Parmesan cheese and olive oil); lobster pie includes asparagus, snow peas and new potatoes; and other yummy items commence the dining experience. Salad offerings are equally creative such as sautéed shrimp with goat cheese, sun dried tomatoes, artichokes, lettuce with a lime vinaigrette. The entree items offer marvelous veal, quail, lamb, salmon and chicken culinary treats. Thoughtfully vegetarian and low-fat cuisine is available on request.

Here is a simple, easy-to-prepare variation of Syzygy's nightly changing "pasta du jour."

Linguine with Shrimp Sauce

1	onion, diced	½	pound cleaned, deveined cooked shrimp
½	pound fresh mushrooms, sliced	4	ounce linguine
1	green bell pepper, diced	1½	quarts boiling water
1	8-ounce can tomato sauce	2	tablespoons grated Parmesan cheese
¼	teaspoon Worcestershire sauce		

Sauté the onion, mushrooms, and green pepper in a nonstick frying pan until they are limp. Stir frequently. Add the tomato sauce and Worcestershire sauce, cover, and simmer for 5 minutes. Add the cooked shrimp and heat through. Meanwhile, gradually add the linguine to rapidly boiling water so that the water continues to boil. Cook, uncovered, stirring occasionally, until tender. Drain in a colander. Serve the cooked linguine topped with shrimp sauce. Sprinkle with grated cheese.

Variation: vegetarians may substitute artichokes (canned in vinaigrette) for shrimp.

THE BROADMOOR HOTEL

Penrose Room
1 Lake Avenue
Colorado Springs, Colorado 80906
(719) 634-7711

Chef Sebanc

Mustard Glazed Salmon Filet on
Stirfried Spinach Leaves, Tarragon Butter

4	(5-6 ounces each) salmon filets	2	ounces olive oil
¼	lemon (juice)	1	ounce butter
Worcestershire sauce		1	cup bread flour
salt		2	ounces chablis
2	ounces dijon mustard		

Season salmon filets with salt, lemon juice and Worcestershire sauce. Mix 1 ounce olive oil with the dijon mustard and spread evenly over the top of the salmon filet. Dredge salmon on both sides in bread flour, heat remaining olive oil and butter in saute pan. Place salmon into hot oil and butter, mustard glazed side down first and sauté for about 3-4 minutes (depending on thickness), turn salmon filets onto other side and complete cooking for another 3-4 minutes, arrange salmon filets on stirfried spinach leaves, deglaze (add) 2 ounces chablis wine to the remaining drippings in sauté pan. Add 3 ounces tarragon butter and melt over low heat, constantly shaking the sauté pan, pour foaming tarragon butter mixture over the salmon. Serves four.

Stirfried Spinach

8	ounces fresh spinach leaves (raw)	1	teaspoon chopped garlic
2	ounces olive oil	1	teaspoon chopped anchovies
2	teaspoons chopped shallots		nutmeg and black pepper to taste

Heat sauté pan. Mix olive oil, shallots, garlic and anchovies, pour into pan. Add spinach, nutmeg and black pepper and stir over high heat for a couple of minutes until spinach is hot.

Tarragon Butter

3	ounces salted butter (soft)	1	teaspoon Worcestershire sauce
juice of ¼ lemon		1	ounce fresh chopped tarragon (not too fine)

Whip soft butter until creamy. Add lemon juice, Worcestershire sauce and tarragon. Refrigerate until ready for use.

THE LITTLE NELL

675 East Durant
Aspen, Colorado 81611
(303) 920-4600

Oven Roasted Salmon with Potato Basil Crust
and Warm Tomato Chutney

4   salmon filets, 6-ounces each
2   sprigs fresh basil
2   potatoes
¼   cup clarified butter or 4 teaspoons lemon juice
salt
white pepper

Chutney:

1   cup diced tomatoes, seeds removed
2   tablespoons shallots, chopped
½   teaspoon garlic, chopped
3   tablespoons red onions, diced
½   teaspoon fresh ginger, chopped
1   teaspoon honey
2   tablespoons St. Mary's Gourmet Vinegar
½   teaspoon pickling spice
3   tablespoons butter
1   tablespoon peanut oil

Chutney:

In 2-quart saucepan, sauté shallots, garlic and red onions in peanut oil over medium heat for 2 minutes. Add vinegar, honey and pickling spice. Reduce until dry. Add ginger and tomatoes. Finish with butter and stir. Remove and keep warm.

Cut off each end of potatoes and stand on end. Cut off corners to form round cylinder. Slice paper thin.

Lay basil leaves over top of filets. Lay potato slices over top of basil to look like fish scales. Cover with clarified butter or lemon juice and chill. Preheat oven to 375°.

In 12-inch sauté pan, over medium heat, add 3 tablespoons of peanut oil. Sauté until edges begin to brown (if salmon slides away from potatoes, simply press back together). Place pan in oven and cook until medium (approximately 4 minutes). Do not turn. Remove and spoon tomato chutney over plate, place salmon on top, potato side up. Garnish with basil. Serves 4.

THE WILDFLOWER INN

174 East Gore Creek Drive
Vail, Colorado 81657
(303) 476-5011 ext. 170

Oysters With Crackling For Six

24 oysters, prefer spinney creeks
2   skins from breast of chicken
1   shallot, fine diced
2   tablespoons Italian parsley, chopped
1   lemon
fresh black pepper
extra virgin olive oil

Place skins of chicken on baking sheet with a little kosher salt. Bake until crisp, let cool and break into very small pieces.

Open oysters, careful not to lose juice and place on plate.

The next step is to place a "little" shallot, a "little" crackling, a "little" parsley (by a "little" we mean almost a pinhead of each. If too much is used it overpowers the oysters), two drops lemon, ½ turn black pepper and a drop of olive oil on each oyster.

Repeat process, serve.

The key to this dish is balance of ingredients. First and foremost, one should taste the oyster and the other flavors should be in the background. Serves 6.

FERN'S RESTAURANT

Denver Hilton South
7801 East Orchard Road
Englewood, Colorado 80111
(303) 779-6161

Sous Chef Jeanette Landgraf

Papillotes of Lobster and Shrimp

2   pieces wax paper
1   large lobster tail
6   large shrimp
1   bunch cleaned spinach
fresh, crushed garlic

lemon
oyster mushrooms
butter
salt and pepper

Cut wax paper into a large heart. Shape. (Easily done if paper is folded in half.) Open, set spinach, ½ lobster tail, 3 shrimp, lots of fresh garlic, fresh lemon juice, oyster mushrooms, chopped, large pieces of fresh whole butter and salt and pepper on ½ half of heart-shaped wax paper. Double-fold the edges all the way around and fasten with a paper clip. The food must be tightly and completely enclosed. The wrapping will swell in the oven and should be opened before the guests are seated. Repeat step for second serving. Cook in a 375° oven until done. Serves 2.

POMODORO

601 South Broadway
Denver, Colorado
(303) 698-9864

Pomodoro is Denver's only four-star Italian restaurant, as rated by the *Rocky Mountain News* dining critic, Bill St. John. It is the second successful venture of Zenith owners Janet Wright and Kevin Taylor. In his review Bill St. John commented, "So Denver has too many Italian restaurants. It could never have too many Pomodoros!"

Pomodoro has mastered the trick to creating contemporary and traditional Italian cuisine. Starters range from the traditional Carpaccio and Antipasto to the very popular Frito Misto. The salads are combinations of lush greens and delightful light accompaniments. Dinners are a wonderful choice of homemade pastas, and delicately grilled items, ranging from lamb and veal, to seafood and fish. Tirmai su, gelati, and light fruit sorbets headline the list of delicious homemade desserts which add a delightful ending to guests' meals.

It is no wonder Pomodoro's is so popular.

Pesce Spade Alla Siciliana
(Sicilian Style Swordfish)

2	tablespoons olive oil
4	swordfish steaks, ¾ inch thick
2	cups Italian plum tomatoes, seeded and chopped with their juices
1	small onion, julienne cut
2	garlic cloves, thinly sliced
6	anchovy filets, chopped
1	cup Italian red wine (Chianti)
½	cup black olives, pitted
1	tablespoon capers, rinsed
¼	cup julienne basil leaves
1	roasted, peeled and julienned red pepper

salt and pepper to taste

Heat olive oil to near smoke point. Quickly brown swordfish one minute on each side and remove from pan (swordfish should still be raw in center). Add tomatoes, onions, garlic, anchovy and red wine and cook until onions become translucent.

Add rest of ingredients and season. Place swordfish back into sauce and finish cooking until fish is warm throughout. Ladle sauce on swordfish steaks and serve with vegetable, pasta or risotto.

OFF BELLEVIEW GRILL

8101 East Belleview
Denver, Colorado
(303) 694-3337

Opening a new restaurant is such an exhausting enterprise that some often wonder why does anyone do it? But for Dean Peterson this is not the case. Opening a new restaurant is challenging but mostly great fun. And in Denver no one does it better! Off Belleview Grill had scarcely been open a year when it was awarded "Denver's Favorite New Restaurant" for 1987.

The restaurant is Southwestern in decor with stucco walls, granite in-laid floors and famous original Southwestern art. The sophistication and interest in art is apparent in every touch, from the tasteful decor to the beautiful arrangements of food on the plates.

Off Belleview Grill is noted for its French rotisserie and wood-fired Italian Pizza Oven. The rotisserie offers spit-roasted chicken, roast duck, and beef tenderloin; swordfish and Florida Red Snapper are grilled. Other specialties include homemade pastas and California gourmet pizzas.

The wood-fired oven was imported from Italy and has been installed in the center of the restaurant. It provides decor in motion. Guests see the pizza maker throwing the dough, the pasta being cooked and the salads being tossed.

This "upbeat" bistro has become a favorite for lunch, dinner and cocktails. The chef's innovative menu and stylish simplicity in presentation and cooking has helped the restaurant earn its 4-star rating.

Red Snapper Louisiane

2-3 pounds Gulf Red Snapper filets in 4 portions
1   egg
1   cup milk
6   tablespoons butter
salt and pepper to taste
½   cup flour for dipping
2   cups cooking oil
8   artichoke hearts
4   large fresh mushrooms, sliced
1   teaspoon Worcestershire sauce
1   teaspoon lemon juice
1   teaspoon tarragon vinegar
½   cup sliced almonds

Beat together egg, milk and 2 tablespoons melted butter. Salt and pepper to taste.

Dip filets into batter, then in flour. Sauté in oil (as needed) until lightly browned and just done. Keep warm.

In another pan, sauté artichokes and mushrooms in 2 tablespoons butter. Add Worcestershire, lemon juice and vinegar. Cook until tender.

Toast almonds in 2 tablespoons butter under broiler.

Place filets on serving platter. Top with artichokes and mushrooms. Sprinkle with toasted almonds. Serves 4.

Preparation: 10 minutes
Cooking: 20 minutes

RENAISSANCE

304 East Hopkins
Aspen, Colorado 81611
(303) 925-2402

Chef Charles Dale

Salmon A La Provençal with Flageolet Bean Compote

4   seven ounce salmon filets

Provençal Breading

¼	ounce basil leaves	½	cup white breadcrumbs, unseasoned
1	clove of garlic	½	teaspoon salt
½	cup extra virgil olive oil	¼	teaspoon freshly ground pepper
¼	cup grated Parmesan cheese	¼	cup pure olive oil for sauteing

Flageolet Bean Compote

1   8-ounce box dry flageolet beans (available through specialty markets)
1   Spanish onion, finely diced
2   cloved of garlic, pressed or finely diced
1   teaspoon tomato paste
1   branch fresh thyme, or ¼ teaspoon dry
1   branch fresh rosemary, or ¼ teaspoon dry
2   tablespoons salt
¼   teaspoon pepper

For the Bean Compote: Cover and soak the beans overnight in the refrigerator, then drain them the next day. Sauté onion in 2 tablespoons olive oil until limp, add chopped garlic and tomato paste, stirring 1 minute. Add beans and herbs, and water to cover by two inches. Bring to a boil, then lower to a simmer for 2 to 3 hours, or until beans begin to get tender. Add salt, and cook 1 more hour, or until beans are tender, adding water if necessary. Remove beans to cook, saving the cooking liquid, but removing any fresh herb branches that remain.

To prepare the salmon: Put garlic, basil, and olive oil in a blender, and puree on high speed. Remove to a bowl, and mix with cheese and breadcrumbs, adding more oil as necessary (mixture should hold together, yet be malleable). Add salt and pepper, and spread evenly over each filet, pressing down to set the breading firmly on the salmon. One may prepare the dish ahead to this point.

To finish: Place beans in a casserole with the cooking liquid and 2 tablespoons of sweet butter. Heat to simmer and hold. Preheat a 12- to 14-inch, heavy duty sauté pan, add olive oil, and cook salmon filets, *bread side down,* for 1 minute. Season the back side with salt and pepper to taste, turn heat to medium low, then turn salmon bread side up. Continue cooking 3 more minutes, while plating the beans. Place salmon over the beans, garnishing with a basil leaf or parsley sprig, and serve. Serves 4.

THE BROADMOOR HOTEL

Charles Court
1 Lake Avenue
Colorado Springs, Colorado 80906
(719) 634-7711

Salmon Newburg

6	cups flaked salmon	3	egg yolks
6	tablespoons butter	2	cups cream
1	teaspoon shallots	½	teaspoon salt
2	tablespoons flour		dash cayenne pepper
⅓	cup cooking sherry		

Cook salmon and shallots in butter for 2 minutes, sprinkle with flour and stir well. Add sherry slowly and cook for 2 minutes longer. Combine egg yolks and cream, add slowly to the salmon, stirring constantly. Place over hot water and stir until it thickens. Add salt and cayenne. Serve over rice or toast. Serves 4.

TANTE LOUISE

4900 East Colfax Avenue
Denver, Colorado
(303) 355-4488

For seventeen years, Tante Louise has been committed to providing a most memorable dining experience. Chef Margaret Bradley creates a new menu balanced between traditional French cuisine, and the innovations of new American cooking. A seasonal changing of the menu allows for using the freshest products the market has to offer. Freshly baked breads and desserts that are irresistible are created daily by the pastry chef.

Tante Louise has consistently been chosen as the most romantic restaurant in Denver. It is easy to see how the comfort and charm of a renovated bungalow, featuring hardwood floors, candlelit tables, the emanating glow of the fireplace, and classical music softly playing in the background, create a warm and welcoming ambiance.

A national award winning wine list of over 250 imported and domestic wines is maintained by a full time wine steward, with the great vintages well represented.

The staff, owner and chef are available every evening to take care of any special needs or services guests may have and look forward to an opportunity to serve you and your guests.

Salmon Tartare

1   pound very fresh salmon filets, boned and skinned
¼   cup olive oil
juice of 2-3 lemons, depending on taste
2   tablespoons chopped fresh dill
¼   cup finely diced red onion
2   whole anchovies
1   teaspoon chopped garlic
2   teaspoons worcestershire sauce
½   teaspoon Tabasco
2   tablespoons dijon mustard
2   egg yolks
splash of armagnac
salt and pepper
2   tablespoons capers

Chop salmon with sharp knife until finely and evenly diced. Hold over ice, covered, until ready to use, for up to 30 minutes. Meanwhile, in blender, combine juice, olive oil, garlic, anchovies, worcestershire sauce, Tabasco, dijon and egg yolks. Blend until emulsified. Adjust seasonings to taste. Toss onions, capers, and dill with salmon. Pour sauce over salmon and stir. Serve immediately with dark rye bread.

FLAGSTAFF HOUSE RESTAURANT

1138 Flagstaff Road
Boulder, Colorado 80302
(303) 442-4640

"Pack up all your cares and woes — you'll have to pawn them to pay for dinner — and head for the ritziest restaurant in the rockies — Flagstaff House!" Thus begins *Denver Magazine's* rave reviews about this sensational Boulder restaurant which rates 5 stars in food, service, and ambiance by local and national reviewers.

And if the stars could rate higher Flagstaff would earn even more.

Whether from the spectacular terraces on a sparkling summer eve, or the elegant inside dining rooms on an enchanting, snowy night, "Flagstaff House" imparts to its guests the beauty and spirit of Flagstaff Mountain itself.

But wait. Then there's the food and the service.

Chef Mark Monet has been trained well by his father, Don Monet, and the two make a winning team. Chef Mark seldom strays from the stove, where his experience in Manhattan's, France's, and Hong Kong's finest restaurants brings fabulous cuisine to guests' tables: not only the classics but nightly exotic chef's creations.

The *Wine Spectator's* Grand Award for the "Greatest Wine List in the World" has been bestowed on the Flagstaff House for the past 8 years, where rare 1988 vintage bottles may go for $8,000 — down to selections of today's contemporary and affordable wines.

Service is elegant, efficient and attentive. Guests are treated like royalty.

So for ambiance, service, and food and a dinner to put in guests' "savings account of memories" it is a meal at the Flagstaff House.

Salmon with Lobster and Truffles

1	pound filet of salmon		1	pinch saffron
4	ounces fresh lobster meat			salt
1	ounce truffles, chopped			white pepper
2	sprigs fresh tarragon, chopped			

Celery Pureé

¼ cup heavy cream
1 bulk celery root, peeled - ¹/₅ cut into thin slices and ⁴/₅ cubed
1 cup water
salt and pepper
cayenne

Niçoise Olive Sauce

2 fresh tomatoes, peeled, chopped and seeded
½ cup extra-virgin olive oil
1 clove garlic, chopped
4 ounces combined: chopped fresh thyme, marjoram, oregano and tarragon
Niçoise olives, seeded and diced

Slice the salmon in half and keep in one piece. Pound thin. Spread the lobster, truffles, tarragon and saffron over the salmon. Salt and pepper. Roll tightly and wrap in cellophane. Take out of cellophane and roll in parchment paper. Tie and portion. Sear on both sides.

Celery Puree

Cut the celery root into thin slices and deep fry. Cut remaining celery root into cubes and boil until soft. Put softened cubes into food processor and add hot cream until pureed. Season to taste.

Niçoise Olive Sauce

Heat olive oil with tomato, garlic, herbs and olives. Simmer and spoon over salmon. Serves 2.
BON APPETIT!

RUDI'S

4720 Table Mesa Drive
Boulder, Colorado 80303
(303) 494-5858

Chef Faith Stone

Salmon Wrapped in Filo with Brie

3   pounds fresh salmon filet boned and skin removed
1   package filo dough
1   pound butter melted
6   ounces Brie cheese
a few sprigs of fresh dill or tarragon
pastry brush

Divide the salmon into 5 eight ounce portions.

Spread the filo sheets flat and cover with plastic wrap. Take one filo sheet, laying it flat and brush it with melted butter. Lay another sheet of filo on top and brush it with butter also. Place a third sheet on top and brush it with butter. Take one salmon filet and place it in the center at the bottom of the buttered sheets, top it with one ounce of sliced Brie and sprig of dill or tarragon. Fold the sides of filo dough toward the center and gently fold the fish forward, rolling strudel style. Repeat the same procedure with the other 5 portions.

Bake the salmon stuffed filo in a 350° oven for 20-25 minutes or longer, depending on the thickness of the fish. Cut through the bottom of one strudel to check for doneness. The fish should be opaque throughout. Transfer to serving dishes and top with Hollandaise (see Sauce section). Serve immediately.

TAKAH SUSHI

420 East Hyman
Aspen, Colorado
(303) 925-8588

Sashimi*

1   large salmon
1   teaspoon salt
2   cups rice wine vinegar
2   cups short grain rice, soaked in cold water for 1 hour and drained
2½ cups water

Garnish:

1½ inch piece of fresh green ginger, peeled and grated
5   scallions, finely chopped
1½ cups soy sauce
2   teaspoons green horseradish, mixed to a paste with two teaspoons water

Salt the salmon filet and refrigerate for an hour. Cover the rice with water in a saucepan and bring to a boil, cover and simmer until the water is absorbed, about 15 to 20 minutes. Keep hot in a serving bowl. Remove salmon filet from the refrigerator and soak in vinegar another hour, then remove from vinegar and pat dry. Cut vertically into ½ inch pieces, arrange on serving dish with grated ginger and scallions. Pour soy sauce into individual bowls along with individual portions of horseradish mixture. Mix horseradish to taste into the soy sauce and dip the salmon pieces into the sauce before eating with the rice. Serves 4.

* Variation

BOCCALINO'S

158 Fillmore
Denver, Colorado
(303) 393-6544

Sautéed Scampi and Fettuccine Alfredo*

1	pound scampi	2	cloves garlic
¼	cup olive oil	1	lemon rind, grated
¼	cup butter	1	teaspoon oregano
2	eggs, beaten	3	tablespoons lemon juice
1	tablespoon flour	1	pound fettuccine
1	teaspoon salt	½	cup butter
2	tablespoons worcestershire sauce	2	eggs
pinch red pepper		2	teaspoons black pepper
2	tablespoons fresh parsley		

Clean scampi and remove from their shells. In a bowl, mix the eggs, flour and salt. In a skillet, melt the butter in the olive oil. Add the garlic and brown. Remove. Dip the shrimp into the batter and drop into the skillet. Cook until they are brown and crisp and remove. Return the garlic to the pan and add the parsley, lemon rind, lemon juice, red pepper, oregano and worcestershire sauce. Blend quickly over a hot flame.

Add the scampi but do not stir. Cook the noodles in plenty of salted boiling water until they float to the top. Drain them in cold, running water and return to the pot. Mix the eggs, pepper and butter quickly with the pasta until the noodles are coated. Put on a warm serving dish. Arrange the sauteed scampi on top of the pasta. Spoon the sauce over the whole platter and serve with additional Parmesan cheese.

* Variation

THE WILDFLOWER INN

174 East Gore Creek Drive
Vail, Colorado 81657
(303) 476-5011 ext. 170

Scallops Niçoise

6   ounces fresh scallops
4   ounces Cioppino Sauce (see Seafood section)
¼   cup white wine
2   anchovies
2   black olives, chopped
minced garlic

Sauté garlic in butter, add scallops and saute for a few minutes. Add wine and reduce while scallops continue cooking. Add Cioppino Sauce, anchovies and olives. Serve in casserole dish or shallow boat. Serves 1.

UTE CITY BANQUE

501 East Hyman
Aspen, Colorado
(303) 925-4373

Scallops Parisienne*

Combine and boil 15 minutes:

3¾	cups white wine	10	sprigs parsley
2	coarsely chopped medium onions	3	bay leaves
3	coarsely chopped shallots	¾	teaspoon thyme

Strain and reserve the liquid.

Wash and dry:

2½ pounds fresh bay scallops

Add scallops to reserved liquid and cook them until liquid almost boils. Drain scallops, reserving liquid, and spread out to cook quickly. Sauté until browned lightly:

1¼ pounds quartered mushrooms in about ½ cup butter, add more butter when needed.

Add and cook 3 minutes:

4 tablespoons flour

Add and cook until thickened:

¾	cup milk	2	cups reserved liquid

Remove from heat and add:

¾	cup grated imported Gruyere cheese	1	teaspoon salt
¹/₈	teaspoon pepper		

Place scallops in lightly buttered casserole and top with the sauce. Sprinkle lightly with bread crumbs and dot with butter. Bake at 450° until lightly browned, about 15 minutes. Serves 5 to 6.

* Variation

LA BOHÉME

315 Gateway Building
Aspen-Snowmass, Colorado
(303) 923-6804

Maurice Couturier and his wife, Brigitte, have provided a heavenly gastronomic experience for guests visiting Snowmass. Here is a variation of one of their nightly changing entrées.

Shrimp Baked with Feta Cheese and Tomato

1½ pounds fresh shrimp	¼ cup fresh parsley
1 cup feta cheese, crumbled	2 tablespoons fresh dill
½ can tomato paste (6 ounces)	3 cloves minced garlic
½ can tomato sauce	½ teaspoon dried mustard
2½ cups fresh or canned tomatoes (drained)	2¼ cups onions, finely chopped
3 tablespoons olive oil	1 cup dry white wine
1½ cups olive oil	

Heat the oil in a saucepan and add onion, cooking until light brown. Add the parsley, dill, garlic and mustard. Blend together. Then add the tomato paste, tomato sauce and tomatoes and cook slowly for ½ hour.

Clean shrimp (peel, devein and rinse) and add them to the mixture. Cook for 5 minutes or less. Pour the ingredients into a 2-quart casserole and add wine. Spread feta cheese over the top and bake in a preheated over at 425° for 10 minutes or until feta cheese is melted. Serves 4.

MOSTLY SEAFOOD

303 Sixteenth Street
Denver, Colorado
(303) 892-5999

Shrimp Chile Rellenos

6   eggroll wrappers
6   green chiles (canned, already roasted and peeled)
6   large shrimp, peeled and deveined
3   ounces sharp cheddar cheese, grated
1   egg
½   cup water
1   cup wheat germ or breadcrumbs
milk for dipping
cooking oil

Beat egg and water together. Lay one eggroll wrapper flat. On it lay one shrimp, one green chile and ½ ounce of the cheese side by side. Roll the wrapper around the contents. Moisten the edge of the wrapper with egg and water to seal it. Fold each end toward the center and moisten with egg and water to hold the ends down on the relleno. Dip the relleno in the egg and milk, roll in crumbs. Let rest for a few minutes. Deep fry in oil until golden brown. Cover with pork and shrimp green chile.

PIÑON'S

105 South Mill
Aspen, Colorado
(303) 920-2021

Shrimp Dijonnaise*

6   ounces heavy cream
½   tablespoon shallots, minced
¹/₈ cup white wine

1   tablespoon dijon mustard
    salt and pepper to taste
    roux

Sauté shallots and deglaze with the white wine. Reduce heat slightly. Add mustard and cream and thicken to a medium consistency. Season with salt and pepper. Strain sauce. Sauté 5 shrimp per person in butter and a little white wine. Remove to casserole and top with 2 ounces of sauce and fresh, chopped parsley. Serves 4.

* Variation

SMUGGLER BAR AND RESTAURANT

415 East Hopkins
Aspen, Colorado
(303) 925-8624

Smoked Mussels in Mustard-Cream Sauce*

1	teaspoon minced scallion green
1	teaspoon minced garlic
½	cup smoked mussels from can, drained
1	tablespoon clarified butter (procedure follows)
1	teaspoon dijon mustard
2	tablespoons dry white wine
¼	cup heavy cream
1	tablespoon minced fresh parsley leaves

In a skillet cook the scallion, the garlic, and the mussels in the butter over moderate heat, shaking the skillet gently, for 1 minute; add the mustard, the wine, and the cream, stirring gently, and cook the mixture, stirring, until it comes to a bare simmer. Spoon the mixture onto 2 heated plates and sprinkle the parsley over it. Serves 2 as a first course.

To Clarify Butter

Unsalted butter, cut into 1-inch pieces

In a heavy saucepan melt the butter over low heat. Remove the pan from the heat, let the butter stand for 3 minutes, and skim the froth. Strain the butter through a sieve lined with a double thickness of rinsed and squeezed cheesecloth into a bowl, leaving the milky solids in the bottom of the pan. Pour the clarified butter into a jar or crock and store it, covered, in the refrigerator. The butter keeps indefinitely, covered and chilled. When clarified, butter loses about one fourth of its original volume.

* Variation

CASTAWAY'S

107 Manitou Avenue
Manitou Springs, Colorado
(719) 685-5626

Smoked Oysters and Shallots Vinaigrette

1 can smoked oysters	1 tablespoon shallots, chopped fine
juice of 1 lemon	¼ teaspoon salt
¼ cup St. Mary's Gourmet Vinegar	black peppercorns
½ cup water	

Put the oysters carefully into a colander and rinse under running lukewarm water, being careful not to let the force of the water break the oysters. Rinse off all traces of oil and place the oysters in a plastic bowl. Sprinkle chopped shallots over the top of the oysters. Pour vinegar into a saucepan and add water and salt and heat until the mixture comes to a boil. Cook the vinegar mixture for a few minutes, then pour it over the oysters and shallots. Cool to room temperature, then refrigerate for several hours.

To serve, drain the oysters and place them with the shallots on a serving dish. Spoon 1 or 2 tablespoons of the vinaigrette sauce on the oysters and shallots. Add the lemon juice and grind black pepper coarsely over the top. Serve with buttered dark bread. Makes 4 servings.

THE LITTLE NELL

675 East Durant
Aspen, Colorado 81611
(303) 920-4600

It is no wonder that *Bon Appetit* magazine labeled the Executive Chef at Aspen's newest deluxe hotel "Up and Coming." Little Nell's Chef Richard Chamberlain specializes in American Alpine cooking which reflects the needs of cooking on a mountain top: the use of smoked and cured meats; dried fruits; and vegetables and herbs braised in moisture as a corrective to dry air.

His superb cookery is served in a room that is understated and elegant with a view of the Little Nell's pool and in the background the ski run, Little Nell, itself.

A meal at Little Nell's is a most memorable and enjoyable, first-class gastronomic experience.

Smoked Trout with Papaya, Avocado and Cucumber

8 smoked trout filets	4 tablespoons water
1 avocado, diced	½ teaspoon ginger
1 cucumber, diced	1 tablespoon honey
2 papayas, diced	5 tablespoons peanut oil
juice of half lemon	1 teaspoon dill, chopped
1 egg yolk	

Combine in blender one papaya, lemon juice, egg yolk, water, ginger and honey. Slowly add peanut oil and season with salt and white pepper. Pour sauce on plates, sprinkle with avocado, cucumber, remaining papaya and dill. Lay trout over sauce in criss-cross fashion and serve. Serves 4.

CHEZ THOA

158 Fillmore
Denver, Colorado 80206
(303) 355-6464 or 355-2323

Tom Chien Lan Bot (Hot and Spicy Prawns)

1	pound large green shrimp	1	clove garlic
1	cup flour	1	onion, diced
½	cup rice flour	2	tomatoes, chopped
1	cup water	½	teaspoon hot Szechuan dried peppers
salt and pepper		½	cup cornstarch, diluted in water
2	cups peanut oil		diced green onions for garnish

Peel and butterfly the shrimp, leaving the tails intact. Mix all flour with water, salt and pepper to make a batter. Heat oil in a wok or deep-frying pan. Dip the shrimp in flour batter and coat completely. Fry shrimp in hot oil until it turns golden brown. Remove shrimp from the pan and set aside on a warm plate. Pour out all but 2 tablespoons of oil. Sauté garlic, onion and tomatoes until soft (about 5 minutes). Add hot peppers, seasoning with salt and pepper. Thicken with cornstarch and water mixture. Arrange the fried shrimp on a plate and pour sauce on top. Sprinkle with some diced green onions. Serve shrimp and sauce while hot with steamed rice. Serves 4.

ANTONIO'S ITALIAN RESTAURANT

301 Garden of the Gods Road
Colorado Springs, Colorado
(719) 531-7177

Two cousins of Sicilian heritage have brought fine Italian dining to the Springs. Chef Giglia's fresh seafood and pasta specialties are rivaled only in the Sicilian seaports where they originated. Here is a variation of an Italian favorite.

Tonno Con Salsa Di Pomodoro
(Fresh Tuna with Tomato Sauce)

2   pounds fresh tuna fish: 4 slices, 1½ inches thick
4   tablespoons olive oil
1   tablespoon chopped parsley
3   cloves garlic, minced
1   small onion, diced
1   can tomato paste

Rinse tuna and set aside.
Pour oil in skillet; add onion, garlic, parsley; cook 5 minutes or until soft.
Blend tomato paste in 2 cups of hot water; add to mixture in skillet; cover; simmer 20 minutes, stirring occasionally. Add fish; cover; cook 15 minutes or until tender.
Serve very fast. Serves 4.

TRANSALPIN

Seventh Avenue at Logan Street
Denver, Colorado 80203
(303) 830-8282

To experience Transalpin is to experience culinary artistry and visual art as well — all created by the Chef of Cuisine Martha Keating. Her two fish plates with two different fish filets in two different sauces, cooked in two different ways has become the seafood pinnacle in Denver; has become the seafood dish or star of excellence by which other restaurants' seafood dishes are compared. Her menu is as creative as her artwork. French, Bali, Chinese, Italian, Scottish, and Louisiana and more countries' famous dishes as well as Denver dishes and Chef Martha Keating's creative specials have thrilled guests and have earned Transalpin rave reviews in the *Denver Post* and the *Rocky Mountain News*.

What fun to go to an art gallery and dine beautifully. Artist Martha Keating's Oil Wall Murals change every five or six weeks as they rotate to galleries and enter the treasured assets of major corporations.

Trout Poached In Lemon Grass Broth
Served over Spinach and Topped with Pineapple Ginger Sauce

8 to 12 large spinach leaves	2 cloves garlic, minced
4 cups chicken broth (see Sauce section)	4 boneless trout filets
1 lemon grass stalk, finely chopped	

Prepare Pineapple Ginger Sauce several days ahead of time or 10 minutes before serving (see Sauce section).

Poach fresh spinach leaves in chicken broth, lemon grass and garlic. Then remove spinach from liquid and place in warm oven to keep warm. Also place 4 individual porcelain plates in oven. Take liquid mixture (chicken broth, garlic, and lemon grass) and add 4 boneless trout filets. Poach 7 minutes.

While this is poaching, assemble spinach leaves; top with poached trout filets. Pour Pineapple Ginger Sauce over the filets. Serve on warmed plates. Serves 4.

PICASSO'S

The Lodge at Cordillera
Vail-Edwards, Colorado 81632
(303) 926-2200 or 949-7112
(800) 548-2721

Chef Philippe Van Cappellen

Since its opening, Picasso's has become a 4-star restaurant. *Rocky Mountain News* says, ''Picasso's is superb dining, flawless at every turn, and an enormous pleasure to experience.'' Many dignitaries, including former President Gerald Ford, and celebrities agree and regularly thrill to Picasso's marvelous haute cuisine with an emphasis on fresh, regional products.

Original Picassos grace the walls. Guests dine in an atmosphere of European elegance amid Rocky Mountain splendor. Piccasso's is in the Cordillera, a beautiful lodge atop a high peak overlooking a pristine mountain view twenty-five minutes west of Vail.

Executive Chef Philippe E. Van Cappellen, who has earned Diplome de' Honneur du Club des Gastronomes de Belgique plans the menus and supervises the preparation of his fabulous creations. Here he shares the secrets of a few of his popular dishes.

Tuna Tartare with Chives

1 ½ cups tuna, diced (raw, such as yellowfin or albacore)
¾   cup cream
juice of 2 lemons
3   tablespoons fresh chives, chopped
salt and pepper to taste
mache leaves for garnish (lamb's lettuce) or parsley

Mix together cream, lemon juice, chives and salt and pepper. Toss tuna, diced very small, in cream mixture. Serve cold and garnish with leaves of mache (lamb's lettuce). Serves 4.

H. BRINKER'S

I-25 and Arapahoe Road
Denver, Colorado
(303) 792-0285

Turrine of Fish

¼	pound skinless, boneless salmon			grated nutmeg
2	eggs		½	pound scallops
2	egg whites		10	ounces skinless sole filets
	juice of lemon		2	cups heavy cream
	salt and pepper		6	tablespoons spinach pureé

Grease 1½ quart turrine or loaf pan and line with greased parchment paper.

Cut the salmon into strips and process with 1 whole egg, 1 egg white, lemon juice, salt, white pepper and grated nutmeg to taste. When mixture is smooth transfer contents to a mixing bowl. Chill while preparing the rest of mixture.

Wash out the bowl of the food processor and process the scallops with 1 egg, 1 egg white, lemon juice and seasoning. When smooth, chill as before. Last, process the sole with the remaining whole egg, egg white, lemon juice and seasoning. Chill.

Transfer the chilled salmon mixture to the bowl of mixer and beat well. Gradually beat in ⅓ of cream. Mixture should be very thick. Set aside and repeat with scallop mixture, set aside. Last, beat the remaining cream into the sole mixture with spinach puree.

Spoon half the sole mixture into the turrine and spread evenly until level. Spread mixture of salmon on top then make a layer using remaining sole. Last, cover with the scallop mixture.

Cover with greased parchment paper and a lid or foil. Stand turrine in a water bath and bake at 350° for 30-40 minutes.

Serve slices with parsleyed mayonnaise. Serves 4.

CHINA TERRACE

1512 Larimer Street
Denver, Colorado 80202
(303) 592-1032

Volcano Shrimp

10	ounces Chinese cabbage		4	ounces ground pork
2	ounces soybean oil		2	water chestnuts, finely chopped
3	tablespoons water		4	black mushrooms, finely chopped
⅓	teaspoon salt		3	green onions, finely chopped
½	teaspoon sugar		½	teaspoon soy sauce
½	teaspoon cornstarch		1-2	ounces 151 rum

Chop Chinese cabbage into 3 x 2-inch chunks. Heat 1 ounce of the soybean oil in wok over high heat. Add Chinese cabbage; stir-fry for 1 minute. Add water, salt and sugar. Stir another minute. Pour in cornstarch and cook ½ minute. Put cabbage mixture on a dish and set aside.

Remove shells from shrimp, leaving tail intact. Use a sharp knife to cut down the front of the shrimp. Open and flatten. Remove the back vein. Mix pork together with all remaining ingredients (except rum). Spoon pork mixture into each shrimp, pressing pork into the shrimp with the back of the spoon. Preheat the wok over medium heat for 1 minute. Pour in remaining 1 ounce soybean oil; heat oil ½ minute. Carefully put shrimp into wok, pork mixture side down. Cover the wok and cook for 10 to 15 minutes, or until pork turns light brown. Remove shrimp and arrange them on the cabbage base with tails in the center of the plate. Pour rum over shrimp; light with match. Serve flaming with side of steamed rice. Serves 1 or 2.

ENTREES
FOWL IX

P. McClure

ENTRÉES FOWL, IX

Avocado Pancake filled with Smoked Duck and Wild Rice (Sweet Basil) — p. 1
Baked Chicken in Orange-Almond Sauce (The Deacon's Bench) — p. 2
The Bowl of the Wife of Kit Carson (The Fort) — p. 2
Campaigne Chicken (Friendly Country Chicken) (Delfannies Restaurant) — p. 3
Cashew or Almond Chicken (China Dragon Restaurant) — p. 3
Charbroiled Quail with Shiitake Mushrooms and Wild Rice (Strings) — p. 4
Chestnut Chicken (Asia) — p. 4
Chicken a la Français (Mother Lode) — p. 5
Chicken a la King (The Golden Dobbin) — p. 5
Chicken Breast Boursin with Red Wine Sauce (Ute City Banque) — p. 6
Chicken Breast Tina Louise (Maxie's) — p. 6
Chicken Green Chili Stew (Marina Landing) — p. 7
Chicken Kiev (Sweet Basil) — p. 7
Chicken Marengo (The Golden Eagle Inn — Introduction) — p. 8
Chicken Quenelles with Mushroom Sauce (Rudi's) — p. 9
Chicken with Garlic Sauce (China Terrace) — p. 10
Chicken with Orange Sauce (Chanticler — Introduction) — p. 11
Chicken with Red Chiles, Mint and Oregon Raspberry Wine (John's Restaurant) — p. 12
Cornish Hen Glazed with Orange and Ginger (Craftwood Inn) — p. 13
Ducks with Orange and Grand Marnier Sauce (H. Brinker's — Introduction)) — p. 14
Grilled Achiote Chicken with Chipolte Salsa and Shallot Sauce (Sweet Basil) — p. 15
Grilled Breast of Chicken with Avocado Cream Sauce with Sundried Tomatoes (Firefly Cafe) — p. 15
Jalapeño Lime Marinated Chicken with Corn Bread Dressing (Duggan's — Introduction) — p. 16
Kai Yand (Garlic Chicken) (Chao-Praya Thai Restaurant and Lounge) — p. 17
Kung Pao Chicken (Little Shanghai Cafe) — p. 17
Marinated Turkey Breast with Coriander-Lime Sauce (The Market) — p. 18
Mini Meat (Ground Turkey) Loaves (Turntable Restaurant) — p. 19
Peppered Chicken (Hunan City) — p. 20
Plum Wine Chicken (Golden Dragon) — p. 20
Pollo Asado a la Parrila (Señor Pepe's) — p. 21
Portuguese Chicken (The Bristol at Arrowhead — Introduction) — p. 21
Potato-Stuffed Roast Goose or Turkey (Pepi's Restaurant and Bar) — p. 22
Poulet Alexander Stuffed Chicken Breasts (Le Central) — p. 23
Vit Quay (Roast Duck) (Chez Thoa — Introduction) — p. 24
Sautéed Boneless Quail with Poppies Potato Cake, Raspberry Vinegar Demi Glace Sauce and Fresh Thyme (Poppie's Bistro Cafe) — p. 25
Sesame Chicken Breasts with Lemon Cream (Tamarron Inn) — p. 25

Avocado Pancake filled with
Smoked Duck and Wild Rice

6   eggs
1½ cups milk
2   cups all-purpose flour
1   tablespoon baking powder
14 ounces avocado
5   ounces butter, melted
salt and pepper to taste
2   cups diced smoked duck
2   cups cooked wild rice

Purée the avocado. Beat the eggs, add the milk and mix. Stir in the avocado purée. Sift in the flour and baking powder, blend, do not overmix.

Stir in the melted butter and salt and pepper.

Spread about 3 ounces batter to 4″ diameter in heated skillet. Sprinkle 2-3 tablespoons diced smoked duck and 2-3 tablespoons cooked wild rice on each pancake.

Cook for 4-5 minutes, flip and cook additional 4-5 minutes.

Serve the pancakes on a heated plate with a dollop each of herbed sour cream and salsa and a nice sprig of cilantro. Serves 4 to 6.

Herbed Sour Cream

1   cup sour cream
2   tablespoons mixed herbs - chives, sage, parsley

Salsa

5   tomatoes, seeded and diced
½   red onion, diced
½   cup peeled, diced Anaheim chile
1   tablespoon jalapeno chile, chopped
¼   cup chopped cilantro
2   tablespoons lemon juice
2   tablespoons olive oil
salt and pepper to taste
mix well — best made the day before

THE DEACON'S BENCH

106 Stone
Morrison, Colorado 80465
(303) 697-8211

Baked Chicken in Orange-Almond Sauce

1	fryer, cut into pieces		a dash of ginger
½	teaspoon salt	¼	teaspoon salt
¼	cup butter	1½	cups orange juice
2	tablespoons flour	½	cup sliced almonds
1/8	teaspoon cinnamon	½	cup seedless raisins

Season the chicken pieces with ½ teaspoon salt and brown lightly in butter. Arrange chicken skin side up in a flat baking dish. Add the flour, cinnamon, ginger and ¼ teaspoon salt to the drippings in the skillet to make a smooth paste. Add the orange juice, almonds and raisins to the skillet and stir till thickened and boiling. Pour over chicken. Bake, covered, at 350° for 25 minutes, then uncover and continue baking 30 more minutes. Serves 4.

THE FORT

19192 Highway 8 at U.S. 285 (West Hampden)
Morrison, Colorado 80465
(303) 697-4771 - Morrison
(303) 758-3388 - Denver

Sam Arnold

The Bowl of the Wife of Kit Carson

This wonderfully delicious "dinner-in-a-bowl" is properly called Caldo Tlalpeno, but Kit Carson's grand-daughter, Miss Leona Wood, told me that she remembers eating it as a youngster. The "K.C. Bowl" (as we called it at the Fort) requires a special smoked chile pepper called the chile chipotle adobado, available from Mexican groceries in cans.

¼ cup chopped chicken breast, raw meat
1 cup rich chicken broth
pinch (small) leaf oregano
¼ cup cooked rice
¼ cup cooked garbanzo beans
¼ chopped chipotle pepper
¼ avocado, sliced
¼ cup cubed Monterey Jack or Muenster cheese

Heat broth to boiling — add chicken and other ingredients except cheese and avocado. Serve in large, individual bowls. Add cheese and avocados last, just before serving. Serves 1.

DELFANNIES RESTAURANT

215 East Foothills Parkway
Fort Collins, Colorado 80525
(303) 223-3354

Chef Peter Osterfelt

Campaigne Chicken
(Friendly Country Chicken)

1   six-ounce boneless, skinless chicken breast, floured
2   ounces butter
pinch salt   pinch dried thyme
pinch black pepper   1   artichoke heart, quartered
pinch dried tarragon   2   medium mushrooms, quartered
pinch dried oregano   1   tablespoon diced onions
pinch dried basil   2   ounces white wine
pinch dried parsley   3-4 ounces heavy cream

Sauté chicken breast in butter and dry spices until done. Add mushrooms, artichokes and onions. Deglaze with white wine. Add cream and reduce until sauce will coat the back of a spoon. Serves 1.

CHINA DRAGON RESTAURANT

820 Wilcox Street
Castle Rock, Colorado 80104
(303) 688-2300

Cashew or Almond Chicken

1   teaspoon sugar
¼   cup chicken stock
1   cup celery, diced
1   cup onion, diced
1   cup bamboo shoots
2   tablespoons cornstarch
3   tablespoons soy sauce
8   water chestnuts (optional)
2   tablespoons sherry or rice wine
3   tablespoons peanut oil or salad oil
1   pound uncooked chicken meat, cut into cubes
½   pound almonds or cashews

Mix cornstarch, soy sauce, and sugar and marinate chicken for ½ hour.
Heat pan, add oil and sauté chicken until tender. Add chicken stock to the chicken and heat thoroughly.
All vegetables should be sautéed slightly and added to the chicken mixture. Serve hot. Serves 4 to 8.

STRINGS

1700 Humboldt
Denver, Colorado 80218
(303) 831-7310

Charbroiled Quail with
Shiitake Mushrooms and Wild Rice

8   pieces of quail
16 shiitake mushrooms

Marinade Mix

2   ounces olive oil
reduce ¼ of lemon
4   sprigs fresh thyme
½   clove garlic, diced
salt and pepper

   Marinade quail in mix for ½ hour.
   Charbroil quail until crisp and moist.
   Take 16 shiitake mushrooms (whole — remove stalk). Dip in marinade mix and charbroil.
Serve shiitake mushrooms on top of quail with a light white wine brown sauce.

ASIA

132 West Main Street
Aspen, Colorado
(303) 925-5433

Chestnut Chicken

1   teaspoon salt
1   teaspoon sugar
4   tablespoons soy sauce
2½ cups hot water
½   teaspoon fresh ginger, diced
1   teaspoon sherry or rice wine
2   cups onions, sliced lengthwise
2   tablespoons peanut oil or salad oil
36 chestnuts
½   cup fresh mushrooms, sliced
1   pound uncooked chicken, cut into strips

   Heat half the oil in a saucepan and then add chicken and onion. Sauté until light brown.
Add mushrooms, mix soy sauce, salt, sugar, sherry and cornstarch and add it to the first mixture.
Stir until thickened. Add the hot water, ginger and slightly chopped chestnuts. Boil for 20 to 30
minutes until chicken is tender. Serve hot.

MOTHER LODE

314 East Hyman
Aspen, Colorado 81611
(303) 925-7700

Chicken a la Français

8   ounces boneless chicken breast
4   teaspoons flour
1   egg
1   lemon
1   shot white wine (table wine)
1   teaspoon parsley, finely chopped
2   teaspoons butter
2   teaspoons olive oil

Pound out chicken breast. Dip the chicken in flour and then into beaten egg. Heat the pan and put in the olive oil. When the oil is heated, put the chicken in the pan and saute each side of the chicken. Add the juice of the lemon, white wine and butter. Let simmer for a couple of minutes until the sauce is thickened. Garnish with chopped parsley and serve with vegetables. Serves 1.

THE GOLDEN DOBBIN

519 Wilcox
Castle Rock, Colorado 80104
(303) 688-3786

Chicken a la King

½   cup butter
1   cup flour
4   cups lukewarm chicken stock (or milk)
1   tablespoon salt
½   teaspoon pepper
1   cup fresh mushrooms, sliced
5   cups cooked chicken, diced
½   cup diced pimiento
1   package frozen peas

Make cream sauce with butter, flour and stock. Season with salt and pepper. Sauté mushrooms. Add chicken, pimiento, sauteed mushrooms and cooked peas to cream sauce. Cook slowly for about 10 minutes, stirring constantly. Serve with rice. Serves 8 to 10.

UTE CITY BANQUE

501 East Hyman Avenue
Aspen, Colorado
(303) 925-4374

Chicken Breast Boursin
with Red Wine Sauce (see Sauce section)

4   whole chicken breasts, boned
salt and pepper
4   small, thin slices of prosciutto ham
5   ounces round Boursin cheese
2   tablespoons white wine

Preheat oven to 450°. Skin the chicken breast and sprinkle with seasonings on the inside. Place a thin slice of prosciutto in the center of each breast. Divide cheese into quarters and put one quarter in the center of each breast. Form the breasts around the cheese and ham and place them seam side down into individual buttered casseroles. Place in 450° oven at least 20 minutes or until golden brown. Top each baked chicken casserole with red wine sauce (see Sauce section). Serves 4.

MAXIE'S

600 South Colorado Boulevard
Denver, Colorado 80222
(303) 759-3341 ext. 755

Chicken Breast Tina Louise

8   ounces chicken breast, skinned
2   cups Boursin cheese
¼   cup white wine
2   cups wild rice
mushroom glaze

Mushroom Glaze

2   pounds fresh mushrooms
2   pounds mirepoix
1   tablespoon cornstarch

Glaze: Simmer fresh mushrooms and mirepoix (diced vegetables, herbs and bacon) in water until stock is reduced by ¾. Thicken with corn starch. Strain sauce through china cup.

Skin and tenderize chicken breast. Fill with Boursin cheese and broccoli buds. Dust lightly with flour and place small amount of olive oil in sauté pan. Brown chicken breast lightly, then place in 350° oven and finish baking until breast is done, about 20 mintues. Place chicken breast on bed of wild rice. Sauté mushrooms in white wine. Place mushrooms on top of chicken and add mushrooms glaze and serve immediately. Serves 1.

MARINA LANDING

8101 East Belleview
Denver, Colorado
(303) 770-4741

Chicken Green Chili Stew

3 large onions, diced large
2 pounds large diced raw chicken, boned and skinned
4 seeded jalapeños, diced fine
1 tablespoon fresh garlic, diced fine
1 teaspoon black pepper
½ cup chopped fresh cilantro
10 cups chicken stock (see recipe)
2 large cans green chilies, cut into strips
1 large can hominy, drained
butter to saute chicken
½ cup flour
2 tablespoons chicken base
salt and pepper to taste

Salt and pepper chicken and toss in flour coating well. Sauté floured chicken in butter until lightly browned. Add onion, jalapeños, garlic and sauté lightly. Add chicken stock and bring to a boil. Add green chili and simmer approximately 40 mintues. Add cilantro, chicken base, hominy and cook 15 minutes. Serves 6.

SWEET BASIL

193 East Gore Creek Drive
Vail, Colorado 81657
(303) 476-0125

Chicken Kiev

4 chicken breasts, boneless
4 tablespoons butter, unsalted
1 tablespoon fresh parsley, chopped
2 cloves garlic, minced
1 teaspoon dijon mustard
salt and pepper
1 tablespoon chives, minced
¾ cup flour
3 eggs, beaten
1 cup bread crumbs
oil to fry

Pound chicken breasts between sheets of plastic wrap until ½-inch thick. Combine butter, parsley, garlic, mustard, salt, pepper and chives to make herb butter. Divide this herb butter into 4 parts and place 1 part in the center of each chicken breast. Roll each breast and twist gently so that ends are well closed. Dredge breasts with flour, then eggs, then bread crumbs. Refrigerate for at least 20 mintues. Bake at 450° until browned and fully cooked. Serves 4.

THE GOLDEN EAGLE INN

Village Hall
Vail-Beaver Creek, Colorado
(303) 949-1940

Beaver Creek Resort and The Golden Eagle Inn complement each other. Vail pioneer restaurateur Pepi Langegger saw the need in this fast growing, world-class resort. Don Bird, Pepi's longtime assistant at the Tyrolean Inn, and Steve Jones, another valuable and dedicated assistant, make guests' visits to The Golden Eagle a time to remember. Although The Golden Eagle Inn's "Chicken Parmigiana" is "top secret," here is a chef's popular alternative variation.

Chicken Marengo

2	3-pound frying chickens
¼	cup vegetable oil
1	onion, thinly sliced
3	tablespoons brandy
2	1-pound cans Italian tomatoes, drained
½	cup dry white wine
2	cloves of garlic, pressed
½	teaspoon dried thyme
1	bay leaf
4	sprigs of fresh parsley
1	cup basic chicken stock
1	teaspoon salt
½	teaspoon freshly ground pepper
1	cup small cleaned shrimp
½	pound fresh mushrooms, sliced
¼	cup butter
2	tablespoons lemon juice
2	tablespoons freshly minced parsley

Remove the skin from the chickens, then cut each chicken into quarters. Pour the oil into a large, heavy skillet and place over medium heat until hot. Add the onion slices and sauté, stirring frequently, until golden brown. Remove the onions from the skillet with a slotted spoon and set aside. Add the chicken to the oil remaining in the skillet and cook until browned on all sides. Heat the brandy and pour over the chicken. Ignite the brandy and flame, shaking the skillet until the flame dies. Place the tomatoes in a blender container and process until puréed. Add to the skillet. Add the wine, garlic, thyme, bay leaf, sprigs of parsley, stock, tomatoes, salt and pepper and sautéed onions. Cover the skillet and simmer for 1 hour or until the chicken is tender. Remove the chicken from the sauce and keep warm. Strain the sauce, if desired. Add the shrimp to the sauce and simmer for 5 minutes. Saute the mushrooms in the butter in a saucepan until tender, then stir in the lemon juice. Add to the sauce and heat through. Arrange the chicken pieces on a heated serving platter and pour the sauce over the chicken. Sprinkle with the minced parsley. Garnish with croutons. Serves 8.

RUDI'S

4720 Table Mesa Drive
Boulder, Colorado 80303
(303) 494-5858

Chef Faith Stone

Chicken Quenelles with Mushroom Sauce

1½ pounds raw chicken breasts, skinned and boned
3   eggs
1½ cup heavy cream
¾   teaspoon tarragon
¾   teaspoon salt
dash freshly grated nutmeg
½   ground white pepper
2   dashes Tabasco
3   cups chicken stock
garnish — 2 tablespoons green onions, sliced
             1 tablespoon freshly grated Romano

Chop the raw chicken meat. Put it in the container of a blender or food processor with the eggs, cream and process to a smooth paste. Mix in the tarragon, salt, nutmeg and Tabasco.

Chill the mixture while making mushroom sauce. Recipe follows.

Keep sauce warm while heating stock for poaching quenelles. Bring the stock to a simmer and drop in quenelle mixture 1 tablespoon at a time. Poach for 10-15 minutes or until cooled through. Cut one in half to check. Cook the quenelles in several batches to keep them from overcrowding the pan.

Drain the cooked quenelles and keep warm on a platter. Spoon the hot mushroom cream over the platter and garnish with sliced green onions and a sprinkle of Romano.

Mushroom Cream

3   tablespoons butter
½   pound Colorado mushrooms wiped to remove dirt
2   cloves garlic
2   cups heavy cream
½   teaspoon salt
pinch pepper and grated nutmeg
¼   cup sherry

In a heavy saucepan bring the cream to a simmer and cook until reduced by half. Meanwhile melt the butter in a skillet and saute the garlic and mushrooms until tender, but not mushy. Then stir the mushrooms into the reduced cream and season with salt, pepper, nutmeg and sherry. Serves 6.

CHINA TERRACE

1512 Larimer Street
Denver, Colorado 80202
(303) 592-1032

Chicken with Garlic Sauce

⅓   ounce wan yee (tree) mushrooms
2   teaspoons hoisin sauce
2   teaspoons soy sauce
2   teaspoons cooking sherry
2   teaspoons vinegar
½   teaspoon salt
2   dashes chili oil*
2   dashes white pepper
12 ounces chicken breast meat
3   tablespoons soybean oil
¼   ounce ginger root, finely chopped
1   clove garlic, finely chopped
3   ounces water chestnuts, shredded
2   ounces water
1   green onion, finely chopped
1   teaspoon cornstarch dissolved in 2 tablespoons water

Soak wan yee mushrooms in warm water for ½ hour. Cut chicken into very small pieces. Mix together hoisin sauce, soy sauce, cooking sherry, vinegar, salt, chili oil and white pepper to make a sauce. Heat oil in wok over very high heat. Fry ginger root and garlic, then add chicken meat and stir-fry for 1 minute. Add wan yee mushrooms and water chestnuts, then add water. Cook another minute. Pour in the sauce and stir for about 30 seconds. Add cornstarch mixture. Serve immediately with steamed rice. Serves 1 to 2.

*Chili oil can be made by adding Szechuan dried peppers to olive oil or sesame oil and letting them blend together over a period of 1 week.

CHANTICLER

710 West Lionshead Circle
Vail-Lionshead, Colorado
(303) 476-1441

Vail is blessed with some of the world's best skiing. Vail is also blessed with some of Colorado's finest restaurants. At the Chanticler restaurant, guests' host Thomas Lundgaard and Chef Arnold have created a dining experience one will not want to miss and will be certain to remember. Relax and enjoy superb continental dining in a charming country French atmosphere.

Chicken with Orange Sauce *

1   tender chicken, jointed (or duck)
salt and cayenne
3   tablespoons butter or olive oil
12   almonds
½   cup seeded raisins
1   cup pineapple, chopped
1/8 teaspoon ground cloves
1/8 teaspoon ground cinnamon
2   cups orange juice
1   tablespoon flour
garnish: avocado slices and pomegranate pips

Season chicken and brown pieces on all sides in olive oil. Blanch almonds. Remove skins; chop and add with raisins, pineapple, spices and orange juice. Cover tightly and simmer until chicken is tender. Work flour smooth with 2 tablespoons cold water and add here and there, shaking pan to mix well. Simmer 5-8 minutes until gravy thickens. Take up chicken on hot platter. Pour some of the gravy over the garnish platter with half-moon slices of avocado and pomegranate pips. Serve remaining gravy in a gravy boat.
Serves 4 to 6.

*variation

JOHN'S RESTAURANT

2328 Pearl
Boulder, Colorado 80304
(303) 444-5232

Chicken with Red Chiles, Mint and Oregon Raspberry Wine

4   boneless chicken breasts, skin on
2   tablespoons ground red New Mexican chile
3   cloves garlic
2   tablespoons flour
2   tablespoons olive oil
1   teaspoon butter
pinch of teaspoon oregano and thyme
dash of worcestershire
2   teaspoons sugar
few sprigs of fresh mint
4   ounces Oregon Raspberry Wine (such as Paul Thomas)
fresh red raspberries

Start with 4 boneless chicken breasts (skin on) and rub with garlic. Sprinkle with salt and a little ground red New Mexican chiles. Dust lightly with flour. Brown on both sides in a large, heavy skillet with two tablespoons of olive oil. When brown, pour off all oil and any rendered chicken fat.

Add to pan two cloves of garlic (chopped), one teaspoon butter, one teaspoon mild red New Mexican chile powder, ¼ teaspoon each oregano and thyme, two teaspoons sugar, one sprig of fresh mint. Sauté together one minute fifteen seconds.

Add two teaspoons of flour to pan and stir in, deglaze pan while stirring with four ounces of raspberry wine and a dash of worcestershire sauce.

Simmer one minute with low to medium heat until sauce has thickened to sauce-like consistency. Place chicken breasts on platter and finish in oven at 350°, strain sauce and spoon into chicken. Garnish with mint tops and fresh red raspberries. Serves 4.

CRAFTWOOD INN

404 El Paso Boulevard
Colorado Springs-Manitou Springs, Colorado
(719) 685-9000

Owners Rob Stephens and Cris Pulos, longtime standout local chefs, have restored this grand old Tudor-style mansion. The decor is subdued and romantic with great views of Pikes Peak and lots of tucked away twosome tables and earned the award "Most romantic restaurant" in *Best of the Springs 1989*.

The menu is varied and seasonal featuring pheasant, quail, duck, venison and seafood.

Cornish Hen Glazed with Orange and Ginger*

1   Cornish hen (1½ to 2 pounds), skinned
¼   teaspoon each dried sage and rosemary, crumbled
1   clove garlic, crushed
1   teaspoon minced fresh ginger or ¼ teaspoon ground ginger
¼   teaspoon black pepper
1   strip orange peel, 3 inches long and ½ inch wide
1   tablespoon olive oil
¼   cup orange juice
1   tablespoon honey
1   tablespoon St. Mary's Gourmet Vinegar
1   teaspoon grated orange rind

Preheat the oven to 375°. Remove and discard all excess fat from the hen. Rub the body cavity with the sage, rosemary, garlic, ½ teaspoon of the ginger, and $1/8$ teaspoon of the pepper; tuck the strip of orange peel inside.

Truss the hen, place breast side up on a rack in a shallow roasting pan, brush with the olive oil, and sprinkle with the remaining pepper. Roast, uncovered, for 35 to 40 minutes or until a leg moves easily in the hip socket.

While the hen roasts, combine the orange juice, honey, vinegar, mustard, and remaining ginger in a small saucepan, and bring to boil over moderately high heat. Adjust the heat so that the mixture bubbles gently and simmer, uncovered, stirring often, for 5 minutes or until the mixture is syrupy; set aside.

When the hen is done, transfer it to a carving board and halve lengthwise. Increase the oven temperature to broil. Return the hen to the roasting pan, breast side up, and spoon the orange and honey sauce over each half. Place in the broiler, 4 to 5 inches from the heat, and broil for 2 to 3 minutes or until the hen is golden brown. Sprinkle with the grated orange rind and serve. Serves 2.

*variation

H. BRINKER'S

I-25 and Arapahoe Road
Denver, Colorado
(303) 792-0285

   H. Brinker's represents a departure from any other Denver restaurant. Its facade is dominated by a 70-foot windmill, and the vanes can be seen for miles.
   The plank boardwalk leading up to H. Brinker's entrance and the water wheel that flows water gracefully into a pond enhances the Dutch influence and decor.
   The cocktail lounge is built under and around the windmill and one can actually see it working for stories high.
   H. Brinker's has an extensive menu specializing in mesquite grilled fresh fish, steak, prime rib slow cooked in their special ovens, and pan-fried trout from their 800-gallon fresh fish tank.
   The Executive Chef is a master in New American Cuisine and creates exciting daily specials that use the freshest herbs and spices. Two honorable mentions would include H. Brinker's grilled shrimp wrapped in pro-scuitto and mixed with a lemon pasta in a zesty lemon cream sauce; or the Dutch Pepper Steak which is a New York strip finished in a six blend peppercorn Brandy cream sauce.
   Of course, everyone's passionate conviction of Brinker's Pie, and Buttermilk Chocolate Cake with Chocolate genache sauce are awaiting guests.
   For two consecutive years, H. Brinker's has been awarded "Favorite Place for Weekend Brunch."

Duck with Orange and Grand Marnier Sauce

2   4-pound ducks
2   oranges
1   tablespoon brown sugar
1   teaspoon tomato paste
2   teaspoons honey
¼   cup Grand Marnier
flour

   Roast the ducks, carve into slices and keep warm. Break up the bones of the carcass and put with roasting juices into a saucepan with juice and pared rind of the orange. Add 2 teaspoons of the sugar, tomato paste, honey and Grand Marnier. Allow to boil for 3-4 minutes. In a separate saucepan, brown the remaining sugar. Add the strained orange mixture, skim the top and thicken the sauce with flour. Serve with sauteed fine green beans, peas, asparagus and zucchini. Serves 4.

SWEET BASIL

193 East Gore Creek Drive
Vail, Colorado 81657
(303) 476-0125

Grilled Achiote Chicken with Chipolte Salsa
and Shallot Sauce (see Sauces and Dressings section)

½   cup achiote (crushed annatte seeds)
¼   cup lemon juice
2   cups orange juice
2   tablespoons fresh or 1 tablespoon dried oregano
2   tablespoons minced garlic
3½ pound free range chicken, cut into serving portions

Season the chicken with salt and fresh pepper. Coat with achiote mixture and refrigerate for 24 hours.

Prepare Shallot Sauce and Chipolte Sauce and Black Bean Tortilla (see Bread section).

To assemble: Grill the achiote chicken over mesquite or applewood. Cook until medium rare, then let sit 5 minutes to rest. Grill again 1 minute then serve.

Spoon Shallot sauce onto plate.

Cook tortilla and place on top of sauce.

Top with Chipolte Salsa, chicken and sautéed spinach.

FIREFLY CAFE

5410 East Colfax Avenue
(303) 388-8429

Grilled Breast of Chicken with Avocado
Cream Sauce with Sundried Tomatoes

6   boneless, skinless chicken breasts about 6 ounces each

Avocado Cream Sauce

1   pint heavy cream   salt
3   shallots, minced   ½   teaspoon vegetable oil for grilling the chicken
3   ounces white wine   ½   cup soaked sundried tomatoes
1   avocado, pureed

Heat an iron skillet over high heat and add enough of the oil to leave a film on the skillet. Season the breasts lightly with salt and white pepper and pan grill on each side, approximately 3 minutes per side or until golden brown. Remove the breasts and cover to keep warm until service.

After removing the breasts from the skillet, reduce the heat to medium high and add the shallots and deglaze with the wine. Reduce the wine until it is almost evaporated. Add the cream and reduce by about ⅓ and add the avocado. Adjust the seasoning with salt and pepper.

On the serving plates place a pool of the sauce and top with the grilled chicken breasts. Serve with vegetable garnish and the starch of one's choice. The Firefly Cafe recommends plain sauteed summer squashes with basil and roast new potatoes with garlic, salt and pepper. Serves 6.

DUGGAN'S

South Federal at Belleview
Denver, Colorado
(303) 795-1081

An Irish hunting lodge provided the inspiration for this warm neighborhood gathering place. Duggan's is located in Denver's southwest area at Belleview and South Federal. In addition to being a congenial, well-run, bustling neighborhood restaurant, Duggan's has a wonderful kitchen. The menu could be best described as "something of everyone's taste." In a nutshell — "GREAT American Country Cooking" such as Yankee Pot Roast and meatloaf with apples.

The variety, choice and reasonable price range are as significant as the personal supervision and care that goes into Duggan's food quality.

Duggan's is famous for its weekend brunch and has been awarded for that mention the past three years in Denver's Dining Out Survey.

The chef has developed a style to satisfy the patrons and in the process has expanded everyone's taste.

Specialties include some Southwestern dishes, BBQ ribs, great Mexican food, steak and fresh seafood.

The desserts satisfy one's old-fashioned American sweet tooth with Hot Fudge Brownie Sundaes and Armenian Bread Pudding.

The ambiance of Duggan's reminds one of an Irish Country Club: friendly, generous, unpretentious. People in the immediate neighborhood treat it as their dining room away from home.

Jalapeño Lime Marinated Chicken with Corn Bread Dressing

4   chicken breasts, skin on
2   tablespoons garlic salt
2   medium jalapeños
2   tablespoons chopped cilantro (finely chopped)
½   cup lime juice
½   cup olive oil
1   cup chicken stock

Rub chicken with garlic salt, cilantro. Purée jalapeños in blender using just enough lime to moisten. Rub over chicken. (Be certain to wash hands well afterwards).

Place chicken in non-metallic container, cover with remaining lime juice and olive oil. (Let marinate at least 2 hours).

Prepare Corn Bread Dressing (see below).

Sauté chicken in two tablespoons oil, skin side down until brown. Turn chicken over; cook 2 minutes and then add chicken stock to pan. Bring to a boil and place in a 375° oven approximately 10 minutes.

Remove chicken to plate and keep warm. Reduce sauce in pan for 1 to 2 minutes. Pour over chicken. Place dressing next to chicken and garnish with cilantro. Serves 4.

CHAO-PRAYA THAI RESTAURANT AND LOUNGE

5411 Quebec Street
Commerce City, Colorado
(303) 287-2210

Kai Yang
(Garlic Chicken)

2   pounds chicken breasts
6   cloves garlic, crushed
2   teaspoons salt
2   tablespoons black peppercorns, coarsely ground
4   bunches fresh coriander, including roots
2   tablespoons lemon juice

Cut breasts in halves. Crush garlic with salt. Wash and chop fine the fresh coriander, including roots, stems and leaves. Mix garlic, salt, peppercorns, coriander and lemon juice and rub into the chicken breasts. Cover and let stand for at least 1 hour or overnight in refrigerator. Put under a hot grill approximately 6 inches from heat. Cook, turning every 5 minutes until chicken is tender and skin crisp. Serve with boiled rice, fresh tomatoes sliced and seasoned with a dash of chili powder and salt and lemon juice to taste. Serves 4.

NOTE: This is especially good cooked on a barbecue grill.

LITTLE SHANGHAI CAFE

460 South Broadway
Denver, Colorado 80209
(303) 777-9838/722-1292

Kung Pao Chicken

Peanut oil for frying
½   pound boneless chicken meat
    clove garlic, chopped
3   dried chili peppers
1   tablespoon hoisin sauce
1   bell pepper, chopped
½   pound sliced bamboo shoots
2   tablespoons soy sauce
½   carrot, finely cubed
3   tablespoons water

a few drops sesame oil

Heat oil in a wok over high heat for 5 minutes. Add chicken and fry until brown. Pour off all but 2 tablespoons of oil. Saute garlic, peppers and hoisin sauce for 45 seconds to 1 minute. Add all the rest of ingredients except water and sesame oil. Stir-fry for 1 to 1½ minutes, then add water and cook for another 1 to 1½ minutes. Add a few drops of sesame oil on top and serve. Serves 2.

THE MARKET

1445 Larimer
Denver, Colorado 80020
(303) 534-5140

Marinated Turkey Breast
with Coriander-Lime Sauce

Broiling the turkey breast before roasting browns it and seals in the juices; so if your broiler and oven operate on one dial, don't forget to reduce the temperature after you're finished broiling.

1   whole turkey breast with bone (about 8 pounds) thaw if frozen

Marinade

½   cup dry white wine
¼   cup dark oriental sesame oil
¼   cup soy sauce
3   tablespoons fresh lemon juice
4   teaspoons minced garlic
1   tablespoon fresh thyme or 1 teaspoon dried
1   teaspoon crushed red pepper

Coriander-Lime Sauce

2½ cups mayonnaise
2   cups loosely packed fresh coriander (cilantro)
3   teaspoons fresh lime juice
1½ tablespoons seeded and finely chopped fresh jalapeno pepper
1   tablespoon soy sauce
2   teaspoons minced garlic
1½ teaspoons dijon mustard

Garnish: fresh coriander leaves or parsley.

Remove skin from the turkey, then cut each breast half from the bone in one piece (or have the butcher do it). You should have about 6 pounds of meat.

Mix all marinade ingredients in a large glass, earthenware or stainless-steel bowl. Add turkey breasts, and turn to coat well on all sides. Cover and refrigerate at least 12 hours or overnight or leave at room temperature for 2 hours.

Mix Coriander-Lime Sauce ingredients in a large bowl. Keep refrigerated until ready to serve.

Remove turkey from marinade (reserve marinade) and place skinned side up in a shallow roasting pan. Broil 2 to 3 inches from heat source 10 to 12 minutes, without turning, until browned.

Heat over to 375°. Pour reserved marinade over turkey. Roast 50 to 60 minutes until juices run clear when meat is pierced with a knife. Remove from oven and let stand 10 minutes.

Slice turkey across the grain and arrange on a platter. Garnish with fresh coriander or parsley. Pass sauce separately, and let guests spoon on amount they wish. Serves 8 to 12.

TURNTABLE RESTAURANT
Exit 171
Vail-Minturn, Colorado
(303) 827-4164

Mini Meat (Ground Turkey) Loaves

1   tablespoon olive oil
2   small carrots, peeled and chopped fine
1   medium-size yellow onion, chopped fine
½   small sweet green pepper, cored, seeded, and chopped fine
2   cloves minced garlic
½   small sweet red pepper, cored, seeded, and chopped fine
1   teaspoon dried sage, crumbled
1   large egg white, lightly beaten
1   pound lean ground turkey
1   cup soft white bread crumbs (2 slices)
⅓   cup homemade ketchup (see Sauce section)
2   ounces Swiss cheese, cut into ¼ inch cubes
¼   teaspoon black pepper

Melt the olive oil in a medium-size heavy saucepan over low heat. Add the carrot, onion, green pepper, red pepper, garlic, and sage; cook, covered, stirring occasionally, until the vegetables are soft — 8 to 10 minutes.

Preheat the oven to 375°. In a large bowl, combine the egg white, ground turkey, bread crumbs, ketchup, cheese and black pepper. Add the cooked vegetables and mix well.

Place 10 2½-inch foil cupcake liners in the cups of 1 large or 2 small muffin pans. Spoon ⅓ cup of the turkey-vegetable mixture into each of the lined cups. Bake, uncovered, for 25 to 30 minutes or until the meat loaves are lightly browned and firm to the touch.

Cool the meat loaves in the pan upright on a wire rack for 10 minutes, then cover the pan with plastic wrap and refrigerate until ready to serve. Remove the meat loaves and wrap each one in plastic or aluminum foil. Makes 10 small meat loaves.

HUNAN CITY

7115 Sheridan
Arvada, Colorado 80002
(303) 429-4825

Peppered Chicken*

1   teaspoon salt
1   cup chicken soup stock (see Soup section)
1   hot pepper, diced
1   tablespoon cider vinegar
1   cup onions, diced
3   tablespoons soy sauce
4   green peppers, diced
1   green cucumber, diced
2   hot red peppers, diced
1   pound uncooked chicken meat cut into 1½-inch pieces
peanut oil for frying

Marinate chicken meat with 2 tablespoons cider vinegar, soy sauce and 1 cup chicken stock for 2 hours. Fry chicken in deep peanut oil until brown and tender. Drain. Sauté all vegetables with remaining ingredients and stir constantly. Combine meat and vegetables. Serve hot. Vegetables may be made in advance and reheated with chicken meat. Serves 4 to 6.

*variation

GOLDEN DRAGON

903 South Eighth Street
Colorado Springs, Colorado 80906
(719) 632-3607

Plum Wine Chicken

6   ounces chicken breast, diced
½   ounces snow peas
1½   ounces broccoli
1½   ounces mushrooms, sliced
1½   ounces white onion, chopped
½   cup chicken stock or water
1   ounce plum wine
1   tablespoon Ai Kan Sweet & Spicy Sauce
1-2 teaspoons corn starch

Blanch the broccoli and set aside. Heat the oil in a wok or saucepan and stir-fry the chicken. Add vegetable and chicken stock/water. Stir and add the seasonings. Bring to a boil and simmer for a few minutes (1-2 minutes) or until the vegetables change color. Add corn starch to thicken the gravy. Serve with rice. Serves 1.

SEÑOR PEPE'S
1422 Poplar Street
Denver, Colorado 80220
(303) 321-1911

Pollo Asado a la Parrila

½ frying chicken
olive oil
salt and pepper
lemon juice

Wash and dry fryer half; sprinkle with salt and pepper to taste. Coat with oil and lemon juice and place on broiler. When side of fryer close to the fire is fairly brown, turn to other side and coat with oil and lemon juice, so it will be nice and moist. Cook until second side is brown. Serves 1 to 3.

THE BRISTOL AT ARROWHEAD
Post Office Box 960
Edwards, Colorado
(303) 926-2111

Chef Dennis Corwin and owner Jim King have worked together for more than eight years — first at the Clubhouse Restaurant at the Vail Golf Course and now in their fourth year at The Bristol. Chef Corwin is a graduate of the Culinary Institute of America. King got his start in the bar and restaurant business while in Washington, D.C. The ambiance, decor and great food are all pluses at The Bristol.

Here is a variation of some of their nightly changing specials.

Portuguese Chicken

1   large fryer, cut up
1   small jar pimientos
1   small jar artichoke hearts
3   tablespoons capers
1   cup stuffed green olives
1   medium can pear tomatoes or 1 cup chopped fresh tomatoes
½   pound fresh mushrooms, sliced
juice of 2 lemons
4   cloves garlic, minced
1   teaspoon crumbled oregano leaves
4   tablespoons olive oil

Place chicken in an 8½ by 11 inch pan. Pour all ingredients over the top and place in a 350° oven for 1 hour. Turn the chicken frequently and make sure it is covered with the vegetable mixture. When the chicken is done, remove to a hot plate and spoon all ingredients over it. Serve over rice.

PEPI'S RESTAURANT AND BAR

Gasthof Gramshammer
231 East Gore Creek Drive
Vail, Colorado
(303) 476-5626

Pepi's Restaurant is a cornerstone in Vail's fine dining and a "must experience" for every Vail visitor. This great restaurant has traditional continental fare as well as unique, wild game dishes. Here is a variation of one of their wild game dishes.

Potato-Stuffed Roast Goose or Turkey

Potato Stuffing

3   cups hot mashed potatoes
1   large onion, diced
3   tablespoons minced fresh parsley
½   cup celery, diced
2   egg whites, beaten
¼   teaspoon marjoram
1   teaspoon sage

Mix together all ingredients. Let cool and fill cavity of bird.

Goose

1   goose, 10 to 12 pounds
¼   cup St. Mary's Gourmet Vinegar
fresh cracked white peppercorns
6   cloves garlic, minced
2   cups St. Mary's Style Chicken Stock (see Soup section)
2   tablespoons celery seed
½   cup low-sodium soy sauce

Dip cloth in St. Mary's Gourmet Vinegar and sop goose inside and out (this will tenderize goose). Mix cracked peppercorns and minced garlic and rub goose inside and out with mixture. Stuff goose with potato stuffing and place breast side up in roasting pan. Mix soy and celery seed and pour over goose. Place in a 350° preheated oven for 2 hours. Afterwards, baste goose with pan drippings every 10 minutes for the next 30 minutes. Serves 8.

LE CENTRAL
112 East Eighth Avenue
Denver, Colorado 80203
(303) 863-8094

Poulet Alexander Stuffed Chicken Breasts

6   boneless chicken breasts
4   tart apples
½ to ¾ cup Roquefort cheese
1   pint ricotta cheese
1   pint sour cream
1   teaspoon thyme
1   teaspoon salt
juice of ½ lemon
2   ounces of cognac
½   cup chopped parsley
1½ cups bread crumbs
1   quart chicken stock
Curry-Ginger Sauce (see Sauce section)

Pound chicken breasts to uniform ¼-inch thickness. Set aside. Core and dice apples. Place in large bowl and mix in all other ingredients except chicken stock. Mold a large handful of stuffing into an oblong ball. Place it on one side of a pounded breast, wrapping the rest of the breast to cover all stuffing. Repeat for all breasts. Steam over rich chicken stock until done. Top with Curry-Ginger Sauce. Serves 6.

CHEZ THOA

158 Fillmore
Denver, Colorado 80206
(303) 355-6464

To enter Chez Thoa is to experience an envelopment in tasteful decor of mauves, burgundies, beiges, and etched glass. Long-stemmed, fresh roses on each table. The quality of decor, cleanliness, and good taste hints of the delicious creations that consistently come from the kitchen which have earned Chez Thoa's rave restaurant reviews. The petite and beautiful proprietor-hostess, Thoa Fink, offers a wonderful combination of French-Vietnamese cuisine. Spicy shrimp, marvelous soups such as the crab-asparagus cream, wonderful veals, a delicate lemon chicken and more greet guests. At lunchtime fashionable shoppers and Cherry Creek business professionals crowd into Chez Thoa. At night, with candles glowing from each table, the who's who of Colorado and connoisseurs of good eating can be seen experiencing the dining pleasures of this wonderful restaurant, Chez Thoa.

Vit Quay
(Roast Duck)

3   green onions, mashed
½   tablespoon soy sauce
1   tablespoon five-spice powder
¼   cup sugar
½   cup white wine
¼   cup orange juice
1   tablespoon fresh ginger, mashed
2   ducks
3   quarts water
½   package dried rice noodles
2   green onions, minced
2   tablespoons olive oil
hoisin sauce (available at oriental grocery)

Combine first seven ingredients to make a marinade sauce. Marinate the ducks overnight (the longer the better), turning several times. Pour some marinade inside the duck. Preheat oven to 350°. Place ducks on a rack in roasting pan in the oven. Roast for 45 minutes, then reduce heat to 300°. Roast for 1 hour longer, turning twice. While roasting the duck baste with remaining marinade. Meanwhile, bring water to a boil, add the noodles and boil for maximum of 5 minutes. Drain through a colander under cold running water. Allow the noodles to dry. Set aside. Sauté minced onions in oil. Arrange the noodles on a large platter, pour the sautéed green onions over. Bone and cut the duck into bite-sized pieces. Arrange it on a platter. Serve with rice noodles and hoisin sauce. Serves 4.

POPPIE'S BISTRO CAFE

834 West Hallan
Aspen, Colorado 81611
(303) 925-2333

Sautéed Boneless Quail
with Poppies Potato Cake (see Vegetable section)
Raspberry Vinegar Demi Glace Sauce
and Fresh Thyme (see Sauce section)

4	semi-boneless quail		½	cup clarified butter
	whole thyme sprigs		2	teaspoons olive oil

Use hot black, steel pan. Pour in clarified butter. Place quails in pan, skin side down. Sauté till crisp, flip over. Cook till medium rare. Drain excess oil. Place cooked quail on plate. Prepare Raspberry Vinegar Demi Glace Sauce (see Sauce section). Ladle sauce onto quail. Garnish with thyme sprigs. Serve Poppie's Potato Pancakes (see Vegetable section) with the quails. Serves 2.

TAMARRON INN

Le Canyon Gourmet Room
40292 U.S. Highway 550
Durango, Colorado
(303) 247-8801, ext. 1123

Sesame Chicken Breasts with Lemon Cream*

Sauce Ingredients:

½	pint cream
1	egg yolk
5	teaspoons lemon juice or 1 whole lemon
2	tablespoons dry white wine
1	tablespoon powdered chicken stock base
½	teaspoon dijon mustard
¼	teaspoon salt
½	teaspoon onion powder
1	teaspoon dry chives
2	dashes white pepper
½	teaspoon flour
2	cups fresh mushrooms, sliced, stems removed

Mix all ingredients, except mushrooms, in a saucepan. Cook over medium-high heat and simmer until reduced to medium-thick sauce. Stir often and fold in mushrooms before serving.

Sesame Chicken

Brown 4 boneless chicken breasts (skins removed) in butter until almost done. Remove and dip chicken pieces in beaten egg, coat chicken with mixture of rolled sesame crackers and whole sesame seeds and place in shallow pan under broiler until brown. Spoon sauce over chicken and serve on a bed of your favorite seasoned rice. Serves 4.

*Recipe created by Kurt Chiles, variation

ENTREES MEAT X

ENTRÉES MEAT, X

Armenian Shish Kebab (Mataam Fez at Vail) — p. 1
Beef Stroganoff (Sopris Restaurant and Lounge — Introduction) — p. 2
Bolivian Chili (Muddy's Java Cafe — Introduction) — p. 3
Bresaola (Spice Cured Beef Tenderloin) (Bibelot Restaurant) — p. 4
Côte de Boeuf Bordelaise (Left Bank — Introduction) — p. 5
Cuisses De Grenouilles Au Riesling or Frog Legs in Riesling Wine (Normandy French Restaurant) — p. 6
The Golden Dobbin Meatloaf (The Golden Dobbin) — p. 6
Hazelnut Crusted Colorado Rack of Lamb (Cliff Young's Restaurant — Introduction) — p. 7
Hot Shredded Spiced Beef (Milan's — Introduction) — p. 8
Kapusta (Soren's) — p. 9
Lamb Chops Parmesan (Maxie's) — p. 9
Lamb Chops with Barbecue Sauce (The Charter — First Season) — p. 10
Lamb Shanks for Six (The Wildflower Inn — Introduction) — p. 11
Loin of Lamb with Sweet Peppers in Strudel (Flagstaff House Restaurant) — p. 12
Manchurian Beef (China Sun Restaurant) — p. 12
Ma-Po Style Bean Curd (China Terrace — Introduction) — p. 13
Marinated Sirloin Steak (Rick's Cafe) — p. 14
Meat Balls with Egg-Lemon Sauce (Monaco Inn) — p. 14
Mongolian Beef (Little Shanghai) — p. 15
Moroccan Couscous (Mataam Fez at Vail) — p. 16
Pariser Schnitzel (The Golden Horn) — p. 17
Paté Maison (Le Central — Introduction) — p. 18
Pork Cutlets (Hotel Sonnenalp) — p. 19
Rabbit Loin Stuffed with Cornbread and Andoville Sausage (Cliff Young's Restaurant) — p. 19
Roast Crown of Lamb Bouquetière (Brown Palace) — p. 20
Roast Leg of Lamb Venison (Gold Hill Inn) — p. 21
Roast Pork (Imperial Chinese Seafood Restaurant) — p. 21
Roast Venison (Black Forest Inn — Introduction) — p. 22
Sauerbraten (Black Forest Inn) — p. 23
Scaloppine di Vitella al Marsala (Abetone Restaurant) — p. 23
Steak Tartare (Brown Palace — Introduction) — p. 24
Stuffed Breast of Veal with Marsala Wine Sauce (St. Bernard Inn — Introduction) — p. 25
Sukiyaki (Takah Sushi) — p. 26
Sweet and Sour Pork with Pineapple and Peppers (Little Shanghai) — p. 27
Sweetbreads aux Marsala (Cafe Giovanni — Introduction) — p. 28
Thai Sausage (T-WA Inn) — p. 29
Tian of Colorado Lamb with Shiitake Mushrooms, Spinach, Tomatoes (Bibelot Restaurant — Introduction) — p. 30-31
Tournedos au Poivre Vert (The Tower Magic Bar & Restaurant) — p. 32
Tournedos Diane (Wellshire Inn) — p. 32
Tournedos Toscana (The Greenbriar) — p. 33
Veal A La Oscar (The Red Onion) — p. 33
Veal with Roasted Red Bell Peppers Beurre Blanc (Fern's Restaurant-Denver Hilton South) — p. 34
Veal with Rosemary Chili Sauce and Walnuts (Piñon's) — p. 34
Wiener Schnitzel (Wienerstube Restaurant) — p. 35

MATAAM FEZ AT VAIL

Vail Run Building in Sandstone
Vail, Colorado
(303) 476-1818

Armenian Shish Kebab

½ cup vegetable oil
¼ cup lemon juice
1 teaspoon salt
1 teaspoon marjoram
1 teaspoon thyme
½ teaspoon freshly ground pepper
1 clove of garlic, halved
¼ cup chopped onion
2 tablespoons minced fresh parsley
2 pounds boneless leg of lamb, cut into 1½-inch cubes
16 mushroom caps
4 tomatoes, quartered
2 green sweet peppers, cut into large squares
2 Spanish onions, cut into eighths

Combine the oil, lemon juice, salt, marjoram, thyme, pepper, garlic, chopped onion and parsley for marinade. Pour the marinade over the lamb cubes. Cover and refrigerate for 6 hours or longer. Remove the lamb from the marinade and drain on paper towels. Spear the lamb cubes, mushroom caps, tomato quarters, green pepper squares and onion quarters alternately on skewers. Broil over a barbecue grill or in the oven broiler, turning occasionally, until cooked to desired degree of doneness. Push foods off the skewers onto plates with the back of a fork to serve. Sixteen cherry tomatoes may be substituted for quartered tomatoes. Serves 8.

SOPRIS RESTAURANT AND LOUNGE

7215 Highway 82
Glenwood Springs, Colorado
(303) 945-7771

Chef Kurt and his lovely wife, Elizabeth Wigger, attend nightly to guests' culinary enjoyment at the popular Sopris Restaurant and Lounge.

Chef Kurt Wigger is just waiting to tantalize guests' taste buds. He has been cooking for 32 years, including 17 years as Executive Chef at the well-known Red Onion in Aspen. Kurt is very proud of the fact that he has prepared meals for and satisfied people such as Clint Eastwood, John Wayne (one of Kurt's favorites), the Kennedy family, Rock Hudson, Henry Fonda, Lee Marvin, John Denver, Franz Klammer, Wally Schirra, Lucy, Sandy Koufax, Buddy Hackett, George C. Scott, Charles Bronson, Cybill Shepherd and Jill St. John, to name but a few.

Beef Stroganoff

2	tablespoons butter	½	fresh tomato (sliced)
1	pound lean filet of beef (cubed)	6	fresh mushrooms (diced)
1	tablespoon onion (chopped)	1	tablespoon dill pickle (diced)
1	teaspoon fresh parsley (chopped)	2	jiggers red wine
salt, pepper, and paprika		8	tablespoons brown gravy
1	jigger French brandy	2	teaspoons sour cream
1	teaspoon butter		dash of heavy cream

Melt the butter in gourmet pan until bubbling. Add meat, sauté 2 minutes for medium rare. Add onion, parsley, salt, pepper, and paprika; saute another 20 seconds. Flame with French brandy; remove from heat. Place meat on separate plate. Heat gourmet pan, adding 1 teaspoon butter, tomatoes, mushrooms and pickle and sauté; stir in wine and brown gravy; then cook until bubbling. Add meat and cook together for 10 seconds. Add sour cream and heavy cream; stir. Serve with noodles and vegetable garnish. Serves 2.

MUDDY'S JAVA CAFE

2200 Champa Street
Denver, Colorado 80202
(303) 298-1631

Muddy's first opened its doors in September 1975 and since then has become one of the most popular little haunts in Denver. True to the coffeehouse of 18th century England, Muddy's specializes in coffee, conversation and camaraderie. Guests don't need reservations and need not feel rushed. Guests also delight in homemade soups, sandwiches, or salads and cups of the finest coffee in town. When guests are at home, they may try this recipe and pretend that they are at Muddy's — it will do until they can experience this intimate Denver haunt.

Bolivian Chili

5	cups rich beef stock
3	medium potatoes
1	medium onion
2	cloves garlic
1	pound choice bottom round
2	tablespoons butter
1	can whole tomatoes (or 4 fresh tomatoes, peeled)
1	tablespoon fresh parsley

Seasonings

1	teaspoon oregano
½	teaspoon basil
½	teaspoon cumin
1	bay leaf
¼	cup chili powder (a dark red chili is best)
salt to taste	

Garnish

feta cheese and parsley sprigs

Heat the beef stock in a 2-quart pan. Scrub the potatoes and cut them into ½-inch slices. Add the potatoes and the seasonings to the stock and bring to a boil. Reduce the heat and simmer gently.

While the potatoes are cooking, chop the onion and garlic. Melt ½ the butter in a large frying pan and sauté the onion and garlic lightly. Add to the soup.

Trim the beef and cut into 1-inch cubes. Brown the meat on all sides in the remaining butter and add to the soup. Simmer, covered, for about 1 hour.

Quarter the tomatoes, mince the parsley, and add to the soup 15 minutes before it is done. Correct the seasonings and garnish each bowl with a tablespoon feta cheese and a sprig of parsley. Serve with good French bread and a tossed salad.

Bolivian Chili is Muddy's most requested soup and is delicious year 'round. We developed it from a verbal recipe that one of our traveling cooks brought back from Central America. We hope you can stop in some evening and enjoy a bowl and have a cup of cappuccino, Muddy's specialty! But if you can't make it to Muddy's, you can make a pot of chili and pretend you're there!

BIBELOT
RESTAURANT

1424 C Larimer
Larimer Square
Denver, Colorado
(303) 595-8400

Chef Ken Moody

Bresaola
Spice Cured Beef Tenderloin

1   whole beef tenderloin trimmed of all fat and sinew (about 4 pounds)
3   tablespoons sugar
3   tablespoons sweet paprika
1   tablespoon fresh ground black pepper
1   tablespoon crushed red pepper
1   tablespoon ground fennel seed
3   tablespoons kosher salt

Rub tenderloin with sugar and all spices except the salt. Wrap in a single layer of cheesecloth, place in a non-corrosive container. Refrigerate for 2 days, turning once each day. At the end of 2 days, unwrap and rub with the kosher salt. Rewrap with cheesecloth and refrigerate 8 more days, once again turning daily.

To serve, slice very thin and arrange over arugala. Sprinkle with Pecarino Romano cheese, chiffanade, (finely sliced or chopped) basil, and extra virgin olive oil. Serves 6 to 8 salad entrees.

LEFT BANK

183 Gore Creek Drive
Vail, Colorado
(303) 476-3696

Liz and Luc Meyers have a magic touch when it comes to making a restaurant work. Luc's training under Madame Point at the highly acclaimed three-star Restaurant de la Pyramide in Vienna, France, taught him the secrets of exquisite gourmet cuisine and service. These expert secrets nightly draw casually dressed, international power (financial, political, and beauty) figures into the linen-tabled, flower-topped Left Bank to drink, dine, and discuss. Luc specializes in his pastries and desserts — a Grand Marnier souffle is a "must experience" for those guests lucky enough to visit this delightful place — or better yet, for those even luckier, who are able to make dining at the Left Bank a habit.

Côte De Boeuf Bordelaise

7   prime rib steaks
salt
white pepper
8   shallots
2   cups red wine
1   bay leaf
2   anchovy filets
2   ounces butter
½   ounce flour
beef extract
fresh lemon juice
7   marrow bones
chopped parsley

Take a small western cut prime rib, with 2 to 3 weeks aging, and slice it into 7 steaks so that each one will have a bone. Trim excess fat and sprinkle meat with salt and pepper. Broil over a very hot fire. It takes 5 to 7 minutes broiling on each side over a hot flame to have the meat medium rare. When broiling meat rare, the broiler should be at the highest temperature.

In a heavy sauté pan, place 8 finely chopped shallots, red wine (Bordeaux), bay leaf, chopped anchovy filets and cook to reduce to half the quantity. Add butter which has mixed with flour, a little beef base, salt, pepper, and a few drops of lemon juice. This sauce should be strained and smooth.

Poach 7 marrow bones, then take out the marrow and put it on top of the steak and pour over the very hot sauce. Add a little chopped parsley.

Serve the following vegetables: fresh spinach, string beans and sautéed potatoes. Serves 7.

NORMANDY FRENCH RESTAURANT

1515 Madison Street
Denver, Colorado 80206
(303) 321-3311

Cuisses De Grenouilles Au Riesling
(Frog Legs in Riesling Wine) from Alsace

8	pair of frog legs - medium size	2	shallots
	enough flour to dust the legs	½	clove garlic
6	tablespoons butter	1	tablespoon parsley, finely chopped
	salt and pepper, freshly ground	1½	cup of Alsatian Riesling
	dry white wine, sufficient for marinade	½	cup heavy cream or crème fraiche
	small sliced onions		pinch of nutmeg

Place frog legs in white wine with sliced onions. Marinate for 1 to 2 hours.

Dry off frog legs and dust with flour and sauté in butter lightly until tender. Salt and pepper to season. Add pinch of nutmeg, optional.

Remove from skillet and keep warm.

In same skillet and butter, sauté the shallots and garlic until lightly browned. Add Riesling and parsley, reduce for 20 minutes. Add crème fraiche or heavy cream.

Blend well, off fire. Add additional seasonings as needed. Pour over frog legs. Serves 4.

THE GOLDEN DOBBIN

519 Wilcox
Castle Rock, Colorado 80104
(303) 688-3786

The Golden Dobbin Meat Loaf

1	cup chopped onions	2	pounds lean ground beef
1	tart apple, peeled and diced (winesap)	½	cup fine dry bread crumbs
2	tablespoons butter	2	eggs
2	teaspoons curry powder		
1½	cups milk	¼	teaspoon pepper
2	tablespoons St. Mary's Gourmet Vinegar	½	cup sliced almonds, toasted
2	tablespoons sugar	6	whole bay leaves
2	teaspoons salt		

Sauté the onion and apple in butter over medium heat until soft, about 10 minutes. Stir in curry, cook about 1 minute, then turn into a bowl.

To the ground beef, add bread crumbs, one of the eggs, ½ cup of the milk, St. Mary's Gourmet Vinegar, sugar, salt, pepper, and almonds. Add apple/onion mixture. Combine the ingredients well, then pack loosely into a baking dish (about 8 x 12 inches or 9 x 13 inch oval). Arrange bay leaves on top, and bake in a 350° oven for about 50 minutes.

Lightly beat together the remaining 1 egg and 1 cup of milk. Remove dish from oven, drain off excess fat and slowly pour mixture over the top. Return to oven for 10 minutes. Makes about 6 servings.

CLIFF YOUNG'S
RESTAURANT

700 East Seventeenth Avenue
Denver, Colorado 80203
(303) 831-8900

No trip to Colorado would be complete without a visit to "the Best Restaurant of Denver," recently featured in *Bon Appetit Magazine;* Cliff Young's is synonymous with exquisite dining. *Travel/Holiday Magazine* rates Cliff Young's "as one of the outstanding restaurants in the world." And so it goes.

Cliff Young's rave reviews in the *New York Times, USA Today, National Restaurant News,* and other local and national acclaim continue to regularly draw movie celebrities such as Robert Redford, Kiefer Sutherland; as well as famous designers, Oscar de la Renta and Victor Kosta; sports personalities, Mike Ditka; national cuisine authorities, Julia Child, who recently thrilled to a special cake created by Cliff Young especially for her; and national and international business entrepreneurs and dignitaries — to name but a few.

And what is the secret to Cliff Young's success that has earned his restaurant "the Five-Star Award Status"? Is it the bone china and crystal and exquisite decor of the Amethyst Room (created by the designers of the Helmsley Palace Hotel in New York City: Marc Roth and James Pfister)? Is it the superb, creative cuisine that is prepared by the former chef of Malcom Forbes' yacht, The Highlander? Is it the inventories in the remarkably comprehensive wine and cognac offerings? Or the individually hand-painted menus (works of art in themselves)? Or perhaps, it is the elegant service which treats everyone as if he were the royalty of the world.

It is all of the above and more. Cliff Young, the owner, earned a Phi Beta Kappa degree in Philosophy at Colorado College in Colorado Springs while he worked his way up from bus boy at the Broadmoor Hotel. His Phi Beta Kappa philosophy works, "Give the best, present the best, offer the best and treat everyone the best. Oh, yes, and hire the best!"

Enthusiasm, energy, and pride transfer from his personnel to guests' tables.

Cliff Young's magic works miracles. National stores host perfume promotions at Cliff Young's; relatives host wedding banquets; businesses host special luncheons; and the list goes on of intimate and grand functions that take place in the private and main dining rooms of Cliff Young's.

It is no wonder that Cliff Young's draws crowds. It is the meeting place for business and fun luncheons; the extra-special dinner occasions; the people watchers; the cuisine enthusiasts; regular guests accustomed to the best; and for special group functions. But above all, it is the place to lift guests' spirits with the best of the best!

Hazelnut Crusted Colorado Rack of Lamb
with Herbal Buerre Rouge (see Sauce section) accompanied with
Wild Rice Potato Cakes (see Vegetable section) and Baby Vegetables

4	ribbed frenched lamb racks	4	teaspoons kosher salt
4	tablespoons hazelnut oil	¼	teaspoon freshly cracked white pepper

Preheat oven to 475° fahrenheit. Place lamb on roasting tray, seasoned side down and roast 10-12 minutes. After 8 minutes, turn the racks over to insure even cooking, continue roasting until cooked to taste. Using meat thermometer 125° for rare, 130° for medium-rare, 135° for medium. (Slightly under-roast before putting on hazelnut crust.)

Hazelnut Crust

4	tablespoons Creole mustard	1	teaspoon brown mustard seed
1	cup fresh bread crumbs	4	ounces crumbed goat cheese
1	cup toasted hazelnuts (roughly chopped)		

Combine bread crumbs, hazelnuts, and mustard seed together and set aside, paint preroasted rack of lamb with Creole mustard, then press hazelnut-crumb mixture and top with crumbled goat cheese. Place back in oven and continue roasting until cheese is melted and crust is golden brown.

Herbal Buerre Rouge

2	cups Merlot or Zinfandel wine	1	teaspoon chopped thyme
1	cup veal glace	1	teaspoon chopped marjoram
4	teaspoons unsalted butter (softened)	1	teaspoon chopped mint

Deglaze roasting pan with the wine, scraping up all the brown bits of meat with a wooden spoon. Pour into saucepan and reduce by half, add veal glaze and reduce by half. Over a very low flame slowly whisk the butter into the reduction, add chopped herbs and season to taste.

To serve: Slice each rack into four chops. Place ¼ of the sauce on each heated plate and place meat over the sauce. Garnish with fresh thyme, mint and marjoram. Serves 4.

MILAN'S

304 East Hopkins
Aspen, Colorado 81611
(303) 925-6328

Milan's has something for everyone — from American cheeseburgers to oriental entrées, from continental to creative cuisine, thanks to owners Milan Prikryl and Richard Walbert and Chef Kenneth Botka. Its versatility makes Milan's a popular Aspen spot for lunches and dinners.

Hot Shredded Spiced Beef*

2   tablespoons soy sauce
1   tablespoon sherry
2   teaspoons cornstarch
1   tablespoon water
2   cups peanut oil or sesame oil
½   pound lean beef, shredded
3   scallions, cut into 2-inch pieces and shredded
2   (¼-inch) slices ginger root, shredded
2   tablespoons beef or chicken broth
1   teaspoon sugar
½ to 1 teaspoon crushed red pepper flakes (or more to taste)
¼   teaspoon sesame oil

Combine soy sauce, sherry, cornstarch and water. Add beef. In a wok, heat oil until smoking. Add beef and scallions and quickly stir the mixture through the oil for 15 seconds. Immediately pour the contents of the wok through a strainer set over a heat-proof bowl. Drain all the oil from the food into the bowl.

Return 2 teaspoons oil to the wok. Add beef mixture and ginger and stiry-fry for 30 seconds. Add broth, sugar and pepper flakes and stir-fry 30 seconds. Sprinkle with sesame oil and serve immediately. Serve with rice.

* Variation

SOREN'S

315 Detroit
Denver, Colorado 80209
(303) 322-8155

Kapusta

1	pound can tomato paste	3	cloves garlic, chopped fine
1½	pounds Polish sausage, sliced thin	2½	tablespoons thyme
1½	cups sauerkraut, drained and rinsed	1½	tablespoons white pepper
4	carrots, sliced	½	tablespoon caraway
1	bunch celery, diced	1	cup Burgundy wine
2	cups diced red cabbage	3	bay leaves
4	medium-sized potatoes, diced		

Sauté onion, garlic, carrots and celery in olive oil. Add red wine, caraway, pepper and bay leaf. Add tomato paste and 6 cups water or soup stock. Add potatoes, red cabbage, sauerkraut and Polish sausage. Let soup simmer for 1 hour to 3 hours — the longer the better. Add salt and pepper to taste. This is a hearty stew that can be served at lunch or Sunday supper with imported cheese, French bread and butter, and a tossed green salad. As with many stews, it improves with age and can be made a day ahead and reheated the next day. Garnish with a dollop of sour cream. Serves 6 to 10.

MAXIE'S

600 South Colorado Boulevard
Denver, Colorado 80222
(303) 759-3341 ext. 755

Lamb Chops Parmesan
on Sautéed Spinach and Vegetables

2	lamb chops 3 ounces each	½	cup olive oil
1	cup flour	1/8	cup fresh rosemary
1	cup egg beaten	1/8	cup fresh basil
½	cup grated Parmesan cheese		

Sauteed Spinach and Vegetables

½	cup sliced mushrooms	3	cloves minced garlic
½	cup diced tomatoes	½	cup fresh spinach
	shallots, chopped	¼	cup white wine

Bread lamb chops with flour, beaten egg and Parmesan cheese. Heat olive oil in sauté pan (insure oil is hot enough so cheese coating will not stick, about 200°). Place chops in skillet to brown evenly. Add spices after chops are browned and place in a 350° oven to finish.

While chops are baking, sauté mushrooms and tomatoes with shallots and garlic, then add spinach. Sauté spinach just enough to wilt it, add white wine and sauté. Place sautéed spinach and vegetables on plate for bed. Arrange chops on top. Serve with wild rice. Serve immediately. Serves 1.

THE CHARTER

First Season
Vail-Beaver Creek, Colorado
(303) 949-6660 or (800) 824-3064

Lamb Chops with Barbecue Sauce*

¼ cup prepared mustard
½ cup St. Mary's Gourmet Vinegar
½ to ¾ cup olive oil

1 tablespoon catsup
2 cloves garlic, crushed

Mix all ingredients together. Lay lamb chops in bottom of pan, pour sauce over. Marinate for 2 to 4 hours at room temperature before grilling over hot coals. Baste with sauce as the meat cooks. Makes approximately 1½ cups.

* Variation

THE WILDFLOWER INN

174 East Gore Creek Drive
Vail, Colorado 81657
(303) 476-5011 ext. 170

The Wildflower Inn located at The Lodge at Vail is truly one of Vail's finest culinary delights. The five star restaurant, under the direction of Executive Chef Jim Cohen and Maître d'Hotel Gray Ferguson, offers a variety of fine American cuisine. The ever changing seasonal menu provides for a unique dining experience throughout the year. The garden setting at the base of Vail Mountain allows for spectacular views of the slopes, the Gore Range, and Vail Village. Summer dining is also available with an outside patio surrounded by flower gardens. Special events such as Winemaker Dinners, Guest Chefs, The Gastronomic Affair, and other events are featured throughout the year. The Wildflower Inn serves dinner nightly in the winter season, and breakfast, lunch and dinner in the summer.

Lamb Shanks for Six

6   lamb shanks, approximately 1 pound each
1   onion, diced
1   head garlic, cut in half
½   fennel bulb, sliced
6   tablespoons dijon mustard
1   carrot
2   celery stalks, diced
bay leaves
peppercorns

2   cups white wine
2 to 3 cups flour
6   cups lamb stock or chicken broth
½   cup olive oil

Season shank and dust with flour.
Heat olive oil and sear shank until golden brown, remove from pan and put in a pan in which you can braise the shanks.
Add onion, carrots, celery, and fennel to the pan that seared shanks and sauté until soft.
Add flour left after dusting to vegetables and cook until golden, add white wine, reduce by ½, add mustard, bay leaf, peppercorns, and garlic, add stock and bring to a boil.
Pour over shanks and place in a 400° oven and cook until very tender, turning shanks every hour.
Remove shanks from liquid and strain.
Reduce liquid until it coats a spoon, check seasoning, and skim fat off.
Reheat shanks in oven, dry with a little Kosher salt.
To reheat shanks that have been refrigerated put shanks in covered pan with a little water for about ½ hour. Uncover last 5-10 minutes.
Place on plate with garlic mashed potatoes. Pour a little sauce over shank and potatoes.
Serves 6.

FLAGSTAFF HOUSE RESTAURANT

1138 Flagstaff Road
Boulder, Colorado 80302
(303) 442-4640

Loin of Lamb with Sweet Peppers in Strudel

1	loin lamb (boned and trimmed)		salt and pepper
	rosemary	3	sheets filo dough
	thyme, chopped		melted butter
	sage	1	red pepper (julienne)
2	cloves garlic (chopped)	1	gold pepper (julienne)

Rub chopped herbs and garlic liberally over lamb.

In a hot pan with oil, sear lamb quickly on both sides. Remove from pan.

Sauté peppers in the same pan with the chopped garlic until mixture is wilted. Let cool.

Place filo sheet on a wet towel. Brush the filo dough with melted butter and then place another sheet of filo dough on top. Repeat procedure until three filo sheets have been used.

Place lamb on the prepared filo dough. Place the pepper and garlic mixture on top of the lamb. Roll the loin.

Bake in preheated oven at 400° for 8-12 minutes.

CHINA SUN RESTAURANT

2594 South Colorado Boulevard
Denver, Colorado 80222
(303) 757-7963

Manchurian Beef

8   ounces shredded beef soaked in marinade sauce for 12 hours

Marinade

½	cup soy sauce	¼	cup sesame oil
1	egg	¼	cup water
1	teaspoon sugar	1	teaspoon cornstarch

After marinating beef 12 hours, stir fry beef in sesame oil and set aside. In skillet, sauté the following ingredients:

3	dried hot red peppers	1	cup chopped green onions
8	ounces fried beef	2	tablespoons soy sauce

Place the ingredients on a bed of mung bean starch (a special Chinese crisp) that has been fried in sesame oil or on rice that has been steamed. (Mung bean starch may be purchased at oriental groceries.) Serves 1 generous portion.

CHINA TERRACE

1512 Larimer Street
Denver, Colorado 80202
(303) 592-1032

Writer's Square has become the home of one of the best Szechuan restaurants in Colorado — the China Terrace. Here the traditional Szechuan favorites, such as great garlic chicken, moo shu pork, sizzling rice soup and more, regularly parade from the kitchen. But besides the well-known favorites, the China Terrace produces some unique delectables such as volcano shrimp (shrimp flattened, stuffed with pork, served on a bed of vegetables and arranged to form a peak, then flamed with rum at tableside), a delicious garlic and ginger lobster; and the masterpiece: a melt-in-your-mouth tender roast duck which must be ordered the day prior to arrival at the China Terrace. All dishes are prepared fresh by the chef who has prepared Szechuan food since the days of his father's restaurant in Canton, China.

Today chef Wong's son, Kim Wong, and the gracious manager, Victor Chan, greet guests and supervise their dining pleasure amidst an exquisite ambience of burgundy carpet and mauves with tapestry booths. Original water colors adorn the walls, as well as gorgeous framed antique, Chinese silk embroideries.

Perhaps this professional experience is why the food is great; service, efficient; the prices, low; and the decor, beautiful! A winning combination for a marvelous Szechuan restaurant!

Ma-Po Style Bean Curd

1	box bean curd (approximately 18 ounces) diced
3	ounces minced pork
3	ounces green peppers, diced
3	teaspoons Hoisin sauce
1½	teaspoons soy sauce
¼	teaspoon salt
1/8	teaspoon minced garlic
3	teaspoons sesame oil
½	cup water
2	teaspoons corn starch mixed with 2 teaspoons water

Preheat the wok for approximately 5 minutes. Add in oil. Allow to stand for 30 seconds. Add garlic. Allow to stand for 10 seconds. Slowly add tofu and pork, and green peppers. Add ½ cup water and then cover wok for 5 minutes. Add Hoisin sauce, soy sauce, salt and stir commpletely. Pour in cornstarch mix and stir slowly. Stir in sesame oil. Serve.

RICK'S CAFE

80 South Madison
Denver, Colorado 80209
(303) 399-4448

Marinated Sirloin Steak

6   10-12 ounce sirloin steaks cut ¾ inch thick
1   cup St. Mary's Glacier Cajun Marinade
1   cup water

Trim any fat off the steaks. Combine the St. Mary's Cajun Marinade and water in a bowl. Marinate the steaks for 15 minutes at least, longer if desired. Grill to desired temperature. Use more St. Mary's Cajun Marinade and less water for stronger flavor. Serves 6.

MONACO INN

962 South Monaco
Denver, Colorado 80224
(303) 320-1104

Meat Balls with Egg-Lemon Sauce*
(Keftaides Avgolemono)

2   slices white bread
1½ pounds lamb, ground twice
1   onion, chopped

1   clove garlic, pressed
salt
freshly ground pepper

Egg-Lemon Sauce

3   egg yolks
juice of 1 lemon
¾   cup water

salt
freshly ground pepper

First soak the bread in water, squeeze dry and crumble. In a blender or mixing bowl, combine the crumbled bread, lamb, onion, garlic, salt and pepper. Blend at high speed (or knead vigorously) until very smooth. Form mixture into small teaspoon-size balls. Drop the meatballs into a pot of lightly salted boiling water and poach over moderate heat until well cooked, about 20 minutes.

While the meatballs are poaching, prepare the sauce: in the top of a double boiler, beat the egg yolks until light; add the lemon juice, water, salt and pepper, and blend well; place over simmering water and heat gently until the sauce thickens slightly. (Do not allow the water under the sauce to boil.) Keep warm.

Drain the cooked meatballs thoroughly, then add them to the egg-lemon sauce and heat through. Serve immediately. Serves 4.

* Variation

LITTLE SHANGHAI

460 South Broadway
Denver, Colorado
(303) 722-1292

Mongolian Beef

1   pound boneless, fat-trimmed beef filet sliced ¹/₈-inch thick and cut into thin strips
½   teaspoon "five-spice" powder
1   egg white
2   cloves garlic, slivered
4   thin slices of fresh ginger root
3   teaspoons cornstarch
5   teaspoons soy sauce
6   tablespoons sherry or rice wine
2   tablespoons water
10 green onions, including tops
2   tablespoons sesame oil

Mix beef in a bowl with 5-spice, egg white, garlic, ginger root, 1 teaspoon of cornstarch, 1 teaspoon soy sauce; let stand 10 minutes. Meanwhile blend rest of the cornstarch, soy sauce, sherry and water. Cut white part of each onion in half, crosswide. Cut sections from green tops, about 1½ inches long. Heat oil in a wide frying pan or wok over highest heat. Add meat mixture and cook, stirring, until meat browns slightly; return to bowl. Add to pan the cornstarch-soy sauce mixture and white part of onion. Cook, stirring until mixture thickens. Add meat and green onion tops and heat, stirring, until simmering. Serve at once. Serves 4.

MATAAM FEZ AT VAIL

Vail Run Building in Sandstone
Vail, Colorado
(303) 476-1818

Moroccan Couscous is a North African dish which is made with semolina, a rice-like grain. Couscous can be a somewhat confusing term: it refers not only to the complete dish (made of semolina, lamb and vegetables), but also to a particular kind of semolina.

In Morocco, Couscous is served in two tajines, or covered earthenware cooking pots: one is for the couscous semolina, the other for the lamb stew. Each diner ladles his own portions and tops it with a delicious raisin sauce. Couscous (the semolina) may be purchased, packaged in a box like rice, in some supermarkets or in gourmet food stores.

Moroccan Couscous

1   medium eggplant
4   medium onions
1½ pounds lean lamb, cut into cubes
1   small head cabbage, coarsely chopped
½   cup butter
1   teaspoon ground coriander
1   teaspoon saffron
1   teaspoon freshly ground pepper
4½ teaspoons salt
4   medium carrots
3   large tomatoes, skinned
1   red sweet pepper, cut into strips
2   cups couscous
2   cups basic chicken stock
1   cup raisins

Peel the eggplant. Slice lengthwise, then cut into strips. Chop 2 onions fine. Combine the lamb, chopped onions, cabbage and ¼ cup of the butter in a large kettle and add enough water to cover. Stir in the coriander, saffron, pepper and 2½ teaspoons salt. Bring to a boil, then reduce heat and simmer for 30 minutes. Quarter the remaining onions. Scrape the carrots and cut crosswise into thirds. Cut the tomatoes into quarters. Add the quartered onions, carrots, tomatoes and sweet pepper to the lamb mixture and simmer for 20 minutes longer or until the lamb and vegetables are tender. Drain off most of the liquid and reserve. Keep the lamb mixture warm. Place the couscous in the top of a double boiler and stir in 2 cups of reserved liquid, chicken stock, remaining salt and remaining ¼ cup of butter. place over boiling water and cook, stirring occasionally, for 5 minutes. Reduce heat to lower and cover. Simmer for 15 minutes or until the liquid is absorbed. Remove from the water and stir lightly with a fork. Strain 1 cup of the reserved liquid and pour over the raisins in a small saucepan. Simmer, covered, for 5 minutes or until raisins are tender and plump. Heat the remaining reserved liquid and pour into a sauceboat. Place the couscous in a serving dish. Place the lamb mixture in a separate serving dish. Serve the couscous and lamb accompanied by the hot gravy and the raisin sauce. Serves 8 to 10.

THE GOLDEN HORN

Cooper and Mill Street
Aspen, Colorado
(303) 925-3373

Pariser Schnitzel*

4   veal cutlets (allow 1 to 2 per person)
flour to coat
2   eggs, beaten
butter to sauté
¾   cup white wine
juice from ½ lemon

Use thin cut, pounded veal, dipped in flour and then in beaten egg. Sauté in butter for 3 minutes on each side. Remove meat to serving platter and add to the pan, wine and lemon juice. Simmer liquid for 3 minutes and pour over meat. Serve with butter noodles. Serves 2 to 4.

* Variation

LE CENTRAL,

Denver's Affordable French Restaurant

112 East Eighth Avenue (8th Avenue and Lincoln)
Denver, Colorado 80203
(303) 863-8094

Le Central brings to Denver a small corner of France complete with marvelous authentic French cuisine at incredibly affordable prices. One might mistake the large, quiet owner/chef Robert Tournier for a football player if it weren't for the mastery with which he creates a pâté de foie or the love he magically bakes into a three-fish souffle of sole, salmon and haddock. Fresh French bread and croissants are baked fresh daily and accompany each meal. This wonderful, intimate French restaurant offers some of the best French cuisine in Colorado with quality ingredients prepared to perfection — at very reasonable prices. Restaurant reviewers from the *Post, Colorado Homes and Lifestyles,* and national publications *New York Times, Gourmet Magazine,* and *Esquire,* repeatedly rave about Le Central. Bon appetit!

Pâté Maison

3	pounds pork shoulder, ⅔ lean, ⅓ fat
2	onions
5	branches parsley
2	cloves garlic
10	cornichons (a small French pickle with sharp flavor)
6	shallots
1	tablespoon pepper
1	cup cognac
½	liter white wine
1	teaspoon salt
5	whole bay leaves
½	teaspoon thyme
1	pound sliced bacon

Grind all above ingredients (except bacon) together in a food processor or blender until coarse. Line loaf pan with uncooked bacon. Fill lined loaf pan with pâté and continue wrapping bacon over the top of the pâté. Place the loaf pan in a "bain marie" (a shallow, water-filled pan) in a 350° oven. Bake 3 hours. Lay foil on top of pâté and cool one night under pressure. (Place a heavy object such as a brick on top of foil, over pâté to guard against crumbling). Serve with croutons, cornichons and a dry, white wine. Serves 12.

HOTEL SONNENALP

20 Vail Road
Vail, Colorado 81658
(303) 476-5656

Pork Cutlets

2	teaspoons salt	½	pound mushrooms, chopped
¼	teaspoon pepper	1	cup dried, old bread, grated
2	cloves garlic		salt and pepper to taste
6	pork cutlets	2	ounces white wine
3	tablespoons butter	12	tablespoons unsweetened whipped cream
2	large onions, chopped	7	ounces mild cheese, grated

Rub salt, pepper and garlic into the pork cutlets. Fry cutlets in 1½ tablespoons butter for 5 minutes on each side. Remove cutlets from frying pan and put them on a flat baking pan. Fry chopped onions and mushrooms in the rest of the butter. Add the grated bread, salt and pepper. Stir in the white wine and whipped cream; boil for several minutes. Spoon this mixture onto the cutlets and add grated cheese on top. Bake at 325° until the cheese is golden brown. Serve with baked potatoes and fresh salad, and accompany with beer or red wine. Serves 6.

CLIFF YOUNG'S

Restaurant

700 East Seventeenth Avenue
Denver, Colorado 80203
(303) 831-8900

Chef Dave Query

Rabbit Loin Stuffed with Cornbread and Andoville Sausage

2	boneless rabbit loins	1	roasted, peeled poblano chili, julienned
2	cups cooked, crumbled cornbread	2	ounces melted butter
½	cup chopped onion	10	slices good, smoked or peppered bacon
1	tablespoon chopped garlic		salt and pepper
1	link andoville sausage		white wine

Pound rabbit loin to ¼-inch thick using meat mallet. Cover meat with plastic wrap making sure not to damage or split rabbit meat. Remove sausage from casing and sauté until fully cooked. Remove sausage from pan and sauté onions and garlic in remaining fat until soft. Deglaze pan with ½ cup dry wine. Reduce by half. Add cornbread, sausage, onion mixture and toss together with melted butter, salt and pepper until moist, adding more butter or wine if necessary.

Place rabbit loins on work surface and lay julienne strips of poblano lengthwise on meat. Press stuffing in consistent layer over entire surface of meat.

Roll loin tightly into log shape. Wrap entire loin with strips of bacon from side to side. (It should take 5 strips per loin.) Tie with butcher's twine or toothpick to secure bacon while roasting. Cook for 20 to 25 minutes, checking for desired doneness. Allow loin to cool for several minutes after cooking. Slice ¾-inch slices and serve over cream polenta, flageolet beans or rissoto. A sauce for this dish could be coarse mustard and green onion, roasted red pepper cream or as at the restaurant, with apricot essence. Serves 4.

BROWN PALACE

17th and Tremont Place
Denver, Colorado
(303) 297-3111

Roast Crown of Lamb Bouquetière*

2	racks of lamb	1	pound lamb bones
1	carrot	1	quart stock
1	small onion	1	bay leaf
1	stalk of celery	3	cloves minced garlic

Bouquetière:

2	1-pound heads fresh cauliflower	6	large potatoes
6	large carrots	1	pound butter
2	pounds peas	½	lemon
6	large mushrooms	3	eggs
2	pounds asparagus spears		salt and pepper

Trim the two racks of lamb of excess fat. Tie racks to form a crown. Season lamb with salt, pepper and minced garlic. Place in a 12-inch braising pan. Place bones around crown of lamb. Cut 1 carrot, 1 onion, 1 stalk of celery into 1-inch pieces, wash and place around crown of lamb with basil leaf. Roast at 400° for 1 hour or until medium. Remove from pan and keep in a warm place. Add 1 quart of stock to pan and reduce to 1 pint. Strain. This is lamb au jus for crown of lamb.

Clean cauliflower and peel carrots. Cut with parisienne spoon. Wash mushrooms and peel potatoes. Cook in individual pots. Cook all vegetables except mushrooms in salted water until tender. Drain. Add 1 tablespoon butter and season to taste with salt and pepper.

Simmer mushrooms in butter until half done. Add juice of ½ lemon and cook until tender.

Duchess potatoes: Mash cooked potatoes. Add 3 raw eggs, 3 tablespoons butter, salt and pepper to taste. Use pastry bag to force potatoes through on an 18-inch platter. Brown until golden brown.

To serve, place crown of lamb in center of the platter. Place the vegetables and mushrooms around the crown. Serve with au jus and fresh mint or Quick Mint Sauce (see Sauce section). Serves 8.

* Variation

GOLD HILL INN

Gold Hill
Boulder, Colorado 80302
(303) 443-6461

Roast Leg of Lamb Venison*

6	pound leg of lamb	½	teaspoon marjoram
	St. Mary's Gourmet Vinegar	½	teaspoon allspice
	buttermilk	1	small carrot, sliced thin
3	cloves of garlic, mashed	10	whole cracked peppercorns, 6 whole cloves
1	large onion, thinly sliced	3	large bay leaves
3	juniper berries, crushed	10	sprigs fresh parsley
½	teaspoon ground mace	6	sprigs green celery leaves

Rub a 6-pound leg of lamb with St. Mary's Gourmet Vinegar and place in a crock. Cover with buttermilk and remaining ingredients. Cover and keep in cool place, turning twice daily, making sure the meat is always covered by marinade. After the fourth day, remove lamb (reserving marinade). Wipe dry and rub completely with salt and pepper.

Place in a roasting pan and insert 2 dozen whole cloves. Pour ½ cup bacon fat and ¾ cup dry white wine over lamb. Roast at 450° for 20 minutes, turning frequently. Lower heat to 350° and allow 18 minutes per pound. Baste frequently with strained buttermilk. When lamb is done, place on serving platter. Strain the pan juices and marinade into a saucepan. Skim off fat and bring to a boil. Add ½ cup red currant jelly and 1 tablespoon lemon, thickening with flour and a little cold water. Pour part of sauce over sliced lamb and serve hot. Serves 6 to 10.

* Variation

IMPERIAL CHINESE SEAFOOD RESTAURANT

1 Broadway
Denver, Colorado
(303) 698-2800

Roast Pork*
with Soy Sauce Marinade (see Sauce section)

Pork can be roasted either in an open pan and basted frequently with a bulb baster, or roasted in a covered casserole. The latter tenderizes the meat more and gets out the fat. Allow about 35 to 40 minutes per pound in a 325° oven. We suggest you marinate the roast before cooking, either overnight or for at least 6 hours.

Save the marinade for possible use as a sauce for the pork. To make the sauce, skim the fat left in the bottom of the casserole or pan. You will be left with the cooking juices of the meat. There are many variations of sauces using the juices (see Sauce section).

* Variation

BLACK FOREST INN

260 Gregory Street
Black Hawk, Colorado 80422
(303) 279-2333 or 582-9971

The Black Forest Inn is located in Black Hawk, Colorado, in the scenic foothills just outside of Denver, and is easily accessible by car, being only 38 miles or 45 minutes from Denver.

The Black Forest Inn is famous for the finest in German food, steaks, fish, wild game, and fowl. Award-winning lobster, great chocolate pie, and numerous other exquisitely prepared meals with generous portions draw crowds, wedding groups, Central City opera fans, lovers, and friends to this — one of Colorado's finest restaurants hosted by one of Colorado master restaurateurs, Bill Lorenz.

Roast Venison

1	venison roast (4 to 5 pounds)
fresh pork	
3	medium onions, chopped
1	stalk celery, chopped
1	carrot, chopped
pepper, salt, cloves	
¼	cup flour
4	cups cream
2	cups button mushrooms
4	cups beef stock

Preheat oven to 450°. Remove any skin from the roast, then lard the roast generously with fresh pork. Place it in a roasting pan with onions, bay leaf, carrot, celery, cloves, and plenty of salt and pepper. Bake for 20 to 25 minutes. Reduce the heat to 300° and allow to cook about 3 hours or until done. Remove the roast from the oven and place it on a warming platter.

Dust the vegetables and drippings moderately with flour, then add beef stock. Cook on top of the stove until this mixture is reduced to 2 cups. Strain the mixture and add cream. Cook again until the stock is golden brown. Add the mushrooms and pour over the meat.

Serve with orange slices, baked bananas, pineapple, cranberry sauce, or butter noodles.

BLACK FOREST INN

260 Gregory Street
Black Hawk, Colorado 80422
(303) 279-2333 or 1-582-9971

Sauerbraten

1	pound per person, lean beef		parsley
	(top or bottom round or chuck roast)		onions
1	quart St. Mary's Gourmet Vinegar	1	bay leaf
1	quart water		several cloves
carrots			peppercorns

Boil one quart of St. Mary's Gourmet Vinegar with an equal amount of water together with rough-cut carrots, parsley, onions, bay leaf, cloves and peppercorns for 15 minutes. Let cool and pour over meat which has been placed in crockery pot. Place in refrigerator for 72 hours.

When preparing the meat, first dry the roast, then place in roasting pan with enough fat to brown meat on all sides in 450° oven. Add marinated vegetables with ½ the strained liquid and reduce temperature to 400°. When liquid turns golden brown after 1 hour, dust roast and broth with flour. Cover and continue roasting another hour. Add remainder of marinade together with 3 ounces tomato paste per pound of meat. Cover and roast for 2½ to 3 hours or until tender. Skim off all fat and strain liquid after roast has been removed to plate. Make gravy by thickening with 2 tablespoons flour with 8 ounces (1 cup) red wine.

Slice roast into 2 generous slices per person. Place on serving tray and totally cover with sauce. To complement this dinner, mashed potatoes, potato dumplings, spaetzle, potato pancakes, or buttered noodles may be served along with vegetables of choice. Serves 6.

ABETONE RESTAURANT

520 East Hyman
Aspen, Colorado
(303) 925-9022

Scaloppine Di Vitella Al Marsala
(Veal Scaloppine Marsala)

12	slices (about 1¼ pounds) prime veal	1	cup Marsala wine
salt and pepper		¼	cup chopped, fresh parsley
½	cup flour	1	lemon, sliced
½	cup butter		bouquet of parsley sprigs

Pound veal until it is about ½ inch thick. Salt and pepper veal, and lightly coat with flour. Melt butter in a large skillet over medium heat. Brown veal quickly on both sides. Add Marsala and simmer for 3 minutes. Put veal in a serving dish. Sprinkle with chopped parsley. Pour sauce on top; garnish with lemon slices and parsley bouquet. Serve immediately. Serves 4.

BROWN PALACE

17th and Tremont Place
Denver, Colorado
(303) 297-3111

In 1892, Mr. Henry Brown built the Brown Palace Hotel in Denver, Colorado, which was then primarily a mining and gold exchange town. In August of 1892, an official opening dinner marked the beginning of elegant gourmet dining complete with imported crystal and china.

Today in the Palace Arms, tuxedoed waiters still attend guests with a royal, yester-year ceremony which includes linen tablecloths, fresh flowers on the table, tableside preparation of classic continental dishes, exquisite fresh and expensive quality ingredients, flatware appropriately shaped for every course, and even silver finger bowls containing warm water and a floating lemon slice (an elegant concluding touch to a memorably fabulous meal).

Because the Brown Palace's dining rooms still offer this almost lost art of attentive royal service, the Brown attracts today's business royalty, the international and national political leaders, corporate magnates and local oil men and bankers who daily gather for coffee, lunches and dinners at the Brown's Ship's Tavern, Ellyngton's, Brown Club, and the favorite room, the intimate Palace Arm's Room.

Local and national restaurant reviewers have repeatedly praised the Brown's prime rib, steak tartare, coffee, freshly squeezed orange juice, breakfast trout, and fine tableside dish preparation and service.

Although the Brown Palace has changed hands over the years, it has maintained a tradition of elegant, quality gourmet dining at its finest and best.

Steak Tartare

1	pound rib-eye steak, freshly ground
½	cup grated onion
1	teaspoon dry mustard
½	teaspoon Tabasco sauce
1	clove pressed garlic
1	teaspoon salt
1	teaspoon worcestershire sauce
½	teaspoon freshly ground pepper
1	egg, slightly beaten
2	tablespoons minced parsley
¼	cup fine chopped (or pressed through sieve) boiled egg
¼	cup capers
¼	cup chopped, cooked red beets
6	small anchovy filets
2	large slices of dark rye bread
several lettuce leaves	

In a large wooden bowl, rub garlic around bowl's inside. Add egg, ground steak, dry mustard, Tabasco, worcestershire, ground pepper, salt and parsley. Add all ingredients (except lettuce, dark rye bread and anchovies). Mix thoroughly, line 2 plates with lettuce, top with a slice of rye bread. Add ½ of Steak Tartare with 3 anchovy filets and serve immediately. Serves 2.

ST. BERNARD INN

103 South Main
Breckenridge, Colorado 80424
(303) 453-2572

The St. Bernard Inn, a popular Italian restaurant in Breckenridge for years, has been transformed into an unusual experience in fine dining. In 1978 the dining room was restored to its original Victorian style and a new kitchen and lounge were added. Soon after, a wine cellar was constructed which now houses one of the finest collections of Italian, French, California and German wines in Colorado.

St. Bernard Inn offers extraordinary Italian food and an impressive selection of wines served in casual elegance; an unusual experience in fine dining.

Stuffed Breast of Veal with Marsala Wine Sauce

Preheat oven to 425°
1   breast of veal bone-in, approximately 10 pounds
1   pound sausage (sweet Italian)
1   pound ricotta
¾   cup Parmesan cheese
4   cloves garlic, crushed
1   cup fresh parsley, minced
3   eggs
2   stalks celery, minced
1   small onion, minced
1   cup breadcrumbs
¾   cup prosciutto, chopped
15 ounces chunky applesauce
pinch nutmeg
salt and fresh ground pepper to taste
¼   cup dry marsala wine
1½ quarts veal stock
olive oil

Cut a pocket in the veal by cutting along the bone. Trim off any excess fat. Combine remaining ingredients except for the veal stock and olive oil, and stuff into the pocket. Close up the pocket with toothpicks. Brush the top with olive oil. Sprinkle with garlic, salt and pepper. Generously splash marsala wine over the top and sides. Bake uncovered for ½ hour. Add 1 quart veal stock, cover and bake for 3 hours at 350°.

Drain juices into a saucepan. Skim off grease. Add approximately 1 cup marsala wine, salt, pepper and ½ quart veal stock. Cook down for 15 to 20 minutes. Thicken with approximately ¼ cup flour. Sauce should be thin and creamy, not heavy like a brown gravy. Serves 8.

TAKAH-SUSHI

420 East Hyman
Aspen, Colorado 81611
(303) 925-8588

Sukiyaki*
Quick-Cooked Beef and Vegetables

2   pounds thin sliced prime rib
12 spring onions, thinly sliced
1   small can winter bamboo shoots, drained and sliced
1   pound fresh mushrooms, rinsed
2   medium onions, thinly sliced
8   ounces fresh bean sprouts
1   small white Chinese cabbage, chopped to bite size
1   packet (2 ounces) cellophane noodles
6   pieces bean curd (tofu), optional
oil or chicken stock
Japanese soy sauce
sugar
sake
beef stock

Arrange all ingredients on platter. At tableside heat an electric frying pan or chafing dish.
Add oil or chicken stock to pan. Add half of each vegetable to pan and fry or poach for
a minute or two until slightly soft. Push to side of pan and add slices of meat in one layer.
When cooked on one side (this should not take long because meat is so thinly sliced), turn
and cook other side. Sprinkle with soy sauce, sugar and sake to taste, add a little stock to
moisten all the meat and vegetables. Mix in noodles and tofu (if used) and heat through.
Serve immediately. Let each person help himself from the pan.

More ingredients are added to the pan and cooked only after the first batch has been
eaten and guests are ready for second helpings. Add more stock, sauce, sake and sugar to
pan and simmer ingredients as required. Serves 6.

* Variation: you may vary noodles and vegetables.

LITTLE SHANGHAI

460 South Broadway
Denver, Colorado
(303) 722-1292

Sweet and Sour Pork with Pineapple and Peppers
(see Sauce section for Sweet and Sour sauce)

1	egg		1	pound oil (peanut or salad oil)
1	pound pork		1	large tomato, cut into sections
½	teaspoon salt		2	green peppers, cut into sections
2	tablespoons flour		4	slices pineapple, cut into sections
1	medium-size cucumber			

Cut the green peppers, cucumbers, pineapple and tomato into sections. Chop the pork into same size though not the same shape. Whip the egg and mix with flour and salt. Drop the pieces of meat into the flour mixture and stir well. Heat the oil until boiling. Fry each piece of pork until it is brown and crisp and drain well.

Frying must be done when the oil is boiling, otherwise the pork will not be crisp. Leave only 1 tablespoon of oil in the pan and pour in the green pepper, tomato, pineapple and cucumber. Add remaining salt and stir for one minute and mix with fried pork. Heat the Sweet and Sour sauce (see Sauce section) and pour on top of the pork. Serve piping hot.

CAFE GIOVANNI

1515 Market Street
Denver, Colorado 80202
(303) 825-6555

Cafe Giovanni is synonymous with excellence in dining. *Esquire Magazine* chose this restaurant as one of the hundred best restaurants in the United States. *Colorado Homes and Lifestyles* chose Cafe Giovanni for a feature on culinary excellence. Restaurant reviewers from the *Post,* the *News,* as well as other local and national publications unanimously sing the praises of Jack Leone's gastronomique delights. Melt-in-your-mouth, fluffy lobster and crabmeat souffles; rich Cappuccino cheesecake; great pasta dishes, and delicate, tender veal entrées make the menu a hit parade of glorious treats.

Jack Leone is the master chef and proprietor of this outstanding restaurant. As a student in restaurant management, he apprenticed in Nice France. He later worked for a restaurant chain before he and his wife, Jan, decided to open a restaurant in Denver. They bought a historic building downtown and renovated the interior with rich wooden paneling from a dismantled Lloyd's Bank of London, marble countertops, plus emerald carpeting and forest-green half-moon banquettes, glowing candles and fresh flowers atop each table and wonderful foods.

At meals guests may enjoy poached salmon, salads, cassoulet (a pork and bean dish from Gascony), or a Niçoise-styled veal stew, or a pasta with crabmeat and clams and many other prepared-to-perfection delights which have won acclaim from critics and connoisseurs who rank Cafe Giovanni as one of the finest restaurants in Colorado.

Sweetbreads Aux Marsala

1½ pounds veal sweetbreads
1   cup dry white wine
2   tablespoons butter
½   pound fresh mushrooms, sliced
1   shallot, finely chopped
½   cup sweet Marsala wine
2   cups Brown Sauce (see Sauce section)
½   cup heavy cream
salt and pepper to taste

Soak sweetbreads in salted ice water for 3 hours. Rinse sweetbreads and place in a kettle with just enough water to cover. Add white wine and slowly bring to a boil. Cook for 5 minutes. Remove from stove and rinse with cold water until cooled. Clean the sweetbreads and peel as much membrane and fat off as possible. Break the sweetbreads into bite-size pieces, removing any membrane. Place cleaned pieces on paper toweling and drain well. In a sauté pan, melt butter, add sweetbreads, mushrooms and shallots and cook until lightly browned. Add Marsala and allow to flame. Add the Brown Sauce and cream and simmer until the mixture is reduced to a rich, velvety sauce. Season to taste with salt and pepper. Serve in small individual puff pastry shells en papillote (in parchment paper) or over toast points.

T-WA INN

555 South Federal Boulevard
Denver, Colorado
(303) 922-4584

Thai Sausage (Sai Krog Thai) *

1	pound lean ground beef	2	cups half & half
½	pound ground pork	1	tablespoon ground coriander
6	large eggs	1	tablespoon red chili
1	cup ground peanuts	1	tablespoon curry mix
1	cup coconut flakes		salt and pepper to taste
1	cup grated carrot		

Combine all the ingredients into a big mixer bowl. Mix well. Take a small portion of the mixture and panfry until done. Taste. If hotter is desired, add red chili and the salt to suite taste. Make into 6-inch patties about ¾ inch thick and fry in the pan until done. Serve on top of a bed of shredded lettuce as appetizer or main dish. Serves 12.

* Variation

BIBELOT
RESTAURANT

1424 C Larimer
Larimer Square
Denver, Colorado 80202
(303) 595-8400

Bibelot's sophisticated, cosmopolitan, open, airy restaurant is Denver's newest rage! And why not? It is Cliff Young's newest fun spot. With the original Cliff Young's restaurant, he made dining "serious fun"! With Bibelot he makes dining "happy fun"! All the while he is using his same wonderful formula for dining success: great food, great service, and great decor.

In the heart of Denver's urban hub, designers Marc Roth and James Pfister have once again worked their award-winning interior magic. Unlike most dark subterranean restaurants, Bibelot sports sparkling glass, mirrors, pastel colors, openness, mauve limestone pillars, a contemporary Monet wall mural, with brass sconce light fixtures creating a stunning, bright, happy atmosphere.

During lunch, shoppers brimming with packages, businessmen and women purring with the chatter of urban excitement make Bibelot, like Jacques of Montgomery Street in San Francisco — a bustling luncheon hub — only better, thanks to Cliff Young. At night the excited purrs are from theater personalities and enthusiasts, tourists, romantics, and the electric, eclectic types who thrive on urban settings.

To ensure "Happy dining at Bibelot" means to ensure fabulous food. Cliff Young does this with Executive Chef Ken Moody. Over the years, this chef ensured the culinary success at Cliff Young's. Now his expertise is overseeing the success of Bibelot's delicious Mediterranean offerings and it is working: "Bibelot climbs near-perfect orbit from launch pad," heralds the *Denver Post*; *Rocky Mountain News* raves, "Service is a hallmark of Cliff Young's new restaurant . . ." Numerous other local and national publications are fast putting Bibelot on the map for American adaptations of marvelous Mediterranean and other delicious delights.

"Make the best, offer the best, treat the best!" is Cliff Young's winning philosophy. (He earned his philosophy degree from Colorado College where he was awarded the honor of Phi Beta Kappa. While attending college, he worked his way up from bus boy at the Broadmoor.) "Oh yes, and hire the best!"

Ken Moody — food overseer, award-winning designers, and everyone Cliff Young hires reflect his philosophy of excellence.

So, for "serious-dining-fun" its Cliff Young's. And for "happy-dining-fun" it is Cliff Young again — this time at his new Bibelot!

Tian of Colorado Lamb with Shiitake Mushrooms, Spinach, Tomatoes Served with Ouzo Essence

lamb filets, approximately 3, boned from the larger side of the loin and trimmed scrupulously
    to leave no trace of fat nor sinew
4   large ripe tomatoes, skinned and seeded
4   ounces (½ cup) olive oil
1   small onion, finely chopped
salt, pepper and basil
1   pound fresh spinach
½   pound Shiitake mushrooms
7 to 10 tablespoons butter, including 4 tablespoons diced, cold butter to finish the sauce
6 to 8 cloves garlic
1¼ cups lamb stock*
1   tablespoon truffle juice
salt and pepper

* for the lamb stock, place the bones and trimming in a hot oven until very brown, then transfer them to a pot, cover them with water (5 cups is enough for 4), and add chopped shallots, ½ carrot, 2 tomatoes, garlic, thyme and a bay leaf. Simmer this slowly for 2 hours, reducing the stock by three quarters of its original volume, then strain. The fat should be skimmed off well before using.

To prepare the vegetables: Prepare the vegetables in advance. They can be briefly reheated in small saucepans before assembly.

Peel and seed the tomatoes. Chop them coarsely and sweat them with a little chopped onion in 2 tablespoons oil. When the moisture has evaporated and the tomatoes are mashable, salt and pepper them and add some freshly chopped basil for flavor. Devein the spinach, wash, blanch momentarily, then refresh it and squeeze all the moisture out by pressing between hands. Chop and sauté the spinach in a little olive oil until they release their water. Remove with a slotted spoon, season with salt and pepper, and set aside.

To cook the lamb:

Season the lamb filets with salt and pepper just prior to cooking. Heat 4 tablespoons butter until hot and sauté the lamb for 4 to 5 minutes, rolling it to brown, well, until it is cooked but pink inside. For taste, add 6 to 8 cloves of garlic to the cooking pan. When cooked, remove the lamb filets to a plate and keep warm, covered, in the oven. Save the garlic for later.

Degrease the pan and add the Metaxa Ouzo. Reduce the Ouzo to a teaspoon or two only, stirring up all the sediment, then add 1 cup of lamb stock. Add the truffle juice, if using it, then salt and pepper the sauce, giving it one good boil while stirring. Strain over a bowl and return to the pan to keep warm.

Reheat the vegetables in small, separate saucepan.

To assemble the Tian:

Rub a little of the fried garlic on the base of each plate and place the rings in the center of each. Put the spinach in the bottom of the rings, in a fine layer, pressing down with a fork to spread and pack them well.

Next make a layer of Shiitake mushrooms on top of the spinach.

Place a layer of tomato purée on top of the mushrooms. Slice the filets of lamb on the vertical extremely fine with a very sharp knife. One should be able to get 2 tians out of 1 filet, but an extra is included in this recipe to be certain. One needs 12 to 15 slices, which are now spread evenly around inside the rings on top of the tomato in a spoke shape.

Lift the rings carefully from each plate to reveal the layered tian. As the dish is difficult to serve hot during the home-plating, put the lamb into a hot oven for about 30 seconds before removing the ring. Quickly stir in 3 tablespoons of cold diced butter into the sauce and spoon around each of the tians. Serves 4.

THE TOWER MAGIC BAR & RESTAURANT

P.O. Box 5514
Aspen-Snowmass Village, Colorado 81615
(303) 923-4650

Tournedos Au Poivré Vert

2	tournedos of beef (3½ ounces each)	4	ounces chicken stock
1	teaspoon shallots	1	teaspoon green peppercorns
2	ounces white wine		salt and pepper to taste
2	ounces madeira		parsley

Sauté tournedos to desired temperature in 1 tablespoon butter, then remove to heated platter.
Sauté shallots in remaining butter until translucent.
Add remaining ingredients and reduce until thickened.
Garnish with parsley. Serves 1.

WELLSHIRE INN

3333 South Colorado Boulevard
Denver, Colorado
(303) 759-3333

Tournedos Diane

1   ounce butter
1   ounce shallots, chopped
2   tournedos of beef (3½ ounces each)
1   teaspoon dry mustard
freshly ground black pepper
2   ounces fresh mushrooms, sliced
½   ounce worcestershire sauce
4   ounces Demi-Glace sauce (see Sauce section)
dash of cognac
chopped parsley

Preheat a suzette pan and in it, brown butter. Add chopped shallots and sauté until clear. Season both sides of tournedos with mustard and black pepper. Brown tournedos on both sides in suzette pan. Remove; set aside on hot dinner plates. In suzette pan, combine mushrooms, worcestershire sauce, Demi-Glace sauce and cognac. Heat and stir until bubbling. Put tournedos in pan and finish cooking to desired taste. Serves 1 or 2.

THE GREENBRIAR

North Foothills Highway
Boulder, Colorado
(303) 440-7979

Tournedos Toscana

2   tablespoons of Béarnaise Sauce (see Sauce section)
2   4-ounce tenderloin of beef filets
1   tablespoon butter
2 or 3 mushrooms, diced
1   spring onion, chopped
2   scallions, chopped
1   teaspoon soy sauce
1   teaspoon Tabasco
1   smoked oyster, chopped
2   smoked oysters, whole
2   artichoke bottoms

Sauté beef filets. In a separate skillet, saute diced mushrooms, butter, chopped onion, and scallions, and chopped smoked oyster, Tabasco and soy sauce to make filling for artichoke bottoms. In another skillet, heat artichoke bottoms in butter and whole oysters.

On two serving plates, stack filet, whole oyster, artichoke bottom and filling (onion, scallion, mushroom, soy, Tabasco, and smoked oyster). Top with Béarnaise sauce. Serves 2.

THE RED ONION

420 East Cooper Street Mall
Aspen, Colorado
(303) 925-9043

Veal A La Oscar

4   loin veal chops, about ½ pound each
salt and pepper (freshly ground)
8   asparagus spears
2½ tablespoons butter
¼   pound lump crabmeat or 4 cooked and peeled shrimp
¾   cup Béarnaise Sauce (see Sauce section)

Sprinkle the chops on both sides with salt and pepper. Skewer the tail of each chop to hold in place. Scrape the sides of the asparagus spears but leave the tips intact. Put in a skillet with cold water to cover and salt to taste. Bring the asparagus to boil and simmer about 3 minutes till crisp-tender and drain. Heat 2 tablespoons of butter in a heavy skillet large enough to hold the chops in one layer. Brown the chops on both sides. Melt a teaspoon of butter in a small skillet and add the crabmeat or shrimp. Cook briefly just to heat through. As the chops cook, prepare the Béarnaise. Arrange the chops on a serving platter and garnish each with two asparagus spears. Spoon Béarnaise sauce over the asparagus and garnish the top of each serving with crabmeat or shrimp. Serves 4.

FERN'S RESTAURANT

Denver Hilton South
7801 East Orchard Road
Englewood, Colorado 80111
(303) 779-6161

Sous Chef Jeanette Landgraf

Veal with a Roasted Red Bell Pepper Buerre Blanc

2	veal filets	1	shallot, finely chopped
1	egg	1	cup heavy cream
	flour	¼	pound unsalted butter
	bread crumbs	1	roasted, peeled red pepper
1	cup white wine		

Pound veal between 2 pieces of plastic wrap until very thin. Dip in beaten egg, flour and bread crumbs. Sauté in butter until browned.

Reduce white wine and shallots to half, add heavy cream and reduce to half once more over medium heat, until lightly thickened. Remove from heat and whisk in butter a little bit at a time.

Take the roasted, peeled red pepper and purée in blender (add a touch of white wine so purée is smooth). Add to Buerre Blanc and top veal. Serves 2.

PIÑON'S

105 South Mill
Aspen, Colorado
(303) 920-2021

Veal with Rosemary-Chili Sauce and Walnuts*

2   rancho chilies, stems and seeds removed, or substitute 3 large dried red chilies
2   tablespoons olive oil
4   veal cutlets, pounded between wax paper until ¼-inch thick
flour for dredging
2   teaspoons chopped shallots
½   cup red wine
2   teaspoons chopped fresh rosemary
¼   cup chicken stock
cornstarch mixed with water
1   tablespoon chopped walnuts

Place the chilies and 1 cup of water in a saucepan and bring to a boil. Remove from the heat, cover and let sit for ½ hour. In a blender or food processor, purée the chilies in the water until smooth.

Heat the oil in a skillet until almost smoking. Lightly dredge the cutlets with the flour and sauté until lightly browned, about 30 seconds on each side. Remove and keep warm.

Sauté the shallots in the oil until soft. Deglaze the pan with the wine. Add the rosemary and simmer until reduced to ¼ cup.

Add the chicken stock and pepper purée; simmer. Thicken the sauce, if necessary, with the cornstarch.

Place the veal on plates, top with the sauce, garnish with the walnuts and serve. Serves 4.

* Variation

WIENERSTUBE RESTAURANT

633 East Hyman Avenue
at Spring Street
Aspen, Colorado 81611
(303) 925-3357

Wiener Schnitzel
(Breaded Veal Cutlets)

2   pounds leg of veal, cut into ¼ inch thick slices
salt
freshly ground pepper
2   eggs
¼   cup flour, to coat Schnitzel thoroughly on both sides
2   cups bread crumbs, home-made with dry French bread and blender
1½ cups vegetable shortening
1   lemon

Prepare the slices of veal, lightly pounding them with a meat mallet to ¼ inch thick cutlets, or marinate them without pounding in a squeeze of fresh lemon juice for about 1 hour in the refrigerator to tenderize the meat. If marinated pat them dry, then sprinkle with salt and pepper, dip in flour and shake off the excess. Then dip the cutlets in the beaten eggs, and lay them flat in bread crumbs, cover them with more bread crumbs and press down lightly to coat all parts with the crumbs, and gently shake off the excess. The meat may be prepared ahead and refrigerated for no longer than 30 minutes.

Heat the shortening in a 12-inch iron skillet until a light haze forms over it, then add the cutlets so they lay flat and do not crowd each other and cook over medium heat, turning gently with tongs, until they are crisp, golden brown. If thicker pieces are used, or slices of turkey/chicken breast, lower the heat so they get done without burning. Serve at once with lemon wedges or serve "a la Hollstein," with one fried egg facing up with strips of anchovies as garnish. Usually the Schnitzel is served with warm, freshly prepared German potato salad. "Preiselbeeren" Lingonberry relish may be added as a condiment. Serves 4 to 8.

Note: boneless turkey breast slices or skinless chicken breast meat may be substituted for the veal.

DESSERTS
XI

DESSERTS, XI

Almond Gratin with Pineapple (Picasso's) — p. 1
Apple-Raspberry Pie (The Tower Magic Bar & Restaurant) — p. 1
Apple Strudel (The Tyrolean Inn) — p. 2
Banana Flambée (Sopris Restaurant and Lounge) — p. 2
Banana Split Ice Cream Pie (Bull & Bush) — p. 3
Blue Corn Pancakes with Caramelized Apples and Bananas (Zenith) — p. 3
Brie Cheesecake on Champagne Crème Anglaise with Fresh Plums (Tante Louise) — p. 4
Caramel Custard (Off Belleview Grill) — p. 5
Carrot Cake (Mayfair Deli and Patrisserie — Introduction) — p. 6
Chart House Mud Pie (The Chart House) — p. 7
Cheese Blintzes (D-J's Crêpes and Omelets) — p. 8
Chocolate Bread Pudding (Zenith) — p. 9
Chocolate Sorbetto with Raspberry Coulis (L'Ostello) — p. 9
Chocolate Torte (La Coupole — Introduction) — p. 10
Chocolate Walnut Crêpe (Hotel Jerome Restaurant) — p. 11
Cinnamon Walnut Cookies (Cliff Young's Restaurant) — p. 11
Crêpe Suzettes (Cafe Franco) — p. 12
Date Souffle (Rudi's) — p. 12
Dessert Crêpe (D-J's Crêpes and Omelettes) — p. 13
Firefly Granola (Firefly Cafe) — p. 13
Gateux a L'Orange (Rudi's — Introduction) — p. 14
Ginger Crème Brulee (L'Ostello — Introduction) — p. 15
Goat Cheese Tart (Zenith) — p. 16
Iron Skillet Peach Cobbler (Duggan's) — p. 17
Lime Vanilla-Bean Ice Cream with Raspberry Sauce (Marina Landing) — p. 18
Mosaic Nut Tart (The Wildflower) — p. 19
Pecan Pie (Rudi's) — p. 20
Pine Nut Brown Sugar Cookies (Marina Landing — Introduction) — p. 21
Pot de Crème (Philadelphia Filly) — p. 22
Ripe Figs with Mascarpone, Toasted Almonds and Port Wine (John's Restaurant) — p. 22
Salzburger Nockerl (Wienerstube Restaurant) — p. 23
Strawberry Base Sauce for Waffle Toppings (Paul's Place) — p. 24
Strawberry Cream (Rudi's) — p. 24
Strawberry Crêpe Supreme (The Magic Pan Crêperie) — p. 25
Sweet Potato Pie (Daddy Bruce) — p. 25
Torta Regine (The Wildflower Inn) — p. 26
White Chocolate Boats (Strings) — p. 26

PICASSO'S

The Cordillera Spa
Box 1110
Vail-Edwards, Colorado 81632
(303) 926-2200

Chef Phillippe Van Cappellen

Almond Gratin With Pineapple

¾ cup sugar
⅔ cup butter
4 eggs

¾ cup almond flour
1½ cups cream, half whipped

In mixing bowl, combine sugar, flour and butter until very soft. Add eggs one at a time. Gently fold in cream. Chill for at least four hours.

Arrange sliced pineapple on plate or in shallow bowl. Cover with gratin mixture. Place in 350° oven for three minutes, the under broiler until slightly brown. Serve immediately. Serves 4.

THE TOWER MAGIC BAR & RESTAURANT

P.O. Box 5514
Aspen-Snowmass Village, Colorado 81615
(303) 923-4650

Apple-Raspberry Pie

Pie Crust

2 cups flour
2 cups butter
¼ teaspoon cinnamon

1½ teaspoons sugar
6 tablespoons cold water

Mix dry ingredients together. Cut in butter with pastry cutter. Sprinkle water over mixture and incorporate with fork.

Roll bottom crust big enough to fit 10″ pie pan.

Roll top crust.

Pie Filling

8 tablespoons unsalted butter, melted
4 tablespoons cornstarch
½ teaspoon cinnamon
¹/₈ teaspoon nutmeg
3 large Granny Smith apples, peeled, cored and sliced

¾ cup sugar
½ cup lemon juice
3 pounds raspberries

Mix corn starch into melted butter.

Mix sugar, nutmeg and cinnamon together. Stir into butter mixture.

Add lemon juice. Stir together over low heat until incorporated.

Mix apples and raspberries together.

Pour butter mixture over fruit and let sit for 15 minutes. Pour fruit into prepared pie shell. Cover with top crust and flute edges. Slit top.

Bake in preheated 450° oven 30 minutes or until golden brown.

THE TYROLEAN INN

400 East Meadow Drive
Vail, Colorado
(303) 476-2204

Apple Strudel

4   pounds fresh apples, peeled and sliced
1   pound puff pastry dough (see Bread section)
1   egg
1   cup sugar
1   cup raisins
½   cup almonds
½   teaspoon vanilla extract
2   ounces cinnamon
1   egg

Bake or steam apples until cooked. Set aside. Prepare puff pastry dough (see Bread section). Roll out dough onto a paperlined sheet pan. Dough must be tissue paper thin. Beat the egg and use it to glaze around the edge of puff pastry dough. Combine cooked apples and the remaining ingredients. Mix well and place in center of the rolled dough in the pan. Seal the edges and glaze with egg over top. Bake in 375° oven for 45 minutes.

SOPRIS RESTAURANT AND LOUNGE

7215 Highway 82
Glenwood Springs, Colorado 81601
(303) 945-7771

Banana Flambée

The secret is to flame and cook this dessert very quickly. Overcooking will destroy the appearance and the taste. The flambée may be done in front of guests as is the custom at the Sopris Restaurant.

2   bananas
1   tablespoon sugar
1   tablespoon butter
orange peel

¼   cup Kirsch (liqueur)
½   cup heavy cream
Grand Marnier liqueur

Peel and slice two bananas lengthwise. Heat a pan and brown the sugar. Add the butter and a thin-sliced orange peel. Put bananas in the pan and turn them over very quickly several times. Flame the bananas quickly with the Kirsch; add fresh cream and cook until it thickens (about 2 minutes). Place bananas on a plate. Add a dash of Grand Marnier to the sauce and pour it over the bananas. Serve with vanilla ice cream.

BULL & BUSH

Cherry Creek Drive at Dexter
Denver, Colorado
(303) 759-0333

Banana Split Ice Cream Pie

1   wafer crust (see Bread section)
3   cups vanilla ice cream
3   cups chocolate ice cream
3   cups strawberry ice cream
6   fresh bananas
1   jar ice cream nut topping
whipped cream
1   small jar red maraschino cherries
1   jar hot fudge sauce

Layer softened ice cream one layer at a time on top of wafer crust. Freeze at least 4 hours. Remove from springform pan and slice into 12 servings. Top each with one-half sliced banana, hot fudge sauce, nut topping, whipped cream and cherries.

ZENITH

901 Larimer, Suite 600
Denver, Colorado
(303) 629-1989

Blue Corn Pancake With Caramelized Apples and Bananas With Caramel Sauce

½ cup milk	¼ cup blue cornmeal
1 package dry yeast	2 tablespoons butter (room temperature)
2 tablespoons sugar	2 eggs whites
¼ cup strong flour (hi-gluten)	salt to taste
1 sour apple, peeled and cut into 8 wedges	½ cup whipping cream
1 ripe banana, sliced	¼ cup toasted walnuts (optional)
about 1 cup sugar	clarified butter or vegetable oil to fry

Combine milk, yeast, sugar and butter, slightly warm until butter starts to melt. Let mix set until yeast activates (about 10 minutes). Sift flour and cornmeal into liquid and whisk until batter is smooth and lumps disappear. Whip egg whites until soft peaks form and slowly fold into batter. Spoon batter into hot pan and let cook on each side until slightly crisp. Set aside and keep warm.

Sprinkle apple wedges with 1 tablespoon of sugar and toss. Heat 1 tablespoon clarified butter of oil until oil starts to smoke. Toss apples into pan and flip until apples are brown and caramelized all over. Add sliced banana to apples and cook until soft. Remove and top pancakes with warm fruit. Rinse out pan.

Add rest of sugar to pan and moisten with water until syrupy. Brown sugar mixture until thick and candy-like. Be careful not to splatter because sugar mix will burn on contact. Slowly pour in cream and pull off heat, stirring rapidly until light brown caramel sauce comes to desired consistency. Spoon over pancakes and sprinkle with toasted walnuts over plate. Serve warm.

TANTE LOUISE

4900 East Colfax Avenue
Denver, Colorado 80220
(303) 355-4488

Brie Cheesecake On Champagne Crème Anglaise
With Fresh Plums

Cheesecake

1   pound and 10 ounces cream cheese
8   ounces ripe Brie cheese, rind removed
2   cups granulated sugar
8   eggs

Champagne Crème Anglaise

2   cups dry champagne or sparkling wine
½   cup granulated sugar
4   egg yolks
2   cups heavy cream
1   tablespoon vanilla extract or 1 vanilla bean, split

For the cheesecake

Lightly butter a 9½-inch springform pan. Preheat oven to 350°. In food processor, combine cheeses with 1¼ cup sugar. Process until mixture liquefies, scraping down sides of the bowl. Add eggs and remaining ¾ cup sugar and process until very smooth. Pour into springform pan. Set into a larger roasting pan and add enough hot water to reach halfway up the sides of the springform pan. Bake 60 minutes, or until the top is just barely brown. Chill.

For the Crème Anglaise

In a non-reactive pan, bring the champagne to a boil and reduce down to 2 tablespoons. Set aside. Place heavy cream, ¼ cup sugar and the vanilla bean (if not using extract) into a stainless steel saucepan. Set over medium high heat. Beat the egg yolk and remaining sugar in a medium-sized stainless steel bowl. Bring the cream to a boil and slowly temper into the egg yolks, whisking constantly. Return the mixture to the saucepan and place over low heat. Continue whisking until the sauce thickens slightly and coats the back of a spoon. DO NOT LET THE SAUCE BOIL. Remove from heat. If using vanilla extract, add it after the sauce has been removed from the heat. Stir in the champagne reduction and chill.

To serve

Remove the pan sides from the cheesecake. Slice into portions. Place 2 ounces of champagne crème anglaise on individual plates. Place one slice cheesecake on each plate. Garnish with fresh plum slices.

OFF BELLEVIEW GRILL

8101 East Belleview
Denver, Colorado
(303) 694-3337

Caramel Custard

¾	cup sugar	6	whole eggs
¼	cup water	1	cup sugar
2	cups milk	¼	cup vanilla
1	cup half & half		pinch of salt
6	egg yolks		

Put ¼ cup of sugar and water in a saucepan and boil over medium heat until sugar becomes golden brown and caramelized. When caramelized, coat bottom of 4-ounce ramekins.

On the stove in saucepot heat milk, half & half, vanilla to a boil. Let cook to room temperature.

In mixing bowl whip up egg yolks, whole eggs, sugar and pinch of salt.

Add egg mixture to milk mixture.

Strain through a fine china cap (strainer).

Put mixture in 4-ounce ramekins and cover each with tin foil.

Cook in a double boiler at 375° for 55 minutes.

Transfer to refrigerator and cool.

Serves 4.

MAYFAIR DELI AND PÂTISSERIE

315 Getaway Building
Aspen-Snowmass Village, Colorado
(303) 923-5938

Brigitte Couturier gets up early and offers coffee and pastries to early-morning skiers and apres skiers. Here is a variation of her renowned carrot cake which is highly recommended with a cup of cappuccino for morning or apres ski.

Carrot Cake*

2	cups sugar
2	cups flour
2	teaspoons soda
1	cup crushed pineapple, drained
1½	teaspoons allspice
4	eggs
1	cup oil
3	cups grated carrots
2	teaspoons cinnamon
1	cup raisins

Sift and mix dry ingredients. Add oil and stir well. Mixture will be very thick. Add eggs, one at a time, and mix well after each. Add carrots and raisins and pineapple and mix. Pour into greased and floured pans. Bake at 350° for 35 minutes.

Cake Filling:

1	8-ounce package cream cheese
1	box powdered sugar
1	cup chopped nuts
½	cup butter
2	teaspoons vanilla

Blend cheese, butter, sugar and vanilla. If too dry, add a little milk. Add nuts.

* Variation

THE CHART HOUSE

219 East Durant Street
Aspen, Colorado
(303) 925-3525

Chart House Mud Pie

½ package Nabisco chocolate wafers
½ stick butter, melted

1 quart coffee ice cream
1½ cup fudge sauce

Crush wafers and add butter, mix well. Press into 9-inch pie plate. Cover with soft coffee ice cream. Put into freezer until ice cream is firm. Top with cold fudge sauce (it helps to place in freezer for a time to make spreading easier). Store in freezer about 10 hours.

To serve, slice Mud Pie into 8 portions and serve on a chilled dessert plate with a chilled fork. Top with whipped cream and slivered almonds.

D-J'S CRÊPES AND OMELETS

Concert Hall Plaza Building
Vail, Colorado 81657
(303) 476-2336

Cheese Blintzes

Blintz crêpe batter:

3 eggs
1¼ cups milk
2 tablespoons oil

1 cup flour
½ teaspoon salt

Combine blintz ingredients in a blender or mixing bowl and mix thoroughly. Using a 10-inch Teflon or silverstone pan, heat pan under moderately high flame for 1½ minutes or until water drops bead and bubble away. (Tip: A well-heated pan is the secret to good, consistent blintzes. Cook them fast to a light golden brown and leave them flexible enough for folding.) Ladle at least 4 ounces of batter to coat pan and pour off excess. Once edges start to curl, loosen with spatula and flip. Cook this side for approximately 20 seconds and flip back on original side. Slide blintz onto wax paper and repeat. Makes 12 blintzes.

Blintz filler

2 cups small-curd cottage cheese
6 ounces cream cheese

½ cup sour cream
4 tablespoons honey

Heat cream cheese to soften for mixing. Mix with sour cream and cottage cheese and blend in blender thoroughly. Sweeten with honey. Fills 12 blintzes.

Blintz assembly:

Add a well-rounded tablespoon of filler to center of blintz. Fold in left and right side to overlap. Then fold bottom and top to overlap, making a square envelope for the cheese filler. Wrap in wax paper and store in the refrigerator for later use. Will keep refrigerated for 4 to 6 days.

Blintz serving:

Heat slowly in a covered and buttered pan until golden brown.

Blintz topping:

1 tablespoon sour cream per blintz
1 cup of sliced fresh strawberries (or fruit of your choice) per blintz

When blintz is golden brown, remove from pan to serving plate. Top with sour cream and smother with sliced fresh fruit. (Also delicious with some real maple syrup.)

ZENITH

901 Larimer, Suite 600
Denver, Colorado
(303) 629-1989

Chocolate Bread Pudding

1	French baguette	8	egg yolks (room temperature)
8	ounces good quality semisweet chocolate	2	whole eggs
3	cups heavy cream	1	tablespoon vanilla extract
1	cup milk	½	cup sugar
pinch of salt		4	ounces unsalted butter, melted

Cut baguette into ¼-inch slices and mix with unsalted butter. Bake in oven until toasted light brown. Set aside. Heat chocolate over boiling water until melted. Set aside. Heat cream and milk until warm to the touch, being careful not to scald. Mix whole eggs, yolks, sugar and vanilla, whisk until fully incorporated. Pour warm cream/milk mixture over eggs and sugar and blend well. Pour this mixture into chocolate and whisk until blended and no lumps of sugar remain.

Lay bread croutons on their sides in a 9 x 12 Genoise cake pan until pan is full (depending on size of baguettes or slices, some croutons may remain unused). Pour chocolate mixture into pan and let rest for 30 to 40 minutes until all bread is soaked. Bake in water bath for 40 to 60 minutes at 350° until inserted knife in center comes out cleam. Let cool overnight.

Slightly warm bottom and slide knife around edges and invert bread pudding to remove from pan. Serve warm (oven or microwave) with crème anglaise, chocolate sauce or caramel sauce.

L'OSTELLO

705 West Lionshead Circle
Vail, Colorado 81657
(303) 476-2050

Pastry Chef Raymond A. Arter

Chocolate Sorbetto With Raspberry Coulis

Sorbetto

2	cups water	⅓	cup sifted cocoa
¾	cup sugar		

Raspberry Coulis

1½	pint fresh raspberries	½	cup sugar

For Sorbetto:

Put water, sugar and cocoa in saucepan and bring to boil. After brought to boil, cool down and run in ice cream machine for 7-10 minutes. Take out of machine and put in freezer until service.

For Sauce:

Purée raspberries and sugar, then strain through fine sieve.
Serve the sorbetto on chilled plate with coulis around it.

LA COUPOLE

2191 Arapahoe Street
Paris Hotel Building
Denver, Colorado
(303) 297-2288

La Coupole makes all their own desserts on premises and are reputed to have some of the best desserts in Colorado. Here is a variation of one of their top secret creations.

Chocolate Torte*
Cake

2 cups unsifted all-purpose flour
1 teaspoon baking soda
½ cup butter or regular margarine
½ cup salad oil
3 squares unsweetened chocolate
2 cups sugar
2 eggs, beaten
½ cup sour milk (place 1½ teaspoons vinegar in a 1-cup measure;
   fill with milk to measure ½ cup)
1 teaspoon vanilla extract

Preheat oven to 350°. Sift flour with soda into large bowl. Grease well and flour two 8-by-8-by-2-inch square cake pans. In small saucepan, combine butter, oil and chocolate; stir over low heat to melt the chocolate. Add 1 cup water. Cool 15 minutes.

To flour mixture, add 2 cups sugar, the eggs, sour milk and 1 teaspoon vanilla; mix with wooden spoon. Stir in cooled chocolate just to combine. Quickly turn into prepared pans; bake 30 to 35 minutes, until surface springs back when pressed with finger.

Cool in pans 5 minutes. Carefully loosen sides with spatula. Turn out on racks; cool.

Filling

1 can (5.3 ounces) evaporated milk
¾ cup sugar
¼ cup chopped seedless raisins
½ cup chopped dates
1 teaspoon vanilla extract
½ cup chopped walnuts or pecans
½ cup chilled heavy cream

In small saucepan, combine milk, sugar and ¼ cup water. Cook over medium heat, stirring to dissolve sugar. Add raisins and dates. Stir with wooden spoon. Cook, stirring until mixture is thickened — about 5 minutes. Add vanilla and nuts. Cool completely in small bowl, beat cream with rotary beater just until stiff. On plate, place layer, top side down; spread with filling, then whipped cream. Top with second layer.

Frosting

1 package (6 ounces) semi-sweet chocolate pieces
½ cup sour cream
dash salt

Melt chocolate pieces in top of double boiler over hot water. Remove top of double boiler from hot water. Stir in sour cream and salt. With wooden spoon, beat until smooth. Cool 5 minutes, until frosting is of spreading consistency. With spatula, frost top of cake, swirling decoratively; use rest of frosting to cover sides. Refrigerate one hour before serving. To serve: With sharp, thin knife, mark top of cake into four quarters; then cut each quarter into four slices. Makes 16 servings.

* Variation

JEROME HOTEL
330 East Main Street
Aspen, Colorado 81611
(303) 920-1000

Chocolate Walnut Crêpe

Crêpe Batter:

2   eggs
1   cup white flour

1   teaspoon nutmeg
1   cup water

Combine ingredients in blender until smooth. Refrigerate one hour before using. Makes 6 to 8 crêpes.

Egg Custard:

6   egg yolks slightly beaten
⅓   cup sugar

2   cups scalded milk
    dash of salt

Stir in a double boiler until it thickens. Cook in refrigerator.

Crêpe Filling:

2   tablespoons custard
½   banana, sliced into coin-sized slices
2   tablespoons dark chocolate sauce (see Sauce section)
1   tablespoon diced walnuts
1   heaping tablespoon of freshly whipped cream

Warm crêpe in pan, add 2 tablespoons custard and ½ sliced banana to each crêpe. Fold crêpe. Top with dark chocolate sauce, 1 tablespoon diced walnuts and whipped cream to each crêpe, and serve.

CLIFF YOUNG'S
RESTAURANT

700 East Seventeenth Avenue
Denver, Colorado 80203
(303) 831-8900

Pastry Chef Gary McCafferty

Cinnamon Walnut Cookies

1   pound butter
7   ounces sugar
pinch salt
1   tablespoon vanilla extract
7   ounces chopped walnuts

15 ounces all-purpose flour
7   ounces brown sugar
1   heaping tablespoon cinnamon
2   egg yolks

In a small electric mixer bowl, cream together butter and sugar; add in yolks, salt and vanilla extract until mixed well. Then add in walnuts, brown sugar and cinnamon and mix. Add flour and mix until just mixed. Roll dough into logs about 10 inches long and $1/8$-inch thick. Cool. Cut in thin slices and place on a sheet pan. Bake in a preheated 350° oven for 10 minutes or until golden brown.

CAFE FRANCO

2160 South Holly
Denver, Colorado
(303) 759-2276

Crêpes Suzettes

18 crepes (see Basic Crêpe)
8 lumps sugar rubbed over rind of 1 orange and 1 lemon until they have absorbed their essential flavor
½ cup butter
1 orange, strained juice
½ cup super fine sugar
2 strips orange rind
2 strips lemon rind
⅓ cup Grand Marnier or Dry Sec
3 tablespoons Maraschino Liqueur
¼ cup brandy

Place rubbed sugar lumps in a bowl and crush them. Mix in the butter and let stand 15 minutes. (This allows butter to absorb the orange and lemon zest, giving this recipe its particular fragrance.) Add in a tablespoon of orange juice and ¼ cup of super fine sugar. Then add in remaining orange juice and mix well in a glass serving bowl. Heat butter and add the following:

¼ fresh orange juice
½ fresh lemon juice
1½ tablespoons sugar

Let stand over low heat for 5 minutes.

At this point brandy is added, heated and flamed, before the crêpes have been heated.

If guests prefer crêpes less saturated with liquor, add crêpes; heat; fold in quarters; and place on heated plates before brandy has been added and flamed. Then add brandy (heated and flamed) and spoon its sauce over crêpes.

RUDI'S

4720 Table Mesa Drive
Boulder, Colorado 80303
(303) 494-5858
Chef Faith Stone

Date Soufflé

8 ounces cream cheese, softened
¼ cup real maple syrup
1 tablespoon lemon juice
3 bananas, mashed
1 fresh pineapple, crushed
½ cup chopped dates
½ cup chopped pecans
1 cup heavy cream, whipped

Cream the cheese in a mixer, beating in the maple syrup, lemon juice and mashed bananas. Stir in the pineapple, dates and pecans. Fold in the whipped cream. Fill custard or dessert cups and freeze for 20 minutes or refrigerate several hours. Serves 10.

D-J'S CREPES AND OMELETS

Concert Hall Plaza Building
Vail, Colorado 81657
(303) 476-2336

Dessert Crêpe

½ sliced banana
1 or 2 scoops French Vanilla (or favorite flavor) ice cream
4 ounces fresh or frozen fruit
hot fudge (optional)
whipped cream for topping

See recipe for basic crêpe batter. Makes 10 to 12 crêpes. Extras may be frozen. Ladle four 2-3 ounces of batter in a hot, dry 12-inch silverstone or Teflon pan. Pour off excess and lower heat. Flip once when edges curl and bottom is golden brown. Cook reverse side for about 30 to 35 seconds. Slide onto plate. Fold the above ingredients into the crêpe, saving whipped cream for topping. Serves 1.

FIREFLY CAFE

5410 East Colfax Avenue
Denver, Colorado 80220
(202) 388-8429

Firefly Granola

1	quart Quaker Quick Oats	1	cup walnuts
2	cups desiccated coconut	¼	cup molasses
½	cup sesame seeds	¼	cup honey
1	cup safflower oil	½	cup raisins

Heat the oil in a saute pan to just below the smoking point and add the sesame seeds. After about 30 seconds add the honey and molasses. Remove from heat and allow to cook for about 10 minutes.

In a large mixing bowl stir together the oats, coconut and nuts. Pour the cooled mixture over the dry ingredients and mix well. Pour the mixture into a large cookie sheet and toast in a 325° oven, stirring every 10 minutes until the mixture is evenly browned. Allow to cool slightly and mix in the raisins and store in an airtight container.

This recipe is very versatile. One may substitute any kind of nuts preferred. One may also choose to replace the raisins with any dried fruit of choice such as apples, apricots, currants or the like.

May be mixed with non-fat yogurt for dessert.

RUDI'S

4720 Table Mesa Drive
Boulder, Colorado
(303) 494-5858
Chef Faith Stone

Rudi's began as a little vegetarian restaurant in the fall of 1975: the creation of Chef Faith Stone and a group of friends. Over the years, Rudi's evolved to include fresh fish, natural poultry and beef, Boulder-grown organic produce when available; filtered water. Rudi's makes its own yogurt and cheese from scratch (no mixes, no instant food, no microwaves).

Rudi's has earned all sorts of local rave reviews and culinary awards, as well as national acclaim in *Gourmet Magazine* and numerous other publications.

Rudi's menu reflects the loving, caring ambiance of the cuisine as it reads,

"We really care about the foods we make. We love cooking, we hope it shows. We're happy to serve you and are glad you come here year after year. We want the quality of our ingredients to nourish your body and the love we put in to feed your spirit."

Gâteau A L'Orange

Cake

6	whole eggs at room temperature
⅔	cup sugar
1	cup plus 2 tablespoons all-purpose flour
2	tablespoons vegetable oil
¾	cup Grand Marnier or Triple Sec for soaking cake

Whip eggs and sugar together in mixer until light in color and trippled in volume. Transfer mixture to a large mixing bowl and gradually fold/work in the flour, sifting it over the surface of the batter and turning it in, with a rubber spatula. When all the flour is incorporated, fold in the oil. Pour the batter into a lined, buttered and floured 8-inch cake pan. Bake at 350° for 30 minutes or until a toothpick inserted in the center comes out cleam. Cool for 5 minutes in the pan, then remove and cool completely.

Filling

1	cup sugar
1	cup water
1	pound butter, softened
6	egg yolks

Boil sugar and water together in a saucepan for 5 minutes. Place egg yolks in a mixing bowl and pour hot sugar over top. Whip immediately at high speed until quadrupled in volume and very light and fluffy. When the mixture has cooled to room temperature, turn the speed on to low and gradually beat in the softened butter 1 tablespoon at a time. When all the butter is added, turn the speed up to medium and whip until smooth and fluffy.

Icing

1	cup marmalade
1	cup toasted sliced almonds

With a serrated knife, split the cake in half. Drizzle half the Grand Marnier over each half of cake. Spread a third of the filling between the layers and ice the sides and top of the cake with the remaining filling.

Freeze the cake for 30-60 minutes to set the icing. Next lightly spread the top and sides of the cake with a thin layer of marmalade and press toasted almonds into the sides. Refrigerate until serving time.

L'OSTELLO

705 West Lionshead Circle
Vail, Colorado 81657
(303) 476-2050

L'Ostello began serving inspired, but not traditional, Italian cuisine to guests on December 15, 1989, in Vail, Colorado. Lewis Futterman, Owner; John Lunsmann, Manager; Michael Schwarts, Chef; and Raymond A. Arter, Pastry Chef, were formerly the team at Andiamo in New York where they gathered rave reviews. Now they have moved to Vail and opened L'Ostello which nightly fills with Vail guests and which ranks as one of Colorado's finest restaurants.

Ginger Crème Brûlée

1	quart heavy cream	¾ cup sugar
10	egg yolks	1 ½ teaspoons chopped ginger

Bring the heavy cream to a boil in one pot and in another dissolve the sugar and ginger in a little water. When the sugar and ginger come to a boil add to the heavy cream. Add this mixture in a little at a time to the egg yolk until it is all incorporated. Put on ice bath immediately. When cool, pour in ovenproof ramekins. Then set them in a water bath and bake at 350° for ½ hour to ¾ hour. Remove from oven and let cool in refrigerator. When cool sprinkle with sugar on top and put under broiler until golden brown.

ZENITH

901 Larimer, Suite 600
Denver, Colorado
(303) 629-1989

Goat Cheese Tart

Makes 1 10-inch tart

Pastry

6	ounces soft butter	8	ounces flour
3	ounces sugar	1	egg
pinch of salt			

Cream butter, sugar and salt together until light and fluffy. Add flour and mix until incorporated. Add egg and finish mixing until dough-like ball occurs. Press into tart mold and bake at 350° for 10 to 12 minutes or until set (dough should be weighted with beans so as not to slide down sides of mold and to hold its shape). Let cool.

Filling

4	ounces good quality goat cheese	¾	cup sugar
4	ounces cream cheese	2	eggs
4	ounces soft butter	1	zest of orange

Mix cream cheese, butter and sugar together until volume doubles (light and fluffy). Add beaten eggs slowly until fully incorporated. Be sure to scrape sides of mixing bowl to eliminate lumps. Add zest of orange and pour into half-baked tart shell and bake at 350° until inserted knife comes out clean (15 to 20 minutes). Tart can be glazed with fruit jam or decorated with fresh berries.

DUGGAN'S

South Federal at Belleview
Denver, Colorado
(303) 795-1081

Iron Skillet Peach Cobbler
With Bourbon Cinnamon Cream

Cobbler Dough

¼ teaspoon nutmeg
2 cups all-purpose flour
1 tablespoon sugar
¼ teaspoon salt
½ pound unsalted butter, cut into chips and chilled
3 tablespoons ice water

Filling

12 large ripe peaches
juice of 1 lemon
¼ cup sugar
¼ teaspoon cinnamon
1 tablespoon sugar, for top of the crust

To prepare the dough:
In a bowl, sift together the dry ingredients and work in the butter with fingertips until the mixture is a mealy consistency.

A little at a time, add the ice water until the dough sticks together. Do not overmix. Shape dough into a ball, wrap and refrigerate for 15 minutes.

Preheat the oven to 425°.

Peel and slice the peaches and toss with the lemon juice and sugar that has been mixed with nutmeg and cinnamon.

Place the peaches in a 10-inch cast iron skillet.

On a floured surface, roll out the dough to fit the pan. Place the dough over the peaches. Dust with the sugar.

Bake for 45 minutes, or until golden brown. Serve warm, with Bourbon Cinnamon Cream. Serves 4.

Bourbon Cinnamon Cream

1 cup heavy cream
1 tablespoon sugar
¼ teaspoon cinnamon
2 tablespoons bourbon

Whip the heavy cream, sugar, and cinnamon together until stiff peaks form. Stir in the bourbon gently.

MARINA LANDING

8101 East Belleview
Denver, Colorado
(303) 770-4741

Lime Vanilla-Bean Ice Cream With Raspberry Sauce and Pine Nut Brown Sugar Cookies (see page 21)

Lime Vanilla-Bean Ice Cream

1	cup milk	2	cups heavy cream
⅔	cup sugar		grated zest of 1 lime
2	vanilla beans, cut in half lengthwise	½	cup fresh lime juice
9	large egg yolks, at room temperature		

Combine the milk, sugar, and vanilla beans in the top of a double boiler and heat over barely simmering water. Lightly beat the yolks. When milk mixture is almost to the point of boiling, pour a little into the yolks to warm them. Stir and add a bit more hot milk.

Pour warmed yolks into the milk in a slow, steady stream, stirring all the while. Continue to cook, stirring constantly, over hot, not boiling water until mixture coats the spoon.

Press a sheet of wax paper onto the surface of the custard and allow to cool to room temperature.

Add cream, lime zest and lime juice to the custard and refrigerate for several hours.

Just before freezing, remove vanilla beans and scrape their seeds into the mixture. Stir and pour into an ice cream maker and freeze according to directions. Serves 6.

Raspberry Sauce

1	pint fresh or frozen raspberries	¼	cup sugar

Mix sugar and raspberries and simmer until mixture starts to thicken, about 5 minutes. Allow to cool and refrigerate.

THE WILDFLOWER INN

174 East Gore Creek Drive
Vail, Colorado 81657
(303) 476-5011 ext. 170

Mosaic Nut Tart

1 ½ cups flour
½ lemon, juiced
½ teaspoon baking powder
2 egg yolks

½ cup confectioners' sugar
¼ pound (1 stick) softened butter
¼ teaspoon salt

Mix egg yolks and confectioners' sugar. Add flour and lemon juice. Add flour, baking powder, and salt. Add butter. Mix until dough is well combined. Chill for one hour. Roll dough to ¼" thick. Form to a 10" tart tin. Partially bake shell at 350° until shell is light brown.

Filling

1 pound (4 sticks) butter
¾ pound honey
¼ pound sugar
1 pound brown sugar
2 ounces pine nuts

2 ounces pistachios
2 ounces pecans
2 ounces macadamias
2 ounces walnuts

Place butter, honey, sugar and brown sugar in a saucepan. Bring to a boil for three minutes. Add nuts. Pour into the prebaked tart shell. Bake at 325° for twenty minutes or until brown and bubbly.

Chocolate Sauce

1 cup cream
1 ½ cups chocolate chips

1 teaspoon vanilla
½ cup milk

In a saucepan bring cream to a boil. Remove from heat. Add chocolate chips and vanilla. Stir until chocolate is well dissolved. Add milk.

Yields 1 10" tart.

RUDI'S

4720 Table Mesa Drive
Boulder, Colorado 80303
(303) 494-5858

Chef Faith Stone

Pecan Pie

1   nine-inch pie shell (your favorite recipe)

Filling

¼   pound butter — melted
1   cup brown sugar
3   eggs beaten
½   cup pure maple syrup

1   teaspoon vanilla
½   teaspoon salt
1¼   cups pecan halves

Fill pie shell with 1 cup dry beans and partially bake approximately 15 minutes in a 350° oven. Cool and remove dry beans. Beat together butter and brown sugar, add eggs and beat until smooth. Add maple syrup, vanilla and salt, beat until well incorporated, stir in pecans. Pour filling into partially baked pie shell and bake pie in a preheated 350° oven for 45 minutes or until set. Remove from oven and cool at least 1 hour before serving. If sliced prematurely, filling is not set and falls apart.

MARINA LANDING

8101 East Belleview
Denver, Colorado 80237
(303) 770-4741

Marina Landing is located just east of I-25 on Belleview in Marina Square. It is billed as a restaurant for all tastes and its extensive menu appeals to all tastes.

When guests enter they pass through double doors enclosing an authentic ship's wheel which had to be disassembled and cut in two before being mounted in the specially built glass doors, and a large ship's wheel in the back dining area came from the Queen City, a famous Mississippi sternwheeler.

The decor is a yachting club motif and the walls are covered with the Rosenfeld Collection of photos from the classic America's Cup Races. The pictures are blow-ups and are spectacular with color. Crafted from wood in the lounge are three hand-carved racing scenes and several exact scale ship models.

For the past three years Marina Landing has been awarded Denver's "Favorite Place for Breakfast and Weekend Brunch."

Marina Landing specializes in fresh seafood and grilled steaks. They also offer light salad entrées, pastas and sandwiches.

Marina Landing invites you to try their wonderful breads, pastries, and desserts that are made fresh daily from their own in-house 5,000-square-foot bakery.

Pine Nut Brown Sugar Cookies
With Lime Vanilla-Bean Ice Cream

1¼ cups sifted all-purpose flour
dash of salt
¼   teaspoon baking soda
¼   cup unsalted butter, softened
¼   cup margarine, softened
8   ounces light brown sugar
1   large egg
½   teaspoon vanilla extract
1   cup pine nuts

Preheat the oven to 350°. Generously grease two cooking sheets.

Combine flour with the salt and soda, then sift again. Set aside.

Cream the butter, margarine, and brown sugar until fluffy, about 3 minutes. Add the egg and the vanilla and combine well. Add the dry mixture in 4 parts, mixing well after each addition. Fold in pine nuts. Drop by teaspoonfuls onto the prepared sheets, leaving room for them to spread.

Bake for 16 to 17 minutes, or until golden. Remove from cookie sheets and cool on a rack. Repeat with remaining batter until used up.

PHILADELPHIA FILLY

278 South Downing Street
Denver, Colorado
(303) 733-2208

Pot De Crème

1   cup half & half
2   cups semisweet chocolate
6   ounces Eggbeaters
1   tablespoon brandy or other liquor (optional)

Scald half & half in a pan over medium high heat. Put chocolate and brandy in blender. Pour hot half & half over chocolate and let sit 30 seconds to soften chocolate. Blend on high speed for 30 seconds. Continue blending as you add the Eggbeaters. Blend 30 seconds more and pour mixture into 8 stemmed glasses, or into one serving bowl. Refrigerate (don't freeze) for 2 hours. Serve with whipped cream.

JOHN'S RESTAURANT

2328 Pearl
Boulder, Colorado 80304
(303) 444-5232

Ripe Figs With Mascarpone, Toasted Almonds and Port Wine

8   fresh ripe figs (4 whole and 4 quartered)
8   ounces of mascarpone
16   whole natural almonds
6   teaspoons powdered sugar
6   ounces port wine

Toast almonds in a skillet or oven. Score four whole figs by cutting an X in the top, three-quarters of the way down and separate the sections slightly, so they look like flower petals.

Stir powdered sugar and two ounces of port wine into the mascarpone. Spoon mascarpone (in a dome shape) into four bowls. Place one whole fig on top of mound. Around the center arrange fig slices and almonds. Pour one ounce of port wine over each dessert. Serves 4.

WIENERSTUBE RESTAURANT

633 East Hyman Avenue
at Spring Street
Aspen, Colorado 81611
(303) 925-3357

Salzburger Nockerl

This soufflé of Salzburg is temperamental like a primadonna, so extra care in handling the ingredients and baking and serving procedure should be followed explicitly.

2	egg yolks	4	egg whites
1	teaspoon vanilla extract		pinch of salt
½	teaspoon grated lemon peel	2	tablespoons of sugar
1	tablespoon of flour or cornstarch		confectioners' sugar

Preheat the oven to 350°. In a medium-size mixing bowl, break the egg yolks with a wire whisk and stir in the lemon peel and vanilla extract.

In another mixing bowl using a clean wire whisk, rotary or electric beater, beat the egg whites with a pinch of salt until half firm. Add the sugar slowly and beat until the whites form a stiff, firm peak. (Overbeating this meringue type mixture will result in breaking the tiny air bubbles, resulting in failure to rise.)

In a folding motion with a rubber spatula, fold the yolk mixture into the egg whites using under-cutting motion while turning the bowl with the other hand. Halfway through this process sift/sprinkle flour into batter. Don't overfold.

In individual fire-proof serving dishes or one large oblong 8 by 12-inch ceramic or decorative glass serving dish, brush with butter on side and bottom. Using the rubber spatula, in individual servings make one mound (Nockerl), if using the large serving dish, make three large mounds of the mixture in the dish. Bake in the middle of the oven about 10 minutes for individual servings and about 15 minutes for the large serving, until lightly brown but still soft on the inside. Sprinkle with powdered or confectioners' sugar and serve at once. The soufflé may be served with hot vanilla sauce or freshly made hot raspberry syrup/sauce as accompaniment. Serves 4 to 6.

PAUL'S PLACE

3000 East First Avenue
Cherry Creek Mall
Denver, Colorado 80206
(303) 321-5801

Strawberry Base Sauce For Waffle Toppings
(Makes the following Toppings)
* Strawberries Grand Marnier
* Bananas Grand Marnier
* Mandarin Orange Grand Marnier

Combine in a saucepan the following:

½   pound frozen strawberries in sauce
½   ounce arrowroot
¼   teaspoon lemon zest

Reduce on stove until desired consistency is achieved. This will keep until ready to use in refrigerator.

When ready to use fold in:

1   ounce Grand Marnier (optional)
1   8-ounce can Mandarin orange segments, drained or
2   pints fresh strawberries, quartered or
3   cups fresh sliced bananas

Serve at room temperature.

RUDI'S

4720 Table Mesa Drive
Boulder, Colorado 80303
(303) 494-5858

Chef Faith Stone

Strawberry Cream

2 cups heavy cream for whipping	½ pint strawberries (1 cup)
2 tablespoons sugar	1 tablespoon sugar
½ teaspoon vanilla	
1 tablespoon fruit liqueur, such as Grand Marnier or Amaretto	

Slice strawberries, sprinkle with sugar and fruit liqueur. Marinate for 10 minutes for juices to blend.

Whip cream with wire whip, electric mixer, or food processor until it holds firm peaks, but not buttery.

Fold marinated berries into whipped cream. Fill a pastry bag fitted with a plain tube and pipe into curled pizzelles or fill pizzelles with a spoon.

THE MAGIC PAN CRÊPERIE

1465 Larimer
Denver, Colorado
(303) 534-0123

Strawberry Crêpes Supreme

6   cups sliced fresh strawberries (reserve 6 whole berries for garnish)
¾   cup brown sugar
2   cups whipping cream, whipped
powdered sugar
½   cup brown sugar
6   cooked crêpes

For best results, slice the berries no more than an hour or two ahead of serving time. It is important not to bruise the berries or allow them to go mushy. Toss the sliced strawberries very gently with ¾ cup brown sugar. At serving time, place 1 cup of sliced, sweetened berries in center of each crêpe. Top each serving with 2 tablespoons of whipped cream. Sprinkle 1 tablespoon brown sugar (per serving) over whipped cream. Fold sides of crêpe over center to enclose filling. Sprinkle with a little powdered sugar over the filled crêpes. Top each crêpe with 1 tablespoon whipped cream. Sprinkle 1 teaspoon brown sugar over whipped cream on each serving and top with a whole strawberry. Serves 6.

DADDY BRUCE

1629 Bruce Randolph Avenue
Denver, Colorado
(303) 295-9115

20th and Arapahoe
Boulder, Colorado
(303) 449-8890

Sweet Potato Pie

2	cups mashed sweet potatoes	2	tablespoons butter
1	cup sweet milk	1	teaspoon salt
3	eggs	6	tablespoons sugar
½	cup sugar		nutmeg, if desired

Beat the yolks of the eggs into the mashed potato, add the melted butter, and then the other ingredients. Pour into a pie pan lined with pastry given below; bake in a moderate oven until the pie is set. (Optional: Make a stiff meringue of the egg whites and mix tablespoons of sugar, spread over the top of the pie, and bake slowly until a delicate brown. One-fourth cup of coconut may be added to the filling.)

Pastry

1½	cups flour	½	cup cold water
1	cup shortening	½	teaspoon salt

Thoroughly mix the flour, shortening and salt. Add just enough of the water to hold the particles together. Toss on a board and roll thin.

THE WILDFLOWER INN

174 East Gore Creek Drive
Vail, Colorado 81657
(303) 476-5011 ext. 170

Torta Regina

8	eggs, separated	2	ounces filberts, finely ground
6	ounces sugar	2	ounces almonds, finely ground
7	ounces chocolate, finely chopped		zest of 1 orange, finely grated
2	ounces pecans, finely ground		zest of 1 lemon, finely grated
2	ounces walnuts, finely ground		

Whip egg yolks with ½ the sugar until pale yellow and thick.

Add finely grated chocolate. Mix until well incorporated. Add zest of orange and lemon.

Whip egg whites gradually until soft peaks form. Add remaining sugar and continue to whip until peaks are firm and glassy, but not dry.

Alternately fold the nuts and whites into the yolk mixture until all is well incorporated.

Spread batter into an 8″ springform pan.

Bake at 325° for 45 minutes. Cool completely.

Chocolate Glaze

2	cups cream	1	pound semi-sweet chocolate
6	ounces sugar		

Heat cream and sugar to a boil.

When sugar has dissolved completely, remove from heat. Add chocolate, stirring until chocolate has completely melted.

Glaze cake while glaze is still warm.

STRINGS

1700 Humboldt
Denver, Colorado 80218
(303) 831-7310

White Chocolate Boats

½	pound white chocolate	1	egg yolk
1	level teaspoon gelatin	7	ounces whipping cream
1	egg		

Filling:

2	ounces raspberry puree	½	pint whipping cream

Melt chocolate in double boiler. Dissolve gelatin in 1 tablespoon boiling water. Using a sturdy whisk, beat egg, egg yolk, and melted gelatin into the warm chocolate until smooth. Allow to cool slightly. Beat whipping cream until very stiff, and then lightly fold through chocolate mixture. Do not overmix, otherwise mix becomes very soft. Pipe into 2″ rosettes on waxed paper. Freeze until solid. Dip halfway into melted bittersweet chocolate while still frozen and allow chocolate to set. Place 2 rosettes upright together into a paper baking cup.

Chip cream until stiff and lightly fold in raspberry puree. Pipe the cream between the 2 rosettes and garnish the top with fresh raspberries and grated chocolate.

SAUCES & DRESSINGS XII

P. McClure

SAUCES & DRESSINGS, ETC., XII

Apple Mint Salsa serve with Lamb Quesadilla (Bull & Bush) — p. 1
Asian Salad Dressing (Rick's Cafe) — p. 1
Béarnaise Sauce (The Red Onion) — p. 2
Black Bean Garlic Sauce (Panda Cafe — Introduction) — p. 2
Black Bean Sauce (Zenith) — p. 3
Blue Cheese Dressing (The Chart House) — p. 3
Blue Cheese Dressing (Sweeney's — Introduction) — p. 4
Brown Sauce (Cafe Giovanni) — p. 5
Champagne Vinaigrette serve with Charbroiled Eggplant (Strings) — p. 5
Chile Relleno Sauce for Chile Rellenos (Los Amigos) — p. 6
Chocolate Sauce (Jerome Hotel) — p. 6
Coriander Dressing for Black Bean and Shrimp Salad (Bull & Bush) — p. 6
Country Mustard (The Silver Queen) — p. 7
Creamy Garlic Dressing (The Silver Queen) — p. 7
Curry Rice Salad Dressing (The Denver Salad Company) — p. 8
Daddy Bruce's Famous Barbecue Sauce (Daddy Bruce — Introduction) — p. 9
Demi-Glace Sauce (Wellshire Inn) — p. 9
Dijon Mustard Sauce (Paul's Place) — p. 10
Fish Sauce Variation I and II (T-WA Inn) — p. 10
French Mustard (A Piece of Quiet) — p. 11
Green Chili (La Bola) — p. 11
Herbal Buerre Rouge for Hazelnut Crusted Colorado Rack of Lamb (Cliff Young's) — p. 12
Hollandaise (Rudi's) — p. 12
Honey Mustard Poppy Seed Dressing (Flagstaff House Restaurant) — p. 13
House Dressing from Sopris Restaurant (Sopris Restaurant) — p. 13
John Denver's BBQ Sauce for Grilled Shrimp (The Tower Magic Bar & Restaurant) — p. 14
Ketchup (Turntable Restaurant) — p. 14
Lavender Butter Sauce for Lochinvar Scottish Salmon (Alfredo's) — p. 15
Lemon Tarragon Vinaigrette for Grilled Asparagus and Shiitake Mushrooms Salad (Sweet Basil) — p. 15
Light Ginger Soy Sauce (Panda Cafe) — p. 15
Marinara Sauce (The Saucy Noodle Ristorante) — p. 16
Mayonnaise (Flagstaff House Restaurant) — p. 16
Mayonnaise Variation (Low Cholesterol) (Canterbury Cheese) — p. 16
Mornay Sauce (Rudi's) — p. 17
Mustard Dressing (Wellshire Inn) — p. 17
Niçoise Olive Sauce (Flagstaff House Restaurant) — p. 17
Parmesan Dressing (Rudi's) — p. 18
Picante Sauce (Jerome Hotel) — p. 18
Pineapple Ginger Sauce for Trout (Transalpin) — p. 19
Pineapple Salsa (The Denver Salad Company) — p. 19
Quick Mint Sauce for Lamb (A Piece of Quiet) — p. 20
Raspberry Vinegar Demi-Glace Sauce with Fresh Thyme (Poppies Bistro Cafe) — p. 20
Raspberry/Walnut Dressing for Broiled Barberry Duck Salad "Framboise" (Wienerstube Restaurant) — p. 21
Red Wine Sauce for the Chicken Breast Boursin (Ute City Banque) — p. 21
Salsa (Botana Junction) — p. 22
Salsa Crude (The Blue Bonnet Cafe and Lounge — Introduction) — p. 22
Sambal Ulek (Hot Chili Paste) (T-WA Inn — Introduction) — p. 23
Shallot Sauce (Sweet Basil) — p. 23
Smoked Tomato Salsa for Avocado Red Pepper Quesadilla (Uptown Grill) — p. 24
Soy Sauce Marinade (Imperial Chinese Seafood) — p. 24
Sweet and Sour Sauce Dip (Asia Chinese Restaurant) — p. 25
Szechwan Sauce (Imperial Chinese Seafood) — p. 25
Teriyaki Marinade (Minturn Country Club — Introduction) — p. 26
Thai-Vinaigrette Dressing for Thai-Chicken Pasta Salad (The Denver Salad Company) — p. 26
T.L.C. Butter (La Bola) — p. 27
Tomato Sauce (The Villa at Palmer Lake) — p. 27

BULL & BUSH

Cherry Creek Drive at Dexter
Denver, Colorado
(303) 759-0333

Apple Mint Salsa
serve with Lamb Quesadilla (see Appetizer section)

2	cups fresh apple, diced	½	cup apple mint jelly
½	cup red onion, diced	¼	cup red bell pepper, diced
1	tablespoon fresh jalapeño, diced fine		

Mix all above ingredients well.

RICK'S CAFE

80 South Madison
Denver, Colorado 80209
(303) 399-4448

Asian Salad Dressing
(Rick's Cafe House Specialty)

½	tablespoon ginger	¼	cup lime juice
¼	cup sugar	2	tablespoons sesame oil
¾	cup soy sauce	½	cup hot oil
¼	cup water		

Combine all the ingredients except the oil in a mixing bowl, gradually whip the oil and set aside. Pour oil over Asian Salad (see Salad section) and toss. Then add the rest of mixture and toss again.

THE RED ONION

420 East Cooper Street Mall
Aspen, Colorado 81611
(303) 925-9043

Béarnaise Sauce
First prepare Hollandaise Sauce

Hollandaise

2   egg yolks
¼   teaspoon salt
dash cayenne pepper
½   cup melted butter
1   tablespoon fresh lemon juice

With egg beater or electric mixer, beat egg yolks until thick and lemon-colored: add salt, cayenne.

Add ¼ cup melted butter, about 1 teaspoon at a time, beating constantly.

Combine remaining ¼ cup melted butter with lemon juice. Slowly add, about 2 teaspoons at a time, to yolk mixture, beating constantly.

Then prepare Béarnaise addition:

To sauce, add 1 teaspoon each minced onion and parsley and 1 teaspoon minced fresh, or ½ teaspoon dried, tarragon, or 1½ teaspoon St. Mary's Gourmet Vinegar. Makes ½ cup.

PANDA CAFE

1098 South Federal Boulevard
Denver, Colorado
(303) 936-2500

Chef Billy Lam has turned a former fast food spot into one of Denver's finest and most fashionable Chinese restaurants. Guests for lunch and dinner include many of Denver's most prominent restaurateurs who enjoy the Panda Cafe's fresh, creative fare.

Black Bean Garlic Sauce*

2   tablespoons canned black beans, rinsed and mashed
2   cloves fresh garlic, crushed
2   tablespoons light soy sauce
2   tablespoons dry sherry or Chinese wine

Mix above ingredients and top over pork or duck.

* Variation

ZENITH

901 Larimer, Suite 600
Denver, Colorado
(303) 629-1989

Black Bean Sauce

2 cups black beans soaked overnight
1 serrano pepper
2 tablespoons cumin powder
juice of 1 lime

5 tomatillos
water or chicken stock
salt and pepper to taste

Cook black beans with rest of ingredients until beans are soft. Continue to keep covered with liquid, but not totally immersed. Adjust seasoning to your liking and in a bar blender or food processor blend beans until smooth. Adjust consistency of sauce to your liking.

THE CHART HOUSE

219 East Durant Street
Aspen, Colorado
(303) 925-3525

Blue Cheese Dressing

Best made 24 hours in advance and refrigerated.

¾ cup sour cream
½ teaspoon dry mustard
½ teaspoon black pepper
½ teaspoon salt

⅓ teaspoon garlic powder
1 teaspoon worcestershire sauce
1⅓ cups mayonnaise
4 ounces imported Blue Danish cheese

Blend the first six ingredients at a low speed for two minutes. Then add mayonnaise and blend an additional half minute at low speed. Stir in crumbled cheese. Blend no longer than 4 minutes. Makes 2 cups.

SWEENEY'S

1644 Animas View Drive
Durango, Colorado 81301
(303) 247-5236

Sweeney's has long been one of the most popular gathering spots for imbibers and steak enthusiasts. The bar area is always packed with those enjoying "juice" as they wait in merry company to be seated and served fine steaks and more for dinner. Here is a variation of Sweeney's delicious Blue Cheese dressing.

Blue Cheese Dressing

6	egg yolks	¾	teaspoon salt
¾	teaspoon paprika	½	teaspoon dry mustard
6	cups olive oil	9	tablespoons St. Mary's Gourmet Vinegar

Beat egg yolks; add salt, paprika and mustard. Add part of oil slowly and continue beating until thick. Add 9 tablespoons of vinegar a little at a time, alternating with remaining oil.

6	ounces blue cheese, crumbled	2	teaspoons minced garlic
¾	cup sour cream	3	tablespoons St. Mary's Gourmet Vinegar
¾	teaspoon celery salt	¾	teaspoon onion salt
2	teaspoons Worcestershire sauce	½	teaspoon white pepper

Mix remaining ingredients thoroughly; blend into oil mixture. Makes about 6½ cups of dressing.

CAFE GIOVANNI

1515 Market Street
Denver, Colorado 80202
(303) 825-6555

Brown Sauce

5	tablespoons butter	4	tablespoons flour
½	medium-size onion, diced	6	cups canned-beef bouillon, hot
2	stalks celery, diced	2	tablespoons tomato paste
2	carrots, diced	¼	teaspoon thyme
3	strips bacon, blanched		

Brown Sauce may be prepared in the classical manner or by the following shortcut method. Melt butter in a heavy saucepan. Add onion, celery, carrot and bacon and cook over low heat for 10 minutes. Add the flour and blend thoroughly. Cook an additional 10 minutes or until the flour is golden brown. Watch carefully, stirring often so that the flour does not burn. Add the hot bouillon, tomato paste and thyme. Mix vigorously. Simmer over low heat about 2 hours or until sauce lightly coats a spoon. Strain. Makes 1 quart. (Serve with Sweetbreads Aux Marsala in Entree Meat section.)

STRINGS

1700 Humboldt
Denver, Colorado 80218
(303) 831-7310

Champagne Vinaigrette
Serve with Charbroiled Eggplant (see Vegetable section)

½	cup champagne vinegar	½	teaspoon white pepper
2	teaspoons brown sugar	¼	cup olive oil
⅛	cup mustard, prepared	½	cup cottonseed oil
½	teaspoon salt		

Mix well, then add slowly olive oil and cottonseed oil. Serves 4.

LOS AMIGOS

318 East Hanson Ranch Road
Vail, Colorado
(303) 476-5847

Chile Relleno Sauce
for Chile Rellenos (see Vegetable section)

4	ounces butter	2	8-ounce cans diced green chiles
¼	cup olive oil	2	tablespoons salt
½	large onion, diced	½	tablespoon pepper
2	garlic cloves, minced	½	teaspoon coriander
5	cups tomatoes, diced		

In a large skillet melt butter with olive oil. Sauté onion and garlic over medum heat until onions are transparent. Add tomatoes and chiles. Cook for 5 minutes. Add seasonings and simmer for one hour. Serve over rellenos immediately as they come out of the oven.

JEROME HOTEL

330 East Main Street
Aspen, Colorado 81611
(303) 920-1000

Chocolate Sauce

1	cup semisweet chocolate pieces	1	tablespoon butter
½ to ⅓	cup white corn syrup	¼	teaspoon vanilla extract
¼	cup light cream		

In double boiler, heat the chocolate pieces with the corn syrup, stirring, until blended. Stir in the cream, butter, and vanilla extract. Serve warm. Makes 4 servings.

BULL & BUSH

Cherry Creek Drive at Dexter
Denver, Colorado
(303) 759-0333

Coriander Dressing
for Black Bean and Shrimp Salad (see Salad section)

5	tablespoons chopped coriander leaves	10-15	drops Tabasco sauce
2	garlic cloves, chopped	¼	teaspoon salt
¾	cup red wine vinegar	¼	teaspoon freshly ground black pepper
1	tablespoon fresh lemon or lime juice	⅓	cup safflower oil
2	tablespoons dijon mustard	¼	cup olive oil
2	tablespoons honey		

Put all the ingredients, except the oils, in a blender or food processor and process for 15 seconds. Add the oil slowly and process until smooth, about 30 seconds.

THE SILVER QUEEN

500 Sixth Street
Georgetown, Colorado
(303) 569-2961 — local
(303) 670-1307 — metro

Country Mustard

½ cup black mustard seed
St. Mary's Gourmet Vinegar
1 clove garlic, optional

1 tablespoon finely chopped fresh ginger
2 teaspoons sugar
salt to taste

Put mustard seed into a glass or earthenware bowl and pour over enough vinegar to cover. Let stand.

Next day, put the mustard and vinegar into container of electric blender together with garlic and ginger and blend on high speed until seeds are pulverized. Add sugar and salt to taste. Store in a clean, dry jar.

THE SILVER QUEEN

500 Sixth Street
Georgetown, Colorado
(303) 569-2961 — local
(303) 670-1307 — metro

Creamy Garlic Dressing

1 cup plain non-fat yogurt
1½ teaspoons country mustard
   (see Sauce section)
½ teaspoon finely grated lemon rind

$^1/_8$ teaspoon cayenne pepper
2 tablespoons minced parsley
2 cloves garlic, crushed

In a medium-size bowl, whisk together the yogurt, mustard, lemon rind, and cayenne pepper. Stir in the parsley. Thread the garlic onto a toothpick and add to the dressing. Cover and chill for 6 hours or overnight.

Remove the garlic and discard before serving the dressing. Store any leftover dressing in a tightly covered jar in the refrigerator and shake well before each use. Makes 1 cup.

THE DENVER SALAD COMPANY
2700 South Colorado Boulevard
Denver, Colorado 80222
(303) 691-2050

THE DENVER SALAD COMPANY
14201 East Public Market Drive
Aurora, Colorado 80012
(303) 750-1339

THE BOULDER SALAD COMPANY
2595 Canyon Boulevard
Boulder, Colorado 80302
(303) 447-8272

Curry Rice Salad Dressing

2   cups sour cream
1½ cups mayonnaise
⅓   cup rice wine vinegar or St. Mary's Gourmet Vinegar
3   tablespoons curry powder
1   tablespoon sugar
1   tablespoon dijon mustard
2   teaspoons pepper, white
1   teaspoon salt

Mix together sour cream, mayonnaise, vinegar, curry powder, dijon mustard, sugar, white pepper, and salt for the dressing.

DADDY BRUCE

1629 East 34th Avenue
Denver, Colorado
(303) 623-9636

20th and Arapahoe
Boulder, Colorado
(303) 449-8890

Daddy Bruce will be somewhere in his 90s this February 15 and he's still going strong producing his fabulous (hot) barbecue sauce — bottled Daddy Bruce Barbecue Sauce; smoking his slabs of pork and beef ribs; running his eatery which he has been operating for the past 18 years; cooking the best sweet potato pie, spicy pinto beans, and barbecue in the city; and, of course, periodically taking off to cat-fish on the Pine Bluff River in Arkansas.

"My grandmother, Laura Hart, who lived to be 107 years of age and died in the 1940s, was a wonderful woman. She was an Arkansas slave but had it made because she was a fantastic cook. We ran around together and had a great time. She taught me how to cook. I loved cooking with her. She made it fun. It still is," reminisces Daddy Bruce, who was born in 1900.

The Broncos and business people pack Daddy Bruce's for lunch; oil companies regularly request Daddy Bruce for barbecue catering; housewives from all over the area flock in to pick up his sauce.

But what has made Daddy Bruce so famous is his grand generosity. Every Thanksgiving Daddy Bruce feeds literally thousands of disadvantaged people.

Daddy Bruce's Famous Barbecue Sauce

1	cup catsup	1	cup brown sugar
½	cup hot sauce	1	tablespoon salt
¾	cup worcestershire sauce	½	tablespoon pepper
2	cups St. Mary's Gourmet Vinegar	½	cup lemon juice, freshly squeezed
4	cloves garlic, chopped		

Heat ingredients to dissolve sugar and bottle. Improves with time and shaking.

WELLSHIRE INN

3333 South Colorado Boulevard
Denver, Colorado
(303) 759-3333

Demi-Glace Sauce

1	cup brown sauce	4	tablespoons tomato purée
½	cup Madeira wine		

Bring brown sauce to simmering; add wine and tomato purée. Reduce mixture to half. Season to taste. Serve over Tournedos Diane (see Entree Meat section). Serves 1.

Curry Ginger Demi-Glace

For curry ginger — add fresh ginger and ½ teaspoon curry powder.

PAUL'S PLACE

3000 East First Avenue
Cherry Creek Mall
Denver, Colorado 80206
(303) 321-5801

Dijon Mustard Sauce

1   cup plain non-fat yogurt
2   tablespoons dijon or brown mustard

1   tablespoon basil
    juice from 2 average size lemons

Blend together and chill before serving. Great on fish and other sandwiches. Makes 1½ cups mustard.

T-WA INN

555 South Federal Boulevard
Denver, Colorado
(303) 922-4584

Fish Sauce Variation I

1   cup light soy sauce

1   teaspoon of shrimp paste

Wrap shrimp paste in foil and bake until shrimp paste is dry and crumbly. Crumble into powder and add to soy sauce. Shake bottle before each use.

Fish Sauce Variation II

2   tablespoons dried shrimp
1   teaspoon dried shrimp paste (kapi)
4   cloves garlic
2   teaspoons ground chiles (sambal ulek) or 2 fresh red chiles
2   teaspoons sugar
2   tablespoons lemon juice
1½ tablespoons soy sauce
3   tablespoons water

Wash shrimp and soak in hot water for 20 minutes. Rinse the shrimp thoroughly. Wrap dried shrimp paste in aluminum foil and put under a hot grill for 3 minutes on each side. Put drained shrimp and dried shrimp paste in blender container with garlic, chiles, sugar, lemon juice, soy sauce and water. Cover and blend until smooth. Pour into a bowl and serve with other ingredients arranged around the sauce.

If blender is not available, use a mortar and pestle to pound the shrimp and garlic. Use sambal ulek (see Sauce section) instead of chiles. After grilling dried shrimp paste, dissolve in the liquid ingredients, then combine everything.

A PIECE OF QUIET

1585 South Pearl Street
Denver, Colorado
(303) 744-2520

French Mustard

1	clove garlic		dash Tabasco sauce
1	onion, quartered	½	cup dry mustard
1	cup St. Mary's Gourmet Vinegar	2	tablespoons olive oil
1	teaspoon salt	1	teaspoon tarragon

Blend ingredients together until smooth. Store in covered jar to use as wanted. Makes 1 cup.

LA BOLA

900 Jersey Street
Denver, Colorado 80220
(303) 333-3888

LA BOLA VIVA

6830 South University
Littleton, Colorado 80122
(303) 771-4464

LA BOLA GRANDE

8000 East Quincy Avenue
Denver, Colorado 80237
(303) 779-0191

LA BOLA GRILL

Gaylord and Mississippi
Denver, Colorado
(303) 871-0444

LA BOLA

14561 East Alameda Avenue
Aurora, Colorado 80012
(303) 341-4968

Green Chili

2½ pounds pork roast, fresh shoulder preferred
1 pound pork soup bones
44 ounces canned tomatoes (28-ounce and 16-ounce cans)
23 ounces tomato sauce (15-ounce and 8-ounce cans)
3½ cups hot water (28 ounces)
21 ounces diced green chili strips (Ortega brand preferred, 3 7-ounce cans)
⅓ to 1 ounce diced hot peppers (Ortega brand preferred, ¼ of a 3½ ounce can)
1 tablespoon sugar
1½ tablespoons salt
1 tablespoon garlic

Cut pork into ½-inch squares and with the pork bones, fry over low heat until brown and the meat is slightly dry. If pork is very fat, pour off all but 4 or 5 tablespoons of the grease.

Using a colander, strain tomatoes into an 8-quart saucepan and coarsely chop tomatoes. Combine tomatoes, tomato sauce, hot water and cooked pork and bones in the same saucepan. Bring to a rapid boil and continue boiling for 20 minutes. Add spices, chopped hot peppers and chopped chili strips. Continue boiling another 20 minutes.

Finish by cooking on medium heat until desired thickness, usually about another 20 minutes. Remove bones and green chili is ready to serve. Makes 3 quarts.

NOTE: May be kept refrigerated for a week or frozen for 3 months. La Bola uses green chili to cover burritos, chili rellenos and most of their specialities. Melt an equal amount of grated sharp cheddar cheese and green chili for a chili con queso dip.

CLIFF YOUNG'S
RESTAURANT

700 East Seventeenth Avenue
Denver, Colorado 80210
(303) 831-8900

Chef Dave Query

Herbal Buerre Rouge
for Hazelnut Crusted Colorado Rack of Lamb (see Entrée Meat section)

2	cups Merlot or Zinfandel wine		1	teaspoon chopped thyme
1	cup veal glace		1	teaspoon chopped marjoram
4	tablespoons unsalted butter (softened)		1	teaspoon chopped mint

Deglaze roasting pan with the wine, scraping up all the brown bits of meat with a wooden spoon. Pour into saucepan and reduce by half, add veal glace and reduce by half. Over a very low flame slowly whisk the butter into the reduction, add chopped herbs and season to taste.

To serve: Slice each rack into four chops. Place ¼ of the sauce on each heated plate and place meat over the sauce. Garnish with fresh thyme, mint and marjoram. Serves 4.

RUDI'S

4720 Table Mesa Drive
Boulder, Colorado 80303
(303) 494-5858

Chef Faith Stone

Hollandaise (made in a blender)

6	egg yolks		1	cup melted butter
4	tablespoons lemon juice		¼	cup cream
pinch cayenne or Tabasco				

Place egg yolks, lemon and Tabasco in a blender. Turn on high and add the hot melted butter in a slow, steady stream. Sauce will be emulsified and ready to top main dishes. If sauce thickens, reblend it adding 1 to 2 tablespoons hot water, or more lemon juice. (For a richer sauce, transfer emulsified Hollandaise to a bowl and stir/fold in heavy cream.)

Hollandaise-Béarnaise Sauce

For Béarnaise, reduce dried tarragon in St. Mary's Gourmet Vinegar until vinegar is almost gone. Add 1 heaping teaspoon of reduced tarragon to 1 cup of Hollandaise.

FLAGSTAFF HOUSE RESTAURANT

1138 Flagstaff Road
Boulder, Colorado 80302
(303) 442-4640

Honey Mustard Poppy Seed Dressing

1   quart mayonnaise (see Mayonnaise in Sauce section)
½   cup dijon mustard
1   cup yellow mustard
½-1 cup honey
1   teaspoon chopped fresh tarragon
1   lemon
dash of red wine vinegar
salt and pepper to taste
¼   cup poppy seeds

Mix above ingredients and pour over Spinach Salad (see Salad section).

SOPRIS RESTAURANT AND LOUNGE

7215 Highway 82
Glenwood Springs, Colorado 81601
(303) 945-7771

House Dressing from Sopris Restaurant

1   quart mayonnaise
½   onion
1   garlic clove
¹/₅ of a bunch of parsley

dash of thyme
dash of rosemary
½   cup St. Mary's Gourmet Vinegar

Mix all ingredients in blender. Add the mix to the mayonnaise. Squeeze ½ lemon, salt, pepper, little Tabasco and Worcestershire sauce to tast. Stir well.

THE TOWER MAGIC BAR & RESTAURANT

P.O. Box 5514
Aspen-Snowmass Village, Colorado 81615
(303) 923-4650

John Denver's BBQ Sauce for Grilled Shrimp

4	teaspoons dry mustard	1	cup sherry
4	teaspoons onion salt	1	cup white wine
2	teaspoons cayenne pepper	1	cup Worcestershire
¾	cup Grey Poupon	⅔	cup lemon juice
⅔	cup St. Mary's Gourmet Vinegar		

Mix John Denver's BBQ Sauce; marinate the 24 large peeled, deveined, and rinsed shrimp for 1 hour.

Skewer shrimp and grill until opaque. Baste shrimp with John Denver's BBQ Sauce while grilling.

Serve over a bed of rice or fettuccine and top with some heated marinade.

TURNTABLE RESTAURANT

Exit 171
Vail-Minturn, Colorado
(303) 827-4164

Ketchup

6   large ripe tomatoes (about 3 pounds), peeled, cored, seeded, and chopped
1   medium-size yellow onion, chopped fine
3   tablespoons dark brown sugar
2   cloves garlic, minced
1   large bay leaf, crumbled
¼   teaspoon each celery seeds, ground allspice, and cinnamon
$^1/_8$ teaspoon ground cloves
⅓   cup St. Mary's Gourmet Vinegar

Place the tomatoes and onion in a large heavy saucepan. Set over moderate heat and cook, covered, stirring often, until soft — 20 to 25 minutes. Remove the vegetables, then put them through a food mill back into the saucepan, discarding any solids left in the food mill.

Stir in the brown sugar, garlic, bay leaf, celery seeds, allspice, cinnamon, cloves, and vinegar, and bring to a boil over moderate heat; adjust the heat so that the mixture bubbles gently, then simmer, uncovered, stirring often, until it has the consistency of ketchup — 35 to 40 minutes. Store tightly covered in the refrigerator. Makes about 2 cups.

The ketchup will keep well for about two weeks if stored tightly covered in the refrigerator.

ALFREDO'S

The Westin Resort Vail
1300 Westhaven Drive
Vail, Colorado 81657
(303) 476-7111 ext. 7014

Lavender Butter Sauce
for Lochinvar Scottish Salmon (see Fish section)

36	ounces Chablis	1	pound butter (cold chunks)
½	cup chopped shallots	4	ounces heavy cream
2	tablespoons dried Lavender	1	ounce dry sherry

Reduce on medium heat the Chablis, shallots and Lavender to about 10 ounces. Add the cream and reduce again to about 5 ounces slowly.

Remove from heat and slowly whisk in the cold butter chunks until all is absorbed.

Add a little salt and white pepper to taste. Add the sherry. Strain (remove just 1 teaspoon of the Lavender from the strainer and mince it very fine — then add to the sauce). Keep warm until serving.

SWEET BASIL

193 East Gore Creek Drive
Vail, Colorado 81657
(303) 476-0125

Lemon Tarragon Vinaigrette
for Grilled Asparagus and Shiitake Mushroom Salad (see Salad section)

2	tablespoons fresh tarragon, chopped	1	teaspoon salt
⅓	cup lemon juice	½	teaspoon white pepper
⅓	cup champagne vinegar	2	cups light olive oil

Mix well. Toss with Grilled Asparagus and Shiitake Mushroom Salad.

PANDA CAFE

1098 South Federal Boulevard
Denver, Colorado 80219
(303) 936-2500

Light Ginger Soy Sauce

1	teaspoon very finely grated ginger	2	tablespoons lemon juice
½	cup light soy sauce		

Mix above and use as dip with appetizer or as a marinade.

THE SAUCY NOODLE RISTORANTE

727 South University Boulevard
Denver, Colorado 80209
(303) 733-6977 or 778-9735

Marinara Sauce

1   can whole Italian pear tomatoes
6   cloves garlic

oregano, basil, red pepper, salt to taste
olive oil

In a frying pan line bottom with olive oil. Brown 3 cloves garlic cut in half, then remove and discard. Crush tomatoes by hand and place in frying pan. Spice to taste and cook 15 to 20 minutes, simmering.

FLAGSTAFF HOUSE RESTAURANT

1138 Flagstaff Road
Boulder, Colorado 80302
(303) 442-4640

Mayonnaise

5   egg yolks, room temperature
1   tablespoon St. Mary's Gourmet Vinegar
¾   quart olive oil

1   lemon
1   teaspoon boiling water

In a blender, whip egg yolks, St. Mary's Gourmet Vinegar, lemon, and boiling water at high speed. With blender turned on, trickle a needle thin stream of olive oil into whipping mixture until all of olive oil has been added. Refrigerate and use as needed. Makes one quart.

CANTERBURY CHEESE

26 North Tejon
Colorado Springs, Colorado
(719) 635-3337

Mayonnaise Variation (Low Cholesterol)

1   cup non-fat yogurt

½   cup St. Mary's Oil Free Dressing

Mix thoroughly and use as mayonnaise on sandwiches and in salads. Keep refrigerated.

RUDI'S

4720 Table Mesa Drive
Boulder, Colorado 80303
(303) 494-5858

Chef Faith Stone

Mornay Sauce

1½ cups steaming hot milk
Roux (2½ tablespoons butter and 2 tablespoons flour mixed to a paste, melt butter, then stir in flour)
2   ounces grated Swiss cheese
2   tablespoons heavy cream (optional)
a pinch of nutmeg, salt and Tabasco

Rapidly whisk the steaming milk into the roux. Whisk briskly to prevent lumps and stir until thickened. Gently whisk in Swiss cheese, cream and seasonings.

WELLSHIRE INN

3333 South Colorado Boulevard
Denver, Colorado
(303) 759-3333

Mustard Dressing

1   cup homemade mayonnaise
½   cup olive oil
¼   cup St. Mary's Gourmet Vinegar

1   tablespoon dijon French mustard
1   teaspoon Coleman's mustard powder

Blend thoroughly. Season to taste. Serve with Leo's Spinach Salad (see Salad section).

FLAGSTAFF HOUSE RESTAURANT

1138 Flagstaff Road
Boulder, Colorado 80302
(303) 442-4640

Niçoise Olive Sauce

2   fresh tomatoes, peeled, chopped and seeded
½   cup extra-virgin olive oil
1   clove garlic, chopped
4   ounces combined: chopped fresh thyme, marjoram, oregano and tarragon
niçoise olives, seeded and diced

Heat olive oil with tomato, garlic, herbs and olives. Simmer and spoon over Salmon with Lobsters and Truffles (see Seafood section). Serves 2.

RUDI'S

4720 Table Mesa Drive
Boulder, Colorado 80303
(303) 494-5858

Chef Faith Stone

Parmesan Dressing

3	tablespoons freshly grated Parmesan	1	teaspoon oregano
1	tablespoon honey	1	clove garlic, minced
1	cup yogurt	¼	teaspoon salt
1	egg		pinch pepper
2	tablespoons St. Mary's Gourmet Vinegar	½	cup olive oil
1	tablespoon basil		

Combine all ingredients, except vegetable oil, in blender and blend briefly. Add vegetable oil, while blending, in a slow, steady stream.

Will keep at least two weeks in refrigerator.

JEROME HOTEL

330 East Main Street
Aspen, Colorado 81611
(303) 920-1000

Picante Sauce

2   yellow onions, chopped into small pieces
3   green peppers, chopped into small pieces
2   garlic cloves, crushed and minced
1   tablespoon ground cumin
½   cup cider vinegar
2   tablespoons olive oil
½   cup tomato juice

Mix ingredients and marinate in vinegar, olive oil and tomato juice in refrigerator — will last two weeks — and use as a base to many Mexican dishes and sauces.

TRANSALPIN

Seventh Avenue at Logan Street
Denver, Colorado 80203
(303) 830-8282

Pineapple Ginger Sauce
for Trout (see Fish section)

¼ cup lemon juice
¼ cup water
¼ cup pineapple juice
2 slices fresh pineapple

1 clove garlic, finely diced
½ teaspoon fresh ginger, finely minced
¼ cup soy sauce

Add all ingredients, except soy sauce, in skillet and poach at medium heat for 3 minutes. Refrigerate. Just before serving reheat in skillet for about 5 minutes. Add soy sauce to skillet 1-5 minutes before serving. Spoon ¼ of sauce over each of 4 trout filets. Serves 4.

THE DENVER SALAD COMPANY

2700 South Colorado Boulevard
Denver, Colorado 80222
(303) 691-2050

THE DENVER SALAD COMPANY

14201 East Public Market Drive
Aurora, Colorado 80012
(303) 750-1339

THE BOULDER SALAD COMPANY

2595 Canyon Boulevard
Boulder, Colorado 80302
(303) 447-8272

Pineapple Salsa

1 pineapple
1 tablespoon jalapenos, diced
½ bunch cilantro, chopped fine
¼ cup rice wine vinegar or St. Mary's Gourmet Vinegar
1 cup pineapple juice

Wash, skin and core pineapple. Chop up ½ of pineapple into small pieces. Chop up remaining pineapple and put into food processor. Put pineapple pieces and dice in a bowl and add jalapenos, cilantro, and vinegar. Mix well and add 3 cups of Pineapple Salsa to Santa Fe Tabouli (see Salad section).

A PIECE OF QUIET

1585 South Pearl Street
Denver, Colorado
(303) 744-2520

Quick Mint Sauce for Lamb

1 cup fresh, washed mint
1 tablespoon sugar
½ cup St. Mary's Gourmet Vinegar
½ cup lemon juice

Blend until mint is chopped fairly fine. Serve hot or cold. Keep what is left in a covered jar. Flavor develops as it stands. Makes 1 cup.

POPPIES BISTRO CAFE

834 West Hallam
Aspen, Colorado 81611
(303) 925-2333

Raspberry Vinegar Demi-Glace Sauce with Fresh Thyme

½ cup red wine
½ cup raspberry vinegar
splash cassis
pinch of black peppercorn

3 bay leaves
 basil and thyme stems
¼ pound whole butter (unsalted)
2 cups chicken or duck demi glace

Combine red wine, raspberry vinegar, cassis, black peppercorns, bay leaves, a few thyme and basil stems in a saucepan. Reduce to a thick glace. Add demi glace to the reduction. Reduce to sauce consistency. While at a rapid boil, mound in ¼ pound cold butter. Whisk until incorporated. Strain sauce through a strainer. Salt and pepper to taste. Add chopped thyme. Serve with Sautéed Boneless Quail (see Fowl section). Serves 2.

WIENERSTUBE RESTAURANT

633 East Hyman Avenue
at Spring Street
Aspen, Colorado 81611
(303) 925-3357

Raspberry/Walnut Dressing
for Broiled Barberry Duck Salad "Framboise" (see Salad section)

½ cup puréed seedless fresh raspberry and liquid
4 tablespoons of raspberry vinegar
¼ cup walnut oil
¼ cup safflower oil
½ cup fresh jalapeño pepper, finely
   chopped
1 tablespoon fresh shallot
1 teaspoon English dry mustard seed
   powder
1 tablespoon sugar
salt and pepper to taste

In a blender, add the puréed fresh raspberries (strained from seed), raspberry vinegar, walnut oil and safflower seed oil, jalapeño pepper, shallots, dry mustard, sugar and salt and pepper to taste. Blend the ingredients until homogenized and adjust the salt/vinegar balance at this time. Chill and toss with the Broiled Barberry Duck Salad "Framboise" (see Salad section). Serves 4 to 8.

UTE CITY BANQUE

501 East Hyman
Aspen, Colorado
(303) 925-4373

Chef David Zumqinkle

Red Wine Sauce
for the Chicken Breast Boursin (see Fowl section)

Saute until lightly browned in 2 tablespoons butter:
1 cup minced scallions   ½ cup minced mushrooms
1 teaspoon minced garlic

Add and cook 3 minutes:
3 tablespoons flour

Add and cook until slightly thickened:
½ cup red wine   1 teaspoon Worcestershire sauce
2 cups beef stock   pinch of cayenne

BOTANA JUNCTION

742 Highway 86
Elizabeth, Colorado
(303) 646-4444

Salsa

4 to 6 green chiles, skinned, chopped
2   jalapeños, chopped
4   tomatoes, chopped
1   medium red onion, chopped

2   cloves garlic, minced
2   tablespoons chopped cilantro
2   tablespoons olive oil
1   tablespoon fresh lime juice

Combine all ingredients and allow to sit for at least an hour before serving. Makes 2 cups.

THE BLUE BONNET CAFE AND LOUNGE

475 South Broadway
Denver, Colorado
(303) 778-0147

The Blue Bonnet Cafe has long been one of Denver's most popular Mexican restaurants. Here is a variation on their popular salsa.

Salsa Crude

1   large tomato, peeled and finely chopped
2   tablespoons finely chopped onion
1   tablespoon finely chopped green pepper
1   tablespoon finely chopped canned green chili
2 to 4 teaspoons finely chopped jalapeño peppers
2   cloves minced garlic
1   tablespoon fresh cilantro, minced

Mix above ingredients. Cover and refrigerate 2 hours to blend flavors.

T-WA INN

555 South Federal Boulevard
Denver, Colorado
(303) 922-4584

This is one of Denver's best Vietnamese restaurants. Here is a variation of one of their hot sauces.

Sambal Ulek
(Hot Chili Paste)

25 fresh red banana chiles or 2 cups dried crushed chiles
enough vinegar to cover chiles (St. Mary's Gourmet Vinegar)
salt (optional)

Pour into blender and make a paste. Pour into sterilized bottle and store in refrigerator.

SWEET BASIL

193 East Gore Creek Drive
Vail, Colorado 81657
(303) 476-0125

Shallot Sauce

12	shallots, sliced thin	2	cups heavy cream
3	cloves garlic, minced		salt and fresh pepper
2	cups chicken stock	1	tablespoon butter

Saute shallot in butter for 2 minutes, add the garlic and cook 1 more minute. Do not let the shallots turn brown. Add the chicken stock and simmer until reduced by half. Then add the cream and simmer 10 minutes. Finish with salt and pepper, do not strain.

UPTOWN GRILL

472 East Lionshead Circle
Vail, Colorado 81659
(303) 476-2727

Smoked Tomato Salsa
for Avocado Red Pepper Quesadilla (see Appetizer section)

4	ripe tomatoes, cut in ½, deseeded		1	tablespoon St. Mary's Gourmet Vinegar
¼	red onion		2	tablespoons olive oil
½	bunch cilantro		1	teaspoon lemon juice
1	Anaheim chile			salt and pepper to taste
2	teaspoons chopped garlic			

To smoke tomatoes: use the trusty Weber Grill. Get hot, add favorite wood smoking chips to coals and let smoke. Put tomatoes on grill and close lid. Tomatoes will only take 5-6 minutes to obtain a good, smoky flavor as well as being cooked. Let cook. skin and chop.

Chop cilantro, dice onion and Anaheim chile. Mix all ingredients together and let sit at room temperature at least 1 hour. Serve at room temperature. Serves 4.

IMPERIAL CHINESE SEAFOOD

1 Broadway
Denver, Colorado
(303) 698-2800

Soy Sauce Marinade*

1   cup soy sauce
2   cloves garlic, crushed
2   tablespoons dry sherry

Mix all ingredients together. Roll roast in the mixture until it is completely covered. Let it stand for at least 6 hours or overnight.

* Variation

ASIA CHINESE RESTAURANT

132 West Main Street
Aspen, Colorado
(303) 925-5433

Sweet and Sour Sauce Dip

½ cup brown sugar
1 teaspoon salt
½ cup rice vinegar or St. Mary's Gourmet Vinegar
1½ tablespoons cornstarch
4 teaspoons catsup
¾ cup pineapple juice
1 cup crushed pineapple

Cooking: Mix cornstarch and pineapple juice in a sauce pan. Add remaining ingredients. Stir over medium-high heat until sauce thickens. Add more liquid if sauce needs thinning or more cornstarch if a thicker sauce is desired. You may use additional juice or vinegar depending on how sour you want the sauce to be.

Do-ahead notes: Make sauce, cool, place in glass jar, freeze. To reheat, thaw and reheat in small saucepan. Makes 3 cups.

IMPERIAL CHINESE SEAFOOD

1 Broadway
Denver, Colorado
(303) 698-2800

Szechwan Sauce*

2 chili peppers
2 slices fresh ginger
1 clove garlic
3 tablespoons Tabasco sauce
½ cup dry sherry
⅓ cup soy sauce
1 teaspoon sugar
salt and pepper
2 tablespoons peanut or vegetable oil

Mince peppers, ginger and garlic finely. Mix together Tabasco, sherry, soy sauce, sugar and seasoning. In a skillet heat oil. Quick-fry peppers, ginger and garlic for about 2 minutes. Add Tabasco-soy mixture and bring to a boil. Remove from heat and serve at once. Makes about 1 cup.

* Variation

MINTURN COUNTRY CLUB

Main Street
Vail-Minturn, Colorado
(303) 827-4114

Minturn Country Club, Vail's suburban, down-home steak house, offers the best meal buys in the Vail area. Prices range from under $10 to $15 for the entree and an all-guests-can-eat full service salad bar with breads and cheeses. But without a doubt, the best part of dining at the Minturn Country Club is socializing with guests from all over the country as people grill their entrées (kabobs, chicken filets, 16-ounce sirloins and more) over the huge indoor community grill. Here is a variation of their popular Teriyaki sauce.

Teriyaki Marinade

½   cup soy sauce
⅓   cup dry sherry
⅓   cup brown sugar
¼   cup vinegar or St. Mary's Gourmet Vinegar
2   tablespoons vegetable oil
1   clove garlic, minced
½   teaspoon ground ginger

Mix together and brush over beef, chicken, pork, or seafood while it is on the grill.

THE DENVER SALAD COMPANY

2700 South Colorado Boulevard
Denver, Colorado 80222
(303) 691-2050

THE DENVER SALAD COMPANY

14201 East Public Market Drive
Aurora, Colorado 80012
(303) 750-1339

THE BOULDER SALAD COMPANY

2595 Canyon Boulevard
Boulder, Colorado 80302
(303) 447-8272

Thai-Vinaigrette Dressing
for Thai-Chicken Pasta Salad (see Salad section)

¾   cup soy oil   1½ cups St. Mary's Gourmet Vinegar
2   cloves garlic, minced   1   cup light soy sauce

Whisk all ingredients in a large bowl and add water to taste. Toss over Thai-Chicken Pasta Salad.

LA BOLA

900 Jersey Street
Denver, Colorado 80220
(303) 333-3888

LA BOLA VIVA

6830 South University
Littleton, Colorado 80122
(303) 771-4464

LA BOLA GRANDE

8000 East Quincy Avenue
Denver, Colorado 80237
(303) 779-0191

LA BOLA BRAVO

Gaylord and Mississippi
Denver, Colorado
(303) 871-0444

LA BOLA

14561 East Alameda Avenue
Aurora, Colorado 80012
(303) 341-4968

T.L.C. Butter

2	pound lightly salted butter	4	ounces Sauza Gold Tequila
½	cup fresh cilantro	2	tablespoons salt
1⅓	cups freshly squeezed lime juice		

Bring butter to room temperature. Place all ingredients in food processor and blend until smooth and well mixed.

Form butter in rolls approximately 2 inches in diameter, wrap in plastic film and freeze.
Cut into medallions and use to sauté or top any broiled or grilled fish, shrimp or chicken dish.
May also be brushed on fresh vegetables before grilling.

THE VILLA AT PALMER LAKE

75 Highway 105
Colorado Springs-Palmer Lake, Colorado
(719) 481-2222

Tomato Sauce*

¼	cup water	2	tablespoons chopped fresh parsley leaves
2	tablespoons olive oil	1	tablespoon dried oregano
1	large onion, finely diced	1	bay leaf, crushed
3	cloves garlic, minced	1	teaspoon black pepper
1	35-ounce can tomatoes, pureed		

Heat the oil in a nonstick frying pan. Add water, onion and garlic and saute until the onion is translucent. Add remaining ingredients and simmer for 15 minutes. Makes 3 cups. Serve over Gnocchi (see Pasta section) or cooked pasta.

* Variation

COMPREHENSIVE INDEX

Achiote Chicken with Chipolte Salsa and Shallot Sauce..........15, IX
Ahi Tuna in Mustard Crust with Red Pepper Nage..............1, VIII
Alfredo, Fettuccine....................................8, VII
Almond Gratin with Pineapple............................1, XI
Almond or Cashew Chicken................................3, IX
Almonds, Stir-Fried String Beans and....................14, VI
Anchovies and Garlic, Vermicelli with...................23, VII
Apple Bacon, Chowder of Corn, Wild Rice and..............6, II
Apple Mint Salsa for Lamb Quesadilla.....................1, XII
Apple Pancake..1, V
Apple-Raspberry Pie.....................................1, XI
Apples and Bananas, Blue Corn Pancakes with..............3, XI
Apples, Pecans and Lime, Chicken Salad with.............10, III
Applestrudel...2, XI
Apricot Nut Bread, Swedish.............................12, V
Armenian Cheese Boreck..................................1, I
Armenian Shish Kebab....................................1, X
Arroz a la Mexican (Mexican Rice).......................1, VI
Artichoke Florentine...................................2, VI
Artichoke Hearts, Spaghetti with Garlic, Capers and.....17, VII
Artichoke Hearts, Swiss House..........................15, I
Artichoke Salad, Hearts of Palm with...................11, III
Artichoke Soup, Cream of................................7, II
Artichoke, Pita Chips with..............................9, I
Artichokes, Vegetable-Cheese Salad with................26, III
Asian Salad..1, III
Asian Salad Dressing...................................1, XII
Asparagus and Crabmeat Soup, (Mang-Tay Nua Cua).........12, II
Asparagus with Mushroom Salad and Tarragon Vinaigrette..10, III
Asparagus-Mushroom Omelets.............................1, IV
Aubergines Farci (Eggplant).............................3, VI
Avocado Melon Salad....................................1, III
Avocado Pancake Filled with Smoked Duck and Wild Rice...1, IX
Avocado Red Pepper......................................1, I
Avocado Soup with Rock Shrimp...........................1, II
Avocado, Egg, Cheese, Mushroom, Sprouts, Crepe..........2, IV

Baby Canadian Lobster Tails with Curry Sauce............2, VIII
Bacon, Potato Skins with Cheese and....................10, I
Baked Chicken in Orange-Almond Sauce....................2, IX
Baked Macaroni and Cheese...............................1, VII
Baked Salmon with Tequila Coriander Beurre Blanc........3, VIII
Banana Flambee...2, XI
Banana Nut Bread..1, V
Banana Split Ice Cream Pie..............................3, XI
Bananas and Apples, Blue Corn Pancakes with.............3, XI
Barbecue Sauce, Lamb Chops with.........................10, X
Basic German Pancake...................................2, V
Basmati Rice...3, VI
Bean Curd, Ma-Po Style.................................13, X
Bean and Shrimp Salad with Coriander Dressing, Black....2, III
Beans, Green Piquant...................................11, VI
Bearnaise Sauce..2, XII
Beef Stroganoff..2, X
Beef Tenderloin, Spice Cured Bresaola...................4, X
Beef, Hot Shredded Spiced...............................8, X
Beef, Manchurian.......................................12, X
Beef, Mongolian..15, X
Bisque, Tomato...17, II
Black Bean Garlic Sauce.................................2, XII
Black Bean Sauce.......................................3, XII
Black Bean Tortilla.....................................2, V
Black Bean and Shrimp Salad with Coriander Dressing.....2, III
Blackened Tenderloin Caesar Salad.......................3, III
Blintzes, Cheese.......................................8, XI
Blue Cheese Dressing...................................3, XII
Blue Cheese Dressing...................................4, XII
Blue Corn Pancake with Caramelized Apples and Bananas...3, XI
Blueberry-Dijon Vinaigrette, Vail Mountain Summer Salad with.....25, III
Bob's Homemade Pasta....................................1, VII

Bob's Special Fettuccine................................2, VII
Boef Bordelaise, Cote de................................5, X
Bolivian Chili...3, X
Boreck, Armenian Cheese.................................1, I
Bowl of the Wife of Kit Carson..........................2, IX
Braised Belgian Endive with Chevre and Nicoise Olives...4, III
Bread Pudding, Chocolate................................9, XI
Bread, Banana Nut.......................................1, V
Bread, Ginger...10, V
Bread, Honey Walnut....................................10, V
Bread, Lemon Pecan Tea.................................11, V
Bread, Swedish Apricot Nut.............................12, V
Bread, Zucchini.......................................14, V
Breadsticks..3, V
Bresaola (Spice Cured Beef Tenderloin)..................4, X
Brie Cheesecake on Champagne Creme Anglaise with Fresh Plums.4, XI
Broccoli Polonaise.....................................4, VI
Broccoli Salad, Pasta..................................16, III
Broccoli, Creme du......................................8, II
Brodo..1, VII
Broiled Barberry Duck Salad "Framboise".................5, III
Brook Trout, Saute Meuniere............................4, VIII
Brown Sauce..5, XII
Bulghur Pilaf..4, VI

Cabbage, Artichoke and Caper Slaw......................22, III
Caesar Salad...6, III
Caesar Salad, Blackened Tenderloin......................3, III
Cake, Carrot...6, XI
Cake, Poppies Potato...................................11, VI
Campaigne Chicken (Friendly Country Chicken)............3, IX
Cannelloni with Ricotta and Peas........................2, VII
Cantina Rellenos..5, VI
Caper Sauce, Linguine with Tuna-.......................10, VII
Caper Slaw, Cabbage Artichoke..........................22, III
Capers and Artichoke Hearts, Spaghetti with Garlic.....17, VII
Caramel Custard..5, XI
Carrot Cake..6, XI
Carrot Mint Soup..2, II
Cashew or Almond Chicken................................3, IX
Champagne Vinaigrette for Charbroiled Eggplant..........5, XII
Champignon Elegante....................................2, I
Charbroiled Eggplant with Champagne Vinaigrette.........5, VI
Charbroiled Quail with Shiitake Mushrooms and Wild Rice.4, IX
Chart House Mud Pie.....................................8, XI
Cheese Blintzes..8, XI
Cheese Boreck, Armenian.................................1, I
Cheese Danish, Cherry...................................4, V
Cheese Salad with Artichokes, Vegetable................26, III
Cheese and Bacon, Potato Skins with....................10, I
Cheese, Baked Macaroni and..............................1, VII
Cheese, Field Greens Served with Roma Tomatoes and Goat.9, III
Cheesecake on Champagne Creme Anglaise with Plums, Brie.4, XI
Cheesecake, Smoked Salmon..............................13, I
Cherry Cheese Danish....................................4, V
Chestnut Chicken.......................................4, IX
Chevre and Nicoise Olives, Braised Belgian Endive with..4, III
Chicken Breast Poursin with Red Wine Sauce..............6, IX
Chicken Breast Tina Louise..............................6, IX
Chicken Breast, Poulet Alexander Stuffed...............23, IX
Chicken Carbonara Fettuccine............................3, VII
Chicken Green Chili Stew................................7, IX
Chicken Kiev...7, IX
Chicken Marengo..8, IX
Chicken Pasta Salad, Thai.............................24, III
Chicken Quenelles with Mushroom Cream, Appetizer........3, I
Chicken Quenelles with Mushroom Sauce...................9, IX
Chicken Salad with Apples, Pecans and Lime.............10, III
Chicken Salad with Tomato Basil Vinaigrette............18, III
Chicken Salad, Market Curry............................12, III

Chicken Stock..2, II
Chicken Stock Substitute, Vegetarian—Hot and Spicy.............3, II
Chicken Stock, St. Mary's Style..............................3, II
Chicken Vegetable Soup.......................................4, II
Chicken Velvet and Corn Soup.................................7, II
Chicken a la King..5, IX
Chicken and Potato Salad, Dilled.............................8, III
Chicken and Procini Mushroom, Three Cheese Lasagne with...20-21, VII
Chicken in Orange-Almond Sauce...............................2, IX
Chicken with Avocado Cream Sauce, Sun Dried Tomatoes........15, IX
Chicken with Chipolte Salsa and Shallot Sauce, Grilled......15, IX
Chicken with Cornbread Dressing, Jalapeno Lime Marinated.....16, IX
Chicken with Garlic Sauce...................................10, IX
Chicken with Lemon Cream, Sesame............................25, IX
Chicken with Orange Sauce...................................11, IX
Chicken with Red Chiles, Mint and Oregon Raspberry Wine.....12, IX
Chicken, Cashew or Almond....................................3, IX
Chicken, Chestnut..4, IX
Chicken, Friendly Country....................................3, IX
Chicken, Garlic...17, IX
Chicken, Kung Pao...17, IX
Chicken, Peppered...20, IX
Chicken, Plum Wine..20, IX
Chicken, Pollo Asado a la Parrila...........................21, IX
Chicken, Portuguese...21, IX
Chicken, a la Francais.......................................5, IX
Chile Relleno Sauce for Chile Rellenos.......................6, XII
Chile Rellenos, Shrimp......................................30, VIII
Chili Rellenos with Sauce....................................6, VI
Chili Stew, Chicken Green....................................7, IX
Chili, Bolivian..3, X
Chilled Lime and Honeydew Soup...............................5, II
Chilled Noodle Summer Entree.................................3, VII
Chinese Hot and Sour Soup with Shrimp........................6, II
Chinese Pancakes...5, V
Chips with Artichoke, Pita...................................9, I
Chips, Tortilla...13, V
Chocolate Boats, White......................................26, XI
Chocolate Bread Pudding......................................9, XI
Chocolate Sauce..6, XII
Chocolate Sorbetto with Raspberry Coulis.....................9, XI
Chocolate Torte...10, XI
Chocolate Walnut Crepe......................................11, XI
Chowder of Corn, Wild Rice and Apple Bacon...................6, II
Cinnamon Rolls...5, V
Cinnamon Walnut Cookies.....................................11, XI
Cioppino...5, VIII
Clam Chowder, New England Style.............................13, II
Clam Sauce, Linguine with White.............................11, VII
Clams and Mussels Luciano....................................5, VIII
Cobbler, Iron Skillet Peach.................................17, XI
Coho Salmon Tortellini with Orange Brandy Cream Sauce........4, VII
Cointreau, Kiwi Scallops.....................................6, I
Consomme...7, II
Cookies, Cinnamon Walnut....................................11, XI
Cookies, Pine Nut Brown Sugar...............................21, XI
Coquilles St. Jacques A La Parisienne........................6, VIII
Coriander Dressing for Black Bean and Shrimp Salad...........6, XII
Corn Soup, Chicken Velvet and................................5, II
Corn, Country Shrimp and Lemon...............................7, VIII
Corn, Wild Rice and Apple Bacon, Chowder of..................6, II
Cornbread and Andoville Sausage, Rabbit Loin Stuffed with....19, X
Cornbread, Mexican..11, V
Cornish Hen Glazed with Orange and Ginger...................13, IX
Cote de Boeuf Bordelaise.....................................5, X
Country Mustard..7, XII
Country Shrimp and Lemon Corn................................7, VIII
Couscous, Moroccan..16, X
Crab Cakes...9, VIII
Crab Salad...7, III

Crab and Pasta Salad...7, III
Crab, Curried..8, VIII
Crabmeat Salad Crepe...6, III
Crabs, Fried Chili..11, VIII
Cream of Artichoke Soup......................................7, II
Cream of Zucchini..8, II
Creamy Garlic Dressing.......................................7, XII
Creme Brulee, Ginger..15, XI
Creme du Broccoli..8, II
Creme, Strawberry...24, XI
Crepe Supreme, Strawberry...................................25, XI
Crepe Suzettes..12, XI
Crepe, Avocado, Cheese, Mushroom, Sprouts....................2, IV
Crepe, Chocolate Walnut.....................................11, XI
Crepe, Crabmeat Salad..6, III
Crepe, D-J's Basic Recipe....................................7, V
Crepe, Dessert..13, XI
Crepes, Eggplant...7, VI
Crust, Wafer..13, V
Cucumber Yogurt Soup, Iced..................................12, II
Cucumbers with Romaine, Sauteed.............................12, VI
Cuisses De Grenouilles Au Riesling (Frog Legs in Riesling)...6, X
Curried Crab...8, VIII
Curried Squash Soup..9, II
Curry Chicken Salad, Market.................................12, III
Curry Rice Salad Dressing....................................8, XII
Curry Rice Salad with Shrimp.................................8, III
Custard, Caramel...5, XI
Cyrano's Egg Mignons topped with Mushrooms...................2, IV

D-J's Basic Crepe Recipe.....................................7, V
D-J's Special Avocado, Egg, Cheese, Mushroom, Sprouts Crepe..2, IV
Daddy Bruce's Famous Barbecue Sauce..........................9, XII
Danish, Cherry Cheese..4, V
Date Nut Roll..6, V
Date Souffle..12, XI
Deep-Fried Prawns with Chiles................................9, VIII
Demi-Glace Sauce...9, XII
Dessert Crepe...12, XI
Dijon Mustard Sauce...10, XII
Dilled Chicken and Potato Salad..............................8, III
Dilled Potatoes and Sour Cream...............................6, VI
Dim Sum, Vegetarian...17, I
Duck Salad "Framboise," Broiled Barberry.....................5, III
Duck and Wild Rice, Avocado Pancake Filled with..............1, IX
Duck, Vit Quay..24, IX
Ducks with Orange and Grand Marnier Sauce...................14, IX
Dumplings, Gnocchi Potato....................................8, VII
Dumplings, Steamed Meat.....................................14, I
Dungeness Crab Cakes...9, VIII

Egg Drop Soup..9, II
Egg Lemon Sauce, Meatballs with.............................14, X
Egg Mignons with Mushrooms...................................2, IV
Egg Noodle Dough...7, V
Egg Roll...4, I
Egg with Mushrooms, Steamed..................................6, IV
Eggplant (Aubergines Farci)..................................3, VI
Eggplant Crepes..7, VI
Eggplant with Champagne Vinaigrette..........................5, VI
Eggs Benedict, Scrambled.....................................5, IV
Eggs, Huevos Jerome and Picante Sauce........................3, IV
Empanada Dough...8, V
Empanadas, Vegetable..17, VI
Endive with Chevre and Nicoise Olives, Braised Belgian.......4, III
Escargots Bourguignonne......................................4, I
Escargots Maison...5, I

Feta Cheese on French Bread.................................13, V
Fettuccine Alfredo...8, VII

Fettuccine Alfredo, Scampi and . . . . .27, VIII
Fettuccine, Bob's Special . . . . .2, VII
Fettuccine, Chicken Carbonara . . . . .3, VII
Figs with Mascarpone, Toasted Almonds and Port Wine . . . . . . .22, XI
Firefly Granola . . . . .13, XI
Fish Pie, Lemon . . . . .15, VII
Fish Sauce Variation I and II . . . . .10, XII
Fish Stock . . . . .10, II
Fish Turrine . . . . .36, VIII
Flan of Lobster and Scallops with Two Caviars . . . . .10, VIII
Florentine, Artichoke . . . . .2, VI
Florentine, Omelet . . . . .4, IV
Florida Red Snapper Napoletana . . . . .10, VIII
Flour Tortillas . . . . .8, V
French Bread with Warm Feta Cheese . . . . .13, V
French Mustard . . . . .11, XII
French Toast Topped with Pecans, Bananas and Grand Marnier . . . . .9, V
Fresh Field Greens served with Roma Tomatoes and Goat Cheese . .9, III
Fresh Lochinvar Scottish Salmon with Lavendar Butter Sauce . . .11, VIII
Fresh Peach Muffins . . . . .9, V
Fresh Tuna with Tomato Sauce . . . . .33, VIII
Fried Chili Crabs . . . . .11, VIII
Fried Noodles with Shrimp . . . . .12, VIII
Fried Rice with Shrimp . . . . .12, VIII
Frog Legs in Riesling Wine . . . . .6, X

Garlic Chicken . . . . .17, IX
Garlic Rice with Pinon Nuts . . . . .7, VI
Garlic Tamales, Roast . . . . .12, I
Garlic, Capers and Artichoke Hearts, Spaghetti . . . . .17, VII
Garlic, Vermicelli with Anchovies and .23, VII
Gateux a L'Orange . . . . .14, XI
Genovese, Pesto alla . . . . .16, VII
German Pancake, Basic . . . . .2, V
Ginger Bread . . . . .10, V
Ginger Creme Brulee . . . . .15, XI
Ginger and Orange, Cornish Hen Glazed with . . . . .13, IX
Gnocchi Potato Dumplings . . . . .8, VII
Goat Cheese Tart . . . . .16, XI
Goat Cheese, Field Greens served with Roma Tomatoes and . . . .9, III
Golden Dobbin Meatloaf . . . . .6, X
Goose or Turkey, Potato-Stuffed . . . . .22, IX
Grand Mere from Bourgogne, Gratin Dauphinois Chez . . . . .8, VI
Granola, Firefly . . . . .13, XI
Gratin Dauphinois Chez Grand Mere from Bourgogne . . . . .8, VI
Greek Fisherman's Soup . . . . .10, II
Green Beans, Piquant . . . . .11, VI
Green Chili . . . . .11, XII
Green Chili Stew, Chicken . . . . .7, IX
Greens served with Roma Tomatoes and Goat Cheese, Field . . . .9, III
Grilled Achiote Chicken, Chipolte Salsa and Shallot Sauce . . . . . .15, IX
Grilled Chicken Salad with Apples, Pecans and Lime . . . . .10, III
Grilled Chicken with Avocado Cream Sauce, Sundried Tomatoes . . .15, IX
Grilled Halibut Filets with Melon and Mango Salsa . . . . .13, VIII
Grilled Jumbo Shrimp with Kentucky Bacon and Fresh Basil . . . . .13, VIII
Grilled Tuna with Herbed Tomato, Garlic, and Lemon Sauce . . . . .14, VIII
Guacamole . . . . .5, I

Halibut Filets with Melon and Mango Salsa . . . . .13, VIII
Hazelnut Crusted Rack of Lamb . . . . .7, X
Hearts of Palm and Artichoke Salad . . . . .11, III
Hearty Lentil Soup . . . . .11, II
Herbal Buette Rouge for Hazelnut Crusted Rack of Lamb . . . . . . .12, XII
Hollandaise . . . . .12, XII
Homemade Spinach Noodles "Al Pesto" .9, VII
Honey Mustard Poppy Seed Dressing .13, XII
Honey Walnut Bread . . . . .10, V
Honeydew Soup, Chilled Lime and . . . . .5, II
Hot Shredded Spiced Beef . . . . .8, X
Hot and Sour Soup . . . . .11, II

Hot and Sour Soup with Shrimp, Chinese . . . . .6, II
Hot and Sour Soup, Szechwan . . . . .16, II
Hot and Spicy Prawns . . . . .33, VIII
Housedressing from Sopris Restaurant .13, XII
Huevos Jerome and Picante Sauce . . . . .3, IV

Ice Cream Pie, Banana Split . . . . .3, XI
Ice Cream with Raspberry Sauce, Lime Vanilla-Bean . . . . .18, XI
Ice Cream, Lime Vanilla-Bean with Raspberry Sauce . . . . .18, XI
Iced Cucumber Yogurt Soup . . . . .12, II
Iron Skillet Peach Cobbler . . . . .17, XI
Italiano, Spinach . . . . .13, VI

Jalapeno Lime Marinated Chicken with Cornbread Dressing . . . . . .16, IX
John Denver's BBQ Sauce for Grilled Shrimp . . . . .14, XII

Kai Yand (Garlic Chicken) . . . . .17, IX
Kapusta . . . . .9, X
Ketchup . . . . .14, XII
Kiev, Chicken . . . . .7, IX
Kit Carson, Bowl of the Wife of . . . . .2, IX
Kiwi Scallops Cointreau . . . . .6, I
Kung Pao Chicken . . . . .17, IX

Lamb Bouquetiere, Roast Crown of . . . . .20, X
Lamb Chops Parmesan . . . . .9, X
Lamb Chops with Barbecue Sauce . . . . .10, X
Lamb Loin with Sweet Peppers in Strudel . . . . .12, X
Lamb Quesadilla . . . . .6, I
Lamb Salad with Raspberry Vinaigrette .15, III
Lamb Shanks for Six . . . . .11, X
Lamb Tian with Shiitake Mushrooms, Spinach & Tomatoes . . . . . .30-31, X
Lamb Venison, Roast Leg of . . . . .21, X
Lasagne Roll-ups, Spicy . . . . .18, VII
Lasagne with Chicken and Porcini Mushrooms, Three Cheese . .20-21, VII
Lasagne, Zucchini, Mushroom and Pimiento . . . . .24, VII
Lavender Butter Sauce for Lochinvar Scottish Salmon . . . . .15, XII
Leek Soup with Smoked Mussels and Spinach, Puree . . . . .14, II
Lemon Fish Pie . . . . .15, VII
Lemon Pecan Tea Bread . . . . .11, V
Lemon Prosciutto Shrimp . . . . .15, VIII
Lemon Tarragon Vinaigrette for Grilled Asparagus and Salad . . . .15, XII
Lentil Pilaf, Mujedera . . . . .10, VI
Lentil Soup, Hearty . . . . .11, II
Leo's Spinach Salad . . . . .11, III
Light Ginger Soy Sauce . . . . .15, XII
Lime Vanilla-Bean Ice Cream with Raspberry Sauce . . . . .18, XI
Lime and Honeydew Soup, Chilled . . . . .5, II
Lime, Apples and Pecans, Chicken Salad with . . . . .10, III
Linguine and Lobster Tails Diabla . . . . .16, VIII
Linguine with Shrimp Sauce . . . . .16, VIII
Linguine with Tuna-Caper Sauce . . . . .10, VII
Linguine with White Clam Sauce . . . . .11, VII
Lobster Tails Diabla, Linguine and . . . . .16, VIII
Lobster Tails with Curry Sauce . . . . .2, VIII
Lobster and Scallops with Two Caviars, Flan . . . . .10, VIII
Lobster and Shrimp Papillotes . . . . .19, VIII
Lobster and Truffles, Salmon with . . . . .25, VIII
Loin of Lamb with Sweet Peppers in Strudel . . . . .12, X

Ma-Po Style Bean Curd . . . . .13, X
Macaroni and Cheese, Baked . . . . .1, VII
Manchurian Beef . . . . .12, X
Mang-Tay Nua Cua (Asparagus and Crabmeat Soup) . . . . .12, II
Mangione, Pasta . . . . .13, VII
Marengo, Chicken . . . . .8, IX
Marinara Sauce . . . . .16, XII
Marinara with Shrimp, Pasta . . . . .14, VII
Marinara, Spaghetti . . . . .16, VII
Marinated Mushrooms . . . . .7, I

Marinated Sirloin Steak..............................14, X
Marinated Turkey Breast with Coriander-Lime Sauce.........18, IX
Mark's Pasta Primavera Salad with Oil Free Dressing.........13, III
Market Curry Chicken Salad..........................12, III
Mascarpone, Toasted Almonds and Port Wine, Figs with........22, XI
Mayonnaise.......................................16, XII
Mayonnaise Variation (Low Cholesterol).................16, XII
Meat Dumplings, Steamed............................14, I
Meat Loaves, Mini (Ground Turkey)....................19, IX
Meatballs with Egg Lemon Sauce......................14, X
Meatloaf, Golden Dobbin.............................6, X
Mediterranean Pasta Salad...........................14, III
Melanzane Alla Parmigiana...........................9, VI
Melon Salad, Avocado...............................1, III
Melon and Prosciutto...............................7, I
Mexican Cornbread.................................11, V
Mexican Rice.....................................1, VI
Mini Meat Loaves (Ground Turkey)....................19, IX
Mint Soup, Carrot..................................2, II
Mongolian Beef...................................15, X
Mornay Sauce....................................17, XII
Moroccan Couscous................................16, X
Mosaic Nut Tart...................................19, XI
Mountain Meadow Lamb Salad with Raspberry Vinaigrette.......15, III
Mud Pie...7, XI
Muffins, Peach Fresh...............................9, V
Mujedera Lentil Pilaf...............................10, VI
Mushroom Cream, Chicken Quenelles with...............3, I
Mushroom Salad with Tarragon Vinaigrette, Asparagus with......10, III
Mushroom and Pimiento Lasagne, Zucchini.............24, VII
Mushroom-Asparagus Omelets........................1, IV
Mushrooms, Marinated..............................7, I
Mushrooms, Three Cheese Lasagne with Chicken and Porcini..20-21, VII
Mussels and Clams Luciano..........................5, VIII
Mussels and Spinach, Puree of Leek Soup with............14, II
Mussels in Mustard Cream Sauce, Smoked...............31, VIII
Mussels with Sauce Verte............................8, I
Mustard Dressing..................................17, XII
Mustard Glazed Salmon on Spinach Leaves, Tarragon Butter.....17, VIII

New England-Style Clam Chowder......................13, II
Newburg, Salmon..................................23, VIII
Nick's Special Omelet...............................3, IV
Nicoise Olive Sauce................................17, XII
Nockerl, Salzburger................................23, XI
Noodle Dough, Egg.................................7, V
Noodle Summer Entree, chilled.......................3, VII
Noodles "Al Pesto," Homemade Spinach.................9, VII
Noodles with Shrimp, Fried..........................12, VIII
Nut Bread, Banana.................................1, V
Nut Bread, Swedish Apricot..........................12, V
Nut Tart, Mosaic..................................19, XI

Oignon Gratinee, Soup a L-..........................15, II
Olives, Braised Belgian Endive with Chevre and Nicoise........4, III
Omelet Florentine.................................4, IV
Omelets, Asparagus-Mushroom........................1, IV
Onion Potato Salad, Red.............................17, III
Orange Brandy Cream Sauce, Coho Salmon Tortellini with.......4, VII
Orange and Ginger, Cornish Hen Glazed with.............13, IX
Orange and Grand Marnier Sauce, Ducks with.............14, IX
Orange, Gateux...................................14, XI
Orange-Almond Sauce, Chicken in.....................2, IX
Oriental Vegetables................................18, VI
Oysters and Shallots Vinaigrette, Smoked...............32, VIII
Oysters with Crackling For Six........................19, VIII

Pancake with Smoked Duck and Wild Rice, Avocado.........1, IX
Pancake, Apple...................................1, V
Pancake, Basic German.............................2, V

Pancakes with Carmelized Apples and Bananas, Blue Corn.......3, XI
Pancakes, Chinese.................................5, V
Papillotes of Lobster and Shrimp......................19, VIII
Pariser Schnitzel..................................17, X
Parmesan Dressing................................18, XII
Parmigiana, Melanzane Alla..........................9, VI
Pasta Del Giorno (Pasta with Spinach Sauce)..............12, VII
Pasta Mangione...................................13, VII
Pasta Marinara with Shrimp..........................14, VII
Pasta Primavera Salad, Mark's.......................13, III
Pasta Riviera....................................14, VII
Pasta Salad with Basil Pesto.........................17, III
Pasta Salad, Crab.................................7, III
Pasta Salad, Mediterranean..........................14, III
Pasta Salad, Summer...............................22, III
Pasta Scampi.....................................15, VII
Pasta and Broccoli Salad............................16, III
Pasta from Scratch...............................5-6, VII
Pasta, Bob's Homemade.............................1, VII
Pate Maison.....................................18, X
Pate de Foie.....................................9, I
Pea and Potato Soup, Split..........................15, II
Peach Cobbler, Iron Skillet..........................17, XI
Peach Muffins, Fresh...............................9, V
Peas, Cannelloni with Ricotta and.....................2, VII
Pecan Pie.......................................20, XI
Pecan Tea Bread, Lemon............................11, V
Pecans, Apples and Lime, Chicken Salad with............10, III
Peppered Chicken.................................20, IX
Pesce Ala Siciliano (Sicilian Style Swordfish)............20, VII
Pesto alla Genovese...............................16, VII
Pesto, Pasta Salad with Basil........................17, III
Picante Sauce....................................18, XII
Pie Dough.......................................12, V
Pie, Banana Split Ice Cream.........................3, XI
Pie, Fish Lemon..................................15, VIII
Pie, Mud..7, XI
Pie, Pecan......................................20, XI
Pie, Raspberry-Apple..............................1, XI
Pie, Sweet Potato.................................25, XI
Pilaf, Bulghur....................................4, VI
Pilaf, Mujedera Lentil..............................10, VI
Pimiento Lasagne, Zucchini, Mushroom and.............24, VII
Pine Nut Brown Sugar Cookies.......................21, XI
Pineapple Ginger Sauce for Trout.....................19, XII
Pineapple Salsa...................................19, XII
Pineapple, Almond Gratin with.......................1, XI
Pinon Nuts, Garlic Rice with.........................7, VI
Piquant Green Beans...............................11, VI
Pita Chips with Artichoke...........................9, I
Plum Wine Chicken................................20, IX
Plums, Brie Cheesecake with.........................4, XI
Pollo Asado a la Parrila.............................21, IX
Polonaise, Broccoli................................4, VI
Poppies Potato Cake...............................11, VI
Porc aux Trois Poivres, Rillettes de....................11, I
Pork Cutlets.....................................19, X
Pork, Roast......................................21, X
Pork, Sweet and Sour with Pineapple and Peppers..........27, X
Portuguese Chicken................................21, IX
Pot de Creme....................................22, XI
Potato Cake, Poppies..............................11, VI
Potato Cakes, Wild Rice............................18, VI
Potato Dumplings, Gnocchi..........................8, VII
Potato Salad, Dilled Chicken and......................8, III
Potato Salad, Red Onion............................17, III
Potato Skins with Cheese and Bacon...................10, I
Potato Soup, Split Pea and..........................15, II
Potato-Stuffed Roast Goose or Turkey..................22, IX
Potatoes and Sour Cream, Dilled......................6, VI

Potatoes, Truffled Creamy Mashed..............................16, VI
Poulet Alexander Stuffed Chicken Breast.....................23, IX
Prawns with Chiles, Deep-Fried...................................9, VIII
Prawns, Hot and Spicy...33, VIII
Primavera Salad, Mark's Pasta..................................13, III
Prosciutto, Melon and...7, I
Pudding, Chocolate Bread..9, XI
Pudding, Yorkshire..14, V
Puree of Leek Soup with Smoked Mussels and Spinach.........14, II

Quail with Mushrooms and Wild Rice............................4, IX
Quail with Potato Cake, Raspberry Demi Glace and Fresh Thyme..25, IX
Quenelles with Mushroom Cream, Chicken, Appetizer............3, I
Quenelles with Mushroom Sauce, Chicken........................9, IX
Quesadilla Vegetarian..10, I
Quesadilla, Lamb...6, I
Quick Mint Sauce for Lamb..20, XII

Rabbit Loin Stuffed with Cornbread and Andoville Sausage.......19, X
Rack of Lamb, Hazelnut Crusted...................................6, X
Raspberry Coulis, Chocolate Sorbetto with........................9, XI
Raspberry Pie, Apple...1, XI
Raspberry Sauce, Lime Vanilla-Bean Ice Cream with..............18, XI
Raspberry Vinaigrette, Lamb Salad with...........................15, III
Raspberry Vinegar Demi-Glace Sauce with Fresh Thyme.......20, XII
Raspberry/Walnut Dressing for Broiled Barberry Duck Salad......21, XII
Red Onion Potato Salad..17, III
Red Pepper, Avocado...1, I
Red Snapper Louisiane...21, VIII
Red Snapper Napoletana...10, VIII
Red Wine Sauce for the Chicken Breast Boursin.................21, XII
Rellenos with Sauce, Chili..6, VI
Rellenos, Cantina..5, VI
Rice Potato Cakes, Wild...18, VI
Rice Salad with Shrimp, Curry.....................................8, III
Rice with Pinon Nuts, Garlic.......................................7, VI
Rice, Basmati..3, VI
Rice, Mexican...1, VI
Rice, Sushi..15, VI
Ricotta and Peas, Cannelloni with.................................2, VII
Rillettes de Porc aux Trois Poivres................................11, I
Ripe Figs with Mascarpone, Toasted Almonds and Port Wine......22, XI
Riviera, Pasta...14, VII
Roast Crown of Lamb Bouquetiere.................................20, X
Roast Garlic Tamales...12, I
Roast Leg of Lamb Venison..21, X
Roast Pork..21, X
Roast Venison...22, X
Roll, Date Nut...6, V
Rolls, Cinnamon...5, V
Romaine, Sauteed Cucumbers with................................12, VI
Romano Crusted Chicken Salad with Tomato Basil Vinaigrette.....18, III

Salad "Framboise," Broiled Barberry Duck.........................5, III
Salad Crepe, Crabmeat...6, III
Salad with Coriander Dressing, Black Bean and Shrimp............2, III
Salad, Asian...1, III
Salad, Avocado Melon..1, III
Salad, Blackened Tenderloin Caesar................................3, III
Salad, Caesar...6, III
Salad, Crab...7, III
Salad, Crab and Pasta...7, III
Salmon A La Provencale with Flageolet Bean Compote.........22, VIII
Salmon Cheesecake, Smoked.......................................13, I
Salmon Newburg...23, VIII
Salmon Salad..19, III
Salmon Tartare..24, VIII
Salmon Tortellini with Orange Brandy Cream Sauce, Coho........4, VII
Salmon Wrapped in Filo with Brie..................................26, VIII
Salmon on Spinach with Tarragon Butter, Mustard Glazed........17, VIII

Salmon with Lavendar Butter Sauce..............................11, VIII
Salmon with Lobster and Truffles.................................25, VIII
Salmon with Tequila Coriander Beurre Blanc.......................3, VIII
Salmon with Tomato Basil Crust and Warm Tomato Chutney......18, VIII
Salsa..22, XII
Salsa Crude...22, XII
Salzburger Nockerl..23, XI
Sambal Ulek (Hot Chili Paste).....................................23, XII
Santa Fe Tabouli..20, III
Sashimi...26, VIII
Saurbraten..23, X
Sausage, Thai...29, X
Sauteed Cucumbers with Romaine.................................12, VI
Sauteed Scampi and Fettuccine Alfredo...........................27, VIII
Scalloppine di Vitela al Marsala..................................23, X
Scallops Cointreau, Kiwi...6, I
Scallops Nicoise...27, VIII
Scallops Parisienne..28, VIII
Scallops and Lobster with Two Caviars, Flan.....................10, VIII
Scampi and Fettuccine Alfredo....................................27, VIII
Scampi, Pasta...15, VII
Schnitzel, Pariser..17, X
Scrambled Eggs Benedict...5, IV
Scrambled Tofu..12, IV
Sesame Chicken Breast with Lemon Cream........................25, IX
Shallot Sauce...23, XII
Shish Kebab, Armenian...1, X
Shrimp Baked with Feta Cheese and Tomato......................29, VIII
Shrimp Chile Rellenos...30, VIII
Shrimp Dijonnaise...30, VIII
Shrimp Fried Rice..12, VIII
Shrimp Salad with Coriander Dressing, Black Bean and............2, III
Shrimp Sauce, Linguine with.......................................16, VII
Shrimp and Lemon Corn..7, VIII
Shrimp and Lobster Papillotes.....................................19, VIII
Shrimp with Curry Rice Salad Dressing, Curry Rice Salad with.....8, III
Shrimp with Kentucky Bacon and Fresh Basil......................13, VIII
Shrimp, Avocado Soup with Rock...................................1, II
Shrimp, Chinese Hot and Sour Soup with..........................6, II
Shrimp, Fried Noodles with..12, VIII
Shrimp, Lemon Prosciutto...15, VIII
Shrimp, Pasta Marinara with.......................................14, VII
Shrimp, Spaghetti and...17, VII
Shrimp, Volcano...37, VIII
Skins with Cheese and Bacon, Potato..............................10, I
Smoked Mussels in Mustard-Cream Sauce.........................31, VIII
Smoked Oysters and Shallots Vinaigrette..........................32, VIII
Smoked Salmon Cheesecake.......................................13, I
Smoked Tomato Salsa for Avocado Red Pepper Quesadilla......24, XII
Smoked Trout with Papaya, Avocado and Cucumber.............32, VIII
Smorgasbord Salad..21, III
Snapper Louisiane, Red..21, VIII
Snapper, Napoletana..10, VIII
Sorbetto with Raspberry Coulis, Chocolate..........................9, XI
Souffle, Date..12, XI
Soup a L-Oignon Gratinee..1, II
Soup, Split Pea and Potato...15, II
Soup, Szechwan...17, II
Soy Sauce Marinade...24, XII
Spaghetti Marinara..16, VII
Spaghetti and Shrimp..17, VII
Spaghetti with Garlic, Capers and Artichoke Hearts...............17, VII
Spaghetti, Swiss...19, VII
Spanakopita..13, VII
Spicy Lasagne Roll-ups..18, VII
Spinach Italiano...13, VI
Spinach Noodles "Al Pesto," Homemade............................9, VII
Spinach Salad with Honey Mustard Poppy Seed Dressing.........21, III
Spinach Salad, Leo's..11, III
Spinach Sauce, Pasta with (Pasta Del Giorno)....................12, VII

Spinach, Puree of Leek Soup with Smoked Mussels and.........14, II
Split Pea and Potato Soup....................15, II
Squash Soup, Curried.....................9, II
St. Mary's Cabbage, Artichoke and Caper Slaw...............22, III
Steak Tartare.....................24, X
Steak, Marinated......................14, X
Steamed Bao.......................14, I
Steamed Egg with Mushrooms..................6, IV
Steamed Meat Dumplings...................14, I
Stir-Fried String Beans and Almonds................14, VI
Stock Substitute, Vegetarian—Hot and Spicy, Chicken....3, II
Stock, Chicken.......................2, II
Stock, Fish........................10, II
Stock, St. Mary's Style, Chicken................3, II
Strawberry Base Sause for Waffle Toppings...........24, XI
Strawberry Cream.....................24, XI
Strawberry Crepe Supreme..................25, XI
String Beans and Almonds, Stir-Fried..............14, VI
Stroganoff, Beef.....................2, X
Strudel, Loin of Lamb with Sweet Peppers in..........12, X
Stuffed Breast of Veal with Marsala Wine Sauce.........25, X
Sukiyaki.........................26, X
Summer Pasta Salad....................22, III
Summer Salad.......................23, III
Sunomono........................15, I
Sushi Rice........................15, VI
Swedish Apricot Nut Bread..................12, V
Sweet Potato Pie.....................25, XI
Sweet and Sour Pork with Pineapple and Peppers........27, X
Sweet and Sour Sauce Dip..................25, XII
Sweetbreads aux Marsala...................28, X
Swiss House Artichoke Hearts................15, I
Swiss Spaghetti......................19, VII
Swordfish, Sicilian Style..................20, VIII
Szechwan Hot and Sour Soup................16, II
Szechwan Sauce......................25, XII
Szechwan Soup......................17, II

T.L.C. Butter......................27, XII
Tabouleh........................23, III
Tabouli, Santa Fe....................20, III
Tamales, Roast Garlic....................12, I
Taquitos........................16, I
Tarragon Vinaigrette with Asparagus and Mushroom Salad.......10, III
Tart, Goat Cheese....................16, XI
Tart, Mosaic Nut.....................19, XI
Tea Bread, Lemon Pecan..................11, V
Tenderloin Caesar Salad, Blackened..............3, III
Teriyaki Marinade.....................26, XII
Thai Sausage.......................29, X
Thai-Chicken Pasta Salad with Thai-Vinaigrette Dressing........24, III
Thai-Vinaigrette Dressing for Thai-Chicken Pasta Salad.........26, XII
Three Cheese Lasagne with Chicken and Porcini Mushrooms..20-21, VII
Tian of Lamb with Shiitake Mushrooms, Spinach & Tomatoes....30-31, X
Tina Louise, Chicken Breast..................6, IX
Tofu, Scrambled.....................12, VI
Tom Chien Lan Bot (Hot and Spicy Prawns).............33, VIII
Tomato Basil Vinaigrette, Chicken Salad with............18, III
Tomato Bisque......................17, II
Tomato Sauce......................27, XII
Tomatoes and Goat Cheese, Field Greens served with Roma.......9, III

Tonno Con Salso Di Pomodoro (Fresh Tuna with Tomato Sauce)..33, VIII
Torta Regina.......................26, XI
Tortellini........................22, VII
Tortellini with Orange Brandy Cream Sauce, Coho Salmon.......4, VII
Tortilla Chips......................13, V
Tortilla, Black Bean....................2, V
Tortillas, Flour.....................8, V
Tournedos Diane.....................32, X
Tournedos Toscana....................33, X
Tournedos au Poivre Vert..................32, X
Trout Poached in Lemon Grass Broth..............34, VIII
Trout with Papaya, Avocado and Cucumber, Smoked..........32, VIII
Trout, Saute Meuniere...................4, VIII
Truffled Creamy Mashed Potatoes................16, VI
Tuna Tartare with Chives..................35, VIII
Tuna in Mustard Crust with Red Pepper Nage..........1, VIII
Tuna with Herbed Tomato, Garlic and Lemon Sauce..........14, VIII
Tuna with Tomato Sauce..................33, VIII
Tuna-Caper Sauce, Linguine with..............10, VII
Turkey or Goose, Potato-Stuffed................22, IX
Turkey with Coriander-Lime Sauce, Marinated...........18, IX
Turkey, Mini Meat Loaves..................19, IX
Turrine of Fish.....................36, VIII

Vail Mountain Summer Salad with Blueberry-Dijon Vinaigrette.....25, III
Vanilla-Bean Ice Cream with Raspberry Sauce, Lime...........18, XI
Veal a la Oskar......................33, X
Veal with Roasted Red Bell Peppers Beurre Blanc.........34, X
Veal with Rosemary-Chili Sauce and Walnuts...........34, X
Veal, Stuffed Breast of..................25, X
Vegetable Soup, Chicken..................4, II
Vegetable-Cheese Salad with Artichokes.............26, III
Vegetables Empanadas....................17, VI
Vegetables with Oriental Touch................18, VI
Vegetarian Dim Sum....................17, I
Vegetarian, Quesadilla...................10, I
Venison, Roast......................22, X
Vermicelli with Anchovies and Garlic..............23, VII
Vinaigrette Dressing, Thai Chicken Pasta Salad with.........24, III
Vinaigrette, Tarragon with Asparagus and Mushroom Salad.......10, III
Vit Quay (Roast Duck)...................24, IX
Volcano Shrimp......................37, VIII

Wafer Crust.......................13, V
Waffle Toppings, Strawberry Sauce..............24, XI
Walnut Bread, Honey....................10, V
Warm Feta Cheese on French Bread..............13, V
White Chocolate Boats...................26, XI
White Clam Sauce, Linguine with..............11, VII
Wiener Schnitzel.....................35, X
Wild Rice Potato Cakes...................18, VI
Wild Rice and Apple Bacon, Chowder of Corn...........6, II
Wild Rice, Avocado Pancake with Smoked Duck and..........1, IX

Yogurt Soup, Iced Cucumber..................12, II
Yorkshire Pudding....................14, V

Zucchini Bread......................14, V
Zucchini, Cream of....................8, II
Zucchini, Mushroom and Pimiento Lasagne............24, VII